The author, c.1970

About the Author

Mike Stephenson has played in folk clubs and been part of a rock band. He is also an artist and a music composer. He plays guitar, harmonica, ukulele, and piano. He likes cats and curries and reckons The Beatles are the best band *ever*.

Rock around the Crocks:
The Fall and Rise of a Legendary Rock Band

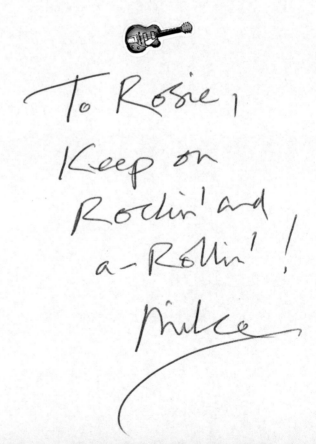

To Rosie,
Keep on
Rockin' and
a-Rollin'!

Mike

Mike Stephenson

Rock around the Crocks:
The Fall and Rise of a Legendary Rock Band

Olympia Publishers
London

www.olympiapublishers.com
OLYMPIA PAPERBACK EDITION

A CIP catalogue record for this title is
available from the British Library.

ISBN: 978-1-80074-684-8

First Published in 2023

Olympia Publishers
Tallis House
2 Tallis Street
London
EC4Y 0AB
Printed in Great Britain

Dedication

TO ADRIAN 'FUNKYDRUMMER' SHAW
THANKS FOR THE NOTES

Acknowledgements

My grateful thanks to my publisher, Olympia, for believing in this book and Kristina for guiding me through the process. Also huge thanks to Adrian Shaw for all the invaluable help and information he provided, from notes about drumming to touring to band transport to the Red Lodge Cafe to just about everything to do with being in a rock band. Thank you also to Abbey Road Studios for answering my questions. Various rock histories came courtesy of the Wonderful World of Wikipedia and the following books: 'Halfway to Paradise: The Birth of British Rock' by Alwyn W. Turner (V&A Publishing), 'The Restless Generation' by Pete Frame (Rogan House), and 'Tour: Smart: and Break the Band' by Martin Atkins (Soluble LLC). Finally, as ABBA put it, and to all great singers and bands: Thank you for the music.

Rock On

They charge onto the stage, like The Beatles at Shea Stadium, holding their guitars like rifles. The singer shakes his tambourine at the crowd who scream in response. 'We luv you, PHILLY!' shouts Danny into his microphone. 'WE LUV YOU DANNY B!' scream the girls in near-hysteria. He does a count-in for the band but they can't hear him over the banshee wails so he stamps his feet instead, 1-2, 1-2-3-4 and they launch themselves into their first song, 'Rock Island Line'.

The noise of the crowd, mainly female, is feral. Animals in pain, it sounds like, not girls in worship. 'MARRY ME MICKEY!' says a sign held up by one adoring fan but it's quickly pulled down by the girls behind whose view is obstructed. A catfight breaks out, spitting, scratching, but is quickly over as Mickey, lead guitar, plays a heavenly solo.

The band can't hear what they're playing but they know the songs so well it don't matter; they play by instinct, led by Tank the drummer's steady beat. He waves his sticks at the start of each number and the crowd wave back. Danny the singer's words are lost, he might as well be singing gobbledegook, and sometimes he does, just out of mischief, for instance: 'The Rock Island Line is a mighty fat toad.' No one notices, not even his bandmates who can't hear anyway. The volume is intense; no wonder Tank suffers from tinnitus.

It is 1981 and the venue is the massive John F. Kennedy Stadium in Philadelphia, U-shaped with the stage at the open end. Capacity one hundred thousand bodies, but this band have only managed to half-fill the space – 'Not to be sneezed at,' is Tank's verdict though on the fifty thousand crowd. The Beatles played there in '66 and the Stones in '78, and later on this year, in September, the Stones will do two shows. In the company of Gods, the lads think. 'The Supremes were here in '65,' so says bass guitarist Tone who's a font of pop and rock knowledge.

In the way of things Rock 'n' Roll, teenage girls are swooning and medics are on hand to revive them. Cops are plentiful to block the tide of stage-invaders who'll charge any barrier, storm any blockade, to reach their idols. One girl gets through the police cordon by crouching down and squeezing through the cops' legs. Before they can stop her, she's on stage and hugging Danny. Then she's led off, weeping, hysterical, and happy.

The band plough through their play-list, performing by rote, interspersed with Danny's spoken intros that no one hears. Then it's all over. A forty-five-minute set that the audience has been queuing hours for. The four lads wave goodbye to their fans, then come back for an encore – their 'Beat, Beat, Beat' mega-hit.

They leave their instruments on stage for the roadies to collect, race out through back exits to waiting people-carriers, darkened windows, towelling off sweat, then hotel, shower, order room service, watch TV, sleep. The same as last night, the night before, every night. 'Tone the Phone', as he's known, needs must ring his missus, no matter what the time difference – 'How was it?' 'Same as always.' 'Where are you?' 'Philadelphia, I think, how're the kids?' 'Same as always. They miss you.' 'I miss you.' 'Love you.' Rings off.

The band, called Rock Ireland Line, comprises Danny, Mickey, Tank and Tone. It is 1981 and yes, it's true, every gig is just like any other gig in any other city or country. But still as exciting as hell! Rock on forever!

1
Rock Island Line

Rock on forever and ever, Amen!

Danny Boy, Tone, Mickey and Tank. The boys in the band. Or rather, the *old* boys in the band. Total combined age: two hundred and sixty-five years in this Year of our Lorde 2016. That would take you back to 1751 if you went back in history. They're all in their late sixties. Danny Boy is the youngest at sixty-four, then Tank at sixty-five, Mickey sixty-seven and Tone knocking on at sixty-nine. 'You're only as old as you feel,' says Tank with a leery grin as he mimes fondling an imaginary pair of boobs. Well, truth to tell, he's fondled a few hundred pair in his time. 'But it were so long ago,' he says, 'it feels like a distant mammary.' And they laugh fit to burst.

They meet up every Thursday evening in Tone's garage to rehearse and try out new material when Tone's wife is off late-night shopping in Tesco. They call themselves a rock *band,* not a rock group. There's a subtle distinction, 'band' meaning music while 'group' simply means a number. They formed in the late 1960s, and they're still going strong today – or strong-ish. Or weak-ish in some cases, to tell the God's honest, as they're all martyrs to some old guy's ailment or other but they soldier on.

Tone's wife gets back from Tesco laden with bags, and the boys help her get them in the house, which is a signal for rehearsing to stop as Tone's wife, who's called Aggie, can't stand the noise, 'let alone the neighbours complaining!' For the while then, the band is banned – instruments packed away, microphones switched off, goodnights said. The remnants of the last song – the classic 'Rock Island Line' – drift off into the atmosphere and far off into the big black yonder as sound waves to be picked up in one millennium by some alien nation. Or maybe the sound just dies, you'd have to be a scientist to know. The speed of sound is 760 mph, travelling at 343 metres a second. Aggie reckons the faster it buggers off, the better.

Where to start? Well first, a pen portrait:

Danny Boy is the leader and the singer. He's Irish, hence the moniker 'Danny Boy'. Still good-looking today with his receding hair greased back and tied in a ponytail, partially concealing the monk-like bald spot. Danny Boy has tried everything to retain his hair, rubbing in expensive hair restorer lotion from Boots to getting pills on prescription, but they messed with his libido so he stopped using them, considering sex to be more important, on balance, than a full head of hair. 'I'd rather be good in bed and bald, than a flop with locks!' And they all laugh fit to burst as pretty much nothing is sacred or secret in this band of brothers.

Danny Boy is tall, but with a potbelly which he tries to disguise on stage with a cummerbund tied tight around the protuberance. A bit like Aggie with her Spanx pants. He has piercings, various, about his ears and, it's rumoured, one 'below the belt', characteristically known as a Prince Albert. He won't confirm or deny this and the rest of the band have never been able to verify the metallic presence as Danny Boy's shower sessions are private, and even a sly shuftee in the Gents affords no *visual* as Danny employs the overhand approach to his public micturition.

Stage-clothes can be anything from a Nigerian-style decorated kaftan affair (again to hide the paunch) to crimson and gold embroidered slippers acquired from the Raffles Hotel in Singapore during the band's more salubrious touring days. Sometimes a Rhinestone Cowboy hat when the mood takes him (straw, tea-stained with rhinestone appliqué). Or he just wears a sharp suit. His voice is magical – strained and raucous when required (Stones songs), soft and gentle for a dollop of Lovin' Spoonful.

Tone (short for Tony), the bass guitarist, is 'The Quiet One'. Generally morose, although he has no reason to be, as he's kept all his hair despite his sixty-nine years on God's Good. And it's not just any old hair but black curls cascading down past his shoulders like a waterfall, and black due to the Men Only hair dye he applies to hide the grey. The others try to persuade him to go grey but Tone won't be swayed. The black waterfall of hair continues to flow dark.

Otherwise, Tone is average. Average height, average build, average personality. However, his idea of clothes belies this averageness as Tone favours colours. Unfortunately, they're old man's colours – the sort of palette that retired men adopt when they cast off the grey pinstripes and adopt *pink* trousers with *light blue* shirts, *yellow* socks etc. This is Tone's 'look', on- and off-stage. Tone is multi-toned. His bass-playing is far from average tho' – he makes those four thick strings *sing*.

He is the band's 'Encyclopaedia-of-Rock', knows everything there is to know about Rock 'n' Roll history. If he was ever on TV's *Mastermind* it would be his specialist subject. But he's modest about his knowledge and often uses the phrase, 'if memory serves'. It usually does.

Mickey. After 'Mouse'. Cos he's a short-arse and has a squeaky voice. He's a mean guitarist, alternating between rhythm and lead. Sometimes plays a twelve-string electric Knoxville Deluxe – ash body, maple neck, rosewood fingerboard. Otherwise, the classic six-string Fender Stratocaster in Sonic Red. Or an electrified Eko acoustic.

His harmonies are like motorway caffs – always there when you need them (and Danny Boy does need them now and again when he tries to hit those high notes. Mickey's squeaky voice can reach F5, he says, being the second F above middle C, he says, and no one else has the musical know-how to argue).

Mickey can be temperamental and nasty at times – 'like most tiny fuckers,' says Danny Boy. His temper is legendary, and he's been known to sock a six-foot-five bolshie roadie in the smacker without batting an eyelid (he just has to reach up a bit).

His stage clothes are tee-shirt-based, bearing various messages, his favourite being LA HIGHWAY PATROL, his second favourite being WEMBLEY STADIUM SECURITY. Jeans of course, then Crocs slip-on shoes as he has trouble with his feet these days. Bunions, corns, the works, so sometimes he hobbles and they call him 'Pegleg', or 'Long John' and Mickey just scowls and calls them 'Wankers'. He's skinny and bony, so the tee-shirts sit well on his slender frame.

Mickey's a Midlander and his lazy accent betrays his Middle England upbringing – he says 'torlet' instead of 'toilet', for instance. Meanwhile, Tone has a soft voice, posh accent, brought up in the Surrey commuter belt. They've never heard Tone raise his voice, but, for that matter, they often can't hear him anyway.

The subject of hair, and a lack of, is a touchy one for Mickey as he is balding (God's great joke on mankind). He doesn't attempt to disguise this or wear hats, but he is self-conscious about his dome being shiny, so before going on stage he puffs talcum powder onto his head to dull the glow. Of course, under the lights or in the hot atmosphere of a pub, his head soon starts to sweat, so you can see rivulets of perspiration bisecting the talc and running in parallel lines down his forehead.

But his guitar-playing… oh, his guitar-playing… is sheer bliss!

Tank, the drummer. Tank, because he's built like one, from his double chin all the way down to his chubby ankles. Tank, because he's like a Sherman or the mighty Churchill charging through the French undergrowth on D-Day. Even in his younger, leaner days, he was still Tank, being stocky and muscular and squat. And Tank, because of his fondness for 'tanking' (his word for 'shagging') the groupies that followed the band around from gig to gig in the olden golden days. Tracy, Shirley, Tina. Generally flat-chested and skinny, living on drugs, little food, a lot of booze and urgent sex. Bend over, knickers down, another box ticked, another rock idol shagged. Thus it was that Tank would make regular visits to the Clap Clinic for his supply of antibios – 'Here again, Mr Sandercock? My, you lead a charmed life,' says the receptionist (and yes, Tank's surname really is Sandercock, being Cornish in origin and not, as you might suppose, knowing Tank, anything SM-related).

But Tank is past all that nowadays, and he sits, denim-clad, like some squatting blue Buddha in his island of percussion. Cymbals, hi-hats, tom-toms, bass drums (x 2). Of course, he has to be heavy built, humping all his gear from gig to gig. Time was, they had 'roadies' do it all for them – when the venues were dance halls and stadiums and not the pubs they play in now. Even the two guitarists have to haul their amps now, and heavy buggers they are too. It's a hard life on the road, especially when you're of State Pension age.

Finally, hair – that all-important factor of the male psyche. Tank is blessed with blonde hair, which he fluffs up with a hairdryer, taking care to cover, as best he can, the bald spot at the crown, and this blonde hair also covers the hearing aids that he has to wear behind his ears. The whole coiffure is set off nicely with a neat goatee beard.

They talk of 'packing it all in', the band do – but they don't mean it. Haul away, heave away, ho! They soldier on.

They're called 'Rock Ireland Line' after Lonnie Donegan's 1950s hit skiffle record 'Rock Island Line'. And they changed 'Island' to 'Ireland' cos of Danny Boy's heritage. There was something of a fashion in those far-off days for bands to have punning names – the famous one being 'Beatles' instead of 'Beetles'.

Professor Tone: 'The song "Rock Island Line" started life as a 1930s American folk song about a railroad. The first recording was made by American prisoners in Arkansas – in the Cummins State Farm Prison, if memory serves. Then Lonnie Donegan took it up in 1955 and scored a major hit and pretty much launched the era of skiffle music with its fast rhythms and delivery.'

The skiffle era was short-lived though. Some skiffle groups used homemade instruments like a washboard for percussion and a string tea-chest for the bass, so just about anybody could form a skiffle group with a cheap guitar from Woolworths, a bit of DIY and your mum's laundry utensils. But the skiffle craze was in a time before this band was formed. The boys would have been just, well, *boys* then. In their teens, their rock heroes would be the Rolling Stones and Jimi Hendrix. Bands like Cream and The Who. This would be their world. Tank idolised Ginger Baker, exponent of the virtuoso drum solo, while Mickey idolised the great Hendrix. Danny Boy's hero was Mick Jagger obviously, sometimes Roger Daltrey of The Who. Tone had no particular bass guitar mentors, although he'd sometimes cite Jack Bruce of Cream, McCartney, of course, and for a while he adopted a peculiar stance – bass guitar held straight upright as opposed to played waist level.

Like many, probably all, bands, they toyed with various band names (The Beatles, for instance, in their very early days, called themselves The

Silver Beetles).

At first, they thought they'd use their own teenage names like a rollcall: Danny Boy, Tone, Mickey and Tank; but soon after that, a pop group emerged into the limelight called Dave Dee, Dozy, Beaky, Mick and Tich, so the name Danny Boy etc. etc. bit the dust. They tried variations on 'Rock' like Brighton Rock, after the book and film, but as none of them came from that seaside town, the name was dead and buried six foot under. Rock, Stock and Barrel was a contender for a while but was voted down because it didn't have a ring to it – 'We need something catchy,' says Mickey. 'Balls,' says Tank, 'they're catchy!' and they laugh fit to burst. Then there was The Rockaneers (a pun on Buccaneers) and they thought they'd cracked it, but as Tank couldn't spell Rockaneers, that name too hit the trash.

Who thought of Rock Island Line and the ingenious variation, Rock 'Ireland' Line? Mickey lays claim to the former, Tone to the latter. But who knows and who's telling? Lost in the mists of time, but the name sticks like Gorilla Tape.

There was, however, a worry in the mid-70s with the IRA bombings in the UK – could the Irish connection make the name unpalatable? As it happened, no. But all the same, why didn't they try a different name altogether? Well, they said they'd gotten used to Rock Ireland Line and anything else they just couldn't agree on. Once a band settles on a name, it usually sticks to it, no matter what. After all, The Beatles were always The Beatles once they'd moved away from The Silver Beetles, same with the Rolling Stones, Bee Gees, Led Zeppelin…

And yet now, here and now, in their old-age dotage, they're toying with a new name to reflect their more mature status as they're still on the road, performing in pubs and clubs and anywhere who'll have 'em.

The Rockin' Crocks is mooted by Tone and well-liked by all until Tank objects to the word 'crocks', and being called a crock, as he still thinks he's God's Gift to Groupies.

The Ol' Tossers – universally disliked by all as they feel that 'Old' or 'Ol' should not be in the name.

Senile Demented is seriously considered but again, that word 'senile' sticks in the craw.

So they decide to stay as Rock Ireland Line. 'It's what our fans expect,' says Danny Boy – as if they have many now. 'As if we have *any* now!' retorts Tone, life-and-soul of the party as long as it's a funeral one.

Anyway, Rock Ireland Line it stays. Unanimous vote. Job done.

They're in a murky pub where they're about to perform. 'ONE NITE ONLY!' the poster says, as if they'd ever be booked for more. No, wait, this is not true. Because they do have followers, female fans 'of a certain age', and often they'll be booked 'For 3 Nights! By Special Demand!' 'Things aren't that bad, Tone,' says Mickey, but Tone is like Eeyore in Winnie the Pooh – the sad, lugubrious donkey who never looks on the bright side of life. 'We're AOK!' says Tank, performing a paradiddle on the pub table, 'We rock!' And they all nod, even Tone.

They're sitting over their pre-gig drinks. Danny B: a pint o' the Black Stuff o' course. Tone: a Gin and Tonic (or '*Tone*-ic' as he likes to call it. The pun wears thin after the 50th outing). Mickey: a lager-top, a legacy of his re-hab days. And Tank? Well, he's off the booze, sticking to orange juice as he's on antibiotics for some unspecified infection (not the clap though, those days are long gone, my friend).

Look at the four of them sitting there around the small table, silhouetted in the frosted window, hunched over their drinks. Comrades-in-arms, it looks like. You can just tell, they're as one, like those Four Musketeers. Tank is in top-to-toe denim over his favourite 'wifebeater' sleeveless vest. He calls it his Tank Top. Grubby trainers on his sockless feet. Mickey is more soberly dressed, in an open-neck check shirt, hoodie jacket and sand-coloured safari trousers – those ones with loads of pockets everywhere but you never put anything in them. His ever-present Crocs preserving his ever-suffering feet. And for Tone? Tone is sporting his usual melange of pastel shades topped off with a deep red cardie – the black curls against the deep red creating a dramatic contrast. Which leaves Danny who is the most elegant of them all. In a suit. Dark and Italian-style. Narrow lapels, tight-cut trousers, almost 'drainpipes', over black crewneck. Shoes: black 'Brothel Creepers'.

Look at the four of them. They don't seem so very wild, this wild bunch, crouched over their drinks which they sip modestly. Mickey excuses himself to go to the Gents – for the second time in just half an hour. He pretends it's to relieve a back strain, that he has to keep moving, but no one believes him. He has the over-sixty year old's pissing habit, and the pint of lager-top doesn't help. 'Goes right through him like a rat through a drainpipe,' says Tank, but no one laughs as they all suffer this to some degree.

Nine p.m. they're on tonight. And it's only eight. It's too early to unpack and set up. So, what to do for an hour? Continual drinking means getting blathered, and, worse, more loo visits. And once you're on stage, you're stuck for an hour before a break. Mickey wears an incontinence pad, but none of the others know this. It's his little secret and if he's caught short while he's performing, well, no one's the wiser.

He returns to the table, making a pantomime of stretching his back to further the myth of getting up to relieve his back not his bladder. 'That's better,' he says, 'bloody back!'

One hour to go. Out come newspapers, paperbacks, mobiles. Anything to pass the time.

2
Summer Holiday

It was still the age of Holiday Camps in England in the 1970s, even though going abroad to the Costa del Sol was taking over from home-grown holidays. The risk of rain at home in July and August meant that the lure of guaranteed perfect weather – sun, sea, sand and sangria – was too much to resist. So Holiday Camps in England, like Butlin's, were struggling against the strong competition of the foreign package holiday. But they were surviving, with a fresh coat of paint and promise of all-round entertainment in the form of pop groups, comedians and singers. Maybe the old days of the Bathing Beauties Competitions or Hairiest Legs had passed, but there were bars and snooker halls for the dads, Bingo and the Princess Ballroom for the mums, and for the kids? Bumpy slides, Ferris wheels, monorails, cable cars, fancy dress… and the Captain Blood Hunt, where a redcoat dressed as a pirate would be chased by squealing kids to the outdoor pool then made to 'walk the plank' i.e. jump off the diving board. Meanwhile, the teen girls would eye up the teen boys in the coffee bars, and the teen boys would ogle the teen girls in their teeny-weeny polka dot bikinis by the pool. Tank gets over-excited at one point when he hears there's a 'Beaver Club', but it turns out it's for kiddies and very much of the semi-aquatic, dam-building variety.

Rock Ireland Line is first booked at the Holiday Camp in Minehead in the summer of 1975 for a month's season for the last two weeks in July and the first two in August. At this time, they've become a tribute band for that 1960s hit pop group, Dave Dee, Dozy, Beaky, Mick and Tich, and, rather than using their Rock Ireland name, they've reverted to using their own names – Danny, Tony, Mickey and Tank – in honour of the Dave Dee band. 'What goes around, comes around,' says Tone, referring to their original idea for their band name. And if anyone doesn't know which band they're tributing, there's a by-line on the poster in brackets: 'Dave Dee Tribute Band', with the songs listed: 'The Legend of Xanadu', 'Bend It!' and 'Zabadak!' Classics, all.

The lads' stage-dress late 1960s-style in floral Carnaby Street shirts, polo necks and suede jackets and flares; but for 'Xanadu' Danny wears Beau Brummell-type regalia with a buttoned high-collared jacket and silk cravat, Mickey in Spanish toreador, Tone sombrero-ed and poncho-ed and Tank as some peasant-brigand type. The Holiday Camp crowds just love 'em, especially when they play the song with its whip-cracking accompaniment, which Danny Boy appears to achieve with a large bullwhip but the sound is really provided by Tank on a percussion instrument called a slapstick. They end with 'Bend It!' (How could they not?) being the Greek-sounding Zorba-tempo song that speeds up and slows down, with the Greek bouzouki played expertly by Mickey, tho' still in his Spanish toreador outfit (what care they for ethnic authenticity?), the audience clapping in time and some ladies on their feet doing the Zorba dance.

The Holiday Camp is a free-love, free-for-all with pubescent mini-skirted daughters out to have a good time, and you can't beat a rock band for a good time. Tank has a field day in this cornucopia of holiday lovelies and as long as an irate father doesn't cotton on, he's safe. As for the rest of the band, they're committed relationship-wise back home so they don't dabble like Tank, who nevertheless has competition from the handsome Holiday Camp staff – but then a rock 'n' roller easily sees off these clean-cut, blazer-wearing, would-be Romeos. As Tank remarks proudly, 'The gals want the grunge.'

Summer Holiday season over, it's time to drive back home in their ramshackle van and try to achieve the seemingly impossible: a recording contract. The boys are only in their mid-twenties, true, but the band seems to have stalled, and fame is elusive.

'We need a manager,' says Danny Boy.

'We've got one. My Aggie handles the bookings, makes the phone calls, does the deals, provides the outfits.' (This is Tone speaking, of course.)

'Sure. But we need a *proper* manager. Someone who can get the contacts in London, get us the big gigs and a record in the charts.'

There is a pause as they all take this in. Where will they find someone to fill the bill? And how can they betray Aggie, who's done so much work for them? How can they let Tone down?

But Tone chips in, 'London. That's where we'll find him.'

Mickey: 'But we're not in London, are we? We're here in the Midlands and Aggie's doing an okay job.'

Danny: 'Aggie *is* doing a good job and we're grateful for that, Tone, honest – but she don't know the people in-the-know, does she?'

They nod. Aggie doesn't. Tone chips in again,

'Aggie won't mind giving it up, we pay her a pittance, and she doesn't even like our music, calls it "caterwauling".'

Aggie (short for Agnieska), who is Polish by birth, brought up in Brum and talks in a Brummie accent with a hint of East European, met Tone at a Rugby Club disco, fell in love, got wed, had two kids. Aggie won't mind at all giving up the managing, 'more trouble than it's bloody worth,' she says when Tone breaks the news. 'Good bloody riddance,' she says – but secretly she likes being married to a rock star, makes her feel 'cool', boasts about her hubby, her Tony, being 'on tour' (a.k.a. Butlin's), meeting Elvis (made-up), jamming with Elton (also made-up), fighting off 'them 'orrible groupies' (ditto).

Where do bands find their managers? Or do the managers find the bands? Like Brian Epstein with The Beatles…

'Take Brian Epstein with The Beatles,' says pop historian-in-residence Tone, 'owner of the NEMS record shop in Liverpool, so had a fair bit of influence. Do you remember back in the '60s when people used to go to record shops and leaf through the singles in racks and ask to hear them in a sound booth with headphones on? All those girls bopping away but you couldn't hear what they were dancing to…'

Tank: 'I remember when Boots used to have a record department.'

Tone: 'Do you remember how great it was to have just bought a record, a 45, in its paper sleeve, and you'd put it on for the first time and hear that crackle at the start? Needle on vinyl, can't be beat!'

They all go misty-eyed as they remember their first-ever record bought.

Tone: 'Walkin' Back To Happiness by Helen Shapiro.'

Tank: 'Walk on By, the wonderful Dionne Warwick.'

Danny B: 'Hey Baby, sung by Bruce Channel.' (He starts to sing it, wonderfully of course.)

Mickey: 'There's something at the Bottom of the Well, by The Moontrekkers.'

There's always one, isn't there. The others look at Mickey questioningly, not having heard of this particular classic.

Everyone remembers their first record as much as everyone remembers where they were when President Kennedy was shot and Princess Diana killed. Everyone remembers their first proper kiss and their first fumble between the sheets. Meanwhile, Tone, resident Professor-of-Rock, is remembering The Beatles and the fortuitous happenstance that gave them the 'Fifth Beatle', as he was sometimes known – or was that epithet given to their producer, George Martin? Or maybe no one should have that title. After all, the Fab Four were just that. Four.

'So Mr Epstein, owner of this successful record store,' says Tone, intoning like a preacher in a pulpit, 'hears talk of The Beatles, sees them advertised on posters around the town and reads about them in the Liverpool pop paper, "Mersey Beat". Then someone comes into his shop and asks if he's got "My Bonnie" by Tony Sheridan and The Beat Brothers, and maybe Mr Epstein says he'll see about ordering it. Then, when he's informed that the so-called Beat Brothers are in fact The Beatles acting as Tony Sheridan's backing group, his interest is piqued. So one lunchtime he goes to see the group at the venue advertised on the posters, being the Cavern Club, and because of his status in the city, he not only gets in free but is announced from the stage by the resident DJ as "someone famous being in". And there they are, The Beatles, up on that tiny stage. Four Liverpool lads, smoking, joking, larking about, and playing their catchy songs and he saw them standing there…'

The boys catch the clever reference to the Beatles song and nod appreciatively.

'Nice one, Tone,' says Danny.

'… and Mr Epstein was impressed, loving their humour and cheekiness and self-confidence, and he afterwards mentioned "their beat" as well, which was a hip thing for him to recognise.'

'And their beat at that time,' says Tank, who has been paying attention, 'was provided by their drummer, Pete Best, as this was before Ringo joined.'

'Correctamondo, my friend,' says Tone. 'This was indeed pre-Ringo and Pete had been their drummer since the Hamburg days of 1960. Ringo joined in '62, but we're getting ahead of ourselves.'

Danny has stopped the van. They've been driving from Minehead for an hour or so on the way back to the Midlands, and Mickey desperately needs a pee. The others decide they need a pee too, so they line up kerbside like four prehistoric standing stones, legs akimbo, not talking, as talking while peeing is verboten in the male psyche.

Back in the van and back on the road, Tone resumes.

'Brian Epstein is enraptured with this group, loving their banter on stage, and decides to offer himself up as their manager. They, in turn, are impressed with this impeccably dressed businessman who they know well from the record shop. They sign with him and he changes their stage "look" to well-cut suits, all identical, so it's like a band uniform. So they played better gigs, got better money, and Epstein went to London record companies and eventually, long story short, got them signed to the Parlophone label under George Martin, and the rest, as they say, is history. Pop history. Pop legend. In my humble, the best pop group that-ever-was and the best combination of individuals: John, Paul, George and Ringo.'

'So they never had to go down to London at that stage?' says Danny. 'Epstein did it for them? Maybe we don't have to up-sticks ourselves. Difficult for you with Aggie and the kids, Tone.'

Tone remains silent, thinking what moving south would mean, but he shakes this off and concludes his pop history lesson.

'Any of you heard of Larry Parnes? A famous manager of the '50s who discovered Tommy Steele? Then had a stable of male pop singers who he re-christened with macho-sounding names: Billy *Fury*, Marty *Wilde*, and Vince *Eager*. Well, there was something Parnes and Epstein had in common, besides being Jewish – they were both gay. But in those days, homosexuality was illegal, and they had to stay shtum about their sexuality. "You've Got To Hide Your Love Away," sang John Lennon, supposedly about "Eppy".'

They're not too far from their homes now, being dropped off in turn, leaving Tank to park the van in the lock-up with most of the heavy equipment still on board. Tone and Mickey have taken their guitars with them, but there's still the amps and the drum kit. Tank will deal with those tomorrow. He phones his current girlfriend from a callbox, finds she's free, and walks the short distance to her house. Husband's away, Tank will play.

3
Hey Joe

They meet in a coffee bar called Gino's. Frothy coffee from the noisy coffee machine fights 'Substitute' by The Who on the jukebox. Mickey has called the meeting as he has an idea about management.

'I used to know this guy, called himself Joe Rainbow. Played bass in the first band I was in. Big fella. Short back 'n' sides. Always wore a suit, shirt and tie. Nice guy, but couldn't master that 17-note bass riff in Hendrix's "Hey Joe". Even though his own name was Joe, he just couldn't handle that bass run.'

And Tone nods sympathetically as if to say, 'I can understand his problem – it's a tricky riff!'

'Anyway,' continues Mickey, 'in this band, I just had a cheap acoustic guitar from Woolworths with an electric pickup. I'd try to get feedback from the amp, but a Woolies' guitar just weren't up to it. Or maybe it was the pickup. We played just Hendrix's songs then – the lead guitarist was good with the solos – and I was on rhythm, playing E major on and on, no variation, bored out of my skull.'

Mickey has drifted off-subject, and the others wait patiently for him to return.

'Anyway,' continues Mickey, back on track, 'Joe Rainbow gets kicked out of the band, same time as I leave, as it happens. Me, fed up with E major, Joe finger-tied on those 17 notes. But Joe Rainbow comes good. His brother plays in the local football team and Joe wangles his way onto the admin side, eventually ending up as manager. And he works wonders. Moving them up the League. Buying in new players and getting sponsorship. Attendance to the games grows as the new "stars" score the goals, and being Pretty Boy Floyds they attract the girls too. Joe Rainbow gives the team a nickname, the Corgis, which sticks and is well-liked by the fans and the players themselves. The girls like the cuteness of the name while the boys recognise that corgis are aggressive little buggers. Joe even gets a crowd-chant going. To the tune of "John Brown's Body" he's re-written the words, so over the "Glory Hallelujah" chorus, it now goes…'

(And here Mickey sings)
'Glory, glory, we're the Corgis,
Glory, glory, we're the Corgis,
Glory, glory, we're the Corgis,
And the Queen loves all of us!'
'And Amen to that,' says Tank.

'So what I'm thinking is this,' says Mickey, who's ultra-serious now, imparting matters of great import. 'Joe's brother, who I'm pals with, tells me that Mr Rainbow is bored with the football job, feels his work is done and is looking for sommat else to do. He likes a challenge, does Mr R – this is what his bro says – and maybe we're just the challenge he might be looking for. He may not know all the Tin Pan Alley cats down in the Smoke, but he has the chutzpah to booze and schmooze 'em I reckon. What do you all think?'

Tone: 'Is he Jewish?'
Mickey: 'I believe so.'
Tank: 'Is he gay?'
Mickey: 'The jury's out.'
Tank: 'Well, one out of two ain't bad!'
And they laugh fit to burst.

After Mickey sounds out Joe Rainbow's brother, and after Joe's brother takes Joe aside at a football match and tells him about this fantastic band and their need for a manager, and after Joe thinks about this for a total of 9.5 seconds, and after Joe says he's interested… after all this, a meet is set up in Gino's Coffee Bar between the band and Mr Rainbow.

First of all, it's just three members of the band as Mickey, who is always late, is late. Overslept, he explains. 'We should be called "Rock Ireland Lie-in"!' Mickey quips nervously. Nervous because he is the instrument of this get-together and doesn't want it to flop. This is a tight band and each has a responsibility to the others.

A Rolls-Royce Silver Shadow swishes up outside Gino's, purrs to a halt and a grey-uniformed, peak-capped chauffeur steps out and goes around to the kerbside passenger door, opens it and salutes. And there stands Mr Rainbow – and boy, are the lads impressed by this show of wealth and success. Mr Businessman and maybe, just maybe, Mr *Manager*.

Perched up on the high stools against the inside window of Gino's, they are peering through the portholes they've created by wiping away the steamy condensation. From the outside, you'd see four expectant faces, each in its own individual circle, as the bell on the door chings, announcing the arrival of this God-of-Commerce – and amazingly from the jukebox comes the song 'Big Spender'.

Mickey gets up and makes the introductions.

'You boys wanna refill?' Joe asks. Good start. Four cups of frothy coffee, please. Don't mind if we do. Joe has a quiet word with Gino, the Italian proprietor, looking like a mini-Godfather, and before you can say 'Gaggia', a frothy coffee – saucer over cup to keep it hot – is whisked out by the Godfather's pretty daughter to the chauffeur outside, who tips his hat to his boss. The lads appreciate this show of magnanimity – or at least they would, if they knew what 'magnanimity' meant.

And so they sit at a table for four now, with an extra soft leather chair brought out from around the back especially for Mr Rainbow, sir. And they sit amongst the Italian memorabilia: plates hung on the walls depicting Florence and Naples, sun-soaked vistas of mountains and beaches, old postcards, faded photos of Gino's kin, present and past, a Nonna in black lace looking stern and stout. The sound of the Gaggia, like someone being strangled, tries to drown out the conversation, but only one person is speaking and he has a booming voice. Joe Rainbow: failed bass guitarist, successful football manager, in his astrakhan coat made from the dark curly fleece of young karakul lambs from Central Asia, and his black Homburg hat made of stiff wool felt with the single dent running down the centre of the crown, dark cashmere suit, striped blue-and-white shirt, spotted bowtie. Then the giant cigar, Churchillian, no doubt a Romeo y Julieta hand-rolled Cuban cigar, creating a blue-grey cloud over Mr Rainbow's head like an erupting Vesuvius.

'Well, boys,' Joe begins in a slightly fey tone with a waspish edge. 'Mickey here has enlightened me as to your situation and a parlous one it is too, if you'll permit me. Chronically short of funds, badly-paid performances, sometimes not paid at all, not a hide nor hair of a record deal and I have to say, if I'm being brutally honest, no future in the music business and, left to your own devices – or "vices" if I'm to believe all I hear of Tank here…'

And at this point Joe pauses, winks, laughs conspiratorially and taps the side of his nose like a market trader, thus establishing himself as 'one of the lads' and endearing himself to Tank who revels in his notoriety as the Bad Boy of the Band – no Johnny B. Goode, he.

'… if left to your own devices your band will split up in maybe a couple of years' time and you'll be back to your day jobs, if I'm not mistaken. And I'm not mistaken, fellas.'

Wow! With this doomsday scenario, there's not a word from the band, not a sip of coffee taken. Even the Gaggia is silent.

'But I'll make a promise to you, boys. One, you'll be on *Top of the Pops* within a year; two, you'll be making dosh, proper dosh; three, you'll be touring, both at home and abroad; four, no more Holiday Camps as you'll be *stars*. But if you *don't* want all that, let's drink up our coffees, shake hands and part as friends. What do you say?'

They *do* want what he's offering. Of course they do. They look at each other, four minds as one in this tight band, and nod yes. They want fame.

'So how can I guarantee this? How can I cross-my-heart-and-hope-to-die promise all these things? I will tell you. Mr Rainbow stands for Mr Success. Joe Rainbow stands for a colourful future. You remember me, Mickey, in that loser-group playing Hendrix songs? Well, I've come a long way in a short time: Mr Football Club…'

'The Corgis,' interjects Danny Boy.

'The Corgis,' resumes Joe. 'Now they're up in the League and climbing and scoring goals and *I* did that. If it weren't for Joe Rainbow, they'd be skulking down at the bottom with just a few fans and now look at 'em. The Corgis! Dogs of war! Hounds of hell!'

Okay, Mr Rainbow is going a bit OTT here, but he is a salesman after all. How does the saying go? Could sell ice cream to Eskimos? Something like that.

'More coffees, Gino!' he bellows, snapping his fingers, taking off his Homburg, sleeking back his black hair. Gino responds, 'Coming right up, Mr Rainbow, sir!' How does Gino know his name? Easy. Joe's chauffeur, who is something of a 'fixer', has phoned ahead, forewarning Gino of the imminent arrival of a VIP who must be treated as such, with the promise of a cash contribution to Gino Incorporated which is Gino's fund to return to Italy and open up a chain of Gino's Italian Coffee Bars. Coals to Newcastle, you might say.

'Let's get down to brass tacks,' says Joe, 'I came to see you the other night in that pub you play in, and I was impressed, I have to say, *well* impressed! Consequence of which, I would like to manage you. Truth is, I've had my fill of football and I want a fresh challenge and pushing a band like yours will be just the ticket. So, let's not beat about the bush – are you fellas interested?'

Interested they are, and they look at each other and nod in agreement.

'Okay, so here's the deal. I take twenty per cent of your gross income then, after deduction of expenses and some nominal tax to keep the taxman at bay – (tap on side of nose, wink wink) – you get the rest. We start a new company called RIL Entertainments and you sign a five-year contract to be re-negotiated after that time with me getting first refusal should you decide to look elsewhere, which I doubt you will as my cut will reduce to fifteen per cent as long as certain targets have been reached, details of which are found in said contract.'

He brandishes said contract, all thirty-odd pages of it, and after a quick perusal and an assurance that 'you won't find anything fairer', they sign on the proverbial dotted with their full names: Daniel Patrick O'Shea, Antony Crichton Tredwell-Johnston, Michael Martin Mills and Jon Kevin Sandercock. Joe signs with his real name, Joseph Aaron Cohen.

So, signed, sealed and delivered unto the care and loving attention of their new bonafide manager and mentor, Rock Ireland Line can look forward to a starry future. But first, down to the nitty-gritty, as Joe calls it.

'We have to base ourselves in London and I'll need you boys with me for demos, meet 'n' greets etc. Let's say it'll take a month to get you on track, so inform your loved ones that you're seeking fame and fortune and you'll be home before they know it – rich and famous!'

And Joseph Cohen, a.k.a. Joe Rainbow, was true to his word.

4

On The Road Again

And so it was, one week later, after tearful goodbyes in some cases and sighs of relief in others (the former being Tone and his brood, the latter being Tank with his married 'bit on the side'), so it was that the boys found themselves crammed in their 1966 blue Ford Transit Custom Camper van with over 100k on the clock, or it would be had the dial not been re-set by a friendly mechanic who set it back to a more presentable 50k.

They call this lady of the road 'Bessie'. Some of the tyres are as bald as Mickey (even at this young age, he's losing it *rapido*), and the exhaust has more patched-up holes than a slice of Edam. This is the transport they've become used to, that they've travelled to Minehead in, and will travel to wherever'll have 'em; that they've slept in head-to-toe and practised their harmonies *a capella*; that they've argued, laughed, thrown up and shagged in; and sung, at the tops of their voices, the newly released 'Bohemian Rhapsody'. This is the van they've called all the names under the sun, stranded by the side of the road with yet another bloody midnight puncture. But equally they've nurtured and tended their oh-so-familiar Bessie – their trusty steed, their female knight (if there is such a thing) in rusting armour.

Consider, if you will, the seating arrangements in Bessie which follow pre-determined set rules. In the driving seat is Danny Boy – fitting that the leader of the band should also be its driver. He sits hunched over the wheel, in advance of a bad back, and uses the horn relentlessly at any unfortunate road-user he considers too slow. Danny is a road-hog and belligerent speedster (but only such as a Ford Transit Custom Camper van can muster) and an impatient bumper-hugger.

Next to him, bolted together, are two decommissioned aircraft seats from an old passenger plane past its prime. These old seats are narrow (which allows for two to be fitted into the space next to the driver) but comfortable enough, they still have working reclining mechanisms so the passengers can grab some shuteye.

So that's three people sat in the front, but where is the fourth man to go as there are no back seats – all taken out so the amps and drum kit and guitar cases can be accommodated? Well, what happens is this: the amps are stacked up to make a kind of throne and whoever's turn it is – because they all, apart from the lucky driver, take turns to sit in amongst the amps – whoever's turn it is piles up some cushions and makes himself as comfortable as poss, what with being bounced around at every angry swerve that Danny makes. But when you're young you don't care, and when you're a member of a travelling band, you don't give a monkey's. This is the life! The life on the road. And better by far than working in the Co-op stacking shelves or labouring on a building site.

On this early fine spring morning in 1976, the van and three of its occupants divert eastwards to collect Mickey who's been staying with his grandparents in Bury St Edmunds, the town where he was born. Having picked up their remaining passenger, and as it's around breakfast-time, they stop off at the famous Red Lodge Cafe on the A11. This 'greasy spoon' all-nighter is a legend amongst the rock bands, bikers and truckers, assured of a slap-up breakfast at a reasonable price, being the 'Red Lodge Cafe Special' with all the trimmings and a liberal helping of baked beans and as much brown sauce as you care to swamp your food in. Pinned on the wall are signed photos of bands who've stopped there and all sorts of memorabilia, and a mug of 'builder's tea' is all you could wish for, strong and sweet at the same time.

'That'll put hairs on yer chest!' an old buffer at the next table says.

The old road still exists today, bypassed by the new A11, and the Red Lodge Cafe still thrives. Bands would stop off there in the early hours on the way back from gigs at the USAF bases at Mildenhall and Lakenheath (the USAF bases regularly booked bands at weekends back in the day). Nowadays, it's trucks.

The Red Lodge Cafe: a legend in its own lunchtime, breakfast and dinnertime.

One More Cup Of Coffee

They went back there recently, the lads – a nostalgic trip down Memory Lane, or Turnpike Road as it's now called. They turned off the

A11 by-pass after a nearby pub gig, and there, as if it were yesterday, was the same single-storey white building, low-slung with one half pitched roof and the other flat.

Regard it now: red-and-white striped awnings above the windows – one long window to the left of the door, three small ones to the right. As pretty a picture as you can imagine, with flower baskets on either side of the door. Pink, red, and white flowers cascade over the sides of the baskets. A sign, however, warns of CCTV surveillance, which belies the friendly atmosphere of the entrance. The double glass-fronted door bears hand-written signs detailing opening and closing hours – no longer twenty-four-hour nowadays, but still pretty good, opening mostly at six and not closing till ten at night. Wooden bench-type tables lined up outside, shaded by blue-and-white striped umbrellas, look out onto the Turnpike Road to the full lorry park opposite. There's a long truck just parking there with a hiss of its hydraulics. 'For all your WALKING FLOOR Requirements', it says on the side. A brawny character steps down from the cab, stretches, scratches his arse and lopes into the cafe.

The boys park their Previa people-carrier in an area, 'For cafe users only' – but given there's nothing much else around here, it's not likely there'll be transgressors. As they enter the caff, another HGV snakes out of the parking area, which is already full, and journeys onward to connect up with the by-pass on its way to Norwich, hooting its horn as a 'be seeing you' to the cafe and its owners. At the same time, another articulated lorry thunders by – why is he not stopping? Why is he on this road when the by-pass surely beckons? But the lads pay him no mind as they venture inside... and look how nothing has changed! Look at the band photos still there on the wall, a mite faded now with the daylight that streams into this bright interior. In the back half of the building, the ceiling is a shallow curve of tongue-and-groove planking; in the front half, the white counter welcomes you with its neat, red trim, cream walls and a clock in the shape of a teapot, 'Time for Tea' it says on the face. It's always time for tea in the Red Lodge. How did the Red Lodge Cafe get its name? Simple, the village of Red Lodge is nearby, so no mystery there.

Ahead of them, as they enter, is the counter, and on the wall behind the counter are three giant menus, laminated, all hand-written with some black marker crossings-out where meal items have been deleted. For decoration, there's a line illustration of a truck in each L-H corner. THIS IS A SET MENU proclaims a further notice – 'So there!' it implies, don't be going off-piste. The woman behind the counter is brisk and business-like as they survey the breakfast offerings: Standard, All day, Large, Mega and Veggie. The 'Mega' basically has two of everything. That's the difference.

'Three Megas and one Veggie, love!' says Tank, speaking for them all and knowing that Danny is more veggie inclined.

'The Veggie isn't strictly for vegetarians as it's cooked in the meat fryer,' says our counter lady. That's okay, Danny isn't strictly veg, just doesn't like meat much so that rules out the bacon and sausage. His veggie sausage, however, will be made of Quorn and looks just like sausage, and probably tastes like it too, so what's the point? thinks Danny.

'Beans or Toms, or Beans *and* Toms?'

'Both please, love, and throw in an extra black pudding for me!' (This is Tank, of course.)

'Toast or bread butter?' White toast all round, and no offer of brown or, Heaven forbid, *wholemeal*! This is an all-England fry-up with carbs on parade.

'Tea or coffee?' Silly question. Tea, of course.

'And plenty of sugar in mine as if I'm not sweet enough!' (Tank again, the saucepot!)

And as if she hasn't heard this a million times, the woman smiles, and Tank has charmed yet another member of the fair sex.

'Sit where you like,' she says. Or sit *where you can* more like, as the place is already full, as evidenced by the number of lorries parked outside. They go into the curved ceiling section that's like an old railway carriage. Buzzing electric slot machines at one end. RETRO ARCADE says one. Strip lighting. Posters on walls. 'Be Slim for Life' says one – not in this establishment, you won't.

The tables are in rows, set with red-and-white gingham plastic, red-covered chairs, squeezed bottles of ketchup and brown sauce. They sit at a table for four next to one occupied by a lone truck-driver with tattooed arms, engrossed in his mobile phone, scrolling up and down with both thumbs, but interrupted by the counter-lady who delivers his plate of food. All-white crockery.

And this is the overall theme of the place: white and bright, cheery and welcoming. And the smells, oh those cooking aromas! Enough to get your tummy rumbling and your mouth watering. Frying bacon – the best smell in the world. Bread toasting – the next best. And coffee brewing – as good today as it's always been, even if it is instant and probably out of a giant catering tin, but hey, it's made with love.

They notice that one leg of their table has some card under it to level it on the ochre-tiled floor. They notice others have the same treatment. Mickey goes outside in the yard where the toilets are and comes back saying, 'Hey, they have showers here!' But yes, they remember that the Red Lodge boasts showers for the truckers. You come in sweaty and leave smelling of roses.

The slot machines buzz and flash with electricity promising wealth and good luck. Tank is up there feeding RETRO ARCADE with his dough. It clangs and clatters as the three Megas and one Veggie arrive, and Tank is beckoned back to the table, miffed that wealth and good luck has not been delivered.

'Back in the day, the Mega breakfast was called the Big Boy,' remembers Danny.

'A "Big Boy" for Danny Boy!' says Tank.

And they laugh fit to burst.

Then they eat every scrap of their huge breakfasts and lean back, replete, fit to burst.

As they leave, they take one last look at the signed photos of the bands and acts who've eaten there over the years.

A collage above the counter is of photos pasted on or pinned at rakish angles: the bands MUD and TWICE AS NICE and HOTWIRED. And T-REX, would you believe! But not *the* T. Rex. So, Marc Bolan never partook of a Mega. There's even the 'Ann Summers Road Show' with a picture of guys in jockstraps and gals in G-strings. Something for everyone.

KITCHEN NOTICE. WHERE THERE'S SMOKE THERE'S TOAST they read last, as the counter-lady asks, 'Anything more for you boys?'

And Mickey, not considering his weak bladder, replies,

'One more cup of coffee?'

On The Road Again (reprise)

Back in time now – some forty years – and the lads finish their breakfasts, make a last loo visit, and pile into Bessie once more for the long drive down to London. 'Let's hit the road, Jack,' says Tank, and as Danny crunches into first gear, they sing the words of the Ray Charles hit. Mickey is in amongst the amps again as he was the last on board and also because he needs, periodically, to avail himself of a new funnel-and-hose arrangement that serves as a travelling lav – or 'travel-lav' as they call it – being a funnel fitted onto a rubber hose, which leads out through a hole in the side of the vehicle to the outside world, or outside verge, which is sprayed liberally with 'gentleman's relish' as Tone calls it, or 'yellow peril' as Mickey calls it. Even at this tender age, Mickey has his weak bladder.

And so they're London-bound in this year of 1976, and if there was a 'spy-in-the-sky' helicopter, it would spot a faded blue Transit van trundling along in the slow lane, charging the backs of lorries as if trying to make them go faster. Danny, road-raging as ever, behind the wheel. Mickey enthroned in the back. Tone and Tank strapped up in the front airline seats, drinking miniatures of vodka nicked from some cheap hotel frigo-bar. On the road again!

5
Waterloo

Joe Rainbow has arranged their London accommodation for them – an address in West Hampstead that is between opposite ends of the social spectrum: posh Hampstead to the east and Irish Kilburn to the west. Danny Boy feels at home here, next door to his fellow countrymen, this Dublin boy who is homesick sometimes, but a few paces west and the familiar brogue is everywhere, and Danny Boy suddenly sounds more Irish too – 'You can take the boyo out of Ireland but not Ireland out of the boyo!' says Mickey.

This area of West Hampstead could be called 'East Kilburn', but the residents would be none too pleased about that as their house values would suffer, they claim. And it's true that at this time Kilburn is a rougher, scruffier area while West Hampstead lives up to its posh Hampstead associations and benefits from the tag even though it is full of student bedsits.

Anyway, here they are now at the door of a house in Kingdon Road.

'A house! A house! My kingdon for a house!' exclaims Tone in a theatrical manner, gesticulating wildly, but his witty adaptation of the Shakespeare quote is lost on the others, until Danny pipes up, 'Now, where have I heard that before?'

'Just now,' says Mickey, which is quite zen of him.

'I'll find something better for you when the money comes rolling in,' Joe has said and, after all, he is bankrolling this accommodation out of his own pocket.

As they stand at the door, they imagine two sharing rooms in this house of bedsits but when the landlord with the keys opens the door, he leads them upstairs, first-floor landing, to one tiny room.

'This is the room Mr Rainbow has pre-paid one calendar month for,' the Polish landlord says, 'it's for one occupier only – hard ruling – are you all together as friends? Who will be the solo occupier pliss?' (Danny Boy raises his hand) 'And you are Mister...?'

'O'Shea.'

'Well, Mr Oshey, I am Mr Zdunowski and I trust you will be happy enough on your accommodating and your friends will have other arrangements make for them?'

They nod in agreement, but no, Joe has not made other arrangements for Danny's friends as he confirms in a letter left for them on the Formica table addressed to 'The Boys' –

'Dear Band,' it says, *'welcome to your new (temporary) home. I'm sure you'll find a way to all fit in but don't tell Mr Zdunowski or he'll turf you out. Mum's the word! I'll catch up with you tomorrow. Meet Waterloo Station front steps, 5pm sharp. See ya! JR.'*

So, how will four grown men fit into and sleep in a room made for one? One bed. Table and two chairs. Armchair. The answer is taking turns, like in Bessie with who sits amongst the gear in the back. They work it out, tossing a coin for who gets to have the bed for a week. Danny Boy is the lucky winner. Then who gets the armchair? Tone gets the armchair. Leaving Tank to have the sleeping bag on the floor. Then Mickey volunteers to sleep in Bessie at night to guard the equipment. Job done. But it's early yet, and there are new surroundings to explore.

Welcome to West Hampstead. Student-land. A haven of laundrettes, Indian takeaways, supermarkets, off-licences – and there's even a Synagogue. So, after dumping their bags, they're off to the nearest pub to consider their unhappy 'lot', which itemises as follows:

– one tiny cramped one-room bedsit in a house full of other one-room bedsits that smell of stale cooking and stale bodies

– one 'kitchen' of sorts behind a plastic curtain with a 'Baby Belling' electric two-ring cooker, sink and cupboard

– one trail of mouse-droppings leading from the cooker to a gap in the draining-board

– one second-floor landing bathroom and toilet shared with the rest of the house's occupants so the sink will serve as bathroom and loo – for peeing anyway

– one Formica table and two chairs plus one moth-eaten collapsed armchair

– one print on the wall of a smoky London landscape

– one alcove for clothes behind another plastic curtain (grubby, never-been-washed, just like the kitchen one)

– one chest-of-drawers containing one sock (male)

– one electric fire fed by a coin-in-the-slot meter and one mini water boiler

– one copy of Mayfair nudie magazine, well-thumbed, hidden behind chest-of-drawers.

'Well, that's a bonus!' says Tank, looking on the bright side. Because the boys accept their situation stoically. It's not going to be forever and they've been in worse, like sleeping head-to-toe in Bessie in a lay-by in the freezing winter months.

They sit in the nearby pub, maybe a touch disconsolate now as reality sinks in. And the pub is strange with interior balconies – a vast emporium with London-priced drinks.

'How much dosh have we got?' asks Mickey. 'What if we pool it all together and find a cheap hotel – two rooms and breakfast thrown in. Where's the nearest railway station? Those hotels are always cheap.'

Pockets investigated, emptied.

'Couple of quid,' says Tone.

'A fiver,' offers Tank.

'A quid and some change,' moans Danny Boy.

'And I've got a tenner,' says Mickey, 'so that's eighteen quid and some change between us, which I reckon is one more round leaving sommat for a takeaway. Not enough for a hotel. Has anyone fed the meter in the room, by the way?'

Shaking heads. No one has fed the meter, but it's a warm spring, and they can wash in cold water.

'I've got my credit card,' says Danny.

The others look up hopefully.

'But it's maxed out.'

The others look down wearily.

'C'mon lads, buck up!" says Danny B, their cheerleader in times of need. 'This is our chance. We're in the Big Smoke, we've got ourselves a manager – so what if we're in one room? It's dry, and we've shared enough times in the past. Just don't peek when I'm peeing in the sink. We're gonna get to the top, boys! In the hit parade, on the telly! This is the Beginning of the Big Time for Rock Ireland Line! C'mon fellas, what do we say?'

And they put their fists together and chant in unison about Getting to the Top, having a Number One, being the Best of the Best.

The Best of the Best. Childish, isn't it? But this is psychology, this school-playground chanting. Or it's like football chanting or that thing American soldiers shout when they're running or marching. They're called cadences, being traditional call-and-response work songs: *They sign you up to go to war, never held a gun before – sound off! Sound off!'* and so on. Tribal, mindless, hypnotic. This is what the band do to keep their spirits up, and it takes a group to do it too; you can't do it on your own – first sign of madness, they say – talking to yourself.

'Didn't The Beatles do something similar in their early days?' asks Mickey.

'If memory serves,' says Tone.

They clink their glasses together and, for want of anything better to do, and not wishing to dwell any more on their inauspicious start in the Big Smoke, they start their favourite pub game:

'I spot Mick Jagger.'

Their Favourite Pub Game: this is a good one, and they all look around, trying to spot the nearest lookalike to the named celebrity. And this is the game: someone nominates a 'celebrity' they think they've spotted amongst the pub customers and the others have to guess which it is. And the trick is: the resemblance to said personality doesn't have to be that accurate, or even accurate at all.

After a lot of craning necks and puzzled frowns, it's Mickey who points –

'Over there by the fruit machine?'

And there, by the fruit machine, is a long-haired geezer – the long hair being the only possible link to one Mick Jagger as the rest of the nominee is quite overweight.

Next, Clint Eastwood.

Another good one. Surely he ought to be easier to identify, the wiry frame, height, quiff of hair, but no, they give up. Not a hint of Clint.

'Standing by the bar, trying to order.'

A short-arse, standing on tiptoe above the crowded bar, trying to attract the attention of the barmaid. It's the quiff, the hair again, that is the only resemblance to the man-with-no-name.

'Lulu!' shouts Danny, and sure enough, a girl sitting at the very next table does look a bit like the vivacious, pretty pop singer. No contest.

So Danny has won, which means it's his round (the rules of the game make no sense), but he has to borrow off Tank. Then, after another round of Spot The Celebrity – Cassius Clay, Roger Moore and Barbara 'Babs' Windsor – they finish their drinks and mosey along to the Taj Mahal, where they slap all their cash onto the counter and say, 'What can we get for this, squire?' and the Indian owner, unused to being called 'squire' and wondering what it means, is able to furnish them with two mains, two sides, rice and poppadoms. A feast! Their bedsit fills with the fumes of curry, adding to the other fumes emitting from other rooms, the communal toilet and blocked-up drains.

'This is the life!' sighs Danny B, cracking open a last Skol, taking a swig to cool off the vindaloo and passing it along. They make the round of curry jokes that they traditionally make: 'Vindaloo?' 'Yes, I went recently.' 'It's chapatti and I'll cry if I want to.' 'Tears on my pilau.' ''Tis a phall, phall better thing I do.' 'Have you read the Korma Sutra?'

Come the morning, and they're all scratching.

The sleeping arrangements have worked out fine with Danny in the bed, Tone in the armchair and Tank on the floor in the sleeping bag, but it's next morning when they realise they're not the only ones sharing this room.

'My god, *fleas*!' shouts Danny as he pulls back the bedsheets and sees little black dots a-leaping, and he tries to catch one but they're too fast, the little beggars! Danny is scratching, the others are scratching, and things are not looking good on this fine morning at the beginning of April in leafy NW6.

In between scratching, Tone, font of all wisdom, has some info to impart:

'If a man was able to jump as high as a flea, he could jump higher than Big Ben.'

'I'm bitten all over,' cries Tank, scratching all over.

'We gotta get some insect spray,' says Danny, 'how much money we got left?'

Tone: 'The bank'll be open in an hour. I'll cash a cheque.'

At that moment, Mickey returns after his flea-free night in the van.

'Why are you all scratching?'

So, while they leave their flea-ridden bedsit and wander around West Hampstead waiting for the bank to open, it is time to reflect on the finances of the band at this moment in their history.

Tone is the only one with a bank account as he has some family money to help him out. He's Surrey born-and-bred with double-barrelled-surnamed kin, but he's dropped the first part of this long moniker as it embarrasses him. Wife Aggie also helps out with the finances doing cleaning jobs while the kids are at school. She 'does' for various women in the nearby more-moneyed end of her neighbourhood and, when pushed, she says she just does it 'for company'.

Mickey moonlights for cash-in-hand at building sites, being employed, sometimes just for a day, other times as much as a month, as a plasterer. The others worry about damage to his precious guitar-playing fingers, but whaddya-gonna-do-about it? Mickey says.

Tank and Danny Boy are on the dole and even though Danny has his credit card, he hasn't been able to use it for months, having abused it for years.

So, Tone is the one with the bank account – hence the cheque book, hence the cash and hence the giant aerosol can of Big D insect spray, itch ointment and subsequent provisions. Soon Tank and Danny will sign on at the Lisson Grove Labour Exchange and get their dole and Mickey will check out local building sites or bum off the rest of them. No one minds. They're a tight band.

Talking of which, there are three different meanings of the word 'tight':

1) 'tight' as in 'drunk'
2) 'tight' as in 'mean'

3) 'tight' as in 'together'

Here, the meaning is 'together'. A tight band. They work as a unit and are friends for life. Is it too much to say they love each other? Like brothers? No, they really do. Like The Beatles did. Like the Rolling Stones still do, must do, for them to still be together and still performing. Pals, mates, muckers, chums.

('The Ballad of the Band' – as composed by Tone, periodically, as and when the Muse takes him.)

Verse (in the key of C major):

'Rock Ireland Line is a band that's tight,
They'll beat the odds, come what might,
They'll rock the halls, most every night,
A band whose bark's as bad as its bite...'

Tone doesn't really understand that last line. He says it's a bit like when Lennon said McCartney should keep the line about 'shoulder' in 'Hey Jude' even though McCartney had intended to change it. So Tone leaves that line as it is.

Chorus:

'Rock Ireland Line, Rock Ireland Line,
Feelin' good, feelin' fine,
Rock Ireland Line, Rock Ireland Line,
Follow the signs to the Rock Ireland Line...'

The hour's meandering is over, and the bank duly hands over cash so the giant aerosol can of Big D can be bought and taken back to the room to be liberally sprayed and entirely emptied onto the bed, on the carpet, over the armchair, in fact in a poison cloud all over the room, whereupon they close the door tight shut, lock it, and go off to the caff for breakfast with their new-found wealth, thanks to Tone.

(It turns out that one of the tenants downstairs keeps a cat – not allowed of course – and the cat keeps fleas and the fleas multiply all over the house until Mr Zdunowski finds out and the tenant and his cat are eventually kicked out – 'No pet allowed, mister, one month notices!')

After the morning's excitement and a walk over to Hampstead Heath to pass the time, and after buying provisions and another giant can of Big

D (just in case), and after checking out the room which still smells of the spray, but judging by some dead specks on the sheets has done its job – after all this activity the lads take the Underground to Waterloo Station where they're due to meet their manager on the steps on the dot of five p.m. They sit expectantly on the steps in a line as commuters move around them, and one city gent even hands them the change out of his pocket, thinking they are homeless. 'Every little helps,' says Mickey.

Five-thirty and they're still waiting. Six p.m., still waiting. At seven, they give up. It's a no-show.

Danny Boy (getting up and stretching): 'That's that then.'

Mickey: 'That's that.'

They start to walk away.

Tank: 'Mebbe he's busy. Arranging meetings and the like. *Managerin'*.'

Danny Boy: 'Yeah, maybe…'

But he doesn't sound convinced.

'… or maybe he's given up on us.'

Tone: 'I had my doubts, I have to say.'

Mickey: 'You never said. Anyway, we all agreed. Signed on the dotted.'

Tone: 'We can get out of that if we have to.'

Tank: 'Don't reckon we can. It was all legal, weren't it?'

Danny Boy: 'I know some fellas'd sort 'im out.'

Mickey: 'Sorry, lads. I feel it's my fault.'

Danny Boy: 'Don't worry, Mickey. It ain't your fault. We all trusted Joe.'

Tank: 'Look fellas, he's only missed the one meet…'

Tone: 'I say we go home, yes? Leave tomorrow.'

They go quiet. They're used to Tone's gloominess, but this is different, this is defeatist talk. Then Tank chips in, 'Look at the sunset.'

Danny Boy: 'Yeah, look at the sunset!'

They are sitting by the Embankment now, near to Waterloo Station, looking west over the River Thames.

'It's a Waterloo sunset,' says Tank, and they start to sing the song by The Kinks. They sing about the river and how Terry met Julie. Pop historian Tone says that Terry and Julie were meant to be references to the Brit film actors Terence Stamp and Julie Christie – both wonderful specimens of the human form and rumoured to be romancing.

Tone: 'The songwriter Ray Davies denied this though, but still people like to think… anyway, you know what day this is? April the first. April Fool's Day. And we've been taken for right fools, I reckon.'

And the sun goes down, a perfect red, over the golden river, and the lads watch till there's no trace left.

'But we don't feel afraid,' says Mickey, roughly echoing the words of that wonderful song.

6

Rock Around the Clock

It's nine p.m. Showtime. The month is October. The year 2016. The venue: the Frog and Parrot – that murky pub of past description. The hour has passed quickly enough, taken up with getting ready for Showtime. Tank is already in his stage gear, so he uses the time to set up his drum kit. There's no stage as such in the Frog, so Tank asks the landlady where to 'put his equipment'. He says this with a wink and a twinkle in his eye, which said landlady chooses to ignore; instead, she helps him shift tables and chairs to make space at one end of the bar. He'll be sat with his back to a bay window with banquette seats that will remain unoccupied, and, as usual, there's a radiator belting out heat right close by – the last thing Tank needs as he gets sweaty enough playing the drums without the Sahara behind him. He has a trick up his sleeve though – or rather, a tool in his bag – which is a pair of pliers to turn the radiator off while the landlady's back is turned (he's torn between eyeing up the landlady's rear end, a comely bum and wiggle, and attending to the radiator – the radiator wins). Next, he places his electric fan next to his seat to keep him cool during the gig. The band jokes – reg'lar as clockwork – that this is his one and only fan, and they laugh fit to burst.

Meanwhile, the others are changing into their stage 'uniforms': Danny Boy shimmies into his kaftan, Mickey pulls on his WEMBLEY STADIUM SECURITY tee-shirt, and Tone admires his symphony of pastels in a mirror, then goes into a pre-show funk. Tank is already a picture in a sleeveless vest and short shorts. They're in their 'dressing-room', which is a back-room where the stores are kept, but they're not complaining as often as not it's the Gents.

They have their various accessories:

Danny is setting out a stand that holds a ring bind folder containing all the songs of the night in running order. He needs this aide-memoire as he can no longer *memoire* all the words to the songs! The audience probably think it's sheet music, which makes him appear to be a real 'muso' – 'clever bugger can read music!' they say.

Meanwhile, with a rasp of Velcro, Tone stretches his elasticated back belt around his waist as he's had back trouble for years, brought on, he reckons, by all the humping of amps etc. The back belt supports his lower back, helps him stand up straight, not slump; but his problem then is bending down, as he's so trussed up, and if he happens to drop his plectrum (or 'pick', as the Americans call it) he has a spare taped to the microphone (but don't drop that one too, my friend!). Some bass players like to finger-pick the strings but Tone favours the plectrum. The others reckon Tone's moroseness is a symptom of his bad back as he preaches 'Sitting is the Enemy', by which he means sitting down for any length of time is a no-no. He's tried physio, acupuncture, osteo, pills, lotions, massage, injections, electro-therapy, aerobics, stretching, powerwalking, as well as therapists who made him strip naked, therapists who tried to get him to find his pelvic floor, and therapists who said, 'imagine you're a tree'. All he wants for Christmas is A New Back Please, but Santa don't deal in no new backs please. So, it's back belts for standing and wedge cushions for sitting down.

Mickey, as noted before, has his bladder problem, which started out as just a 'weak bladder' in his youth but now is a full-blown, piss-every-half hour old man's complaint and is likely due to an enlarged prostate, but Mickey won't go to the doc to confirm this, saying, 'Never mind the finger-up-me-bum malarkey (and I know of a few clubs whose patrons'd happily oblige) but the doc'd only send me for test after test until they succeed in finding sommat wrong and at my age there's probably a lot wrong but do I need to know? No bloody thank you, anyway, whaddya-gonna-do-about it?' This is Mickey's phrase for every eventuality: queue at the post office? Whaddya-gonna-do-about it? Traffic on the M25? Whaddya etc! Going fucking bald? Whaddya... actually there *is* something to be done about that, but Mickey doesn't want transplants thank-you-very-much. So Mickey's stage accessory is the talc he puts on his bonce to dull the shine from the lights. Mickey's other accessory, getting back to the bladder issue, is the incontinence pad he stuffs down his Y-Fronts, and it's his saviour, his glorious bloody best-invention-ever-after-Imodium saviour, during those forty-five-minute sets. And on his feet? Crocs, of course. *Croc*odile Rock!

Tank stuffs in earplugs to protect his damaged hearing. These won't help with his tinnitus though, which is a daily whining high-pitched aggravation and the Devil's own invention to torture the humble soul. Bizarrely, offstage, he wears hearing aids as he can no longer hear high frequencies, and he hides them behind his ears, covered with his blonde hair. So, that's a conflicting pair of conditions – tinnitus on the one hand, partial deafness on the other.

Earplugs in, he can now concentrate on the beat of rock 'n' roll, which is 4/4 time with the backbeat being on beats two and four. Good ol' Rock 'n' Roll! – which will be the theme of this gig. ROCK 'N' ROLL NITE!! screams the poster outside, and their playlist will be songs with the word 'Rock' in the title, starting with their signature song 'Rock Island Line'.

First, they have a sound-check – their audience being just a few people in the pub so far, but it's filling up nicely for the nine p.m. start. The worst gigs they've played were where the landlord would pay only depending on the size of the audience, the logic being the bigger the audience, the more booze'd get sold. One gig they did, the pub was empty, so they just packed up and left without playing a single number – they knew they weren't going to get paid, so go hang! Another one they played had this rule: the band only got paid if, on the door, the punters said they came to see *that particular band*, so the second time they played there, they went up and down the line asking people to say they came especially to see *them*. The ruse worked, and Rock Ireland Line got paid well that night.

Sound-check over and guitars tuned. Tank dunks his hands in an ice bucket to reduce the swelling that would otherwise happen during the gig. Drumming ain't easy; it's punishing on the back, the body, the hands, the ears. Some Heavy Metal drummers wear special drummer's gloves to stop blisters, which is a nice little earner for the drum manufacturers. These specialist gloves have synthetic mesh backs and ventilated palms in stretch Lycra.

Danny Boy bashes a tambourine, both as a prop and also to make him seem more like a musician but, having said that, he can pick up a harmonica and belt out a mean vamping lick – remember his hero is the great Mick Jagger, so he emulates what Mick plays (even though he has neither the moves nor the figure). He sits studying the playlist, wondering how his voice will hold up; it's not what it was way back when – when he was age twenty, thirty, forty… God, in his sixties he is now! But he can still belt out 'I Love Rock 'n' Roll' by Joan Jett and the Blockheads, and the Stones' 'It's Only Rock 'n' Roll (But I Like It)' and Chuck Berry's 'Rock 'n' Roll Music' with that backbeat you can't lose it. They'll end the night with 'Crocodile Rock' courtesy of Elton John and for an encore? 'Rock Around The Clock' of course. The Bill Haley and the Comets song that changed everything.

'But it wasn't till '66/'67 that the word "rock" in the UK was widely used. Up until then, it was "pop music" which sounded a bit "bubble gummy", while "rock" was the biz – (this is University-of-Rock Tone, enlightening them all to their legacy) – "Rock Around The Clock" was the start of a music revolution. It changed everything, changed the climate, changed the 1950s youth of the time, and outraged the elders and the establishment.'

They've heard this lecture a few times now on the Birth of Rock, and Danny B will likely touch on it in his in-between-songs blarney, which he's good at – his soft Dublin accent lulls you into the next song, and you understand its background sure enough. How Before Haley – or 'B.H.' as Tone calls it – you had the crooners, the younger versions of Bing Crosby, spearheaded by Frank Sinatra. These were the smooth Romeos with their slicked-back hair, smouldering Italian looks and sharp suits – while Bing was more homely. Along with Frank, or maybe after Frank, came the Bobby's: Bobby Darin, Bobby Vee, Bobby Vinton. Then along came skiffle with Lonnie Donegan's 'Cumberland Gap' and, of course, 'Rock Island Line'. Skiffle was all about the fast 2/4 rhythm, soon to be replaced, nay, *trounced*, by Bill Haley.

Before Haley (BH) was skiffle.

After Haley (AH) was all hell let loose.

'Ladies and gentlemen, boys and girls, lads and lasses, and not forgetting boys 'n' boys and girls 'n' girls, we're all broadminded here – (pause for laugh as Danny Boy makes his first intro) – tonight, and for one night only, you lucky people are going to be hearing the music of rock 'n' roll, brought to this fair land by Mr Bill Haley and the Comets with his ground-breakin', nay, *earth-shatterin'*, rhythms and his hair-mussin' moves; those of you "of a certain age", and I'm sure I could spot a few of you out there if only I had me specs on – (pause for laughs) – will remember Bill with his cute kiss-curl plastered to his forehead and his rockin' band in their loud check oversize jackets with skinny bowties; picture them now, the sax player playing his instrument lying on his back, we're a bit too geriatric to be gettin' up to those sorts of antics tho' – (pause for more laughs) – while the big double-bass was upended and played upside down and twirled around like a spinning-top; our own bass player, Tone here, may I introduce Tone? – (pause for cheers) – will *not* be playing his instrument upside down, will you Tone?'

Tone shakes his head no, and his long black Charles the First curls flop from side to side in almost slow-motion.

'Most of you are too young to remember this but when Bill Haley performed his song in the UK the audiences'd go mad, ripping up cinema seats, screaming and having hysterics. However, the management of this establishment has requested that you leave the furniture be – (pause for laughs) – but first, back to where it all began: "Rock Island Line".'

And so into their signature song now with a rock-beat and heavier than the Donegan original.

'History-of-Rock' Tone, in reminiscing on the subject, would rhapsodise on the Great Little Richard and Jerry Lee.

'Jerry Lee Lewis, "The Killer", who treated his piano like a weapon, sweeping his clenched fist up and down the keys creating rolling arpeggios and shaking his wavy mane, a lock of blonde falling over his brow because There's A Whole Lotta Shakin' Goin' On, Mama; and Little Richard, largeing it on the baby grand, playing with his back to the keyboard, arms stretched behind him, then one leg cocked up on the piano lid; and there he is in the film *Don't Knock the Rock* singing "Tutti Frutti" in a smart grey suit while the white-suited saxophonists jig up and down in a choreographed routine – and look who's there in the audience with his kiss-curl watching, beating time… why, it's only The Father of

Rock 'n' Roll himself, Mr Bill Haley!'

But Danny has skipped these rock idols to announce their next song, 'Jailhouse Rock', and as he gathers himself up to speak, he cradles the microphone and strokes it like it's an icon or something else (and the girls in the audience think of the 'something else' of course); then, by mistake, he creates the most ear-splitting feedback which penetrates the fortifications of Tank's ears and Tank swears mightily, to the audience's great delight. The evening is going well. Meanwhile, Mickey pisses contentedly into his Level 3 (designed for the 'fuller flow') pad, and Tone holds his bass guitar upright at twelve o'clock as Danny Boy continues:

'All ye gathered here, a moment of silent reverence, if you please, for The King Himself, The Presley, The Elvis! Hush. The Legend That Is Elvis, with his sexy hips that so *enraged* the Bible Belt of the American Southern States, and every aunt, uncle, grandma, grandpa, ma and pa that ever lived in middle-class, middle-aged suburbia with their good-as-gold offspring who are now, Mother of God, dancin' the Devil's fandango to "Blue Suede Shoes", that so-called "sinful music" that spawned mean-lookin', leather-clad rockers like the fabulous Gene Vincent, snarling "Be-Bop-A-Lula" into a chrome microphone, dragging his gammy leg behind him in a parody of Richard the Third, scowling dangerous and mean!'

Whew, follow that! And so they do, with 'Jailhouse Rock' and its guitar slide from E flat to E, the drumbeat synchronising with the slide but adding two beats after. The pub is now rocking, sure enough, dancing around the tables and the landlady, Mine Hostess, serving shot after shot. After the Elvis song, the band go straight into the Chuck Berry number, 'Sweet Little Rock 'n' Roller' about a sweet nine-year-old girl dressed up like a Christmas tree, and there's Mickey's guitar-chugging rhythm that's so distinctive of Chuck Berry.

Danny knows how to work an audience, that's f'sure. It's time for reflection now. A change of pace as he relates the Larry Parnes story.

'Y'know folks, back in the day, or back in the 1950s, to be precise, there was this pop manager – well, more of a "guru" really – called Larry Parnes, who became so successful and rich as a result of his success that he was nicknamed "Parnes, Shillings and Pence", and that was in old money – (pause for laughs from the older audience and puzzled looks from the younger) – and talking of names, it was Larry Parnes who pretty much cornered the market in re-naming his pop stars, who were all boys by the way and yes, Parnes was, as my dear ol' Pa used to say, "queer as a nine-bob note!" – (disapproving boos from the crowd) – I know, not very "woke" of my dear ol' Pa, was it? Anyway, who remembers Tommy Steele? – (hands go up) – real name: Tommy Hicks. Profession: merchant seaman. Parnes saw him perform in the famous 2i's Coffee Bar in Soho, signed him up, and gave him his metallic name *Steele* and Tommy never looked back. And Billy *Fury*? He was originally Ron Wycherley, which didn't sound much like a pop star. Marty *Wilde* was by birth Reg Patterson. Wilde, Fury, Steele – well, you get the picture, don't you? All powerful names. But when it came to Joe Brown, who remembers Joe Brown? – (hands go up) – well, Larry Parnes wanted to re-name Joe Brown: guess what? "Joe Tornado"? "Joe Hurricane"? No, word around the campfire is that it was "Elmer Twitch". Yes, *Elmer Twitch*! Wisely, Joe Brown stuck to his own moniker, thank you very much. Me? My manager wanted to change my name. What to? Well, I'll tell you, he opted for Danny Dogsbollox! – (pause for hilarity, then another pause for comic timing) – my original name was Catsarse!' House brought down and as the laughter subsides, they go into 'Rock with the Caveman', Tommy Steele's early hit.

The first hour is up. Interval now of fifteen minutes before the final one-hour set. The band retire to their 'dressing-room'. Back belt adjusted, tightened; incontinence pad secretly changed, more talc on bonce; songbook folder re-arranged. Tank examines his earplugs: these aren't just ordinary foam earplugs, these are *very expensive,* proper, bonafide, musician's earplugs designed to cut 'damaging transients' (whatever-they-are) while ensuring a 'normal hearing experience'. That's what the brochure said anyway.

Their drinks arrive, and this is all they'll have – one drink pre-show, one in the interval, one post-show. Tank reckons his metabolism soaks up the alcohol pretty sharpish, although, as noted before, he's on fruit juice tonight. Otherwise, he reckons he's okay to drive after his usual three pints of real ale (which is what he has when he's antibio-free). He reckons this as one time he was stopped on his way home from a gig by Mr Plod and was breathalysed, and *zero* alcohol was detected. He attributed this to having metabolised all the booze away due to the physical exertion of drumming – 'Sweated it all out!' he said.

The others stick to the three-drink rule and, if they're driving afterwards, whether it be home or to some B&B, they stop at that. If it's a cheap hotel for the night, they'll hit the bar – even the reformed alcoholic Mickey will hit the bar (as long as Rosie isn't there to stop him). At one time, the band thought they performed better when pissed. They became convinced that the more they supped, the better the music – 'It's like we lose our inhibitions and instinct takes over!'. But then, one time, they listened to a recording of one of those sodden gigs and what they heard was the reverse: under the influence of alcohol, the performance became shambolic. And what's more, they heard the audience's reaction: booze leading to boos.

As to drugs, the boys are past it. Ibuprofen and paracetamol for aches and pains, Regaine for hair loss, Viagra for... well, we know what Viagra's for. The old-style drugs of yesteryear are of no interest to them now; sure, they took marijuana back then, for their nerves. Everyone took marijuana back then, for their nerves. It was good ol' fashioned cannabis resin, not the dangerous hybrid skunk of today. They're all too old and wise for that caper now. And as for cocaine, the hipster's choice? Well, in olden days, their fellow rockers'd snort till their noses dropped off, but nowadays those ol' boys are reformed characters. Either that or they're dead. So that leaves booze: Danny's black stuff, Tone's G&T, Mickey's lager-top and Tank's ale.

The only occasion the band got royally drunk was at a pub gig in Essex that was near-empty. In fact, there were more in the band than in the pub. They played to a crowd of two regulars and one dog, so they just got more and more pissed, blowing their gig-earnings, and ended up in fits of giggles. Irony was, they got paid nothing anyway, but they had a good time even if the two regulars and one dog didn't.

The band call them 'The Loopy Groupies', the three sixty-plus-year-old women who have faithfully followed Rock Ireland Line since forever.

They call themselves 'The Liners' or 'The Cruise Liners'. Hattie, Bet and Trude. Looking like chubby triplets now, but my God, they were beauties back in their day! They, in turn, in the dim and distant, slept with all the boys apart from Tone who remained resolutely faithful to his Aggie – 'She'd have my balls for breakfast!' he'd say.

'No bad thing!' says Tank, imagining a different scenario.

So, in the interval, the ladies visit the band, and the boys welcome their loyalty. The Liners will comment on a performance sometimes, often on stage-wear, but never on physical infirmities; they're too worldly-wise for that. Never be personal with a man, that's their motto. A man's ego is tied up in three things: his hair, his belly and his... well, we know what that is. Otherwise, the ladies praise to the hilt, but they don't have to make it up because Rock Ireland are still great. It's the audience that's changed, wanting rap and reggae, not rock. Ah well.

Hattie: 'You were bustin' tonight! That "Jailhouse Rock" always does it for me!'

Bet: 'Danny, you were sockin' it to me!' (They have an old-fashioned way of speaking like they're stuck in some bygone era, but Bet means well; she's always held a torch for Danny Boy.)

Trude, the diplomat: 'Now Bet, they were *all* great.'

The Frog and Parrot has done the boys proud with the spread of refreshments: crisps, peanuts, pork scratchings, scotch eggs, sandwiches – all pub fare plus their (free) interval drinks. The Liners have brought their own into the dressing-room/broom cupboard, being three G&T's, ice and a slice. They're married, these women, with grown-up kids, and their hubbies have got used to their excursions and accept them – anyway, it's a bit of peace and quiet in their absence, off to the pub for darts and dominoes.

The Liners dress up for the boys in sparkly spangly tops, Lycra leggings, all pink and orange, mutton dressed as lamb but they won't be told. Certainly not by their other halves who don't know anyway as the girls change on the train or coach or whatever. They're last in a long line of the band's female followers though – before them were the skanky skinny ones, the drugged-up and dressed-down, with their 'points' system for rock stars shagged. But even though The Liners have slept with most of the band, they've also undergone a different role, that of substitute girlfriends on the road, ironing clothes, preparing food, providing company and conversation. It's a dedication, a calling even, that they worship the lads and will be their 'rocks' through the days of touring.

But now the boys kiss them politely and suggest they leave them to 'chill'. But 'chill' they won't, because the interval – much like in football when the trainer harangues the team in the dressing-room for their errors – is when Danny B likes to hold a performance 'post-mortem' on how-it's-gone-so-far. Time-honoured tradition and one the others put up with, bearing world-weary expressions, rolling their eyes in exasperation with the occasional behind-the-back V-sign. Because Danny won't hand out praise but rather point out mistakes, never his own of course. And tonight, Tank is the first target. Bullseye!

'Steward's Enquiry!' says Danny. 'Tank, on the last number you ended prematurely and in so doing, you cut off Mickey's guitar solo which would've been much appreciated by the audience t' be sure.' (Danny, lapsing into the Irish vernacular at the end there.) They all look at Mickey who wisely stays shtum. But it's true, it was going to be a great guitar solo.

Tank speaks up in his defence: 'I was following Tone and I thought he nodded for me to finish.' Sneaky move Tank, trying to pull in Tone, who now denies culpability: 'I didn't nod but when you did your big finish I followed suit.'

'Leaving me hanging,' says Mickey, joining the fray.

Tank deflects: 'Sorry, Mickey.'

Mickey demurs: 'No problem, T.'

Danny B: 'We have to learn from our mistakes. How're we gonna stop this happenin' again?'

Mickey: 'I can start my solo early, on the last beat I mean.'

Genius! They all agree that'd work. But Danny has further cause for complaint.

'Regarding the sandwiches so kindly provided by Mine Hostess: may I point out that I, as you all know, am vegetarian but the proportion of meat sarnies to the cheese variety was an unfair three to one. I counted. And yet you lot plunged straight in and scoffed all the cheese ones! This is invariably the case: that, in a meat versus cheese scenario, it is the cheese ones that are nabbed first by you so-called meat-eaters, leaving us veggies wanting!'

'But they had pickle in 'em!' says Mickey, as if that excuses their greed.

Tone: 'Danny's complaint is duly noted and in future he will have first dibs on the sarnies, regardless of the pickle in 'em.' Ever the diplomat is yer Tone. But Danny, unsatisfied (and quite peckish), resumes his post-mortem –

'Chords, Mickey. Chords!'

'Yes, I know. Just got mixed up between me E's and me A's.'

'Learn your chords, Mickey. And Tone, last riff on "Jailhouse"?'

Tone: 'Got stuck. Sticky fingers.' And he wiggles his fingers, miming stickiness.

'Well, we all know what causes that,' leers Tank, 'been playing with The Liners?'

As if, they all think. As if Tone the Saint would ever stray. Never been known. His Aggie must be some gal. Either that or she's a ball-buster.

So, crit over: but who's going to judge Danny Boy, whose voice cracks now on the high notes, whose tambourine beat is wayward compared to Tank's meticulous metronome, whose spoken intros go on too long, leaving the band standing there waiting to start the next number, whose dance moves now are creaky and, at times, embarrassing? 'Dad-dancing', more like. But this is Danny B, who in his mind can't put a foot wrong, even if his big toe joint is bunioned.

Anyway, the interval is over and the band is now back on parade.

Part two. Rock Ireland Line. Rockin' and a-Rollin'.

The first song of the second half is the Led Zeppelin classic 'Rock and Roll' which has Tank ending with a percussive *triumph* emulating the Zeppelin drummer John Bonham's brilliant drumming *tour-de-bloody-force*! Tank, in his cups, once tried to explain his version of the sequence to a fledgling drummer:

'Left and right on the snare, right-right-left, see? Those two right hand beats close together – bangbang! Now six repeats of the pattern on snare, rack, and floor tom. Bass drum. Triplet: left hand rack, right hand floor, bass drum two times. Now watch: three strokes on the snare, right-left-right ending with one almighty sweep, snare, rack and bass. Now you do it.'

But the poor boy can't.

'Never mind,' says Tank, somewhat condescendingly, 'just end with a crash 'n' splash!' (Which is Tank's drumming talk for the two cymbals).

It is in this second half that Tank, in between his sweaty exertions and dabbing down with a towel, begins to notice two females in the audience. What is it about them? One is middle-aged, attractive, smiling, and the other is younger, in her twenties maybe. So, what is it about them? Tank deliberately looks away but, as is often the case in these situations – if one should find oneself in the like – the gaze is soon drawn back to the point of origin, in this case the pair of women.

The younger girl is staring intently at him. Too intently for comfort. When he looks again, they are still in the same pose, the same attitude – one friendly, mocking even, the other earnest. What is it about these two? Tank finds himself unnerved by their brazen stares. No one else in the audience looks like this; the rest of the crowd look relaxed, enjoying the music, chatting amongst themselves. Not *staring*. While these two women – could they be mother and daughter? there's a likeness – stand like statues amongst the dancing all around. They are an island of immobility (and if Tank had thought of that turn of phrase, he might admire his literacy – as it is, he just thinks they're, well, like statues).

he looks the same – fatter now but the same darlin' blonde hair – she doesn't recall it being that blonde before, maybe he uses something like 'Sun-in' to highlight – he would do that, he's so vain, she thinks – and smiles – the goatee beard is new, it suits him sure, brings out the rascal in him she thinks – and smiles – it makes him look like a pirate – God, he dresses the same as ever, terrible vest with those cut-off sleeves, and those shorts! – shorts shouldn't be that short, she thinks and smiles – all the way up to his arse, silly man –but he's still got that devilish twinkle in his eye – and she smiles –

He looks up again, after a few minutes of deep concentration as he completes a complicated string of triplets on the ride cymbal – he looks again and catches the eye of the younger female, but it's not a chance catching-of-the-eye but a determined 'gotcha' holding onto his gaze, defying him to look away but he does, on the pretext of following Mickey or Danny, but he knows she has her eyes on him all right, and they never leave.

could he really be my da? could he really? she wonders and frowns – Ma says so, so it must be – she's rarely wrong – but is this the father she imagined all those years of her fatherless childhood? – the missing 'Daddy'? – she wonders and frowns – she used to imagine a handsome, tall man with a moustache, neat-trimmed, wearing a suit and carrying a briefcase – 'what does he do, Ma?' 'why, he's important in a bank, wears a suit every day to work' – but this one? she wonders and frowns – but he's a character, this one, a piece of work all right – maybe he's all right, she wonders –

Their encore, 'Rock Around The Clock', ends with a percussive crash coinciding with the last heavy E chord from Mickey (played high up on the fretboard as a *barre* chord, 7th fret) as he (Mickey) leaps into the air, upsetting the delicate placement of his incontinence pad – for God's sake, remember your limitations, son! (He turns his back to the audience and re-adjusts himself, and the others don't notice or cotton on, it's just Mickey fiddling with his privates.)

On that last percussive crash on the aptly named 'crash cymbal' and the last splash on the snare, Tank dares to look up again, but the two women have gone. The smiley, older woman and the frowning young 'un. Disappeared like ghosts.

And gradually, creepily slowly, the audience edges in to fill the gap left by the two, as if the space were infected.

7

Rock The Joint

The days go by in West Hampstead in the tiny bedsit, and the boys settle into a routine of boozy nights and getting up late. Not much food to speak of, and they're losing weight, getting skinny, looking like Lowry matchstick men and smoking dope when they can afford it. Not Tone, though. They'll never turn Tone on.

'Unturnable is Tone,' they're wont to say in between deep inhales of a shared spliff.

'I don't smoke, you see. So I'm afraid that puffin' on one of your joints will turn me on not only to marijuana but also to nicotine.' So says Tone and he has a point. The others smoke roll-ups or Player's No 6 (which are dead cheap) so to them a joint is just another variation on a ciggie but more potent of course, as Danny Boy tries to explain to Tone,

'Marijuana, or *weed* or *hash,* lowers your perceptual threshold so y'see, boyo, it *ups* perception, at the same time relaxing and focussing, all these things, it's a wonder drug, t' be sure – (lapsing into the vernacular as Danny becomes *more* Irish the more he inhales or imbibes or whatever-you-want-to-call-it) – and you can finesse the response so if the effect is too soporific to go on stage and perform, you just add a little coke, finances permitting o' course.'

But finances aren't permitting o' course. Tone is no longer the bottomless bank so where's the income? Some dole money, true, but not enough to feed the drug habits of the three of them. And why should Tone fund that anyway, when he's in disagreement in principle, when he's taking the moral high ground?

And talking of 'high', Tank has more to add on the benefits of the 'wacky baccy' –

'More feel for the skins, man – more tactile feedback sensitivity! You can feel the rhythm of the drumbeats in your whole body, man...'

But he drifts off into oblivion and what he doesn't mention is the feeling of paranoia you get when you're high. And that terrible hunger, the so-called 'munchies', which is not welcome when there's not much food they can afford after the outlay on the marijuana – their cannabis-of-choice being the expensive 'Acapulco Gold', which is the bees-knees of hemp.

'The colour of gold.' Mickey will rhapsodise on this, given half a chance. 'It's "connoisseur pot", truly fucking mind-blowin'. Grown under the blazing Acapulco sun, legendary in the '60s, so much more superior to Californian weed. The highest of highs for the rock stars and film stars of the day – "those in the know'd go for the blow!" was the saying.'

'You have to be careful, mind,' says Tank, 'you have to know your sources. You have to avoid the Gold that's been laced with paraquat to make it more golden-coloured. Paraquat's a herbicide and you don't want no weed killer in your weed, man!' And, with that 'man', Tank has become more LA, the effect no doubt of this West Coast drug.

But Tone is not to be persuaded,

'Aggie'd have my guts for garters!'

'And your balls for afters!' So says Danny Boy, chuckling. Then they all, including Tone, bless 'im, laugh fit to burst, knowing that Aggie – Polish, Eastern Bloc-born Agnieszka – is a ball-breaker and a beautiful one at that – a fact they all reflect on quietly to themselves because marijuana increases libido, which is not welcome, given the band's current monk-like existence.

'I need to get laid!' says Tank, going all West Coast again in his vocabulary.

They've mentioned cocaine and how it's not something they can afford, and they've talked about maybe mixing it with hash to help, performance-wise, but they don't indulge in coke as they feel this is a bridge too far, never mind the expense.

'Coke is a bridge too far,' Danny B pronounces, and they all nod their heads in tacit agreement, especially holier-than-thou Tone.

'A bridge you don't want to cross.' Tone is sat leaning forward, elbows on knees, hands clasped together as if in prayer, his long black curls hanging decorously like Jesus.

61

The general way to take cocaine – the method portrayed in movies and the like – is to 'snort' the white powder through the nose. This is called 'insufflation'. This is the technical term for sounding like a foghorn with catarrh. And the way to do this is via the rolled-up banknote – £20 notes are the best – or through hollowed-out pens or cut-down straws. Or, more romantically, or more erotically, whichever way you look at it, off long pointed painted female fingernails. Trouble is the body tolerance strengthens with regular dosage and you need more each time to get the desired effect – that release of energy and feeling of euphoria. So you find you need more and more up your schnozzle, then lo and behold, one too many snorts and your nose gives up the ghost and the bit between your nostrils disintegrates. A bridge too far. A nose bridge too far.

Long story short though, Saint Tone, eventually, in the interests of brotherhood, tries both hash and coke; and the results are disappointing as the marijuana joint he puffs (in between coughing fits) just makes him sleepy, so a line of coke is administered to offset the tiredness. And what does the pop star's choice of stimulus do to Tone? Make him deliriously happy? No. Give him bundles of get-up-and-go? No. Increase his libido? Definitely not. What it does is make him talk at a million miles an hour. No kidding. Fifteen minutes or so of continuous babble that bores his bandmates to catatonic paralysis as follows:

Tone (at 1,000,000,000mph):
    'LookIagreedtotakethisdrugintheinterestsofscienceandresearchonan experimentalbasisandbecauseyouguysjustwouldn'tletupbutasfarasIcanm akeoutthiswonderdrughashadlittleornoeffectonmybehaviourordemeanou rorfeelingofwellbeingasIdon'tfeelespeciallyjoyousorfullofbeansorbuzzi nglikeanoverexcitedteenagersoIconsiderthisexperimenttobeafailureanda wasteofmoneyandquitefranklyIgetmorepleasurefromaginandtonicthanal ineofcocaineandquitefranklyIdon'tseewhatthefussisallaboutbutifIsnorte dittoooftenI'dbeworriedaboutthedamagetomynoseandmynasalpassagesa ndI'dbewaryofnosebleedsbeingasymptomofdamagetothemucousmembr anewhichiswhatI'vereadonthesubjectbeforeIagreedtothisprocedurewhic hcanalsoleadtohallucinationslikeimagininginsectscrawlingallovertheski nandotherproblematicsideefectslikehighbloodpressureabnormalheartrhy

thmanxietyparanoiafidgetingtremblingconvulsionsandcardiacbloodyarr
estsuchisthedownsideofthisabominabledrugwhichhasminimalupsideforI
amawarethatIamnotawareofanysignificantchangeinmydemeanourorbeh
aviouralthoughsuddenlyI'mfeelingmightyhungry…'

– and so he goes on for another fourteen minutes until he slows down
to a dribble, blinks, and says, 'Wha?'

– and they laugh fit to burst, followed by bouts of giggling brought
on more by the marijuana than by any sense of humour.

LSD will figure little in the band's history. This 'psychedelic'
hallucinatory drug – Lysergic acid diethylamide – has had its heyday in
the '60s with its use by many major bands. The resultant distorted
contorted view of life is meant to be mind-opening and Tank tries it once.
He drops acid on a visit to Stonehenge in the company of some Druid
mates. He says that the standing stones came alive and danced around
him in a circle and it was the most *amazing* trip, man! But he doesn't
repeat as later he admits that LSD 'did his head in'.

So, here they are in the tiny bedsit, still taking turns in their sleeping
arrangements, looking like beanpoles, waiting to hear from their absent
manager, Joe Rainbow, who they haven't seen or heard from since the
beginning of April. It is now three weeks on. They're considering giving
up and going home; it was worth a try but hey, whaddya-gonna-do-about-
it? says Mickey.

Then the landlord, Mr Zdunowski, knocks on their door.

'I see you half your friends wiz you again, Mr O'Shee. Very good as
here is parcel delivered downstairs for you all as it addresses "Mr Danny
O'Shee and the Boys" which I'm assume is referring to you all
combined, no?'

Yes. And it's very large and heavy too t' be sure Mr O'Shee as Mr
Zdunowski hands over the parcel which he has been clutching with both
arms. He takes a sly shuftee around the room, checking for any damage
or illegal nailing-up-of-pictures or other such desecration of this ever-so-
humble abode, but he sees none; the walls are bare, the bed is made, a
strange perfumey smell, admittedly, but not offensive, so all is well, and
he takes his leave with a cheery lift of his trilby, a tightening of the belt

around his Macintosh, and a loud cry and salute of 'Do Widzenia!' Goodbye, Mr Z.

The parcel is hamper-sized, which accounts for the contents which are revealed to be… a hamper. From a big London department store. Full of goodies. They look through the food and drink excitedly as their diet to date has been beans and eggs and past-sell-by-date bread. But look what's on offer here, courtesy of the 'Gourmet's Delight' Hamper! Sweet and savoury treats of popcorn and honeycomb dips, fudge chunks, smoked cheeses with paprika crackers, olives suffused in garlic oil, brandy snaps and pâté, accompanied by a bottle of bubbly and the real thing, mind, not the sparkling imitation.

'We should have a picnic,' suggests Tone, 'we've been cooped up here long enough, my friends, and I, for one, am getting cabin fever.'

'Bedsit fever,' interrupts Tank.

'Let's get some fresh air into our lungs instead of your cheap pot,' and Tone is putting his coat on, grabbing the hamper by its handle and making for the door.

Danny B: 'Okay boys, where shall we go? Hampstead Heath?'

Tank: 'Where all the pansies go? Nah, Kenwood House is where it's at, man.'

(And no one present bothers to explain to Tank that Kenwood House is, in fact, on Hampstead Heath but no matter.)

'We're Kenwood-bound!' Mickey squeaks.

And Kenwood-bound they are, humping the hamper and its delicious contents, taking turns with the burden, walking all the way, two and a half miles, turning into West End Lane by the library, then into Frognal Lane, then Frognal, Lower Terrace, and then past Hampstead Observatory, which is on the corner of Heath Street and Hampstead Grove near the Whitestone Pond – a real scientific observatory open to the public; the boys didn't know it existed and vow to visit next time around, but by now they're on Whitestone Walk and about to pass by the famous historic Spaniards Inn on Spaniards Road. There is a tollhouse opposite, still existing, where the road narrows into a single lane; cars get frustrated having to wait, and there are calls to demolish the tollhouse, but common sense prevails.

'Dick Turpin was a regular at the Inn,' says Tone, 'his pa having previously been the landlord, and it was a popular haunt for highwaymen as the road was frequented by wealthy travellers on the way to London. Rich pickings. However, a tree at one end of the road was a hanging tree for highwaymen. Talking of "haunts", Dick Turpin is supposed to still ride by on the heath on his horse, Black Bess.'

'Like our van, "Bessie" – Blue Bessie!' says Mickey.

Onwards then, from the Spaniards Inn where they'd be tempted to stop and take refreshment were it not for:

a) already having a hamper-full, and

b) having no dosh.

From the Inn, they stroll down Hampstead Lane via a heap of trees to the finishing line: Kenwood House. It's taken an hour to get there by shanks's pony.

Why 'shanks's pony'? Tone, fund-of-all-knowledge, might well posit: 'Well, if memory serves, it refers to the shank being the human shinbone or tibia. So "shanks's pony" means literally "travelling by one's own legs".'

And this is where their own legs have taken them. Before them stands the splendid seventeenth-century white wedding cake mansion, long and low, sitting atop a gentle slope which leads down to green, well-kept parkland and large ponds surrounded by trees – and a right beautiful setting it is too for one hell of a picnic.

They settle on the grass in the late April spring sunshine, spreading their coats to sit on, and they pop open the fizz and toast themselves in plastic mugs to their good fortune as there, lying on top of the victuals, is a gold-rimmed embossed card from the Department Store and on it is written a note from their absent, but now hopefully present, manager:

To the Boys in the Band,
Been a Busy Bee on your bee-half!
Buzz Buzz,
Joe R.
P.S.: be outside your gaff, 12pm sharp tomorrow. Dress smart (and if you can't dress smart, dress weird!).

Says Danny, 'Now we can relax and enjoy this feast, knowing that Mr Rainbow has come good after all. Cheers, Mickey!'

And they all cheers Mickey for the introduction, then tuck into the tuck on offer.

Chewing on a chicken leg, Mickey suddenly stops and says, 'What-the-fuck-is-that?' and he points to one of the large ponds opposite. 'Is that a stage I see before me or do my eyes deceive?'

It *is* a stage! A motherfucker of a stage! Classical-concert-sized, set on a promontory jutting out in the large pond (which is in effect a lake but is called the Thousand Pound Pond) with a backdrop of trees. A pure white semi-circular canopy covers the entire stage, which could house a Symphony Orchestra and then some (and indeed, it turns out, it often does, such is its function).

Tank: 'We should be performing. I'm missing the buzz of being on stage, aren't you? Just imagine being on that stage there, the four of us, a success now, a mega-success, so we have an entourage and roadies to hump the amps and *backing singers*, sexy girls, shapely, hip hopping to our beat, and the crowd sitting cross-legged on the grass, our adoring fans, while at the back, over there by the house, it's standing-room-only with some girls hoiked up onto their fellas' shoulders, obligingly pulling their tops up to show their boobs!'

While Tank contemplates this vision, Mickey mimes his lead guitar, 'singing' the bended notes and grimacing as he hits those strings on the uppermost frets, the skinny buggers by the bridge after the 15th fret going up to the 20th, the ones that make the tortured notes squeal as Mickey bends the strings upwards to breaking point.

Then Danny Boy grabs a brandy snap and holds it like a microphone and sings oh-so-sweetly the opening lyrics to the song that Tone has written, that they put as the last song on the demo tape they made before coming down to London. The song is called 'To the Beat, Beat, Beat Of My Heart, Heart, Heart', written for the band and written about Agnieszka, his darlin' wife –

'To the Beat, Beat, Beat of my Heart, Heart, Heart,
You were Mine, Mine, Mine from the Start, Start, Start.
Like the Horse, Horse, Horse before the Cart, Cart, Cart,
We will Never, Never, Never, Part, Part, Part.'

When they first hear it, sung modestly by Tone, accompanying himself on acoustic guitar, Danny accuses it of being 'doggerel', especially the 'horse' and 'cart' bit, but as they rehearse and refine it, they warm to the song, which is just as well as one day it will be a huge, massive mega-hit. One fine day.

As Danny B sings the song, Tank mimics a bass drum noise hitting and echoing the repeated words, 'Beat, Beat, Beat', drumbeat, drumbeat, drumbeat, and Tone mimes the bass note E in strict 4/4 tempo, and Mickey slaps his thigh in time, imitating the dead slap on the mute strings of his Fender Strat.

'Hey, let's check it out,' Mickey says. They leave their picnic and make their way across the bridge that spans the Thousand Pound Pond to find themselves at the back of the stage, where a stage door has been left open for 'Deliveries'.

'Showtime!' whispers Danny.

And they run onto the stage, waving to the cheering crowd, running on like The Beatles at Shea Stadium, their guitars held like rifles. And they race onto the stage, bowing to the multitude, then with a 1-2-3-4 count-in, they launch into their signature song 'Rock Island Line' to the hysterical cheers and screams of the young girls in the congregation.

They're together like Status Quo, singing their first hit, 'Pictures of Matchstick Men'.

Later. Sat on the grass, looking onto the stage.

'If it weren't for meeting Joe tomorrow,' says Mickey lying back and blinking in the sunshine, 'why, I'd be up for legging it back home and playing the first gig on offer, courtesy of your Aggie, Tone, who might just kindly go back to looking after us, making a few phone calls and Bingo! We'd be playing again. Would she do that, do you think?'

'Hold your horses, Mickey. Let's meet with your Joe first and see what transpires, eh?'

They pack up the hamper and leave it next to a rubbish bin round the back of Kenwood House – which is really the front, but who's counting. They walk northwards to a viewing point that looks over the London skyline, which seems a world away from this peaceful spot. The Post Office Tower of Fitzrovia dominates the horizon, then the office blocks of the City, the council monoliths of Camden, the mansion flats of Maida Vale, and cranes like praying mantises that bow over empty scaffolding; and somewhere in this miasma of people is one Joseph Rainbow, née Cohen, their signpost to the future.

'Somewhere over the rainbow,' Danny starts to sing, and the others join in *a capella*. A tight band.

8
Anarchy In The UK

'There's a place for us,' says Danny Boy, 'somewhere there *must* be a place for us!'

What he means is a record company with a deal. The big ones like EMI, Philips and Decca. This is what Joe R has promised, and maybe, just maybe…

Standing outside the front door in Kingdon Road and, please God, may there be a place for them! Five minutes to midday in drizzling rain, standing outside that dismal front door. Danny with his jacket over his head to keep his barnet dry, Tank holding a copy of *The Sun* as an improvised umbrella, getting more sodden by the second, all hunched up in ripped tee-shirt and ripped jeans, Tone decked out in his usual mix of pastel shades, while Mickey is wrapped up in a plastic mac with the hood up. Danny in his habitual black. Hair, for all, is long and greasy. They are hardly dudes, this dishevelled band, nor are they Pretty Things. If you can't dress smart, dress weird, Joe had written, but they can't dress weird either. No money, Joe. Weird costs money, Joe. And smart costs even more money, Joe.

Rock Ireland Line, in their present form, look grungy. However, this is no bad thing as a new four-letter word has entered the pop/rock lexicon, and that four-letter word is PUNK. Ripped tee-shirts are IN, as are safety-pinned jackets – and look! Danny's jacket is held together by safety pins, the buttons having gone AWOL. Grunge. Anti-fucking-establishment. Anarchy in the fucking UK!

What's a band to do in 1976 now punk is here? No more glam-rock or over-produced 'concept' albums. Now it's all stripped-down guitar, bass and drums like in the old days of Buddy Holly. Beanpole Buddy Holly, bespectacled, shirt and tie, with his Fender Stratocaster, which just about every guitarist at the time was envious of. It was a revolutionary look for an electric guitar, and Hank Marvin, lead guitarist of The Shadows, immediately got one, as did the rhythm guitarist Bruce Welch. The Shadows, Cliff Richard's backing group, were also a group in their own right, introducing the concept of the melody-only hit like 'Apache' (which every learner guitarist could play straight off as it's the first four notes on the two upper open strings: B and E – it gets more tricky on the fifth note being a C sharp or D flat, 2nd string 2nd fret, and that's where virgin fingertips would feel the punishing sting of the steel string, as thin as a wire-cutter).

So, what is a band to do in the face of anti-everything punk? When you have the Sex Pistols and Johnny Rotten (née Lydon) snarling out his lyrics about being the anti-Christ (this is in their 'Anarchy in the UK' record released later that year) while there's sweet-sounding Danny Boy with the beat-beat-beat of his heart-heart-heart. Maybe Rock Ireland Line, RIL, could be an *antidote* to the anti-Christ? Who knows? But if you have a savvy manager, then you have the equivalent of the Holy Grail. 'I Will Guide You, My Sons. Have Faith and Believe In Me.'

Here in front of the dismal doorway, though, the Rock Irelanders are as far away from punk as they are from home.

But no, that's not altogether true, they're halfway there with their grunge looks and, as it happens, with the first song on their demo tape, the one that Joe is hopefully hawking around the record companies, which is their version of Buddy Holly's 'Peggy Sue'. Because while Holly's was fairly mild, theirs is a harder treatment with chugging downward chords from Mickey, now in E major rather than the friendlier A major of the original, and Danny Boy's voice is raucous and sounds like he hates Peggy Sue.

The early spring sun peeks out from behind a cloud and catches a gleam, a glint, of silver at the end of the road as Joe's sleek Rolls-Royce Silver Shadow glides up to them. Purrs to a halt. Doesn't bother to park, just stops in the middle of the road, and Joe Rainbow gets out of the back and shakes the boys' hands and hugs them like they've been parted for years. He's decked out in a broad blue pinstripe suit with striped shirt and yellow tie, yellow kerchief draped out of top pocket, yellow rose in lapel. Swanky. Rich-looking.

Then the chauffeur, in grey peaked cap and grey uniform, alights and holds the door open for them as they pile in the back, and Joe sits up front.

'This is Jeeves,' Joe beams, introducing his chauffeur who is a burly fella with tattoos on his knuckles, they notice. R O C K on the left-hand knuckle and R O L L on the right.

'Real name Johnson,' Joe whispers theatrically, turning round to them in the back. 'Ex-con, did five years for GBH – bit a guy's ear off in a pub who owed him money – said he'd take the ear in lieu of payment. Isn't that right, Jeeves?'

Jeeves/Johnson chuckles, then guns the accelerator.

'Where we headed?' asks Tone.

'To the end of the world, my man. World's End, King's Road, capiche, Jeeves?'

Jeeves evidently capiches as he throttles down West End Lane into Abbey Road, past The Beatles Abbey Road Studios. Heads crane back, and a request to stop and take photos on the famous pedestrian crossing is ignored, but who's got a camera anyway?

'Talking of photos,' Joe says, 'I ditched those promo pics we did of you guys; they're just too old-hat.'

He's referring to a photo session that took place just before they came down to London. An acquaintance of his, who Joe had used to take team photos of the Corgis, did them on the cheap in his studio which was really just a back-room in his suburban house with a white sheet draped against one wall. He got the boys to pose formally as a band with their instruments and also some wacky shots with them looning about. Then he printed them in arty black-and-white as Joe said all the best photos were in monochrome. 'Just look at those black-and-white pics on the cover of "with the beatles".'

'We might need to change your band name too,' says Joe.

'We like our name,' says Danny.

And so say all of us, the others think.

'We'll see,' says Joe, in that tone that parents use when responding to their kids' unreasonable demands. 'We'll see.'

The journey continues down Lisson Grove, home of their Labour Exchange, past Hyde Park, through Belgravia, Sloane Square, then along the King's Road, where they see a pub being invaded by uniformed cops, batons raised. The customers are being lined up outside and frisked. What they also see, but the coppers don't, is drugs paraphernalia being chucked out of a side window and being picked up by some lucky freeloaders.

'Welcome to the King's Road, guys!'

They reach the end of the world – World's End as the area is known – to find themselves at 430 King's Road, their destination as it turns out, and what a sight for sore eyes this otherwise inconsequential tiny shop is – inconsequential were it not for the four-foot-high rubber blow-up letters in pink above the shop's door that spell out SEX!

'Welcome to the future!' announces Joe, with such an air of authority and zeal that they have to take note.

At first, the boys are intrigued, especially Tank, being the randiest amongst them, thinking that Joe, for whatever reason, has taken them to a sex shop. Reasonable assumption given the establishment's four-foot-high name. But when they get inside, they see that it's just a clothes shop, albeit a weird clothes shop. There's graffiti scrawled on the walls, rubber curtains, chicken wire, racks of fetish and bondage gear, and tee-shirts like one depicting a huge swastika with the word DESTROY. A sure antidote to Mickey's WEMBLEY STADIUM SECURITY. There's ripped clothing and safety-pinned clothing, and while Danny and Tank kind of fit in, Mickey and Tone definitely don't. The customers are suitably weird too – multi-coloured hair, zombie make-up, plastic trousers, fishnets.

Joe Rainbow again declares that this is NOW and this is the FUTURE! 'Punk' is where it's at, and he wants his band to Adopt and Adapt – to embrace this NEW AGE in clothing, hair and music, and this way he'll make them famous as promised, within a year, and on *Top of the Pops*.

The boys are dumbfounded and watch in a kind of gormless limbo as Joe picks out garments, pays, and leads them back to the Roller to a smirking Jeeves, who then drives them to their next mystery destination. On the way, Joe fills them in on 'punk':

'Malcolm McClaren, who I've had the pleasure of meeting – (this is not true as Joe has *not* had the pleasure) – is this brilliant pop *guru*. He's been in the States managing the New York Dolls, then he's returned to the UK to co-manage the shop SEX with the fashion designer Vivienne Westwood. Two innovative minds destined to change the world of fashion. Now, previous to Malcolm's sojourn in the US of A, he's got to know an English band called The Strand, and some of the members of this group frequent the SEX shop, and Malcolm McClaren gets interested again in the group. Well, long story short, the young band needs a singer and a singer with short hair, if you please, as their style is "short hair" and not the current trend for long locks – like you boys, which is why I'm taking you for your next treat.'

They look at each other doubtfully. Tone fingers his King Charles curls. It's true, they all have long hair, as is the fashion these days. Danny's is lank, brushed back off his forehead, tied in a ponytail. Mickey's hairline is starting to recede at the front, a race between the left-hand side and the right, so he compensates with a centre-parting style. Tank's blonde tresses are shoulder-length, Sunsilk-soft as he conditions regularly. Swears by it. 'You gotta look after your hair, Mickey,' he says, 'even if it is disappearing fast.'

Joe continues:

'A habitué of the King's Road at this time is a nineteen-year-old lad called John Lydon. Now, here's a boy with *attitude*! Green hair, tee-shirt safety-pinned, just the right package for The Strand, now called the Sex Pistols. They meet John Lydon in a pub then, at closing time, mosey along to the SEX shop where Lydon sings along to an Alice Cooper track on the shop's jukebox.'

'Do you know what the track was?' Tone asks smugly.

Joe confesses to not knowing the title of the song.

'"I'm Eighteen" was the track,' says Tone, which earns him a round of applause from his fellow bandmates.

'I stand enlightened,' says Joe. 'So Lydon is IN and becomes "Johnny Rotten". They gig at the 100 Club in Oxford Street and gain their notoriety, abusing the audience (who love them) and with their new lead singer hunched over the microphone sneering like a good 'un, the Sex Pistols legend is born. Right, Jeeves?'

Right, agrees Jeeves.

Then Tone, the walking rock encyclopaedia, chips in again:

'Punk music is rooted in 1960s garage rock with its breakneck tempo, hard-edged melodies, and stripped-down instrumentation. Basically guitar, bass and drums. Like Rock Ireland Line. There's a New York punk band called the Ramones who've just released their debut album – maybe you could get us an advance copy?' (This is directed at Joe who says, 'We'll see,' which means 'No', of course.)

But for now, both Tone's appraisal of things Punk and Joe's history of same is interrupted by their arrival at a high-class gentleman's hairdresser in Conduit Street, just off Regent Street, called Mirrors. 'Mirrors' because the shop boasts two giant mirrors behind each barber's chair, which are opposite each other, so you can see a reflection of the opposite hairdresser's bottom. And what's attractive about this is that the hairdressers, and owners of the shapely behinds, are two young Greek sisters with long dark hair plunging down to pert posteriors clothed in tight Lycra leggings!

Joe announces that the band is too 'hirsute' and demands a 'tidy-up'. Danny B is up for it and so is Tank. But Mickey declines, as does Tone. They sit defiantly at a low table, perusing the out-of-date magazines when not perusing the Lycra-clad Alexia and Andrea.

When they emerge into the sunlit street of Conduit, they are two distinct halves of a single unit – one half long-haired, the other short, and their clothes a mix of styles, no group uniformity for them. They stand by the Rolls, shuffling self-consciously. The silver monster is parked on a double yellow line (as if anyone's gonna tell Jeeves where he can or can't park!), and Joe looks them up and down and sighs.

'I'm going to launch you as a punk band, the next Sex Pistols. You need to change your image, your attitude – you're halfway there, fellas, with your shorter hair – and you *will* need to change your name. Rock Ireland Line is for the birds, fellas.'

'We're not gonna change our name,' says Danny Boy.

'I've got some ideas. At least listen.' And Joe reels off a few vicious-sounding possible band-names like 'Bloodvein', but the lads are shaking their heads.

"We're none of those names, Joe. The band's name stays,' declares Danny as leader and spokesman of the group. 'And what's more, I'm not gonna dress like an eejit just because of some new fad that'll most likely be done and dusted in a year or so.'

Danny Boy is not far wrong. The punk revolution lasts a couple of years, then all but dies out in 1978 with the Sex Pistols disbanding. In that short but brilliant time, they've released 'Anarchy In The UK', been signed by three record labels, sworn on live TV, recruited Sid Vicious as bass guitarist, released 'God Save the Queen' followed by their debut album 'Never Mind The Bollocks', toured the US Southern States and released their third single, 'Holiday In The Sun', and finally, after all this and much, much more... the band split up. Punk is pretty much dead and buried, but still an incredible influence on many bands. In the final US concert at Winterland San Francisco, Johnny Rotten ends the show with the Stooges' song 'No Fun', then, kneeling on stage, he declares that this is no fun, no fun at all. But the audience don't agree; they love the Pistols! Then he smiles, puts down the microphone and leaves the band. Anarchy right to the end and the end of a legend.

Jeeves next drives the boys to the Hilton on Park Lane, where an establishment called Trader Vic's resides, and this will be their next and final port of call for the day.

'Do you like Mai Tais?' asks Joe, and the boys think he's referring to his colourful neckwear, and they reply accordingly, saying he has a flamboyant touch with his choice of ties, and Joe laughs, and Jeeves just smirks. 'It's a cocktail,' he growls. First time they've heard him speak, and it sounds like a threat.

When they enter the wonderful world of Trader Vic's, they're in Tahiti! Polynesian-themed. Golden brown bamboo walls with wicker-plaited backrests on tan chairs. Pictures of old sailing vessels and trading fleets. Seashell lamp covers under bamboo ceiling rafters. Trader Vic's: home of the legendary Mai Tai, a rum-based cocktail 'Paradise in a glass', served in oversize tumblers, 'double old-fashioned' as it's known, a frothy mix of rum, lime juice, orgeat syrup and orange curaçao liqueur, shaken vigorously over shaved ice and garnished with a mint sprig, pineapple cube and Maraschino cherry, served by the Hawaiian-looking barman, Otto, who relates the drink's history as he greets the new arrivals:

'Created in 1934, gentlemen, by our founder Victor "The Trader"

Bergeron, a.k.a. Trader Vic, who opened his first saloon in California and legend has it that one evening, here you are sir – (this, to Joe who Otto serves first, recognising money and prestige) – drink it slowly, sir, and savour the subtle flavours, one evening Mr Bergeron tries out a new cocktail on his friends who exclaim, after just one sip, that's right, gentlemen, *just one sip*, that this magical concoction is "mai tai, roa aé!", which in Tahitian means "out of this world, the best". And so it was that Trader Vic's creation was christened the Mai Tai.'

'And God bless all who sail in her!' says Tank as they take their seats in this golden paradise.

'They say of Martinis,' says Joe, 'that one is not enough, two is enough, and three is not enough. What I would say of Mai Tais is that one is not enough, two is not enough, and three is not enough… another round all round, Otto, if you please.'

They get the picture and, several rounds later…

Tone: 'Joe, we're never gonna make it as a punk band and anyway, why do we have to change? I mean, as well as punk, which is only in its infancy after all, there are still established pop groups around and doing very nicely, thank you. Paul McCartney and Wings, ABBA, Queen, for instance. Now no one's gonna turn ABBA punk, are they?'

'I should think not!' exclaims Tank. '*Mamma Mia!*'

And they all laugh fit to burst, as per. But not Joe.

'Those bands you mention are established, while you're unknown. So you need a hook, and punk could be that hook.'

Danny, slurring: 'By hook or by bloody crook, it's not for us and that's that.'

Undeterred, Joe now goes over all that he's been doing on the band's behalf for the last three or four weeks:

'I started off hawking your demo tape and group pics around the major record companies but, truth is, you have to have the IN to get yourself noticed and what I heard was that demo tapes, unless they're sent by people the company knows, are just tossed to some trainee who listens to the first ten seconds then bins it if they don't like it. Likely bins it even if they do. So I determined on another strategy because you can trust your Uncle Joe to find a way round if the road is all snarled up. Otto, por favor?'

Yet another round, some bar snacks. Joe continues.

'Record labels have their own A&R departments…'

'A&R stands for Artists and Repertoire,' intones Tone.

'Obliged, Tone… who send out scouts to pubs and clubs, and often these talent scouts are freelance, so often as not they're just young kids on not much money. If these young scouts report back favourably, the A&R department guys then go and check out the talent for themselves – comprende? – *so,* I reasoned, it's these freelance scouts who have the IN to the labels!'

It's like – what do they say? – taking candy from a baby, it's so easy. Joe is taking the band from A to B to C and enjoying every second. The salesman's touch. The throwing in of words like 'comprende'. Of course, they comprende when the message is delivered by a master.

'My strategy was to schmooze one of these guys, so I hung around the clubs, see, like the Marquee on Wardour Street: a couple of bottles of bubbs in a bucket, girls in tow, and before you could say "Joe's yer uncle," or "This is Tina and her friend, Sharon," I'd have some talent scout eating out of my hand, or rather, drinking out of my ice bucket. Savvy? I couldn't get the fancypants A&R guys themselves as they had their own entourage, girls, bubbly, drugs and so on, but the freelancers, the *freeloaders,* were the next best thing, mark my words – Otto m'boy, it's a dry ol' ship here!'

The dry ol' ship is duly wetted and the boys sit attentive like schoolboys in front of their headmaster.

'My plan was to find the perfect "mark" and I went to all the clubs: Dingwalls in Camden, the Rainbow in Finsbury Park – which, incidentally, has this *amazing* ceiling of stars and palm trees but, oddly, no rainbow – and it was in the 100 club in Oxford Street that I found my quarry: young, keen, a bit dorky, but open to booze, birds and bribery. Long story short, he listens to your demo tape and you know what? he loves one particular song on it – you can guess which one, the "Beat, Beat, Beat" one of course! He's impressed that it's self-written – well done, Tone – and he promises to play it to his A&R department.'

Joe goes all-confidential now, as if he's imparting some great secret. He leans forward, and the boys follow suit –

'Now, this record label is one of the new small independents who are beginning to rival the biggies and, pay attention here, how it goes is this: the small label finds the talent, signs 'em up, records and promotes 'em, then does a deal with the major player who does the rest. So, in effect, the indie labels are acting as scouts, much like the talent scouts for the A&R guys. Upshot is, my guy's boss likes your demo but thinks the band needs an image, and this is where the SEX shop comes in.'

And at that moment, miraculously on cue, Jeeves enters the scene bearing the bags of gear Joe has bought from SEX. Joe brings out various items ranging from rubber to leather while Jeeves cosies up to Otto, kindred spirits, and tucks into one Mai Tai, then two, then three – obviously following Boss Joe's dictum to the letter.

The lads hate the clobber but by now they're too drunk to take it seriously, and as they pile out onto the pavement and pile into the Rolls, and as Jeeves drives them back to West Hampstead at breakneck speed, they sing out of tune and raucous-loud the 1960s pop song by Mary Wells, 'My Guy', to which they change the words to 'Mai Tai'. Like birds of a feather, this band will stick together.

9

To The Beat, Beat, Beat of My Heart, Heart, Heart

Time to back up a bit…

There is a small demo recording studio and rehearsal room on the outskirts of Market Harborough in the Midlands available for hire, and RIL are here prior to their going down to London. Their manager has paid for them to record a demo tape that he will try to sell to the record companies. The studio, which on the outside is really just a barn in a scruffy farmyard, is called 'Di an' Mick Sound', referring to the owners, Diana and Mick, who've cobbled their names together to make it sound like 'Dynamic Sound' (well, sort of). The corrugated iron-roofed barn with ancient stone walls sits among other farm buildings, and a makeshift sign above the door, hand-painted, does not instil much confidence in the venue. No Abbey Road Studios, this.

The lads roll up in Bessie and step into mud as the yard has not been cleaned, and a distinct animal smell suggests that probably what they've stepped in isn't just mud. Danny takes off one of his Chelsea boots, hops on one leg and sniffs the sole. He grimaces, saying, 'Shit!' and you don't know whether he's describing the residue on the shoe or what he feels about it, but it comes to the same thing. Mickey regrets his open-air Crocs-with-no-socks, and Tone's black shoes are now more brown than black. Tank's trainers are already dirty, so no change there.

They unload their equipment and haul it to the door, which opens to reveal 'Mick', sound engineer and owner, skinny as a telegraph pole, tall as one too, tattooed, long hair, earrings, grubby shirt, frayed jeans. No George Martin, he.

Introduces himself, offering up a high hand-slap rather than a handshake, doesn't help with the carrying but instead lifts a spliff to his lips, which explains the sickly-sweet aroma that mingles with the odour of farmyard.

Inside the studio is a different world. The mooing of some nearby cows that they were aware of outside is now silenced by the soundproofing on the interior walls – a mix of thick carpet and fibreglass insulation applied to every surface. Noticing that they're noticing, Mick says that they're in a hundred per cent 'silence bubble', as he puts it. The layout is a standard recording studio set-up comprising two rooms: one small behind thick glass, which houses the mixing desk and various tape machines, the other being the studio itself.

'State-of-the-art gear,' says Mick, proudly indicating the desk and recording units, 'Nakamichi tape machines, four-head. You don't get better than that. Eight-track desk, natch.' There's a water cooler, coffee station, fridge and sofa. Mick sits in an office chair-on-wheels, and on the back, facing the sofa and its possibly chatty occupants, is a large cartoon of a roaring lion with the word 'QUIET!!!' underneath. Most noticeable is the large reel-to-reel recording set-up using tape two inches wide and the mixing desk itself, which is impressive with the multi-sliders (called faders) and the channels and dials. Two massive floor-standing Celestion speakers on either side will belt out the sound on playback. Their covers are off so you can see the round woofers and tweeters – woofers for low-frequency sounds, tweeters for high – and you can see the woofers pulsating with the bass sounds, just like your own internal organs.

On the other side of the large glass is the soundproofed studio with baffles to separate each player, and the usual array of microphones (known as 'mics' in the trade, pronounced 'mikes'), headphones (known as 'cans'), and a spaghetti junction of trailing wires and cables. It has to be said that Di an' Mick Sound nr. Market Harborough is the Real Deal.

The group set up their instruments and plug into the DI (Direct Input) of the desk, which has its own outstanding feature: a sliding panel at the front which slides back to reveal a stash of hash. This, Mick points out, is the 'hash-stasher', and he makes a gesture of offering up some weed, but the boys aren't biting. They've work to do.

'Take one, Rock Ireland Line, "Peggy Sue".'

This is Mick on the intercom and on a count-in of 1-2, 1-2-3-4 they launch into their high-energy version of the Buddy Holly classic, pitch-perfect and tight as hell. They finish on the four last E major chords and drumbeats and look up to Mick who gives the thumbs-up and mimes 'Playback', making a 'T' shape with his fingers signifying 'Tape', which is the cue for the band to down instruments and go into the control room – Mick's domain – to hear playback on the big speakers.

The sound crashes out at mega-decibels and they almost stagger back at the force of the volume, it sounds great! *They* sound great! Maybe it's those speakers – they're the bees-knees of sound reproduction and the lads are only used to hearing each other perform live, so this is a different ball game – they sound *professional*!

'Let me just try something,' says Mick, and he fiddles with the knobs and the faders, then presses 'Play' again, making that 'T' sign to the boys – and now it sounds *even more* fantastic!

'What did you do?' asks Tone.

Mick settles back, master-of-all-he-records, locks his hands behind his head and swivels his chair around to face them, all lined up like schoolkids on the sofa, which is deliberately low-sprung to make his 'audience' feel inferior.

'I added more *compression*, guys. Compression reduces the audio signal's dynamic range.'

'"Dynamic range" sounds good to me,' says Tone (on a hiding to nothing here). 'Why *reduce* it?'

Mick smiles indulgently, unlocks his hands, leans forward to impart this holy-of-holies info to uninformed Tone:

'Compression closes the gap between the loudest and quietest parts of the track. You may *think* you're all playing at the same volume but my VU meters say different. With compression, the sound is punchier, fuller. That's what you're hearing. Then I added more EQ, then bass, then more bass. You can't get enough bass!'

'It's like making scrambled eggs,' Tone says afterwards. 'The secret to making great scrambled eggs is that before cooking you add a knob of butter, then you add another knob of butter and just to make sure you add another.' (It's like that Martini/Mai Tai theory.)

They move on to song number two.

'Take one. Rock Ireland Line. "Rock *Island* Line".'

Oh-so-familiar territory as they launch into their signature song, which starts with Mickey's blistering lead rendition of the melody line with fuzz and distortion and a bit of wah-wah, which begins slow then builds up in speed until with one crash of the drums – bass, snare, hi-hat – they all join in, and there's Danny Boy doing his strange dance in front of the mic even though there's no audience – but how can he resist?

But wait, wait, there *is* an audience now, as Mick at the desk is joined by Diana (presumably) as she puts her hands on his shoulders in a proprietorial sort of way, then waves at the group with a big welcoming smile. You can't beat a smile. Want to get your way with that officious bastard behind the desk? Smile. Want to get an upgrade on your flight? Smile. Want to complain and be listened to? Smile. Or as the Beach boys have it on their ground-breaking album – 'Smiley Smile'.

The lady with the fetching smile is indeed the 'Di' of 'Di an' Mick Sound' and she's pretty dynamic-looking herself – wild, blonde hair, tousled, striking make-up around the eyes, buxom in a white blouse tied in a loose knot at the waist, lots of cleavage, tight jeans. Surely, she'd break beanpole Mick in two?

'She'd eat him for breakfast, lunch *and* supper!' says Tank to no one in particular as he shields his mouth from the mic in a whisper.

The song ends with a fade-out and Di is clapping the performance and Mick is giving the thumbs-up then the 'T'. In they go to the control room, now inhaling the sweet, sweet scent of female company. The playback is okay but not the best. Should they go for another take? But Mick points to the clock on the wall behind him – Joe has only booked a ninety-minute session which is pretty generous as most demo sessions are one hour and they've been there a half-hour already. There's still one last song to record plus time needed for mixing and mastering, so they decide to move on and come back to 'Rock Island' if there's time left at the end.

The final song: Tone's 'Beat, Beat, Beat', which needs more rehearsing really as they haven't nailed the sound yet. All that's existed so far is a home-recorded cassette with Tone on acoustic guitar singing the song himself in a sort of Country and Western 3/4 time, which is not the band's style. They curse themselves for not being more prepared – they've an hour left, and the clock's ticking.

'We've gotta move from waltz time, Tone,' says Danny B.

'Sure,' says Tone, 'that's just the way I composed it and Aggie likes the waltz, but listen, change it, we'll do it the RIL way, no probs.'

'4/4 then,' says Tank.

'A heartbeat is more 2/2,' says Mickey, 'like a march.'

Tank starts counting a 1-2-3-4 beat, but Mickey's shaking his head, then Di comes on the intercom –

'Listen, guys,' she says, and she takes the desk microphone, opens her blouse, and sticks the mic onto her chest, placing it between her boobs. The boys' cans are filled with a boom-boom (pause) boom-boom (pause) sound. Di's heartbeat.

'So, it's not a straight beat then, we could start off with that interrupted 2/2 beat then move into 4/4 like this,' says Tank, and he demonstrates what he means on the bass drum.

And that's how the definitive version of 'Beat, Beat, Beat' comes about. First, Tank's broken drumbeat on snare and bass drum for four bars, then Tone on bass guitar playing the note E in synch with Tank as he changes to a regular 4/4 time. Then Mickey plays the A major chord – not the E major, so there's dissonance now – and he plays the chord arpeggio-style at first and then resolves to E with hard, percussive strokes, top strings first so playing an up-stroke. Sharp, staccato. Welcome Danny at this point, keeping his voice staccato too in strict tempo –

'To the Beat, Beat, Beat,
Of my Heart, Heart, Heart…'

There is a film by Jean Luc Godard that follows the development in the studio of the Rolling Stones track 'Sympathy For The Devil'. It shows how at the start of the sessions, this classic Stones song is played slowly on acoustic guitars by Keith Richards and Brian Jones with Mick Jagger joining in, following the chords, on guitar also. Richards appears to have open tuning on his guitar. Bill Wyman, on bass, sits and listens. Meanwhile, in the background, Charlie Watts provides some explosive drum breaks to punctuate. At the middle eight, Jagger really comes alive.

What then follows is a slow but methodical progression through styles, a Hammond organ is played at one point, but it's when they change to a samba beat played on the congas – which by its very nature has a dangerous sympathy-for-the-devil-ish feel to it – that the song comes alive. Also shown in the film is the chorus of 'Woo-woos' sung by some of the band and studio visitors. That addition gives the song its character and unique sound. This is what happens when fertile creative minds get together in a recording studio, and Amen to that.

Di applauds their efforts then waves a cheery goodbye, but before playback, Mick has something to offer up. He has kept a track separate for Mickey's guitar solo to be played *backwards*. Now, this is not anything to write home about innovation-wise as The Beatles have been using backwards music since 'Rain' and 'Tomorrow Never Knows', but the lads are staggered by the difference this effect makes to their basic track. It's just the sort of trick to catch the ear because it's so unexpected.

Now it so happens that one of the band is familiar with this backwards-music technique, and that's the songwriter himself, Tone. In his late teens, he'd experimented with music and composition using several tape recorders and a small variety of musical instruments, being acoustic guitar, vamping harmonica and a toy piano…

10
Bricks And Mortar

The tape recorders were a battery portable cassette-type, a basic reel-to-reel and a handsome Revox monster that he'd got second-hand from the father of a girlfriend who owned a hi-fi shop. This machine was the height of technical wizardry and weighed a ton, boasting different speeds, multi-track, superimposition, backwards recording and playing, the ability to create beautiful echo and howling feedback.

So, during his art college education, any time spent at his childhood home, be it weekends or holidays, Tone would be shut in his bedroom, which he'd turned into a makeshift recording studio. Wires trailed over the carpet, microphones placed on chairs and tables, two guitars (one nylon string Kimbara classical tuned standard EADGBE, the other an Eko steel string tuned to open 'delta' tuning – middle two strings standard D and G, bottom strings tuned to G, top strings tuned to D), then some Hohner Echo harmonicas (various keys) and the aforementioned toy piano which surprisingly resulted in a number of effects.

He found that if he pressed the 'record' button a split second after he played a guitar chord, he would catch not the strike of the chord but the decay. This made for a haunting sound. He played around with different speeds: the harmonica, played back ultra-slow, sounded like a church organ instead of a mouth organ, the toy piano treated the same way playing arpeggios sounded like tolling bells, speeded-up guitar sounded crazy, and slowed-down guitar sounded doomful. Add to all these effects *backwards*-playback, echo and tape loops, and Tone was like a George Martin in his Abbey Road bedroom. The superimposition tool was quite something too, allowing for the same sound to be recorded over itself without erasing – a sort of off-synch double-tracking that would phase and create an eerie echo.

In this way, one summer, Tone composed what he considered at the time to be his *masterwork*, sixty-minutes long, which he called 'Genesis'. It began ominously, a doomful steel string guitar chord caught on the decay mixed with a high-pitched single harmonica tone, a dog barking in the distance (an accidental sound caught on tape), then a ghostly snatch of speech repeated on a loop.

Tone was proud of his sixty-minute Opus I – so proud that he never played it to *anyone*. Ever.

No, wait. One other person *did* hear snatches of the 'music' – Tone's mother, who liked Mantovani and Johann Strauss waltzes. And the Seekers with their 'I'll Never Find Another You'. 'I like a proper *tune*,' she'd say, implying that Tone didn't know a proper tune from his elbow. Or was it his arse? She didn't care to conjecture. She could make head nor tail of the 'racket' coming from behind the closed door of her son's bedroom and seeping down through the floorboards into the kitchen below – *her* enclave, which ought to allow *The Archers*, her favourite radio show (an everyday story of country folk), to hold court at 7.05 of an evening, unchallenged by backwards music with echo and feedback!

'What are you up to up there, Anthony?' she'd enquire in her posh lady voice, pronouncing the 'th' of Anthony like the 'th' in 'that'; and An*th*ony would grunt and reply along the lines of, 'Just messing about, Mater.' (And yes, he called his mother 'Mater'.)

There was a lodger now as Mater couldn't afford the mortgage repayments. Their Lord and Master Bastard had ditched her for a younger model and moved away and wouldn't pay for their upkeep. Roger the lodger, in the next-door bedroom to Tone's – the bigger one once occupied by his sister – was fascinated by the sounds coming from Tone's room, as he was young (just a few years older than Tone) and a junior teacher at the local school, and he loved music. He introduced Tone to Albinoni's 'Adagio for strings' and Tone was taken aback by the sheer *modernity* of the sound and consequently re-worked the opening part of 'Genesis' and felt the work now had *gravitas*. So, he allowed someone else at last to hear parts of the piece and was gratified that Roger the lodger was enthusiastic and fulsome in his praise – or was he just sucking up to the landlady's son? (Oh, and by the way, the lodger really *was* called Roger.)

Then, one morning, Mater decreed that Tone should get a holiday job instead of mucking about with that 'pop stuff' in his bedroom all hours. 'Do a bit of hard graft,' she proclaimed in high dudgeon. 'Pay for your keep.'

Now, it so happened that someone on Roger's school staff mentioned a parent who had a building firm, and his current building site was looking for casual labour, and it was that word 'casual' that attracted Tone. So, thus encouraged, he ventured forth to said building site and, for whatever reason, which Tone couldn't begin to fathom, he, this skinny rake of a student, was hired.

There was no foreman on the site, out in the country, building a four-bedroom house, so it was quite relaxed. There was a hierarchy though: the brickie and the chippie (bricklayer and carpenter) were top-of-the-heap, then the labourer, then he, the student, who was mainly employed in brewing up as there were lots of tea-breaks, given the absence of a foreman. It was a warm summer and they'd spend the lunch hour playing cricket on the country lane. A piece of ply fashioned into a bat-shape, tennis ball, and three sticks for wickets stuck in the soil. In their many tea-breaks, they regaled Tone about Art College and what was it like drawing nude models and did he get a 'stiffy'? To oblige them, he said he did, but it wasn't true – the life-drawing was intense as the tutor was merciless: 'Call those tits?' he'd mock at the top of his voice, looking at Tone's drawing. 'Call those TITS?'

One of the jobs he had to do was lugging buckets of 'muck' (cement) to the brickie and these buckets were heavy and he struggled and stumbled. The labourer-guy smirked and didn't help; being a big guy, he could take two at a time, lifting them as if they contained candyfloss. The brickie gave Tone a break and said he only had to half-fill the one bucket.

Another job was 'catching the bricks', which involved standing on the top scaffolding and catching bricks tossed up at him. The thrower, the labourer, was so adept at this that all Tone had to do was hold out his hands in readiness; he could even close his eyes, and the brick'd just land softly in his outstretched hands.

Then he was put onto laying fibreglass roof insulation in the loft area. No one else wanted that job and by the end of the day, Tone could see why. He itched all over and sneezed; his eyes were watering and, when he got home, he had to have a bath straightaway. The glass particles in the glass fibre material had got everywhere, and this was the days before protective masks or protective clothing. There was no such thing as 'Health and Safety' in 1964.

One tea-break, they passed around the topless girl on Page Three of *The Sun* and asked if the models were beauties 'like this 'un 'ere', and Tone said yes as this seemed to be the expected answer, and they went 'Bloody hell!' and 'Lucky bastard!' but again it wasn't true – perfection is hard to draw while a few wrinkles and flabby bellies are more interesting, and this tended to be the type of female model the students were given to draw. Then they had to draw a *male* model, but thankfully he was wearing a 'posing pouch' over his privates so there were no 'bits' to draw – otherwise: 'Call those BALLS?'

The kind brickie offered to teach Tone the art of bricklaying: the right way to hold the brick, the deft use of the trowel, the slick laying of a bed of mortar, the 'buttering' of the end of each brick before tamping it down onto the mortar bed, then the levelling to the brick line followed by a quick scrape of the surplus. He did this so quickly but when Tone tried he made a hash of it and slopped mortar all over the shop and too much mortar was applied and squeezed out like an overfilled cream cake.

'You know who was a famous bricklayer?' said the brickie. 'Winston Churchill, that's who. On his tod he built a red brick wall around his garden at Chartwell, trowel in one hand, cigar in t'other. He was so expert he became a member of the Amalgamated Union of Bricklayers. The trick of bricklaying, son, is not to worry how much there is to do or how high the wall has to be, but to concentrate on each brick as you lay it and think to yourself, "this is just another brick in the wall," and before you know it, you'll have a whole wall built. That's the trick. One brick at a time. Just another brick in the wall.'

'Who's humming?' says Mick through the studio intercom. 'I can hearing someone humming.'

They look at Mickey, who has a habit of humming along to his guitar solos which usually no one in the audience hears due to the surrounding amplification. But the band hear the humming in their rehearsals and usually chorus, 'Shut up, Mickey!', which shuts Mickey up. Here, in the studio with its ultra-sensitive mics, humming is an issue.

Mickey puts his hand up sheepishly like a kid in school admitting to some prank.

'I think that was me.'

'Well, don't!' replies Mick, shaking his head in exasperation. 'Bloody amateurs!' he mutters to himself, but the studio intercom picks it up.

He would likely not be aware of Glenn Gould, the genius classical pianist and exponent of Bach, in particular the *Goldberg Variations*. Bowed over the keyboard, Gould would hum along to his playing, sometimes just on the edge of audibility, other times very obvious indeed, not particularly tuneful and not consistent throughout. The engineer could do nothing about it as that's what you got with Gould – humming, like it or not. But it added something to the personality of the recording; it became more human, and it was unique to that particular performer. No other pianist or solo violin or cello player could get away with it, and neither does Mickey.

'Shut up, Mickey!' they all go.

11
Never Ever

There was at that time, in those careless days, a fine restaurant on the corner of Frith and Romilly Street, in London's Soho, called L'Epicure. French, of course, as one might gather from the name (meaning 'gourmet') and distinctive from the outside for its flaming torch above the doorway that burnt a real flame.

It is here that Jeeves is due to deliver the lads after picking them up the day after Trader Vic's – and, it has to be said, a sorry-looking bunch they are, standing in their West Hampstead doorway, hungover and bleary-eyed.

Jeeves bundles them into the back of the Rolls, not wishing to sully the passenger seats with this riffraff, but he does His Master's Bidding and drives them steadily into Soho – not swerving or braking hard as there is a distinct possibility of vomit over the leather upholstery.

Arriving early and sensing that the boys need a pick-me-up, Jeeves parks the car in Dean Street – just a street away from L'Epicure – and takes them into a pub called the York Minster, colloquially known as 'The French' because of the pub's landlord, one Gaston Berlemont (who is actually Belgian, but the name sounds French).

Enter now the realm of Monsieur Le Gaston: a beaming bear of a man sporting a magnificent handlebar moustache, waxed at the ends, which point due north. He is immaculate in suit and tie, a fleur-de-lys badge in his lapel, and he greets Jeeves like the regular that Jeeves clearly is with a Gallic kissing-of-the-hand and immediate serving of pastis. Jeeves greets him back,

'Ah Gaston, mon brave,' he announces for all to hear and with a flamboyant bow. 'Comment allez-vous?' (and this, without a hint of an attempted French accent but spoken in broad East End).

'Bien, mon ami,' replies Gaston. 'Up to your old tricks?'

'Fingers in pies, my friend,' says Jeeves. 'Fingers in pies. These 'ere acquaintances o' mine are new to The Smoke and in need of refreshment or should I venture, medicine?'

Pastis all round, the milder descendant of absinthe, served from a special tap. Danny B makes the joke that doesn't bear repeating (about absinthe making the heart grow fonder) then tries to order a pint of Guinness but is thwarted because the pub doesn't serve beer in pint glasses, only halves, so Danny sticks with the pastis.

'Why not pints?' Tank asks.

'Story is,' says Jeeves, 'back in the day of those heavy dimpled pint glasses, there was a fight outside with sailors bludgeoning each other about the head, so from that moment on pint glasses were banned. Too much like lethal weapons.'

Of course, this begs the question that any glass can be a lethal weapon, but they let it go. Best not to mess with the intellect of mine host, Jeeves, who, after all, is buying the drinks.

Danny to Mickey (in whispers): 'Don't you think Gaston looks like Jimmy Edwards? D'you remember that programme on the telly, *Whacko!*, with that drunken headmaster who liked using the cane?'

Mickey: 'Yeah, he had that huge walrus 'tache just like this fella. He'd drink beer for breakfast I remember. Yeah, Jimmy Edwards!'

Jeeves hears this and puffs up his chest, playing like he's caught them out.

'That's a shilling fine each for mentioning Jimmy Edwards! Pub tradition!' (Who knows whether it really *is* a pub tradition but who's gonna argue with Jeeves?)

Danny and Mickey only manage to scrape together sixpence each, which goes into the charity box. Tone comes up with the other shilling, which also goes into the charity box. So now the boys are two bob down, which is bad news given how skint they are.

The pub is small for a London pub. One room is all, although there's a room upstairs. Rich brown polished wooden bar, wooden barstools, black-and-white signed photos on every wall of boxers, film stars, singers. Maurice Chevalier, Edith Piaf. Famous Frenchies. Charles de Gaulle wrote his wartime speech in this very spot, and Dylan Thomas left his manuscript for *Under Milk Wood* under a chair. Also, Francis Bacon drank here, ditto Peter Blake. An artist's watering-hole.

Now it's nearly lunchtime, and the bar is wall-to-wall people.

'Drink up lads. It's time to meet your maker!'

Mr J. Rainbow Esq. awaits.

Even though L'Epicure is only a street away, Jeeves bundles them back into the Rolls and drives round the block to deposit them under the flaming torch. The pastis has not yet done its work, and they are led into the restaurant, still bleary-eyed, still weary-eyed, to be greeted by Joe R standing up from a large table, which is also occupied by a young geeky character grinning all over his face (which resides under a bush of ginger hair), who also stands up, knocking a glass over in the process. Water everywhere. Serviette dabbing. Waiter fussing. New tablecloth. Ginger geek trying to shake everyone's hand. Arms crossing over the table space. Waiter trying to get in there. Joe R sitting down, mildly amused at the mayhem. Confusion over who sits down first – the boys or the geek? The boys win. Too knackered to care. Or to stand for too long. Ginger finally takes his seat. Then bursts out laughing. Which endears him to the lads. They laugh too. Ice broken.

Menus. Drinks, boys? Certainly. Bubbly, boys? Don't mind if we do. Snap of fingers. Waiter's ear whispered into. Bubbly in ice bucket. Crisp white serviette around the bottle. Pop of cork. Expertly executed by waiter to avoid both spurts of fizz over customers and wastage. Six flutes poured. Cheers! Here's to a successful partnership! Two large sips, and the boys begin to feel better.

The amazing remedial effect of the Moët et C. Ginger sneezes. And sneezes again. Goes into a sneezing fit. Asthmatic, apparently. Bubbles up nose. Boys pretend to go into sneezing fits too. Restaurant customers look on and disapprove. Swanky establishment. Head waiter whispers to restaurant manager. Manager points to Joe R, indicating VIP. Joe R (VIP) sits back, amused. Menus again. Down to business. Nosebags on. Time to order. Mickey needs the loo. Pastis and fizz straight to bladder. Waiter directs him. 'This way, sir.' Tone follows. Feels queasy. Vomits into basin. Feels better. Back to table. Back to ordering. Nosebags.

91

Joe introduces his tame ginger talent scout. All of nineteen years old. Prone to wearing stripey soccer shirts with a big number on the back. Jeans, of course. Holes in knees. Scruffy trainers. Accent is disguised 'posh', throwing in East End dropping-of-consonants. His name is Raymond. Last name never revealed, but it's Rice. Ray Rice. Sounds like some fish dish. Calls the lads 'chaps' or 'blokes' as in 'you chaps', 'you blokes'. Has a slight lisp, which involves pronouncing, or mis-pronouncing, his 'r's. Which is unfortunate when your moniker employs so many. After this sit-down meal, Tank comments to the others about this speech impediment. 'Couldn't tell his r's from his elbow!' and they laugh fit to burst. Raymond goes for his glass, knocks over a pepper pot. Clumsy fella. 'Expect he trips a lot,' says Tank, smirking. 'Goes r's over tit!' And they laugh again, fit to etc.

Starter's orders. Joe has the pickled herring with a glass of aquavit – a clear drink that tastes a bit like seeded rye bread, which is not surprising as the neutral spirit is flavoured with caraway. They all decide to try it. Aquavit all round. Raymond, spluttering and choking. Allergic to caraway, it turns out. Has to leave room and take strong antihistamine pills. Comes back, red-faced, ginger-haired, complimenting his red-and-black striped sports shirt. A symphony in red. The lads skip starters. Raymond has asparagus. Says Joe: 'Did you know that asparagus makes your pee smell?' *Really?* Yes, really. Something to do with how the body breaks down the acid that's in the asparagus and doesn't quite manage it. The boys decide to try it too and order asparagus all round. 'How long do we give it?' Tank asks after eating the asparagus. 'Well, wait till you want to pee, I guess,' says Joe. They wait, then go as a body, which looks strange to the restaurant clientele, but they're getting used to this uncouth bunch at Table One. Then the clientele hear giggling and groans of, 'Oo, what a pong!' coming from the Gents. The lads exit, again as a body, holding their noses theatrically. Raymond has joined in. Bonding with the boys.

Joe Rainbow has a way of dealing with restaurants. If he's not known there – and L'Epicure is just such a case – and like he did with Gino's – he gets Jeeves to ring ahead explaining that a Very Important Person indeed is about to grace their establishment. Jeeves makes up some guff about aristocratic connections and makes out that 'The Right Honourable Mr Rainbow' is Landed Gentry and Titled. On this occasion, Jeeves has bestowed upon his boss the title of Earl. In this way, the manager gets them the best table and affords said Earl the proper attention and ensures the waiters fawn appropriately (there's a promise of substantial tips). Next, when ordering the wine, Earl Joe ignores the proffered wine list and instead beckons over the wine waiter and signals him to bend down so he can whisper in his ear. And what he whispers loudly, so that everyone can hear, is: 'What's the *best* Bordeaux you have in your cellar?' The best Bordeaux is then religiously brought out, displayed, has the aged dust wiped off, approved by Joe, opened with great ceremony, whereupon Joe smells the newly removed cork, nods, tastes the first drop poured gently and with due reverence by said wine waiter, nods, and the other glasses are filled. Now what the others *don't* hear is that Joe has cunningly set a price limit beforehand to the wine waiter, so that while they might think that this bottle is the most expensive in the cellar it may well not be because Joe has set the limit to £50 which is still a good whack for a bottle of plonk whichever way you look at it. Joe then makes himself known to the other waiters by asking questions, looking them directly in the eye, getting favours, asking their names, demanding to know their opinions about the dishes, so they feel kinda special.

What do they talk about during the meal? What does anyone talk about during a boozy lunch? The food, possibly, although that won't take up much conversation. The wine, according to Joe's expertise, will afford some attention – the Bordeaux vineyards etc. Their personal histories are touched upon: Raymond's dropping out of the LSE – 'Jagger went there,' he says, as if this lends the LSE some kudos. Maybe it does. Joe stays quiet, observing the to-ing and fro-ing, occasional banter, mistruths and exaggerations, self-promotions, self-delusions; he observes like a father figure watching over his offspring, which, in a way, these fellas are. Even Raymond now he treats as one of his own. Adopted, nurtured, owned, bribed!

The food is terrific, and the band find their appetites have been restored after the curative powers of 'hair of the dog' in the form of pastis, aquavit, champagne, and several bottles of Bordeaux. They have fillet steaks and dishes flambéed at the table on a Bunsen burner affair, and by the time the old boy with the wonky eye wheels out the wooden cheese trolley with its selection of digestifs and brandy and port and cigars – of which most partake – they are replete and woozy enough for Joe Rainbow to get down to brass tacks. But first to make *his* pitch is Raymond, who has demonstrated a massive appetite throughout and is called to order after telling his joke about a one-legged nun called Hopalong Chastity.

'Now, fellas. Let's talk about your future,' and this is as far as Raymond gets as the cigar smoke gets up his nose, irritates his asthma and puts him in a sneezing fit all over again, which is only relieved by going outside, leaving Joe to take centre-stage.

'That poor boy. He's in a right state, sneezing and spluttering out there. I can see Jeeves has taken him to the Rolls to recover. Now, what Raymond was going to say was this and I suspect you know what's coming.'

'Yes, we effin' do!' interrupts Mickey, belligerent-pissed now, his hot temper burning, standing up unsteadily, upsetting cutlery and making the other diners tut-tut (although his use of the word 'effin' as opposed to 'fuckin' is to be applauded, however he blows it in the next sentence). 'We're not fuckin' goin' punk! We're *never ever* fuckin' EVER goin' to go punk! So stick that, Mr Rainbow, in your pipe and smoke it!' (Confusing imagery as Joe is smoking a cigar, but Joe lets it pass and answers calmly.)

'Thank you, Mickey, for your frank and open views. Look here, boys. Go back to your digs, Jeeves is waiting to drive you, have a rest and I'll pick you up this evening, say ten o'clock, as there's somewhere I'd like to take you.'

Anticipating more dining out, this seems like a good idea, and Mickey nods meekly, regretting his alcoholic outburst to this manager who is, after all, only trying to launch their rock career.

So, quietly now, he mutters to himself,

'Never ever…'

Ten o'clock. The Rolls purrs up to their front door and hoots twice. Joe and Raymond are on board, and off they all trot to Clerkenwell to a pub with garish posters outside saying TONITE! ONE NITE ONLY! – (and once is surely enough) – THE PLASTIC PUNK ARMY! The lads groan of course.

'Fuckin' punk! He's rammin' it down our fuckin' throats!' (Mickey, his belligerent self once more.)

But they go inside. It's a pub after all, and they're in need of an alcohol top-up.

The wall of sound hits them as they open the door. They could hear bass thumping outside but inside the harsh treble of the distorted guitar smashes them in the face, the ears, the belly. Jeeves brings a tray of beers. The mainly male audience is crazed, hardcore 'moshing', pushing and slamming into each other. Some of the 'moshers' are swinging their arms about, regardless of who they might wallop. The noise is bloody fantastic! The energy, adrenaline. Sweat and a bloody nose here and there as flailing arms make contact. The atmosphere febrile, infectious.

'Fuckin' Nora!' says Danny, slopping his pint as he joins in the 'pogo-ing', jumping up and down on the spot as if on a pogo stick and crushing a few feet into the bargain. Fights break out. Bottles smashed. Jeeves corrals the boys like sheep to protect them from the mayhem. Joe and Raymond hover by the bar.

Look at Joe now, so out of place in this joint: camel-coloured cashmere overcoat with narrow lapels and heavy black buttons down the front, black silk shirt with red bowtie, black homburg. But none of the young crowd bothers him, nor do they pay any heed to Jeeves in his chauffeur's uniform – yes, in this rowdy pub wearing a *chauffeur's uniform*! – *but,* who the hell's going to challenge Jeeves with his menacing look and knuckle tattoos. Raymond stands next to them, same clothes as lunchtime, and he fits in with the crowd here. He is *loving* the sound, proclaiming to anyone who can hear him that Plastic Punk are *twific, twemendous*!

And what of The Plastic Punk Army? String vests, ripped jeans, scowling, spitting, the singer screaming the 'lyrics' of 'fuck you' and 'shit, shit, shit'. The beat is relentless, and Tank is beating time with his hand slapping his thigh as he points out to anyone who'll care to listen, or to anyone who can hear, that the beat is metronomically true, 1-2-3-4 to perfect accuracy. (They say that Ringo Starr, besides being a brilliant, inventive drummer, had this skill. Precision timing. A metronome in his head.)

The guitarist just plays one chord, F major in a barre shape. The skinny bass player wears his huge guitar hung low, much like Sid Vicious of the Sex Pistols will do in future years.

Joe watches his lads, his boys, become seduced by the spectacle. Maybe he can compromise? Maybe they don't have to wear that SEX gear after all? The Plastic Punk Army aren't wearing that fashion, tho' they're a mite scruffy. RIL are scruffy in their own way. Then it hits him: if you can't dress weird, dress smart. Get the boys to be the first punk band to *dress smart*. Play punk music, crouch and scream but dress like The Beatles in their early days. Then he has another revelation: smart but ripped. Smart suits cut up, slashed. Collars ripped. And the name of this band? – because it can't be Rock Ireland Line, too much of a mouthful – could be 'PunkSmart', or maybe 'SmartPunk', yes, that's it! SmartPunk. Joe calls for a beer mat and writes it out, and it looks good. The capital 'P' in the middle of the word. Then he writes '*Smart*Punk', italicising *Smart*. Smiles to himself and watches Danny Boy moshing, Tank beating time, Mickey with his eyes fixed on the guitarist – surely he'll play another chord soon? Tone miming his bass slung low. Then Danny, in the zone, starts singing along with the Plastic Punk Army singer, crouching hunchbacked like that Notre-Dame fella.

Joe takes Raymond to a backroom in the pub and Jeeves stands guard at the door.

'Raymond, this is the plan: Rock Ireland will become the latest punk band but will be a different punk band. They will be the *smartest* punk band ever and they will be called *Smart*Punk. Raymond, with their *Beat, Beat, Beat* hit we will be Top of the Pops. Mark my words, Raymond, you and I are heading for the bigtime. You will be my assistant, my Number Two, after you have sold the boys in their new persona to your A&R department. Raymond, fame beckons, what do you say?'

And Raymond Rice, twice-as-nice in his stripey shirt with his ginger thatch, says, 'Wighto!'

12
Let's Spend The Night Together

'Welcome to our 2017 Village Fete!' announces the PA system amidst howling feedback. It's like being on stage at a Heavy Metal concert. The weather is warm, it's a Sunday afternoon, mid-September. The village name doesn't matter, it's some English-y village-y name that the residents quote proudly. The crowd – although it's not strictly a *crowd* as such, if the definition of 'crowd' means a mass congregation of people – is a smattering, a scattering, of families wandering about, trying to find some attraction that actually *attracts,* though there's not much on offer.

But wait, look! There, under a small blue-and-white striped canopy, with barely enough headroom to stand up – there, here, is Rock Ireland Line, hired to perform all afternoon at this event 'as long as it's not too loud please and no offensive lyrics, mind, as children and families will be present'. So says the organiser, the head of the Parish Council, the 'chair', a Mrs Goodship, voice of the PA system.

The band only just fit into the space provided under the canopy, and they spill out a bit at the sides, especially Tank with his girth and titanic drumkit. They like this kind of gig; it's during the day, which makes a change, and on a Sunday when there's not much else to do and usually no gigs on offer. The money's guaranteed, they won't have to fight for every penny like they do with some pub landlords who want to knock off 'expenses' or apply 'low attendance' penalties. The music will attract a small passing audience, and the kids no doubt'll be enthralled by a 'live' band. There should be some teenagers hanging around, maybe dancing – always good for the soul. They might even sell some CDs: *Rock Ireland Line. Rock the Jam!* Why that title? They don't really know. What does 'Rock the Jam' mean anyway? But the recording engineer – good ol' Mick from Di an' Mick Sound studio – suggested it, and they thought, what the heck? it has a catchy ring to it. They had a quick conference about it and unanimously voted aye. They have a rule, had it since the old days, that any decision affecting the band has to have a unanimous vote. Three to one in favour still means a Nay; four-all means an Aye.

So they've set out their stall, a low table with the CDs neatly stacked, yours for a tenner, two for fifteen quid. Can't say fairer than that. But who buys CDs these days? When you can get everything online. One of the stalls at the fete sells second-hand books, DVDs and CDs. The books sell well, especially the cookery ones, good prices too, and the DVDs sell okay as the older generation, represented here at this stall pretty much one hundred per cent, still watch films on DVD. But CDs? Stacks and stacks of them remain unsold. 'You can't give 'em away,' moans the stallholder, knowing he'll be packing up the whole dam' lot at the end of the day. Keen gardeners might buy some though, to hang from branches to ward off predators. Just think, all those hours in a recording studio arguing over which tracks to include, the blood, sweat and tears spent over this precious CD, the rehearsals, the gaffes, the re-takes – only to end up hanging from a twig! Ah well, what goes around comes around. But the band might sell a few. If they sell five, it's a bonus, a drink.

The Bric-a-Brac Stall does well. People like bric-a-brac, and there the punters are, poring over the wares on offer, upending the pottery to find a maker's mark and the 'silverware' hoping to find a hallmark. They've all watched the antique programmes on the telly where something bought at a car boot sale for a quid turns out to be a precious piece of jade. But here it's old and chipped vases, salt 'n' pepper sets, sherry glasses, decorative plates, the odd picture pretending it ain't a print but a 'hand-painted original'. You should be so lucky!

There's a Plant Stall of course, there's always a plant stall. Selling cuttings in plastic pots. Bigger plants, home-grown. This is the stuff of village fetes. Smoke rises from the BBQ, and look, there's Prosecco on sale in plastic 'champagne' flutes. The mums indulge while the dads go to the beer tent for a pint of Ol' Peculiar, a murky local brew. A day of treats for adults and kids alike. There is also, obviously, because this is Little England after all, tea and cakes. Staple fare. Of the cakes, they're all homemade: fruitcake, lemon drizzle, Victoria sponge. The band have allowed themselves a pint each, and the Ol' Peculiar is indeed peculiar, but they wolf it down all the same – even Mickey, who should be abstaining, but sometimes a lager-top just won't do it.

Then there's the Dog Show. Why is there always a dog show? Answer: because people like dogs, and they like to show them off. And the dogs, the trained ones that is, sit still and obedient like good 'uns, and that's what this dog show is all about as the dogs and their owners (and yes, it's true, the owners *do* look like their dogs!) stand in a wide circle around the perimeter of the fenced-off area. Each dog, to the right of its owner, sits still, panting, looking up at its owner as if to say, 'What's up then, what's occurring?' and the owner says 'Si-i-i-t!' just to remind the mutt of the procedure.

Before the 'Best Dog in Show' is announced by the good Mrs Goodship – who has been partaking of the complimentary Prosecco and is now slurring her words – before this announcement is made, and all the various categories before it like 'Best Puppy' and 'Best Bitch', 'Waggiest Tail' (yes, really) and all that gubbins, Mrs Goodship has a task to perform, which she does with only minimal sarcasm, and that is to award the '*Worst* Behaved Dog'.

Laughter from the crowd, who all look to the northern end of the arena, as does Mrs Goodship, who lets out a hysterical *shriek* of mirth as she says, rather too loudly, 'It's pretty obvious who's going to win THIS one!' as she holds up a tiny plastic silver trophy. Because there, as her pointing long-nailed forefinger confirms, are two little girls trying to pacify a black and brawny monster hound which is chewing frantically at the dog lead attached at one end to its studded collar and at the other end to the two little girls. This bundle of energy is pulling violently at the lead, snarling and dribbling, and the girls are struggling to stand their ground. One calls out, 'It's okay, he's only playing!' and the crowd laugh again at the thought of this Hound of the Baskervilles 'only playing'. Mrs Goodship strides over – well, not exactly strides, more like lumbers; she's an ample woman is Mrs G – to present the cup and interview the girls on her radio-microphone.

'What's your name, young lady?'

'Dolly.'

'And is this your sister?'

Dolly nods.

'And what's your name, dear?'

'Millie,' says the sister.

'And your dog's name?'

The crowd wait expectantly…

'*Ripper.*'

Ripper! The crowd laugh, applaud, the cup is presented. The sisters try to turn to escape, but Ripper is having none of it and pulls afresh at his chewed-up lead.

'C'mon Ripper, home-time,' Dolly says, and it takes the both of them to drag the reluctant beast away.

The other prizes are handed out as the winners, dog-and-owner, trot up to the podium. And don't those owners look proud! And doesn't Mrs Goodship muddle up the cups, trying to read the inscription with her reading glasses looped around her neck! And don't those reading glasses, in their own drunken way, slip off her nose and dangle helplessly!

'Now for this afternoon's entertainment, er, all the way from Ireland, er, Rock…' A garbled announcement from Mrs Goodship. The good ship Mrs G is sinking fast, holed below the waterline by too much fizz.

Another voice takes over: 'Rock Ireland Line! For your listening pleasure!' This is Mrs G's daughter, Gloria. Bright and breezy, two dress-sizes overweight, a jolly-hockey-sticks private education type. Her voice brays through the feedback. Like mother, like daughter.

'They may look a little long in the tooth,' Gloria continues, 'but they're not short on good ol' fashioned Rock 'n' Roll! Rock on, chaps!'

And with that less-than-flattering welcome, the band launches into an old favourite, 'Peggy Sue', dedicated to Gloria, God bless 'er and all who sail in 'er!

'To all you Buddy Holly fans out there,' (of which there are maybe six, including the band).

This is the only introduction that Danny makes as the band have a new trick which is not to pause between numbers, no intros, no speeches, no rock histories. One song ends and immediately merges – 'segues' is the technical term – into the next, making for an energetic show, even if the *chaps*, the boys, the men, the geezers, *are* 'a bit long-in-the-tooth'. At least they still have all their own, they might well reply.

A decent-sized audience gathers and kids start dancing on the spot and mums jig a bit and the teenage girls swing their hips and hold their arms up high. This is a good gig on this sunny Sunday afternoon, and to commemorate this, the band sing The Kinks hit 'Sunny Afternoon', which has some pretty dour lyrics about the taxman and drunkenness and cruelty, but who's to notice as RIL have up-tempoed the song from the original so it sounds, well, *sunnier.*

Tank, at one point, looks up from his drumming – some sixth sense telling him that he's being stared at, more than just audience-watching but like intense *staring*… and it's *them* again! The two women, one middle-aged, one younger. One smiling, the other frowning. The mother-and-daughter lookalikes. And again, these two ain't dancin'. Again, in this small sea of jigging bodies, there is this one island of stillness. And *again,* the crowd shies away from them a bit, not wishing to twitch them as if they're contagious.

Tank, distracted, misses a beat, fluffs a run. The others notice, look round at him, Danny B glares. Tank tries to concentrate. But looks again. He has to. The younger staring, the older amused.

At the end of the set, the women have gone but Tank thinks that they can't be far and he goes in search and there, right at the end of the recreation ground, amongst the novelty stalls like Tin Can Alley and Splat the Rat, he finds them. They have their backs to him, trying to knock coconuts off the stands; they're unaware of him until he speaks –

'So…'

Just that. A simple 'So…' They turn around, shocked. Embarrassed to be confronted. At least the younger girl is flustered, but the ma (if she *is* the ma) just smiles sweetly then lowers her eyes.

'So, who are you? Fans? Stalkers? The Inland Revenue?' But Tank's attempt at humour falls flat. They couldn't look less like the Inland Revenue. They look at each other, this mother and daughter, and seem to come to some mutual agreement. To come clean.

'No, we're not stalkers,' the elder woman says, 'but we know you. That is, *I* know you.'

Something about her face, familiar, from the past, in fact from some twenty years ago, but as Tank's memory only goes back a few weeks he can't place her. But a horrible thought does come to him:

1) Woman and younger girl, could be mother and daughter,

2) Woman familiar to him,

3) He is only familiar with women in one way,

4) Could the younger girl be his *daughter*?

5) But he's always been careful,

6) No, that's not true, not always in the time of the Pill.

'We'll have tea,' the woman says, in her soft Irish accent – a sort of Edna O'Brien-County Clare lilt. She leads them off to a little tea-place under a marquee.

'I'm Mary, this is my daughter Kathleen.'

Tank doesn't offer up his name, and the younger girl called Kathleen keeps throwing stealthy glares at him, downward eyes, hands twitching. Mary leads on smiling, always smiling.

'It'll be this way.'

Tank is compliant, though. Doesn't say anything, although what he should be saying is, 'Why should I go with you? I don't know you.'

But he does, doesn't he?

'You find a table, Kath, I'll get the tea. Do you like cake?' This, to Tank, who nods in a trance. Sits down with the daughter. Ah, now he can say it. The daughter. That's what Mary said, and now it's so bloody obvious. But *his* daughter? She sits opposite him, and for the first time since he clapped eyes on her, she smiles. And his heart melts. It truly does. Such a cliché, but he feels it go. Kathleen looks down shyly. So pretty. Dark-haired like her mother. Pale skin. Eyes with light in them. Shining.

The older woman brings a tray over and goes to pour the tea.

'Shall I be Mother?' And there it is. The acknowledgement. The mother.

To Tank: 'Do you still take sugar? And what do I call you now?'

'Tank,' says Tank. 'I'm known as Tank. On account of my size.'

'I knew you as Jon,' and there it is. The connection.

'When? I don't remember.'

'How gallant of you. Not remembering I mean. Am I that forgettable?'

He flounders. Drinks his tea. Takes a bite of his cake.

'Be nice,' says Kathleen quietly to her ma.

'A long time ago,' continues Mary, 'a very long time ago, let's say, in 1996, you and I, Jon, and I'm blushing, truly I am, to be saying this out loud in front of Kath here – you and I were *friends.'*

'Oh, come on, Mam!' says Kathleen. 'I'm not a child. You had sex, right?'

The older people at the other tables look round, shocked – they just say *anything,* don't they? The youth of today!

'Kath darlin', language please! Be polite!' scolds the mother, but gently. And always with that smile.

Tank becomes Mr Reasonable.

'That was a long time ago. There were many…' But he can't finish this.

'Groupies?' Mary laughs. 'But I wasn't one of them, we went out, you took me out, courted me, even.'

'There were so many, we were touring, getting up to all sorts…'

'Gettin' up to all sorts, he says. Well, thank you, kind sir.'

but she wasn't all sorts – they met in a bar, she was with friends, and he looked over, again and again – and yes, he was handsome! so handsome! – then her friends told her he was in a band, a famous band, something with 'Ireland' in the name, so you've something in common, her friends said, winking their eyes and nudging with their elbows – they had a hit record, this famous band, tho' she'd never heard of them, but she was fascinated – a young twenty, virgin – he comes over! offers to buy her a drink – a Babycham with a glacé cherry – the bubbles went up her nose, she sneezed, he had a clean hanky –

'For the love of God,' she says. 'I wasn't *all sorts*!'

'Of course you weren't, Mam! Don't be so rude, Jon, or is it "Tank", did you say? "Tank"? Jesus, Mary and Joseph, what kind of a name is that?' And they both laugh their tinkling girly laughs.

'Call him "Mr Make-believe",' says Mary.

'I'll call him "Mr Bad-manners"!' says Kath.

Tank recovers himself. Sits up, tries to take charge.

'Ladies. I'm a rock star. You're not the first to come up to me and accuse me of this or that. You know what they say? "What goes on tour,

103

stays on tour". No tell-ee, no like-ee!'

And at that last bit of nonsense, Mother Mary bursts out laughing and takes his hand.

'You darlin' man. Such a child. Always were. That's what I liked about you.'

that's what she liked about him – the blue eyes, blonde hair – a rebel Viking but with a little round tummy – sweet way of talking – and his hands, oh his hands! – calloused through all the drumming – she strokes his hand now, it's like leather –

'You dear, dear man.'

But to the daughter, he's not a dear, dear man. He's fat, paunchy, looking shifty, wanting to escape.

no father mine, this one – old and past it but still thinks he's God's gift, I'll be bound – rock star indeed! – playing at a village fete under a canopy like he's a fairground act – playin' to kids and grown-ups and a few teeny girls who should know better – why are we doin' this, Mam? – why? for fuck's sake, I wanna go NOW!

But her mother can't hear her thoughts, although her daughter kicking her shin under the table should be message enough, plus the glare she's giving – We. Have. To. Go. NOW!

'Kath darlin', my baby, be still.' There it is again. The Irish poetry in her voice, breathy and low but soft to the ears like cotton wool smothered in baby powder.

this is what got you, isn't it, Jon? – my gentle voice whisperin' in your ear, 'let's go someplace away from this bar' – and you took me away from my mates to an Italian restaurant around the corner called Little Italy which had red-and-white check tablecloths and empty Mateus Rosé bottles with candles in dripping wax down the side – we had spaghetti bollock-knees you called it, and the waiter corrected you saying 'Bolognese, sir' – and you whispered in my ear 'bollock-knees', and I near died laughin'! – and it were the first time I'd ever eaten spaghetti that wasn't out of a tin, and it was the first time I tried red wine, and it made me tiddly it was so strong-tastin' – but warm and sexy that red wine, heady and thick it was too, like blood, like Jesus's blood – I loved you from that moment on, you dear, dear man –

and she smiles –

'We slept together and I had a baby and this is Kathleen.'

'And so… how do I know Kathleen's mine?'

'Biology,' Mary says.

'What do you mean, *biology*?'

'We slept together, and nine months later, out popped this darlin' wee child – biology.'

'But how do I know it's mine?'

Kath winces at being called an 'it'.

'Sorry, *she*.'

'You're the only man I slept with. And I was a virgin.' The Virgin Mary.

'You said you were on the Pill.'

'Did I?'

'Yes, I remember.'

now he remembers – she was tipsy, giggling, flirty – he supported her along the street – checked into a small hotel, well, a B&B really – landlady was snooty, disapproving, disbelieving of 'Mr and Mrs Jones', but she took the money, cash, no questions – dingy room, candlewick bedspread, disinfectant smell – Mary up for it – takes her jumper off, then bra, giggles, jeans off, falls over – 'I'm a bit tiddly,' she says – he undresses, she takes her panties off, falls on the bed. inviting – 'You're mine,' she says – he fiddles with a condom – 'Don't bother,' she says, 'I'm on the Pill' – and there it is – on the Pill – five minutes later, it's over – she, crying, but smiling too – crying and smiling – 'I lost my virginity to a rock star,' she says – and he hadn't realised, but sees the blood on the sheets – what will the B&B owner say? – better get out before she can catch us! – they grab clothes and race down the stairs, out into the street, running, laughing – then he forgets her – just another girl in another town – one of so many –

'Well, I wasn't,' says Mary, 'on the Pill, I mean.'

The other customers in the tea-place are listening intently to this exchange, so the three of them down their tea and leave the inevitable tittle-tattle behind – 'Well I never!' 'Who'd a-thought it in a village fete?' 'Disgusting behaviour!' 'I had to cover my ears!'

They walk, the three of them, then stop and sit under a tree.

'So then it's not my responsibility, is it? If you told me it was safe and it weren't,' says Tank. 'Anyway, there's no proof. Your word against mine. In fact, I'm not even admitting it. I'm not even sure I know you, come to that.'

'We have proof,' Mary says, for once not smiling.

Mary, Mary, quite contrary.

13
Be My Baby

They have proof, she says, and for the moment, Tank is panicked. 'Proof' is not a friendly word unless connected to a booze bottle.

It is the end of the afternoon; the band's final set is over, and Tank is again in the company of the two women. Walking by the stalls, not stopping. Mary explains the proof that they have.

'A sample of your DNA we took from a glass you drank out of. We got it at one of your gigs.'

Tank is appalled. 'What? Is that even *legal*?'

'It's legal enough. Proof enough. Your DNA matches half of Kathleen's. The other half matches me. Game, set and match. You're her father.'

But it's not a game, and Tank is pale. Shaking. Angry that they've connived to nick his own personal DNA by surreptitious means. He flounders.

'I… I didn't give permission. Surely you have to get permission? I won't take the responsibility. Anyway, the DNA could be flawed, contaminated. I've heard that can happen…'

Mary replies calmly, '99.99999 per cent accuracy, fella! Good enough for you?'

'What do you want? I can't take the responsibility. Do you want money? I can't pay maintenance, even if she is mine.'

'We don't want you to be responsible,' Mary continues, 'financially, I mean. We don't want your financial support. We don't really want you to be involved. We've done fine so far, Kath and me, with no husband or father. We've been fine, sure enough. But Kath here wanted to meet her real Da', that's all.'

Kathleen looks up at him now. This weak, bruised man is beginning to grow on her. The 'little boy lost' expression. Or maybe it's some father/daughter instinct kicking in.

'Can I call you "Dad"?' says Kathleen.

And quite unexpectedly, and quite movingly really, Tank bursts into tears.

And Kath, his daughter, hugs him.

'Dad,' she says.

14
Crying

'Cry-baby,' mocks Mary gently.

'My baby,' says Tank.

15
Drums

Talking of DNA, Kathleen has inherited her father's drummer genes. She develops a passion for percussion at music college.

Take a walk around the Royal Albert Hall in London's South Kensington and opposite, on one side, you will see a building like a Town Hall. Red brick, towers, grand entrance. This is the Royal College of Music. It's a summer's day, and the windows are open. You hear music, but not coming from the Albert Hall, where all the concerts take place. You might hear a flute high up in its register or a piano practising scales. Then a string quartet tuning up or a trombone playing solo. All coming from inside the RCM's stern walls.

Kath has been accepted there, auditioning as a performer on the clarinet, the wind instrument she has mastered since her baby days on the recorder. Mary, her mother, scrimped and scraped to buy her the best clarinet and pay for lessons, and now she has been rewarded. The *Royal College of Music!*

But the parting-of-the-ways has been a wrench that Mary can hardly bear, accompanying her baby, this person who has been the centre of her existence for eighteen years, who has occupied her heart wholesale, who has been the whole adorable focus of her universe – and what does she do, this mother, this guardian angel? She takes her first-born, her *only-*born, to dingy student lodgings in the distant big city, and… *and… she leaves her there!* She leaves her child there. Where's the logic in that? And she, Mary, travels back home on the train, in copious tears, and the other passengers look at her and don't know whether to ask if she is okay or look the other way. One woman asks this weeping lady what the matter is and is there anything she can do? And Mary answers, in between sobs, just two words: 'Empty nest,' and the woman gets it immediately, as she has experienced the same thing. Empty nest. This bird has flown.

Kathleen makes a great success of music college, enjoying the independence of her new life, the bustle of Knightsbridge, the companionship of her fellow students, the commonality of a love of music, the guidance of the tutors. One of the students in her year is called Sean – Irish, of course, with a name like Sean – and he starts following her around, standing behind her in the refectory queue, engaging in shy small-talk. So she lets him walk beside her, exchanges music views, goes to the cinema when they can afford it, and eventually, as is the way of things, she sleeps with him, both clumsy virgins, and why don't they teach you this at school but then again, how could they? But nature is a quick learner, or teacher, and soon they perfect the art of lovemaking over many practice sessions. Practice makes perfect, both in music and sex.

'We're getting pretty good at this,' says Kath after one particularly energetic session.

'Practice makes perfect,' says Sean. And it *is* perfect. Life is perfect.

Eventually, they get onto the subject of parents and siblings. Sean has a complete set, but Kath lies about her father, saying he died when she was a toddler and she never knew him. But goes on to lavish all her love on her dear mama. Sean's 'full set' is almost textbook. Both parents still married, two younger sisters, all living back in the old country. He lives now though in a world of his music and likes to share his knowledge with Kath and becomes the inspiration for her love of percussion, for this is his love too – the beat, beat, beat of the drum, the crash and hiss of the cymbal.

One day, Sean sets Kath a puzzle. 'Name the only drum solo in opera.'

Of course, she can't. Can anyone? A *drum solo*, à la Ginger Baker, in *opera*? Mozart? Puccini? Verdi?

'Shostakovitch!' says Sean triumphantly. 'Dmitri Shostakovitch in his opera "The Nose"!'

The drum solo – and it really is a solo, albeit played by several percussionists – comes near the beginning of the opera and lasts for a whole *three minutes* using every percussion instrument in the ensemble. Crashing, clicking, clacking, tapping, bashing. Sean plays the LP to her on his ancient Dansette record player back in his 'digs', but not too loud as his landlady'll shout up the stairs, 'Turn your music down, Mr Callaghan, I can't hear myself *think*!'

Kath discovers for herself the relentless side-drum playing in Nielsen's fifth symphony where a repeated tattoo, '− . . − − −', begins a battle with the whole orchestra, trying to disrupt the charted course the orchestra is taking by playing, as instructed on the score, an *ad-lib* cadenza for a near two and a half minutes, using every counter-rhythm the frenzied drummer can muster, hitting stick against stick, stick against metal and pounding the skin on the side-drum at *ffz* dynamic which means AS LOUD AS POSSIBLE! But eventually the orchestra wins out, and the percussion retires, defeated, and dies away with a final last gasp of its insistent '− . . − − −', *poco a poco diminuendo,* meaning quieter, little by little.

'Imagine being the percussionist in Ravel's Bolero!' says Kath, one time, walking in Hyde Park. 'The snare drum has over 4,000 notes to beat out *ostinato* in endless repetition in the fifteen-minute piece, with no variation apart from volume.'

'I wonder if Ravel wrote out every beat on the score or just indicated "Repeat until end but get louder"?' says Sean.

They find the score in the college library, and sure enough, Ravel, or his music inscriber, has printed out all 4,062 identical notes. They go back to Kath's digs and celebrate with some *bravura* lovemaking, *poco a poco accelerando*.

16
Bits & Pieces

In a cramped recording studio just off the Lindenstraat in Amsterdam's De Jordaan district, the headquarters of Radio Amst thrives and bustles as delightful Dutch blondes fuss and flatter around the radio station's star DJ, Tim Smit, and his famous rockstar guest, Tank – or, as Tim Smit calls him, 'Mr Tank'. The year is more or less present-day, give or take, and this is the band's renaissance, hence the interview on Radio Amst's popular prog-rock show, 'Smit's Hits'.

Tim Smit: So welcome Mr Tank to – (pause for jingle) – 'Smit's Hits'.

Tank (pleasantly): It's just Tank, not Mr.

TS: I owe you too much respect, Mr Tank, and may I add how much pleasure we have to welcome you here.

T: The pleasure's all mine, especially to be here in your lovely city.

TS: May I ask some questions please, Mr Tank, that will be welcome for our listeners?

T: Fire away.

TS: Excuse me?

T: Go ahead.

TS: For the second time in your historical career, your band Rock Ireland Line has discovered fame. What is that like for you in your older ages?

T: It's a blast, Tim.

TS: Excuse me?

T: It's great.

(The two languages collide. The polite but stilted Dutch version of English and Tank's more colloquial. The words 'blast' and 'fire' confuse DJ Smit.)

TS: I would like please to interrogate you about your drumming –

how did you ever start? Who were your influencers?

T: Who influenced me? That's easy. I wanted to be a drummer when I first saw Ringo Starr on TV and later Keith Moon of The Who. In the Boy Scouts – do you have those over here? – there was an older lad who played the drums, and I was caught – hook, line and sinker!

(More confusion from Tim at this puzzling phrase.)

TS: What is this 'hooker and sinker', please?

T: I mean, I was captivated. The boy's dad was the village cop, and he'd been a military drummer. He showed me how to hold the sticks *lightly* – 'let the drums do the work,' he'd say. He showed me the basic stuff, and it kinda grew from there. He said as long as you have 'time', that is, a feeling for perfect time, you can make it as a drummer.

TS: When did you get your first drum kit, please?

T: I started with a biscuit tin and my ma's knitting needles for sticks. Then I graduated to a family-size Cadbury Roses tin we got one Christmas – that made a good sound, I remember. Drove my parents mad! What I'd do is place some coins on the tin lid, and when I hit it, the coins'd vibrate like a sort of snare drum effect. For the bass drum, I used a large cardboard box that I'd kick, and for a cymbal, a tin sheet on a pole. I laid some empty tin cans in a row – they were my tom-toms.

TS: How many years did you have then?

T: My age, you mean? I was ten or eleven. My mum and dad took pity on me and bought a plastic snare drum and cymbal kit at a jumble sale. Half a crown it cost, and I was dead chuffed. Excited, I mean. It felt like being a *real* drummer!

TS: What drummers did you follow at this time?

T: Well, Ringo, as I said. He had a great sense of time and a special sound. I could always tell a Ringo beat. Did you know that on the Abbey Road album, he performed his *one and only* drum solo. It was in the medley at the end. Thirteen bars, to be exact, fifteen seconds in all. Ginger Baker would do *ten-minute* solos on stage!

TS: Do you do drum solos when you play live, Mr Tank?

T: Tank, please! Yes. Sometimes the others will put in a slot for my solo. Means they can go off, have a pee, a pint and a quick forty winks!

Tim laughs along with Tank, more to be polite than understanding Tank's baffling phrases. Forty winks? The engineer behind the

114

soundproof glass also rocks back in his chair, mouth open in a parody of hysterics though no sound comes out of that orifice. A delightful Dutch blonde chooses this moment to enter the studio bearing tea etc – the 'etc' being a giant spliff for Tim and one for Tank too. Ah well, when in Amsterdam, as they say.

TS: So, er… Tank. You're a teenager and ready to play drums in a group. How did that happen, please?

T: The first band I played in was a Blues Band. I hung around them as a sort of unofficial roadie. They had a beat-up Ford Thames 15 cwt van that I'd drive. Didn't matter that I was only fifteen or thereabouts, I looked older and, anyway, life was much freer in them days. Sat on a cushion in the driving seat so I looked more grown-up. What happened was there was this one gig and their drummer hadn't turned up. Nor had his drum kit. Now the group knew I could play drums a bit. I'd badgered them enough about it and they'd heard me muck around when drummer-boy was off taking a piss or something – screwing a chick, I dunno – he'd turf me off sharpish when he got back, saying they were *his* drums and *no one* was allowed to touch 'em! Well, this one night he doesn't turn up so they ask me to fill in, so I drive over to Mal's house – the drummer's name was Mal – to get the drum kit. Mal wasn't in, but his drums were present and correct, so I persuade Mal's ma to let me borrow the kit. 'Mal said it'd be okay,' is what I promise, lying through me teeth o' course. I load it all into the van and drive back in triumph to the pub where the gig is. Trouble was, by then, the landlady of the pub had returned from her hols and was bollocking the temporary manager for hiring a band when the pub had no music licence. So, in the end, we were all chucked out on our arses, and I had to return the drum kit to Mal's home, by which time Mal had returned from wherever and gave me a right mouthful and nearly a bunch of fives into the bargain.

TS: Bunch of fives?

(Tank mimes a fist.)

TS: Ah, I see. For our listeners, Mr Tank has demonstrated that a bunch of fives refers to a fist. So, did you actually join that band?

T: I filled in for Mal when he was AWOL – sorry, not around, I mean – but Mal hated me, so I replied to an ad for a drummer in the local paper. Apparently, in this particular group, there'd been a bust-up with the previous guy who'd legged it, so they needed a replacement sharpish as they had gigs booked. The singer, who was the leader of the group, was a right bastard, nasty temper, and would fly off the handle at the slightest thing. Name of Brian – 'Bolshy Bri' as he was known by the band. I got on okay with him cos I kept me trap shut and just played the drums. I had me own kit by then, a full kit bought second-hand.

TS: And what is the 'full kit'? All together, I mean. The bits and pieces.

T: Bits and pieces. Funny you should say that. Title of a song by the Dave Clarke Five. Only line-up that's ever had the drummer up-front. Dave Clarke became known for his clever staccato machine-gun 'fill' in that song.

(And here Tank imitates the Dave Clarke signature fill by slapping the rhythm on the table.)

T: The rest of the band would stamp their feet in time. There was another band called The Honeycombs, who had a female drummer. Beehive hairdo. Appropriate as her name was Honey.

(Tim looks perplexed at 'beehive hairdo' but wisely lets it go.)

T: D'y'know they always make jokes about drummers – 'What do you call a band? Three musicians and a drummer!', 'How do you tell the stage is level? The drummer is drooling equally out of each side of his mouth!' And yet we're the solid rock of the band.

TS: That is most unkind. What other drummers do you follow?

T: Ginger Baker, of course. He had *two* bass drums in his kit! Most drummers have some kind of quirk – Ringo was a left-handed drummer, and I'm pretty sure he played a right-handed kit. I reckon that's what made his sound unique. Drummers like Keith Moon were more flamboyant, playing wild and crazy, while the likes of Charlie Watts of the Stones, Phil Collins of Genesis and Mitch Mitchell of Hendrix's band specialised in great 'chops' as they're known, which is the term for the licks and clever fills. That's my opinion, anyway. John Bonham of Led Zeppelin. All brilliant practitioners of the art of percussion because, Tim, it is an *art*, make no mistake.

TS: What is your favoured part of your drum kit?

T: The snare drum – the simple snare drum with its wires stretched across the lower skin – makes a sharp, staccato sound, the essence of backbeat and the heartbeat of the band, the pulse that gets everyone dancing. The volume can be intense, likened to the blast of a .38 revolver.

TS: What are your problems, if any, of drumming in your advanced years? Please to forgive my impertinence.

T: That's okay, Tim. Comes to us all. It's the hands. Definitely the hands. I need to soak my hands in iced water before every gig to reduce inflammation. Nowadays, my hands tend to be stiff – when I form a fist, it hurts. So I avoid forming a fist, unless provoked, natch.

(Large inhale of the spliff and a nervous laugh from Tim sat opposite Tank and within striking distance of the bunch of fives.)

TS: Lastly, as we are racing out of time, how did you join Rock Ireland Line?

T: Easy, really. Really easy. Friends of friends. I knew Mickey.

TS: Your lead guitarist.

T: Yeah, I knew him from Tech college, and he introduced me to the other two. Auditioned. I guess they liked what they heard. Mickey bigged me up anyway. So I was in the band and Bob's your uncle.

(Of course, this is *double Dutch* to poor Tim Smit – what is this talk of Mr Tank's Uncle Bob?)

But the interview is over, and Tank takes a last enormous drag of his spliff, shakes Tim's hand, and shuffles off, stage-left and into the bustle of the Lindenstraat.

17
Daddy-O

In the Café Américaine, a splendid drinking establishment close to the Marnixstraat in Amsterdam, all-gold interior and art deco styling, Kathleen sits at a small table by the window sipping a dry sherry. Dark hair bobbed, she is wearing an assortment of Bohemian fabrics. White headphones set off her black hair, and she is listening to Revueltas's 'La Noche de los Mayas' – a modern classical orchestral miasma of sound that features fourteen percussionists playing a mass of instruments: bongos, conga, metal rattle, güiro, teponaztli, caracol, Indian drums, suspended cymbal, tam-tam, plus the usual array of snares, bass drum, tom-toms and timpani along with xylophone and piano. They play for extended lengths of time, interchanging rhythms while the rest of the orchestra sit mute. One would not think that such a cacophony is playing in Kath's head, judging by her poised demeanour as she sits waiting for her father.

And there he is, framed in the doorway, pointing out to the female meet-and-greeter the table where Kathleen sits. 'Meeting my daughter,' he says proudly. And the girl smiles warmly as all girls love their dads.

And there he is, this incredible bulk of a man, looking a bit like Meatloaf. Tank, red-faced and sweaty after his tram ride, his 'Sun-in' blonde hair tied back in a ponytail with a rubber band, dressed all in faded denim with a Dragonslayer tee-shirt. Arms stretched wide to greet his darlin' girl, beaming all over his face, his eyeballs betray the recent ingest of weed.

And there he is, weaving between the tables, which are a little too close together for a man his size; he knocks a chair and a cranky old woman tut-tuts, but a kindly waitress clears a way for him.

Then, this bear of a man bear-hugs the petite Kathleen, who says,
    'Hey Daddy-o!' – for this is her new name for him.

18
Remember The Alamo

Back in time to 1976, the end of April and the beginning of Rock Ireland's road to rock-stardom, and introducing, for the first time in this history, the independent record label company called 'YoungDudes Records'.

It is to this company that the band are summoned on the morrow of their viewing The Plastic Punk Army in the Clerkenwell pub. And it is at the behest of their manager Mr Joe Rainbow and his new sidekick, Raymond 'Twice as Nice' Rice, after the momentous revelation on the part of Joe R to make RIL the smartest punk band around, changing their band name to *Smart*Punk (if only the band'll agree). The lads themselves are in blissful ignorance of this plan of action, which is just as well as, if they were, they'd most like be in very bad moods by now, as opposed to the optimistic frame of mind they're in at the prospect of a meeting at YoungDudes Records.

The building in Soho Square is a converted townhouse, four storeys high, but only wide enough to accommodate a staircase and office on each floor. Staff numbers are six, including the boss (of whom more soon). The ground floor houses the reception area, which is presided over by a gum-chewin' chick-in-pink who looks proper bored but somehow cool all the same. Pink polo-neck jumper, hair in bunches. Big hoop earrings.

It is in this reception area, smart and light-beige-carpeted, that a rock band or pop group will congregate, typically nervous and ill-at-ease if they're unsigned newcomers, brash and slovenly if they're already signed. Sandy, the receptionist, can spot the types instantly and treat them accordingly – fawning over the named bands, dismissive over the unknown. And Rock Ireland Line are unknown. There they sit, uncomfortably, flicking through the music papers on the low table, the

New Musical Express and Melody Maker.

The boys are waiting for Joe and Ray, who are late, and Mickey, feeling the need for a pee, announces same to Sandy, who, without bothering to look up, points to the stairs and says, 'First door on the right – marked LOO.' Mickey does his business, comes down the stairs, resumes his seat with the others. Then a record company executive (presumably) comes down the stairs to give an envelope for posting to Sandy who is all over him like a warm duvet and, as he turns to go back up the stairs, he remarks, 'What are these marks on the carpet?' and he goes to take a closer look and says that the marks look like footprints, white shoeprints, and he tries to wipe them off, saying, 'Looks like paint to me. Call Maintenance, will you, Sandy?'

Sandy pushes buttons on her mini-switchboard and summons Andy of Maintenance to present himself pronto with a rag and some turpentine. She then comes out from behind her desk, displaying lots of leg due to her micro-skirt, and investigates the marks on the stairs, bending over to give the boys a pleasing eyeful, and notices that the white footprints are also all over the reception area carpet too. She looks suspiciously at the group, but at this point her brain shuts down, unable to think what to do or say next, so goes back to chewing and thinking of her boyfriend, Delbo, who's giving her a hard time and screwing around, the bastard. Should she dump him? Or get more industry contacts via him as he is a much sought-after rapper DJ who knows all the right people. Mind you, so do I, Sandy thinks – so do I really need his connections? She resolves to stick with him for now and dump him when she finds someone better. Her brain, after all this overdrive, slips now into neutral, and she goes back to concentrating on chewing and filing her nails all at the same time.

Meanwhile, Mickey has been pondering the white footprints in front of him, and a vision comes into his head of the pavement outside and a sign saying, WET PAINT, and a pool of spilt white paint on the road. He remembers avoiding it… or did he? He casually crosses his legs and looks at the upturned sole of his shoe and sees… WHITE! He re-crosses his legs in order to take a peek at the other shoe and sees… WHITE! Panicking now, he pretends he needs some cigs and rushes out, wiping his feet on the mat, on the grass verge and in a nearby puddle. Satisfied that his shoes are now free of the offending paint, he returns, only to meet Joe and Ray by the door.

Enter Joe into the establishment, all a-swagger, and with great aplomb he addresses Sandy thus, in a booming voice: 'MISTER RAINBOW AND MISTER RICE TO SEE MISTER GODBOLD, MY DEAR!' – Mr Godbold being the head of YoungDudes Records, who has Raymond under his wing. They're directed up the stairs, edging past Handy Andy of Maintenance, who has now turned up with a rag and turps and is rubbing away at the stains. A handsome fella is Andy, looking fit in his crisp overalls, and giving a wink now and then to Sandy who ignores him, considering him well below her station.

On the top floor is an open door, and through that door can be seen a large mahogany desk, piled high with cassette tapes, LPs, papers and files and a hi-tech turntable. Behind the desk is a throne of antique origin by the look of it, carved with serpents on its high back, and seated on the throne is a handsome man of about thirty-ish. Tall, by the look of him, sitting bolt upright. Behind the throne and framing the man is a portrait of Chairman Mao, Andy Warhol-style, covering the whole wall.

The man is like a 1950s movie matinee idol, think Douglas Fairbanks or Clark Gable. Pencil-thin 'tache. Slicked-back, black wavy hair with sideburns. In each earlobe, a swashbuckling earring but this is offset by the sombre suit and business shirt-and-tie. However, on closer inspection, the pattern on the tie is of repeated pistols. The shoes, if they could be seen behind the desk, are Italian brogues. The man may be smart, but he's showy, displaying a lack of class and breeding. Any high-class restaurant maître-de or hotel manager would spot his sort a mile off. Nouveau-riche, brash but a good tipper.

Gypsy

In fact, Mr Godbold – for this is he – Mr Godbold's breeding is impeccable, being of traditional gypsy stock, family name 'Goddard', which he's changed to a name he thinks sounds more aristocratic. On the desk is a nameplate which reveals his full name: ALAMO GODBOLD. He gestures them to sit, then leans back, hands in a pyramid shape to his lips, eyes closed and… silent. Silent for what seems like minutes but is, in fact, one minute to the second as Mr Godbold, née Goddard, is counting off the seconds in his head. He opens his eyes at 'sixty' and proceeds to talk in a South London accent interspersed with intervals of 'posh'.

'Danny, Tony, Tank and Mickey. My name, as you will have discerned from the nameplate before you, is Alamo Godbold, but you can call me Al. Unusual moniker, I grant ye, but I was blessed with unusual parentage. Gypsy descent – Romani, not Irish, gypsy. Sorry Danny, can't empathise with your Celtic roots. Danny, Tony, Tank and Mickey – and, not forgetting your esteemed manager, Mr Rainbow, to whom I doff my cap in recognition of his talent-spotting. My Romani blood flows with the clairvoyance of fortune-tellin', or "duckerin' " as my dear ol' mama called it, Gawd rest her soul! My ma was an expert duckerer and she passed on the gift to me. So boys, let me tell you your future...'

He mimes a small circle on the desk, like a globe.

'Imagine a crystal ball, if ye will, and as I clear the mists of destiny, I can see great fuckin' success for yay four. Great fuckin' success! I can see you're gonna be stars. And who's gonna make you stars? Answer: Me. Leading you all by the hand to the Promised Land.'

The boys are already enraptured by this creature, led by some form of mystic hypnotism, or maybe it's just the promise of riches beyond their wildest. The Promised Land has evaded them for so long they never thought they'd get there. They'd be in the dreary 'burbs forever. Alamo now turns to Joe, bowing his head in reverence.

'My good friend Mr Rainbow here has presented me with an idea. A vision, if ye will. A gimmick, to be precise. Nothing wrong with a gimmick if you don't have talent. But equally, nothing wrong with talent that has no gimmick. It don't need it, y'see. Like Concorde don't need different classes of travel. It's *all* First Class! Like you, boys...'

Omigod, they like what they're hearing. Manna from Heaven is what this is. Joe, despite knowing what's coming, is beaming. *His* boys. First Class!

'Mr Rainbow had this notion – a not unfeasible one, yours truly might add – that Rock Ireland Line should not only go punk but go punk-with-a-difference, i.e. punk-in-suits. Smart punk. And that you should change your band name to that very phrase – *Smart*Punk. Here's how he saw it…'

He writes the name on a notepad, indicating the italics, the capital 'S' and 'P', and all in one word. The boys look at each other, horrified. Which, of course, Mr Godbold clocks.

'Ha! I note your discomfort, and well may you look like sommat the cat dragged in and then puked up on the living room carpet. Our Mr Rainbow here doubtless had your best interests at heart but fret not my fine friends, cos I predict that your band name will ever be thus, namely "Rock Ireland Line", cos not only do I like the play on words of "Ireland" and "Island" but also that particular skiffle song was a favourite of mine in my youth, furthermore punk will *not* be a direction you're headin' and no suits neither! Savvy, Mr Rainbow?'

Mr Rainbow savvies.

'Punk is a passing fad,' says Alamo, 'maybe last a year or two but it won't last. What's more, its anti-establishment stance will become establishment, such is the way of things, and soon traditional pop and rock will surface again. And that's where Rock Ireland come in.'

And he's not far wrong; because a year later, Christmas 1977, a love song to a Scottish region, in waltz time, complete with bagpipes and marching band, becomes a massive hit for Paul McCartney and his group, Wings. 'Mull of Kintyre' is the song of course. So, eat your heart out, punk!

'Now then, Raymondo.' Alamo is addressing his erstwhile underling. 'Raymond, Raymond, Raymond! What were ye a-thinkin' of? A posh well-educated plonker like you havin' opinions 'bout what sort of direction a band should take? Take the advice of your elders and betters. Full marks, mind you, for spotting these boys – this is what we hire ye for – and putting them on the path to YoungDudes Records, and ten out of ten for recognising that 'Beat times three' is a fuckin' all-out *one thousand per cent guaranteed hit!* Credit where it's due and on-point, Master Rice. But allow *me*, if you'll be so bold, to lead these tender sheep like the good shepherd that I am. Does that sit well with thee, Master Rice?'

It sits well with Master Rice.

'To continue then. Yours truly is President, Leader, Archbishop,

Head Honcho and fuckin' Head Sharrom of all assembled here at YoungDudes Records. I am the bees-knees, the dogs-bollox and what I says goes. Behind this placid exterior is an iron will and fuckin' tender heart for this company and all who sail in her. Look at the photos on the wall here, peruse them at your leisure. Whaddya see?'

What they see, what they *peruse*, are pictures of well-known bands with Mr Godbold shaking their hands, or he has his arms round them like a doting father. There are female singers too, kissing a beaming Mr G on the cheek. All and sundry appear to worship their Good Shepherd. As well as appreciating the love shown here for their leader, the boys are entranced by the onslaught of words – the ye's, yay's and the thee's – while Joe Rainbow sits back, smiling sweetly, smelling success. What cares he now for his *Smart*Punk idea? Water under the bridge. He realises he no longer needs Raymond as his business assistant and anyway he has other plans for him. Because here, in this business situation, it's clear that Raymond does not impress, fidgeting, taking periodic snorts of his asthma inhaler, at one point colliding with a chair.

Here, There and Everywhere

Alamo Godbold chooses this moment to stand up too. Fucking hell, he must be over six foot! He points to his right to a closed door.

'In the next room is a contract. It's full of small print and the reason the print is small is because I don't want you to waste your precious time readin' it. Savvy? It's full of all sorts of caveats and where-to-fores and here-in-fuckin'-afters and anyway your manager has given it the once-over and the green-o. Do you concur, Mr Rainbow sir?'

Mr Rainbow sir concurs.

'So all that's required of yay, young fella-me-lads, is to go yonder into that room, take up the ballpoint pens so thoughtfully provided by yours truly, and sign your fuckin' lives away, savvy? Now, I will turn my back and face the wall, close my eyes tight shut, and count slowly to twenty; after which I expect to see you four sittin' before me, clutching glasses of bubbly in your ballpoint-pen-ink-stained fingers. Ready? One... Two... Three...'

He counts.

Eyes tight shut.

Facing Chairman Mao.

The boys look at each other.

Shrug and nod in unison.

Unanimous vote of YES.

They journey forth into the next room.

Where Biros await.

Where a blonde beauty awaits.

With a tray of glasses of bubbly.

'Ten… Eleven… Twelve…'

Joe indicates the dotted lines.

Here, there, and everywhere.

He co-signs.

Then they toast their bloody good fortune that at long last they have a record deal! What every band longs for, no matter what. No matter the small print. A Bona Fide Fuckin' Record Deal! Here-to-bloody-fore signed to YoungDudes Records, who will now undertake to record them professionally, promote them tirelessly, and sell them on selflessly to a major company.

For this service, the band will be given an advance on future earnings with all expenses deducted at gross, which will include management fees, finders' fees, food, transport, accommodation, recording costs, publicity junkets, booze, women, drugs and even toilet paper (the small print). This advance is split four ways after Joe's cut and Raymond's slice. So, in effect, a pittance. But what the hell? They're signed!

'… Eighteen… Nineteen… Twenty! Coming, ready or not!'

So says Alamo G as he turns and there the boys are as good as gold with their glasses of bubbly, sitting obediently before their Headmaster. Hands are shaken, backs slapped, glasses clinked. Mr Godbold doesn't imbibe, he says, so his secretary – omigod, just look at her! – brings him a glass of innocent-looking orange juice (that is *actually* laced with a generous shot of vodka, so not innocent at all).

As the boys leave, passing Handy Andy the handsome Maintenance Man on the stairs, still rubbing away with the rag and turps, they say goodbye to Sandy on reception, and Danny Boy, confident now, gives her a sly wink. She thinks that by the way they're acting all uppity and the fact that Mr Godbold from the top of the stairs is bidding them a cheery farewell and a 'See you anon', she surmises, call it feminine intuition or what, that the band has been signed. She's seen it before, the dejected demeanour of the unsigned slinking out, the swagger of the newly signed. So Sandy gives Danny an encouraging smile, in anticipation perhaps of the dumping of Delbo.

They're out on the street. Congratulating each other. What a happy bunch gathered there on the pavement as the street painter brushes the spilt white paint away! And here is Jeeves with the Roller, and they'll be Trader Vic's-bound no doubt. But before that, Mickey shows his upturned soles, still bearing some remnants of the white paint, to the boys, who laugh fit to burst. A tight band is RIL.

Sandy

To complete the history of Sandy, who does not fall for Danny B's charms, nor does she stay with Delbo. Instead, she falls for Andy, handsome as he is. They marry and produce two kids, a boy and a girl. Sandy stays as receptionist at YoungDudes and works her way up to filing and finance as the company expands. Andy starts his own Office Maintenance company called 'Handy Andy's'.

They have a happy life together until, at the ridiculously young age of forty-nine, Andy dies of pancreatic cancer.

Alamo Godbold, now in his early sixties, looks after Sandy and her family, providing financial support until, after a respectable time has elapsed, they marry. They take his yacht to many places overseas, with friends and family and Sandy's children and now grandchildren, until Alamo Godbold has a stroke.

Sandy, now widowed twice, inherits a considerable fortune from Alamo's businesses and moves to Monte Carlo for tax purposes. However, a gambling obsession loses her most of the money, and she returns to England, broke and broken, when she is in her seventies.

Crippled with arthritis, she is looked after by her daughter until she also shuffles off her mortal coil at the grand ol' age of eighty-five. Such is life.

19
Sunny Goodge Street

A recording studio in London's Goodge Street, just off the Tottenham Court Road. Goodge Street is a quiet backwater compared to its busy neighbour, this day in the early summer of '76. It's going to be a long, hot one. Through the months of June, July and August, temperatures will get as high as thirty-five degrees. The popular papers run screamer headlines, SCORCHER! and PHEW! All records broken. It's three months of hell if you're an office worker as there's no aircon in the UK. Still isn't today, pretty much. The Underground becomes a sauna, and on the roads, the tarmac melts. Someone fries an egg on the pavement. One paper headline: SUNNY SIDE UP!

Eventually, of course, England being England and incapable of dealing with any aberration of the weather, a DROUGHT is declared. There are standpipes in the streets, and a nationwide hosepipe ban is introduced with a big fine for miscreants who sneakily try watering their gardens, their brown grass, under the cover of darkness; but beware, because neighbours are encouraged to rat on any late-night hosepiper. Couples are encouraged to share a bath, resulting in a baby boom nine months later. The government springs into action and appoints a 'Minister for Droughts', at which point the heavens open and thunderstorms swamp the scorched earth.

Here in Goodge Street, it's sunny and pleasant in this early June month. The market stalls outside the tube station look appetising with fresh fruit on offer, displayed in all its vibrant colour. The Evening Standard seller is out already with the first editions, looking hot and bothered, wearing too many clothes – 'Stand-ard!' he shouts. 'Get yer Evening Stand-ard!'

THE FILTH AND THE FURY! will scream one newspaper headline in

December of this year when the Sex Pistols appear live on early evening TV and say FUCK on-air (shocking in 1976) and other choice four-letterers. The programme is 'Today' on Thames, and the Pistols have been brought in as a last-minute replacement for the band Queen due to Freddie Mercury's dental appointment, or so the story goes. The interviewer, one Bill Grundy, rather coaxes the Pistols, who are looking suitably anarchic and slovenly, to say something rude. He, in his suit, with his own TV show. Say something outrageous, go on, he says. So they call him a dirty fucker and become famous overnight. Their record 'Anarchy In The UK' has already been released in November. This is anarchy on British television.

But now it's June and sunny in sunny Goodge Street, and Rock Ireland are scheduled to record their first single in a professional recording studio with a professional record producer who has a string of hits to his name. Sitting beside him at the mixing desk is the professional engineer. This is a far cry from Di an' Mick Sound of Market Harborough.

The producer is introduced to them as Simon ('Si') and they don't catch the name of the engineer because he mutters it as he crouches over the desk – his empire of knobs, sliders and meters.

Their equipment is already in position in the recording studio, the guitars are waiting on their stands, the drum kit set out correctly, all done by their new roadie, Raymond 'Twice as Nice' Rice, who over the ensuing months/years will build up his muscles, lugging all the gear about, and the physical activity and fresh air will actually help his asthma. The band grow to cherish their new roadie, and he takes to the work like he was born to it. RayRoadieRice he becomes known as, like it's all one word.

The nameless engineer takes the band's demo tape from Joe and puts it into the machine. Suddenly, in this state-of-the-art studio, it sounds amateur. Crap, really. Si winces and turns down the volume and turns it down even more when Mickey's backwards-guitar starts. Silence when the tape ends. Engineer ejects the tape, and Si hands it back to Joe, holding it by the very edge in thumb and forefinger like it's infected.

'So old-hat, guys. Amateursville!' is all Si says, so the boys go to set up in the recording studio, unsure of how to start or what to do next. But

Si is rooting around in a box of old vinyl records, and he pulls out a BBC Sound Effects Library LP.

'Listen to this,' he says through the intercom and selects a track. Out of the speakers comes the sound of a human heartbeat, which takes them back to a memory of Di placing a microphone between her boobs.

'We know,' says Danny. 'We've been down that road.'

'But I bet you haven't heard this,' says Si, and now out of the speakers comes a deep bass thud, which reverberates through their very bones.

'I've quadrupled the bass signal, taken out all the top end and now I'll put it through a phasing loop. Try playing to this, guys. See how you do.'

Intriguing as the idea is – no, as *stupid* as the idea is – they go along with the idea, play along with the heartbeat and you know what? It ain't half bad against this background of BBC Sound Archive 'Heartbeat, human', track thirteen.

After a few false starts and attempts by Tank to counter the beat, they settle into a rhythm which is quite hypnotic, mesmerising even. And *catchy*.

It's Tank, with his sense of perfect timing, who first notices it.

'It's speeding up gradually, isn't it? You're speeding it up.'

'Well spotted,' says Si. 'We've been speeding it up all the time to give some *tension* to the track. What it does is encourage your own heartbeat to try and keep pace, so you feel this sense of excitement. It takes a hold of you.'

But, having drawn attention to himself, Tank now becomes the target of Si's superiority. Mr Hitmaker now keeps halting the run-throughs, criticising Tank's 'rigid' technique – 'Loosen up, man!' – but Tank, with his perfect timing, can't help but stick rigidly to the backing beat, which Si says is too 'mechanical' – 'You're like a fuckin' metronome, man!' – and he complains of Tank doing too many fills and frills – 'Fills and frills is just what we *don't need*! Feel the beat. Where's your attack?'

Well, by this time, Tank is definitely in 'attack' mode and would happily put Si's lights out; but the nameless engineer stops the recording and Si asks Tank if he wouldn't mind stepping into the control room where he tells Tank that his drumming ain't up to scratch and that the band will work to a 'click track' for the moment, which is about as insulting as it can be to a drummer – to be replaced by a click track. The rest of the band don't hear what's going on as the action behind the soundproof glass is played out like a pantomime: Joe looking worried, Si leaning back in his chair, arms folded behind his head all casual-like, the engineer stooped over the desk... and Tank gesticulating, furious, shouting (obviously), banging his fists on the desk with the engineer trying to protect his precious knobs and sliders... then Tank throwing up his arms in defiance and storming out of the door of the control room and now into the studio where all hell lets loose as Tank fills the boys in on the fuckin' *outrage* that has occurred, the fuckin' *insults* he's had to endure, but what are the boys to do? Walk out in sympathy? Of course, says Tank. Maybe not, they think, having got this far.

'Look, let's work to the click track and bring you in later, eh?' says Danny Boy in leader-mode. But now he's talking to empty space as Tank has stomped out of the studio. Joe Rainbow comes onto the intercom.

'Lads, you're contracted to complete this recording and if you default, we'll get sued to buggery, okay? They're bringing in a session drummer; he'll be here soon.'

A bloody *session drummer*! They can't believe it. Fortunately for Tank's blood pressure, he doesn't know of this development. He, as of this moment, can be found in the One Tun, a nearby hostelry that will play host to this dejected, rejected soul who is now propping up the bar and getting smashed.

'It's in the contract,' continues Joe. 'The small print.' He takes out the contract from his briefcase, flips through some pages, then reads:

' *"Any performer, if it be so deemed to be beneficial, by producer or head of record company or manager or person or persons affecting the recording session(s), can be replaced, without notice, and with immediate effect, by a session musician to complete in said recording session(s). The session player will receive a fixed fee, to be set by the record company, and will not receive royalties from the record or be mentioned, named, or otherwise referred to, on the record sleeve. However, the person or person(s) replaced, as a member of the group, will be named as a contributor, even though he or she may not have*

131

actually contributed. " So saith the small print, fellas.'

He puts said contract back in his briefcase.

And at that moment, the door to the studio opens and a squat figure appears, bald and middle-aged, and takes his place at the drums – 'Nice kit,' he says – and performs a roll, either to warm up or to show off, who knows? but it's an expert cascade of beats, using every dam' item of the kit.

'Guys, this is Monty – Monty, take a bow,' says Si, and Monty does what is requested in such a warm and humble way that the fellas take to him instantly. 'Run-through for Monty, if you please,' and the track is played, minus the click track and minus Tank's drumming.

'Okay, got it,' says Monty. 'Heartbeat speeds up gradually, right?'

'Spot on,' says Si. 'Ready for a take?'

'Ready for a take.'

And they're off! Monty *is* terrific, it has to be said. Full of energy but with real precision too.

He later tells the band about the legendary Hal Blaine, session drummer *extraordinaire* who was part of the American producer Phil Spector's 'Wall of Sound', being the cinematic treatment Spector gave to his recordings,

'Hal Blaine played on thousands of recording sessions, amongst them the famous "Be My Baby" by The Ronettes and the Beachboys hit "Help Me Rhonda". Hal had his own special rubber stamp that he'd put onto music scores and even on the walls of the drum booth. It said HAL BLAINE STRIKES AGAIN.'

'So MONTY STRIKES AGAIN, eh?' quips Danny B after the recording is done, and Monty packs up his drumsticks, thanks them kindly, and bids them a fond. They later find out that Monty's surname is 'Dummer'. Dummer the Drummer, as he's known in the trade.

Time for overdubs. Danny double-tracks himself singing, preferring to do it 'live' rather than rely on ADT (Automatic Double Tracking). Mickey's guitar is also double-tracked, but the nameless engineer overlays the second track at a slightly different speed which makes the end result *zing*. They gather in the control room to hear playback, and they have to admit it's streets ahead of the demo. It sounds like a *real* record! Meanwhile, Si has been making calls, which results in three cello players entering the studio with their bulky cases and earnest expressions. These will be for-hire members of well-known orchestras earning a quick buck on the side, and, as is normal in these circumstances, they've met up in the nearby pub beforehand, the One Tun, and are now nicely lubricated, hence the earnest expressions, trying to look sober.

Si sets them the task of underlying the heartbeat with their lowest register notes, played staccato, and then an overdub of a continuous drone. It's magic. One thousand per cent fuckin' brilliant, Si! We fuckin' love ya, Si. No more so than Tone who gets to hear his simple song, dedicated to Aggie, now become a Magnus Opus.

When it's played to Alamo 'Call Me Al' Godbold back at the ranch, he loves it, then makes his calls to a major record company and the deal is done. 'To The Beat, Beat, Beat of My Heart, Heart, Heart' by Rock Ireland Line, written by (A. Johnston), will be released in August. A summer hit. The girls love the sentiment, the boys love the earthy sound. RIL are on the way.

'What did you do for the B side?' slurs Tank when they find him in the One Tun, well in his cups. He's full of remorse and whisky, and the boys hug him and commiserate. A tight band once more.

' "Rock Island Line" o' course,' says Danny. 'Monty followed your drumming from the demo. Said he couldn't improve on it.'

This makes Tank feel better, and they help him out of the pub, and Jeeves takes him back to the hotel they're staying in now, courtesy of the 'advance'. Jeeves, ever the faithful servant, puts Tank to bed, and Tank falls into oblivion.

Next morning he wakes up, comes to, amidst the most wonderful fragrance. His room is full of flowers, huge bouquets, just like The Beatles did with Ringo that time. The Beatles were a tight band too. A knock on the door, and here is a very attractive woman in a fur coat, which she opens to reveal three silk bows – around her breasts and points south. 'A gift from Mr Rainbow,' she says and sashays in. Mr Rainbow knows what Tank likes, hangover or no hangover.

20
Homeward Bound

Job done, the boys can now return home to their other halves, be they permanent or temporary, or, as in the case of Mickey, non-existent. He will go back to 'Friday night is Disco Night!' at the local Rugby Club where he'll tell all the girls how he's going to be a rock star, but as the disco's so loud they can't hear him anyway. Tone happily returns to wife and kids, Tank to his latest squeeze, and Danny Boy to a rather sordid affair with a married woman (which ends when the husband gets out of prison early).

The bedsit in West Hampstead gets a fresh lick of paint, a new flea fumigation, and is ready to rent out again. The house itself will eventually be known as the 'RIL Pad' and fans will be photographed outside the now-famous front door, much like the Abbey Road pedestrian crossing, or, if they're lucky and get to know the current tenants, get to see *inside* the actual room! Mr Zdunowski, the landlord, will hold interviews sharing his reminiscences of the boys who he loved 'exact like a father'.

RayRoadieRice – 'RRR' or '3Rs' as he's sometimes known (with 'Rs' sounding like 'arse') – is driving Bessie, with the boys crammed in, two of them now having to sit in the back amongst the amps. In future, there will be a second bigger van with proper seats, driven sometimes by Danny, sometimes by a hired driver, and RRR will follow, driving Bessie with all the gear. A brave new world of luxury coaches and Winnebagos awaits, but that's a story for the future.

Meanwhile, Bessie is homeward bound, back to the Midlands, back to ordinary life before things get *extra*ordinary. On the long journey up the M1, Mickey strums his acoustic guitar and the others join in singing their repertoire, with Tank beating the rhythm on Bessie's sides and Tone singing harmony with Danny. And RayRoadieRice lovin' every minute of it! At one stage of the journey, a silver Rolls-Royce overtakes them, and there is Joe waving from the back seat, puffing away on a fat cigar, and Jeeves honking the Roller's adapted horn, which plays a short melody, 'Greensleeves', which Mickey takes up on the guitar and the others hum along to.

So begins the long wait until the record's release, and at times it seems like nothing ever happened. Did they really record the song? Did they really meet with that record company boss? Joe Rainbow has disappeared off the scene, looking for new 'artists' to represent. Says he fancies taking on a girl singer, and he tours the clubs with Raymond in tow, working as Joe's assistant as his requirements as a roadie are not needed. The band have gone back to rehearsing in Tone's garage, new songs, new covers. Tone is composing because he's aware a follow-up may be needed quickly if 'Beat, Beat, Beat' is a Hit, Hit, Hit. Joe has stopped them from doing gigs. 'Keep yer powder dry,' he says.

But the band are relaxed; they feel confident that big things are on the horizon. Tone, happy at home, in the bosom of his family. Danny up-for-grabs now the married-lady affair has ended. He's a good-lookin' boy, so he won't have to wait long. His favourite 'hunting ground' is the record shops – easy to get into a conversation with a pretty girl reading off the back of an LP. 'Do you like that band? Me too, I'm Danny by the way. What's your name?' Other hunting grounds are book shops, art galleries, even supermarkets (looking like a hopeless male shopper needing help from some frustrated housewife – 'Excuse me, where would I find the Ready Meals?'). Aww, poor lonely soul having to cook his own meals, and out comes the mothering instinct. 'You look like you could do with a good square meal inside you's!' Home to a homely kitchen while hubby is out at work and Danny B can be mothered then smothered.

Tank has his own methods, which is his little black book with numbers to ring. 'Hi, remember me?' And Mickey... ah, Mickey! Not the most successful Romeo of the bunch, relying, as mentioned before, on Friday-night-disco-nights where, *if he's lucky,* he might get a midnight snog. He just wants a regular girlfriend, does Mickey, but he's picky is Mickey, as his heart's already been broken, smashed into smithereens, by a pretty girl who he *adored*, poor lamb, but who didn't *adore* him back.

She had a domineering father, a clothes manufacturer with his own small factory – just a warehouse, really – well-respected in the community, big house, big money, who didn't approve of Mickey's long hair and shortness of stature, the father being tall. He, the father, was on the lookout for someone more worthy for his darling daughter. She eventually married someone in the export trade. Mickey remembers being taken out on the family sailing boat and being bossed around by the father, the 'Captain'. Why, in sailing, do they call ropes 'sheets'? Why not 'ropes'? So, when Captain Father tells Mickey to tie the sheets, he looks around for… well, sheets. Then, they all (including the girl) go down below for 'drinkies', leaving him alone at the tiller steering the boat. 'Just keep it parallel to the shore,' says Captain Father loudly. When they come back up on deck again after about half an hour, it turns out Mickey has succeeded in going round in circles and they haven't got anywhere. The bolshy brothers (all tall) mock poor Mickey and, in the girl's eyes, the boy is a failure. He remembers that night, back at her parents' house, the brothers out at the boozer, the mother hitting the gin, the father comatose snoring in the front room, and his girlfriend (soon to be ex) lying drunk and naked in the bath telling him he was no sailor. So it was a case of 'Goodbye Sailor' rather than 'Hello'.

21
Guitar Man

There was an episode of *Coronation Street*, back in the early 1960s, where some young fella had been jilted by some young lass and sought solace in his guitar, playing a melancholy riff. This struck a chord, so to speak, with Mickey. He'd be around eleven at the time and not averse to falling in love with girls and feeling a mite weepy over songs like 'I Guess It Doesn't Matter Any More' by the great Buddy Holly. So Mickey decided that the guitar was to be his saviour in matters of the heart and a good way of singin' the blues. He persuaded his dear mama to buy him a cheap guitar, which, like all things cheap, was something of a mockery compared to the real thing. The metal strings were a million miles away from the fretboard which made pressing down the chords with virgin-soft fingertips like pressing down on cheese-wires, and until the skin hardened, the playing of the instrument was torture. But artists have to suffer for their art and, likewise, love-struck boys have to indulge their angst with poetry and love songs.

Mickey persevered, learning the basic chords of C major, F and G, not easy shapes by any means, but to untrained fingers all chords are tricky. But those three chords were the way into folk classics like 'We Shall Overcome' and Dylan's 'Blowin' In The Wind', and soon Mickey was a pretend-Bob-Dylan in his bedroom.

Then a revelation – a *revolution* – happened.

He was on holiday in Torquay, age fifteen. A promenade photographer captured him with his older sister: she, with a Lulu bob in stripey shirt and short shorts; he, in shirt and pencil tie, trying-to-be-a-Beatle moptop, drainpipe trousers and Chelsea boots, and carrying a transistor radio. There was a coffee bar they'd go to that had a jukebox that *showed videos*! This was very modern at the time (1964) and the videos were all of foreign singers. But this wasn't the revelation.

They went to an evening concert featuring the group, The Yardbirds. Famous group of the time and the draw was the lead singer Keith Relf, who had fringed blonde hair which he set off with Ray-Ban-type dark glasses. Now it so happened that Keith Relf was indisposed on this particular evening and a substitute was on hand to do the honours which was a bit of a disappointment for Mickey's sister who thought Keith Relf was *fab*. But what drew Mickey's attention was the guitar player who was one *Eric Clapton* – and anyone who knows anything about guitarists sure knows who Eric 'Slowhand' Clapton is, but in 1964 he was relatively unknown. What fascinated young Mickey was the thing that Clapton was doing with his guitar, playing a barre shape right up to the 12th and 15th frets, which created a dead, percussive sound like nothing Mickey had ever heard on the guitar before. When he got home from the holiday, Mickey tried to re-create this with his cheap acoustic, but all that resulted was a muffled, unfocussed noise, not at all like what Clapton was producing – but then, Clapton had an *electric* guitar.

An electric guitar was way beyond Mickey's means but what he did get, via various holiday jobs, paper rounds etc, was an electric pick-up and a small amp. He was well into Dylan by now, bought the songbooks, learnt the chords and the words, started to play the folk clubs. Wore a harmonica rack around his neck to play along with the guitar, just like Dylan. Adopted a nasal sort of singing style with some American twangs so he sounded more like Dylan than a lad from the Midlands. The trick was to sound more US than UK. He bought a black corduroy cap with a push-button fastening like Dylan wore on his first LP cover. He found that he learnt the words easily; there are many verses to commit to memory, like in 'Mr Tambourine Man' or 'Chimes of Freedom'.

Then Mickey, like Tone, started to write his own songs, kind of ersatz Dylan, and played them at parties where he was a guest performer, i.e. playing for free. His sister was now going out with a guitarist, who was a couple of years older than Mickey; when he visited the family home, he would bring his guitar along and spend more time jamming with younger brother than canoodling with sis. This caused some friction, but in the end the boyfriend (who was a fine guitar player) formed his own group – *he* had an electric guitar – and asked Mickey to join. So Mickey, plus electric pick-up, joined his first band, and this is where he met Joe Rainbow, who was the hopeless bass player.

By the time he was seventeen, and after many paper-rounds and begging off his parents, Mickey had his own electric guitar. Second-hand of course. He would joke at the time that while Clapton was called 'Slowhand' he could be called 'Secondhand'! His heroes were George Harrison, Jeff Beck, and Clapton of course (Beck, at one time, was also a guitarist with the Yardbirds).

So, Clapton, Beck, Harrison: these are the names that Mickey now includes in his 'Guitar Greats' as he talks to Radio Amst DJ Tim Smit in another of the 2018 band interviews when the band once again finds fame:

TS: Welcome to another of our favourite band Rock Ireland Line slots and their famous guitarist Mickey Mills. Welcome to Mickey. We are all great fans here on Radio Amst and I know our listeners would be pleased to know your influences and which top guitar players you admire?

M: Hi Tim, hi Amsterdam! I have to say Clapton because he is the *maestro* with terrific technique and speed; George Harrison plays *solo melodies*, tunes in their own right, centred around, or variations of the actual song, I'm thinking here of 'And Your Bird Can Sing', where the lead solo guitar is the basis of the song; Queen's Brian May does the same, the lead guitar has its own special *voice*, thinking here of 'We Will Rock You'; Jeff Beck is another example of the lead guitar basis for the song, 'Hi Ho Silver Lining', and the brilliant solo he plays on that song. But Clapton is *the* God, in my humble – the one I think we all aspire to. He played lead on Harrison's 'While My Guitar Gently Weeps', did you know that?

TS: No, that is new information to me. Mickey, may I ask you what is your favourite *guitar solo* out of all these great guitar players?

M: That's easy. Hendrix, who I haven't mentioned yet. The *incomparable* Jimi! 1969. Woodstock. His crazy wild dissonant distorted version of 'The Star Spangled Banner', played live with sustain and feedback, making the sounds of crying and explosions and gunfire and bombs and screaming, and the sound is *tortured*! I was there and half the audience were crying it was so moving. We will never see the like.

TS: Any other great guitar moments?

M: Lemme think… at the end of the 'Abbey Road' album, in the medley section, there's a moment when all three guitarists in The Beatles play solos one after another, and they're all different in their own way and all totally fuckin' brilliant!

TS: But Paul McCartney plays bass surely, yes?

M: Paul McCartney can play just about anything, man! Drums. Piano. On that medley section, he was playing lead guitar.

TS: Ah, I see. All is explained. So, Mickey. I have a question for you, please. When your first hit record came out, there was a rumour that you were replaced by a 'lookalike'. Is this true?

Mickey goes quiet, looks uncomfortable, doesn't answer.

TS: I have it on reliable authority…

M (cutting in): Those rumours, they're all a load of BS, aren't they? Like the 'Paul is dead' rumour, you know, how the VW on the 'Abbey Road' cover had the registration 28IF, so the rumour-mongers reckoned it was code for how Paul would've been twenty-eight *if* he'd lived (in fact, he'd have been twenty-seven). And how the Paul lookalike was barefooted as a sign of a corpse and Ringo was dressed as an undertaker, John the priest, and George a gravedigger! All pure baloney. Paul was barefoot probably cos he was hot – it was a sunny day by the looks of it.

TS: Wasn't Lennon meant to be saying, 'Paul is dead' at the end of 'Strawberry Fields Forever'?

M: I read somewhere that he was actually saying, 'Cranberry Sauce'.

TS: Getting back to my question though: my source says that you disappeared in 1976 and that your management had to put someone in to replace you on TV appearances and some photocalls of the band. I have one here. Is this you, Mickey, or is this a lookalike substitution? I can't tell as it was so long ago and obviously you looked different, but the rumours still survive, so could you please verify or not the rumours?

Mickey is silent. Seething. Finally, he replies.

M: Not fuckin' true. Interview over.

And with that, he tears the headphones off and leaves the booth, finds a cafe, smokes a joint, shaking.

It *was* true. The rumour.

At the time of the record's release, when the band became well known and appeared on TV and had pictures taken of them, Mickey was replaced by a lookalike. It wasn't that difficult as Mickey had that skinny, long-haired look so popular in its day. The replacement was called Phil Sleep, and he was good enough on the guitar to mime the chords for the camera. Actually, being a session musician, he was *well* good enough. They dressed him in Mickey-type clothes and never let him speak or be interviewed. He was a quiet fella, made no trouble, took the money, and swore on the Bible he'd never tell. He never did. Big pay-off from Joe when Mickey finally returned and Phil Sleep went back to obscurity, several thousand pounds the richer.

So, what had happened to the real Mickey?

22
Cold Turkey

While the band were all at their various homes waiting for the record's release, Mickey was back with his parents. Fairly predictably, his father hated the long 'pansy' hair, and the mother was going a bit mental what with the menopause (a devilish perversion of Nature), and the father was getting more and more grouchy in his old age and idle in his retirement. Mickey would spend his days in his childhood bedroom playing his guitar and the evenings round the local.

He gets in with the 'wrong crowd'. A mix of his Rugby Club mates and the lads from the pub. Mickey is already into weed, but its effect is no longer the buzz he's craving. He yearns, in his boredom, for something more. More delirious. More mind-numbing. Or maybe more mind-stimulating, he's not sure. But his life now is a vacuum after the excitement of London and the camaraderie of being cheek by jowl with the boys. Who're all off doing other things and he misses them. But yes, Mickey wants something more than the mild effect of weed. He has the money to spend too with the advance from the record company. A further 'transfer fee' (from the major record company who takes over the contract from YoungDudes) swells the coffers, even though, in the end, it'll all be paid back through future earnings. But what if there are no future earnings? Doesn't bear thinking about. And 'thinking' is not something Mickey is doing much of these days.

Cocaine is the next port of call after pot; first of all snorted, then progressing to liquid cocaine which grabs him like a rabid hound. The pub lads introduce him to mandrax which is more of a sedative, which relaxes him but then he overdoses and gets delirious, so he moves on to mescaline, made from cactus apparently, which Mickey thinks sounds cool and is a Mexican LSD-type drug. He hallucinates in the pub, seeing monsters crawling out of the wallpaper. But what cares he for hallucinations? They're just bad dreams come to life. Anyway, Mickey tries them all, then staggers home in the early hours to be met by an angry father and fretting mother. But, he thinks, he's twenty-seven, an adult, why's he having to kowtow to his bloody *parents*? Because you're living under our roof, boy, says the father. Eating our food. Living rent-free. That's why. We want to take care of you, says the mother. You're not well. Leave me be, says Mickey. Leave me bloody be.

He, sweating, pupils dilated, shaking. Tries to sleep. Can't. Tries to play his guitar. Can't. Tries to write songs. You must be bloody joking.

Heroin is stage three. The feeling of euphoria is intense. The perfect drug. Snorted, which is AOK for him as he has a needle complex. Just as well too, as injected heroin is the very devil. The boys get to hear about this as Mickey's parents contact them, desperate for help. Danny Boy is the first to hear about Mickey's rapid downfall and he calls the others and they rally round. An 'intervention' is arranged. There they all are, sitting in the parents' front room, photos of boy Mickey on the mantelpiece, some with his sister, wedding pics of mum and dad. Baby pics on the sideboard. Tank, Danny and Tone are wedged tight on the sofa, looking like the Three Wise Bloody Monkeys, Mickey slouched in the armchair and the parents standing. Dad, arms folded in authority. Ma, wringing her hands.

They read the riot act: how the band will have to *dis*band. How are we going to perform with you in this state? How did you let yourself get like this? Mickey is shamed but the boys reassure him, somehow we'll get through it, but Mickey, you've got to go 'cold turkey'. Off the heroin, which is the worst cold turkey. Off the coke, which ain't so bad. Stay on the hash, we can live with that. No, he says, he'll give up the lot and get clean. For the sake of the band.

So, Danny Boy stays with him in his room as he goes through the hell of cold turkey. Why do they call it that? It's not like there's anything wrong with cold turkey that you eat on Boxing Day after the roast the day before. Cold turkey and salad are a welcome respite after the Christmas Day blow-out. In the throes of withdrawal, he will ask Danny if he knows why it's called cold turkey, and Danny says that the skin of an addict during the withdrawal period is like a cold, uncooked turkey: clammy, pale and goose-bumped. At this, Mickey will throw up for the hundredth time.

Everything has been prepared for the ordeal. They try to play it down, saying it's just like a bad dose of the flu. The bedroom is made comfortable, kept warm. Danny has a chair and books to read; there's two buckets for vomit, plenty of water to hydrate, and lots of toilet paper as diarrhoea is a symptom. The mother will take over when Danny has to sleep, but Mickey will not sleep, another symptom of the process.

In the first twelve hours, there will be sweating and muscle aches. A feeling of anxiety, irritability and mostly an overwhelming need to just take another dose of heroin to alleviate the discomfort. It's like heroin is the cure, not the cause, at this stage. But Mickey is imprisoned. The peak condition is in the next two days when he will suffer cramping, causing him to curl up in a foetus shape, hugging his knees and moaning. Then the vomiting and diarrhoea. Danny takes up the guitar and plays gentle chords. The street name for cold turkey is 'dope sickness'. Elders and betters would note that you have to be a dope to get so sick.

But there's good news. Light at the end of the tunnel. As Mickey hasn't been on the heroin for that long, and as he wasn't 'shooting up', the next four days are less severe – same symptoms but less. One sick bucket instead of two. He starts to sleep and eat properly. He can keep food down and furthermore it doesn't immediately find its way out the other end. They clean his room, open the windows, change the bedding. The rest of the band come to visit and praise Mickey for his guts and look to Danny as his saviour. Leader, nurse, doctor, comforter, friend and helpmate. Mickey starts to go out, go for walks, avoiding the pub, and the boys go back to their own lives, awaiting news from Joe.

23
Strange Brew

But, sad to say, all is still not well with Mickey. It turns out there's a worse demon than heroin or coke or marijuana, and it's the Devil Drink. The sort of addictive personality that has led him to the drugs now grabs him by the snout and lands him a craving for alcohol.

It starts with a return to the pub, first of all in the evening, then at lunchtime, then opening time. Drinking all day and into the night until closing time and the slobber-drunk crawl home. He favours a local ale which is cloudy and has bits floating in it and is rumoured to cause hallucinations. It's like a beer soup and is called 'Strange Brew Bitter'. He sees giant spiders crawling up the wall, or thinks he sees.

At home, he stashes bottles of brandy under his bed, gets through a bottle in the morning (before opening time) and a bottle last thing, then unconsciousness. He is a belligerent drunk, a bad drunk, morose and aggressive, gets into fights. Staggers home one night, bleeding from a deep cut to his chin, blood-spattered tee-shirt. Turns out he's been at a mate's house, knocking back whisky, and when he leaves he goes out by the back door by mistake. Confusion of doors. And it's dark. Turns out father-of-mate is building a low stone wall in the garden by a trench, which Mickey stumbles into, cracking his chin on the wall. But like all drunks he doesn't feel much, doesn't notice the blood, and the cops find him and return him home. They know where he lives, he's drawn enough attention to himself amongst the local constabulary what with his drug use and the booze. Harmless enough they say, but he'll do himself damage sooner or later.

Things are going downhill fast. It's only been a couple of months since they got back from London. The boys try again with Mickey, trying to get him to go cold turkey again, this time for booze addiction, but it's more dangerous with booze; it can actually be life-threatening as alcohol is more of a dependence in some folk and more of a hill to climb down from. A slippery slope, says Danny.

Rehab

So they try to go through the same routine of withdrawal, but this time Mickey gets seizures, *grand mal* seizures, the doc says; now there's only one course left and that's rehab. There's a clinic in the area that runs an Alcohol Addiction Programme. Victorian country pile, looks like a prison, *is* a prison in some respects. He's signed in, wheelchaired in, and so begins a twenty-eight-day detoxification process, followed by addiction therapy. The actual detoxification will take ten days, then there'll be one-to-one counselling, and then group therapy. It's a disease, is the maxim. To be treated as such. The patient is ill, not just physically but mentally as well. The movie or TV cliché is that, in a group set out in a circle, someone stands up and says, 'My name is X and I'm an alcoholic.' Pretty obvious one would think, as that's the raison-d'être of the place, but apparently it's all about admitting to *yourself* that you have a problem. So Mickey duly goes, 'Hi, I'm Mickey and I'm an alcoholic,' and the group applaud him, yes, *applaud* him as if it's something to be proud of. But no, this is standard therapeutic procedure: address the issue, confront it head-on. And on a simpler level, ban all booze on the premises.

After the ten-day detox, Mickey's day goes something like this –

Morning: woken early, no lying-in here. Healthy breakfast of fruit and cereal. No tea or coffee, water or fruit juice instead. HEALTHY BODY HEALTHY MIND! proclaim the posters dotted around the walls.

Mid-morning: classes of yoga and meditation to bring about a relaxed state. Then a group session led by a therapist focussing on addiction and recovery. Another poster says, ADDICTION, NO! RECOVERY, YES!

Lunch: light, healthy and nutritious (i.e. dull, repetitive, unappetising). 'Body Fuel', they call it.

Afternoon: more intensive. Discussion groups and Cognitive Behavioural Therapy. CBT for short, but they are long sessions. Every other afternoon though, it's Supplemental Therapies (STs) like an Art and

Music course and Dance Classes. Mickey learns to waltz and two-step.

Teatime: is Free Time, and the only time the beverage on offer is not fruit juice or water. Strange just how great a cup of coffee tastes when it's been restricted. Free time is anything from Table Tennis to Pool to Board Games to Reading.

Evening: dinner is served, and this is more substantial than the other meals. Proper meat and two veg. Usually chicken. Water and fruit juice again. No coffee as it's early to bed, early to rise. Lights out at ten. Sweet dreams. No nightmares or DTs.

But all of the above is a lie.

Because even though this routine is what *should* happen every day, and indeed *does* happen to most inmates, Mickey's own version of it is, well, different, and as follows –

Morning: won't get up, sleeps late despite banging on the door from the staff. Eventually, a male nurse has to use a master key and drag Mickey out of bed. Too late for breakfast, so he goes without.

Mid-morning: he thinks yoga's for pansies, and as for meditation? What do you mean I gotta think! That's all meditatin' is, just *thinking*! Been doin' that ME WHOLE FUCKIN' LIFE! Now he's shouting and has to be calmed, restrained even. A pill in his orange juice, which, unbeknownst to the staff, is laced with vodka.

Lunch: wolfs down the meal as he missed breakfast.

Afternoon: doesn't join the discussion groups, but he likes the classes and learns the waltz and two-step.

Teatime: his coffee is fifty per cent coffee, seventy-five per cent vodka (yes, do the maths).

Evening dinner: ditto with the alcohol. Stays up late listening to music on his headphones. Lights out, midnight. Then the nightmares start.

So, where does he get the illicit booze from? Not from his visitors, as they have a vested interest in him getting better.

So, my dear Watson, it has to be someone *on the inside.* Who is he chummy with? Well, Holmes, there is a girl who's a likely candidate. Name of Rosie. Pretty, butter-wouldn't-melt type. Rosie by name, Rosie by nature. But with thorns attached. She is an addict like Mickey and is manipulative, winds folk around her little finger. Especially a boyfriend, who brings stashes of booze to a nearby wood, payment for which is a quick how's-yer-father when she stops on her afternoon walk to collect said booze and then hide it in her baggy clothes.

But she's two-timing said boyfriend with Mickey (and this is how he gets his alcohol), two-timing him in broom cupboards, outbuildings, toilets, but never in their rooms as liaisons between patients are forbidden. But lust will find a way.

When Mickey's twenty-eight days are up, he's due to leave, and the staff have given up on him anyway, but Rosie has more time on the clock. She resents him going and leaving her and smuggles a knife from the kitchen and, in a fit of rage, tries to stab him. Her wild screams and his shouts for help are heard and the male nurses grab Rosie and the knife before any damage is done. No action is taken as it makes the clinic look bad – that a knife, a *metal* knife, was so easily obtained.

So, Mickey, with some relief, will soon leave, and he avoids Rosie like the bubonic. He'll then be back in the real world.

24
Substitute

Meanwhile, the real world has moved on.

'Beat, Beat, Beat' is at last released and moves up the charts, slowly at first, then soars up to the Number Two slot. Only a crooner with a dippy love song stops it from being Number One. But Number Two is considered a 'hit', and Rock Ireland Line are now a band being talked about. Interviews are needed, photocalls, TV appearances… but there is no Mickey.

He is, as it turns out, still at the clinic and not going to be out for another twenty-eight days at least. He was due to leave but on the last night he celebrates with a binge-drinking episode in his room with Rosie, who he has now forgiven for the stabbing episode, and anyway she is contrite, begging his forgiveness and plying him with booze, and he drinks himself near to death. Found next morning by Jeeves, who has come to collect him, lying comatose on the bed in a pool of dried vomit. Ambulance called. Stomach pumped. Back to square one. Jeeves calls Joe. Joe calls Danny. We have a problem. Are they to be a band of three? They hold a meeting in Joe's mansion.

Joe: Lads, Mickey's not going to be able to join us for another month or more, and we've got bookings to honour. We're not gonna hide away. You've got to be *out there*. Capitalise on your success.

Danny: Could it just be the three of us? Who knows we're four in a band? Only we know that.

Tone: But a line-up with no guitar? That doesn't make sense. What, just bass, drums and singer?

Danny: And tambourine and harmonica.

Tone: Okay, granted. But still! No guitar?

Tank: Tone's right. Unless you take up the lead guitar, Tone?

Tone: Then there's no bass. Who's ever heard of a band with no bass.

What about you, Danny?

Danny: I only know three chords.

They're stymied. They could pretend Mickey is ill, indisposed.

Danny: Fine. But it'll still be just the three of us. Imagine The Beatles without Harrison.

Their manager lets them ponder a bit, chooses his moment.

Joe: We're gonna have to get a substitute.

Danny/Tank/Tone: NO!!

Joe: Yes. A replacement. Temporary. Another Mickey. A fake Mickey. Till he gets better. He says this time he means it. The girl who got the booze has been kicked out. Security tightened. He's gonna get clean, he swears. Meanwhile, we fill in with a pretend Mickey.

While the others get more heated, Tone is the more pragmatic.

Tone: No one, apart from us of course, knows what Mickey looks like.

Danny: So who's to know, you mean?

Tone: Exactly.

Danny: What about RayRR standing in?

Joe: Doesn't play guitar. We gotta have a guitar player. Even if he has to mime, he's gotta look right, you know, play the chords or whatever.

Tone: Who do we know?

Joe: I have someone in mind. There's a guy I know we could make look like Mickey. He's already short, skinny. Put him in a wig, long hair down his back. Put him in the right clothes. And he's a guitarist. I've taken the liberty.

Joe takes out a photo. He's had the guy costumed, wigged, and posing with a guitar. In the dark and with the light behind him, he *could* pass for Mickey.

Joe: Just to tide us over. Name's Phil. Phil Sleep.

Tank: Crazy dude name!

Danny: But this is just for now, right? Mickey's part of the band. We've already had one upset with Tank here, replacing him with that session guy.

Tank: Yeah, fuckin' right!

Joe: As long as Mickey gets clean, he'll be back before you know it. Meanwhile, I have some fantastic news. *Top of the Pops* wants you!

Their dream come bloody true! Top of the bloody Pops! Height of fame and recognition!

Danny: You're kidding! *Top of the Pops*, really? Wow!

Joe (beaming): Yes, really!

The boys are laughing and congratulating themselves.

Tank: Hey, we'll get to meet Pan's People!

(He's referring to the sexy all-girl dancers who have a spot on every show, usually scantily clad.)

Joe: A bonus! First though, let's meet with Phil. See if you like him. Here tomorrow, same time, yes?

All three agree yes.

They meet the next day, and they like Phil Sleep. He's quiet and modest. Very polite. Knows his place. Plays guitar for them and he's good. Actually, pretty dam' good but there's no replacing Mickey. In a band, it's just as much the fellowship as it is the talent. No use having a brilliant guitarist if you don't get on. Tensions will always out. Blood spilt. But this is only temporary anyway. Just filling in.

And as for Phil? Well, why not? It's easy money. He'll be paid a salary, which is more than the boys are getting. He's normally a session musician but hey, this'll be fun for a while. Be on TV too, most like. He learns the songs quickly. Gets on with the others, especially Danny Boy who he realises is the boss. Something to tell the kids when they're older – how Daddy was a pop star. But he can't be telling too many people as he's bound contractually to *silence*. Pain of Jeeves's fists if he reneges. So, a salary plus an end bonus of £5K. The kids can know he was in a band, but they can never know *which* band. Pain of Jeeves's fists. With knuckledusters.

25
New York, New York

They never get to meet Pan's People. Reason being Rock Ireland's scheduled *Top of the Pops* slot clashes with the band being in New York as 'Beat, Beat, Beat' has shot up to Number One in the States. Number One! In the US! 'Fuckin' A!' Tank says, 'Fuckin' *U.S.* of A!"

They're whisked off, with Phil Sleep in tow, on Concorde to the good ol' Americas for a guest spot on *The Ed Liners Show*. Ed Liners is not a real name of course, it's a pun on 'Headliners' which is kinda strange as the Yanks don't go a bundle on puns, but there it is. Ed Liners, a.k.a. Ed Schein, is an amiable cove in his forties, sharp suit, big smile, big teeth, big voice. Big musical intro from the resident band, catchphrase: 'Who are the Headliners on tonight's Ed Liners?' Just to drum home the pun, capiche? The headliners on the October show are… 'all the way from Ingerland – *Rock Ireland Line*!' Cue applause. Cue teenage screams from teenagers planted in the otherwise middle-aged studio audience.

They run on stage, the three lads and the substitute, in their smart suits and ties courtesy of Joe R's best Soho tailors, waving to the audience, smiling. Interviewed briefly by Ed with Danny B doing most of the answering: 'Do you like your American fans?' 'We love our American fans.' (But not in *that way*, Tank. They're only teenagers, Tank. This is Biblebelt territory, Tank. So, keep it in yer pants, Tank!)

Ed announces: 'Ladeez and Gentiles, for your listening pleasure, Rock Ireland Line with their Numero Uno smash hit "To The Beat, Beat of My Heart"…' (get the title right, Ed Liners) '… which they will play for you now!' Cue applause and screams as the boys strap on their guitars, Danny takes up his tambourine, Tank sits astride his drums. But look, how there are no leads connected to the guitars! It's a sure-fire giveaway that a song's being mimed if there are no leads. Easy for them to pretend to play the chords, but Danny is required to sing live. It's some union thing or it's in the contract, but Danny is no slouch, he's happy to show off his singing, his soft Irish tenor voice that can change in an instant to hard, growling rock. Phil is being a good boy and playing the right chords in the right order; but Tone, who hates miming, is mucking around, going up and down the fretboard, making no sense of the notes. Tank bashes away on the drums, which've been muffled by layers of felt on the skins.

Leaving On A Jet Plane

The flight over on Concorde was a breeze, with Phil Sleep showing his ignorance by asking if they were travelling First Class (there are no classes on Concorde, it's all First Class). Tank disgraces himself by trying, unsuccessfully, to chat up a stewardess, while Danny B overdoes the free champers and falls asleep, drooling, on Tone's shoulder. RayRoadieRice, boisterous and over-excited, starts playfully punching Jeeves, never a wise move, challenging him to a fight. Jeeves eventually elbows him in the gut which makes Ray want to throw up (after all the booze and food) so he has to rush to the toilet, colliding with the drinks trolley then falling face-first into a woman passenger's lap.

Joe is sat up front, away from all the mayhem, like some God, abstaining from too much libation but savouring the delicious hors d'oeuvres. Tone, as well as being a shoulder to sleep on, reads Steinbeck, his favourite author. *East of Eden.* A classic. RayRR gets back from the toilet and proceeds to have an asthma attack, blaming it on the plane's aircon, and of course his inhaler is packed away so assistance has to be called and a solicitous stewardess makes him breathe calmly and relax. As this is the very stewardess Tank has tried to chat up, Tank gets a mite jealous and now somewhat in his cups, throws a seat cushion at Ray, which encourages Danny to throw a seat cushion back at Tank and soon they are all throwing seat cushions until a male steward puts a stop to the frivolity on pain of municipal arrest at their destination.

Customs and immigration at New York's JFK airport becomes complicated as the boys haven't been briefed as to whether they're coming in to work in the US or on a business trip or holiday. Danny B sails through as he says 'holiday'. 'Have an enjoyable stay in New York,

153

Mr O'Shea.' Tone tells the truth, how they are there to perform on a TV show, and therefore gets in a right muddle as to whether this constitutes 'work' until Joe R has to step in and sort things out, which he does with the confidence of a man-of-the-world, world-traveller, high-powered executive – his camel-coloured cashmere coat draped over his shoulders, silk scarf, homburg hat.

Jeeves winks at the Customs woman, not the best move, but he gets away with it, leans forward and growls, ' 'Oliday, love' with another wink. Tank goes into great detail, saying how they are working but not being paid, at least not in the US and not in dollars but back home in British pounds, which would be taken off their expenses, he points out, so technically are they working at all or just appearing? and anyway, it's not as though they'd *actually* be performing, i.e. playing their instruments, as they'd be miming, sir. He's called the Customs Officer 'sir', which *does* go down well, so he's passed through on a Tourist Visa thingy as 'sir' has only understood one word in five due to, a) Tank's Cornish accent, b) his rapid-fire delivery, and c) his slurring, drink-addled speech.

Honky Tonk Woman

They're on Broadway! Yellow cabs and bustling crowds on a wet October evening, having revived themselves in a honky tonk bar after settling into their hotel, eyeing up the honky tonk blondes. One such honky tonk woman sidles over to them and says how she just *loves* a 'Briddish' accent. Tank is eager to demonstrate, which he does with the blonde around the back of the joint.

It's strange how the rain in the Midlands looks different from US city rain. How the roads and sidewalks look like something from the movies with steam rising from the manhole covers. How the cops, armed and dangerous, look so much more threatening than the English policeman with his pointed helmet. How those yellow cabs look so sleek compared to a London taxi or Midlands' minicab. How the bright lights and neon animations look so vibrant compared to – what, a fluorescent-tubed kebab shop back home with the 'K' missing so it reads *EBABS*? How the broads on Broadway look so dam' attractive compared to the chicks in Chickentown.

How do you *not* fall in love with the Big Apple first time you visit? The Twin Towers of the Trade Centre – still standing proudly at this time in our history – seen through the arch on Washington Square where the chess players compete and bongo players line up on the benches and the Hare Krishna shaven-headed prophets chant. Times Square, where the rolling ticker-tape news, telling of Brezhnev, vies with the flickering sign, ALL-DAY MASSAGE (does it mean the massage takes all day? wonders Tank). LIVE NUDE GIRLS! ONLY 25 CENTS! says another sign, 'As opposed to *dead* nude girls?' Tank tastelessly jokes. There's TOPLESS A-GOGO and cinemas with 18 GIGANTIC SCREENS and C-I-N-E-R-A-M-A, blue-movie houses showing *Deep Throat* and *The Devil in Miss Jones*. Huge neon signs for COCA-COLA and SONY and CANADIAN CLUB, and look! a man near getting killed in traffic with his sandwich-board, JESUS SAID SEARCH THE SCRIPTURES. Jesus said Mind the Traffic. Hot Dog and Burger stalls cluster by the crossings with their WALK and DON'T WALK warnings. You can get arrested for disobeying those signs, it's said. Jaywalking, it's called. Horse 'n' Carriage rides opposite The Pierre and helmeted cops on horseback – how do they compare to our bobbies on bikes? And how does the Yankee Doodle Dandy accent compare to the moany tones of Middle England? The American accent *swings*!

They go skating on the ice rink in Central Park. Useless, of course, falling over, giggling, while the local populace zoom and pirouette by, experts all. 'But it's only one blade to each foot?' complains Tank. 'How're you supposed to keep upright?' 'It's against nature,' says Danny B. Meanwhile, Phil, who's recorded sessions before in NY and learnt the skating, *does* stay upright, and furthermore, completes the circuits with ease, which pisses the boys off no end.

They're staying in a fancy hotel near Central Park. Joe has a suite to himself, Tone and Tank share a room, as do Danny and new-boy Phil. Jeeves and RayRoadieRice have gone off somewhere mysterious – not for them the hotel of choice but a sleazy boarding-house, probably a *bawdy*-house, off Times Square, W 47th Street. Ray is rapidly learning the ways of the world, courtesy of Jeeves's tutelage. (RayRR tells the boys that the reception area of the sleazy hotel they're in is full of prostitutes and the corridors full of junkies. He tells them how Jeeves has taken him to see the 'GIRLS IN CAGES', which makes Tank envious. 'Can we swop hotels?' he asks, but Joe won't have it. The band stays together.)

'They have girls *mud-wrestling* in LA,' says Phil. Tank wants to go to LA.

Glory Days

But first a trip to the Cafe Wha? (no French accent required) situated on the corner of McDougal Street, number 115 to be precise, between Bleeker and West 3rd Street in Greenwich Village, the bohemian neighbourhood of the city near Washington Square. Over mid-morning drinks at a friendly dive, Tone has been filling the boys in on what he knows from his rock history regarding the role that this famous music venue, the Cafe Wha?, has played in providing a performing platform for comedians, artists, poets, bands and singers such as Bob Dylan.

'In the early 1960s, the Cafe Wha? – short for What? I imagine – was not just a coffee bar but a venue for anyone who wanted to play or sing or recite. Get up on the makeshift stage, do your bit, pass the hat around for money. All very bohemian and freestyle. Down a steep staircase into a dark basement with brick walls painted black by the owner to give the place a cave-like feel. The owner, one Manny Roth, if memory serves, laid the floor himself, made up of broken bits of marble. The sort of funky place where you go to listen to music, smoke dope, discuss philosophy, hang out till the early hours; the sort of joint where everyone calls everyone "man". You've heard of Peter, Paul and Mary, right? Well, story is that Mary Travers was a waitress there before fame came a-knockin'. Manny Roth would hold these "Hootenanny nights", where anybody who was nobody could step up, sing a song, tell a few jokes. Woody Allen started there.'

An autumn sun has broken out from behind the clouds, so they take their drinks to the outside tables where they sit and watch the Wild Western world roll by.

'Let me take you back to a freezing cold January in 1961,' says Tone, waxing slightly lyrical now, 'when a young kid who's hitch-hiked across the country with his guitar and little else – oh, maybe a harmonica or two – turns up and asks if he can sing a few songs. "Sure," says Manny and a legend is born. This is twenty-year-old Bob Dylan, and maybe he sings some Woody Guthrie songs, probably some Dust Bowl Ballads. How great to have been there, eh? Gets a meal, somewhere to crash. Ends up playing backup harmonica for one of the singers.'

Tone pauses as a thought strikes him.

'Mickey sang Dylan songs, didn't he? Before he joined RIL...'

The mention of Mickey makes them go quiet, look down into their drinks. Phil says nothing. Respect. Then they raise their glasses, 'To Mickey!' Absent friend.

'Used to be an old horse stable before Manny Roth bought it. Apparently, the basement was bisected by a trough that was used as a channel for the horse shit. Manny transformed the whole shebang into this club that attracted hipsters, beatniks, anarchists, probably communists, pacifists too. Then, in the mid-sixties, there was this fella that appeared there who was called Jimmy James, played guitar something awesome, fronting his own band, The Blue Flames. No prizes for guessing the fella was Jimi Hendrix. Hendrix the Magnificent!'

They raise their glasses in salute. Phil Sleep *actually* salutes. Hendrix is his hero.

'What I'm thinking is this,' says Tone. 'We go there and try and get a gig. Play acoustic maybe. What do you think?'

Sure, why not? They agree. Give it a go. They finish their drinks and head off in a southerly direction to Washington Square and the location of the fabled Cafe Wha?.

Except... it's not there anymore.

'I'm sure this is the right place,' says Tone. '115 McDougal Street, yeah, this is it.'

But it's not. The Cafe Wha? no longer exists. In its place is a Middle Eastern eating establishment called Cafe Feenjon, serving Middle Eastern dishes and featuring Israeli and Middle Eastern music. That's what the poster outside says. They stand there on the corner, not sure what to do, trying to look in, but the Cafe Feenjon is shut. Tone is disappointed, embarrassed at the build-up he's given.

'Sorry, guys. I didn't check. Thought the Cafe Wha? would be here forever.'

Turns out, when they talk to a local, that Manny sold the Wha? in

'68 and Tone's rock history, while documenting the club's golden era, does not extend to its demise. Does the basement still exist? The broken marble floor? The black brick walls? They'll never know. Let things lie; it's for the best. Let the memory of the Wha? stay untarnished. The Glory Days. They slink off, back through Washington Square, and back to the dive they'd started off in, and sink a few more beers.

But they agree their instincts were right, they need to perform *live*, to a real audience not to TV cameras. And definitely not miming, says Tone. Joe has not booked any gigs in NY though. But there *are* clubs in Los Angeles that he now calls, at the boys' urging.

And so it is that Tank gets his wish and they'll be LA-bound soon.

Mud-wrestlin' lovelies await.

'Here's mud in yer eye!' toasts Tank with a Budweiser.

It's My Party

They're invited to a party given in a hotel suite by a Heavy Metal band who've struck it big in the charts. The Heavy Metallers are in full 'Goth' make-up and spangly costumes and coked up to hell and back. Topless waitresses sashay around with trays of champagne and cocaine – take your pick or have both. On the lower half of their shapely bodies they wear G-strings and fishnets. The idea, if you feel so inclined, and most of the men here do, is to approach the topless girl of your choosing and she will write a number on a card which you take. When your number is called is the signal for you to join your chosen 'waitress' in one of the bedrooms. Somewhat demeaning perhaps, but the girls are paid a fortune.

Tank scores, as does Danny. Tone, as usual, declines, faithful to Aggie, but he don't mind ogling all the topless beauties. 'Look, but don't touch,' is his motto. When he gets home, he'll try and persuade Aggie to serve him his evening tipple topless, but she'll tell him not to be so bloody daft, the kids are asleep, don't bring your pop star habits home with you, mister!

Phil isn't present as he's being kept in 'deep background' – that's the phrase Joe uses. Joe is there but doing business, schmoozing the record execs. He doesn't partake of the easy sex on offer, and the boys are still wondering about his inclinations – maybe he *is* gay, after all. He seems pretty close to Jeeves, come to that. And Jeeves? Well, he's been to prison. 'Probably swings like a pendulum do,' says Danny.

Tank exits from the bedroom, zipping his fly and one of the Heavy Metal band members sways over.

'Hey man,' he slurs. 'You the band that did that "Best, Beat, Beat" number?'

'Yeah,' says Tank.

'Crap, crap, crap, ain't it,' drawls the Heavy Metal band member in his Bronx accent.

Tank doesn't reply, tries to get away, but the Heavy Metaller grips his arm.

'Y'see, we're Heavy Metal, man, and that kinda crap pop music, like, *really* pisses us off, yeah? Comprende?'

Tank comprendes but begs to differ,

'Fuck off, Johnny – (not the guy's name but Tank doesn't know the guy's name) – we're a rock band, we don't do pop.'

'Pop-a-doodle-doo, man! That song is pop – going "beat, beat" like that. Soft pop, we call it. Now Heavy Metal, my friend, is all about *volume* and fuckin' *hardness*. It's about fuckin' DECIBELS! The louder the better and the more aggressive the worst! Hey, that's a good title, I might use that.'

Fumbles for pen and writes on hand, or tries to, but the writing hand won't follow what the brain is telling it to do, and the left hand is shaking so much it's tricky to write on it anyway. But by then, 'Johnny' has forgotten what he was meant to be writing anyway.

'What was I sayin'? Oh fuck it, you're a Brit, right? I fuckin' *love* the Brits! Beatles, Stones, Kinks, The Who – fuckin' AOK, man!! You're my friend, I fuckin' luv ya! Hey, Bones, come and meet this fucker from Ingerland!'

'Bones' saunters over, six-foot-plus, straggly beard, painted-on barnet as his own hair is receding, leather trews, Inca-like black and white make-up like 'Johnny', tattoos covering every inch – dragons, whores, pirates, serpents…

'Hey Cy! – (so, this is 'Johnny's' name, short for 'Cyclops' as he has a large eye painted on his forehead) – what's happenin', man?'

'Bones, meet – what's yer name?' says Cy.

'Tank.'

'Bones, meet Tank. Hey, weird name "Tank". Why "Tank"? You shoot GIs or the Vietcong or what?'

And Cy laughs, a terrible high-pitched squawking chortle, so incongruous a sound coming from his death-mask face.

'"Tank" cos I'm big, I guess, like one of your Shermans.'

But the reference is lost on Cy.

Tank turns to Death Mask Number Two. 'Why're you called "Bones"?'

'Cos I play with my sticks, man.'

He means his drumsticks, man, which Tank realises as Bones mimes the sticks, and there's no mistaking the mime, drummer to drummer. So, feeling a kindred spirit in this world of Heavy Metal weirdness, Tank goes to hug this fellow percussionist, but Bones recoils,

'Limey faggot! I ain't queer!'

Tank steps back, hands up in apology.

'Sorry, man. Meant no offence. I'm a drummer too. Just wanted to connect, man.'

It's catching, this 'man' business. Not usually that much in Tank's lexicon, but like flu, it's contagious.

'Cool, dude. Anyway, saw ya with that waitress, so I guess you ain't gay. Mistaken ID.'

Cy pipes up,

'Bones, Tank here is one of those Rock Ireland guys. Got to numero uno with that Beat, Beat song.'

'Pop-lite, my friend,' says Bones. 'Opposite of Heavy Metal. You know what Heavy Metal represents? *Volume*, that's what! Mega-watts of sound punched out like a fuckin' batterin' ram!!'

'So, it's just loud for loud's sake?' says Tank, which doesn't go down well with Bones.

' "Loud for loud's sake?" What-the-fuck does that mean? What does that even fuckin' MEAN? Your music, Tank? Lemme tell you, your shit, your *shit*, it's more like *wank*, Tank... WANK!'

Bones, by now drunkenly aggressive, is nose-to-nose with Tank and spitting in his face, chanting, 'Wank, wank, wank,' and Tank can take no more. He gets that ol' 'red mist'. He's been very Brit up to now, reserved, stiff-upper-lipped, polite, tolerant, but this is One Step Beyond and, given the absence of Mickey, who is the official brawler of the band and, given the presence of mucho alcohol (that harbinger of hullabalaoo), Tank takes on the mantle and headbutts Bones viciously and with *multo strengtho*, forehead to delicate bridge-of-nose and crack! Nose broken. 'Bones' – or, broken bones now – shrieks, clutching his nose which is pouring blood like Niagree Falls.

'You bastard, you've ruined my looks. Call 911, I'm dying!'

At this point in the proceedings, as the other Heavy Metallers become aware of the argument and resulting violence and see the blood streaming down Bones's front, the two sides begin to line up in battle formation: RIL v. Heavy Metal. Jeeves, who's appeared from nowhere, stands in front of Tank, his thin form hardly covering Tank's wide girth, but he has knuckle-dustered fists at the ready and a rubber cosh in his pocket; RayRR joins him, a weedy adversary admittedly, but he brandishes a lethal bottle in each hand; Danny Boy joins forces holding an upended wooden chair; Joe Rainbow, who learnt boxing at school, is ready to put his pugilistic skills into practice, he stands in an old-fashioned boxing stance like Tom Cribb; Tank holds a three-foot-high porcelain statuette of a dog (property of the hotel), ready to inflict some serious canine damage; while Tone is nowhere to be seen, hiding in the loo, probs. Jeeves, Ray and Joe encircle the boys like they're circling the wagons in a John Ford western.

On the opposing side, Cy fronts the other Heavy Metallers, who now comprende fully what's going on and have shouldered arms – chains, knives, glasses. Meanwhile, the topless waitresses have locked themselves in the bedroom.

Let battle commence.

Bones, who has temporarily recovered from his broken nose, grabs RRR in a stranglehold from behind, but Ray uses his elbow to make contact with Bones's ribs, maybe cracking a few, whereupon Broken-Bones falls to the ground, curled up foetus-shape, whereupon Tank uses the guy's head like a football – 'FREE KICK!' he shouts. Cy goes for Joe, but Jeeves leaps onto Cy's back, making the two-backed beast and employs his cosh to Cy's right ear, sending him to Cloud Nine and

Beyond. The rest of the Metallers now pile in but it's a lost cause as they're easy meat for Joe's punches, Jeeves's cosh and knuckledusters, and Danny's chair. Tank's dog also comes into play.

The ensuing mayhem is ended with the cops arriving, called by the hotel management, whereupon Danny and Tank are quickly dragged out by Jeeves, followed by Joe and RayRR – and Tone, who has now emerged ('I thought I heard a noise?') from the bathroom. They all crowd into the elevator then out onto the damp street, where blue and orange lights are flashing and sirens wailing, but they're outta there!

Jeeves protects their backs as they race around the corner, joined by a couple of the topless waitresses, covered up with coats, mindful of the cops arriving and aware that they've outstayed their visas by a year or more and don't want to be deported back to Romania, thank you very much. There is kinship between this motley mix of ne'er-do-wells, which is why they all end up in a downtown bar as Jeeves brings drinks on a tray, with some aspirin for sore heads and raw steak for black eyes. The topless waitresses tend to Danny's and Tank's needs, and all is well with the world.

26
Going To California

New York is a cold, damp city this late in the year, so the boys relish the idea of a change of scene and a change of climate. California is milder and drier. Also, California is LA, and LA is HOLLYWOOD, and they're dead excited to be going to Movieland. Maybe they'll see some real-life film stars there.

So, after some final radio interviews in New York and industry meet 'n' greets and another TV show – this time for a younger audience but with a middle-aged theme: barn dancing in a barn-like set with pretend yee-hah cowgals sat astride saddles perched on hay bales while RIL mime (as per) amongst fake haystacks – after these bookings are completed it's off to the land of Route 66. Go west, young men, to the Promised Land!

On the United flight over, Tone, with his love of John Steinbeck, recalls the book *Grapes of Wrath,* which told of the Great Depression of the 1930s when farmers in Oklahoma ('Okies') were forced out of their homes and livelihood by ravaging dust storms and greedy banks and travelled west to California seeking employment and some kind of future. Compare that national tragedy with these English lads already on the road to stardom, now seeking to be even more famous, make even more money. Tone tries to explain how lucky they are, but like all young bucks, they don't care to look back in either anger or sympathy.

CAL-I-FOR-NIA! The word sounds just great, Cal-i-for-nia. Los Angeles, City of the Angels. Which sounds great too. Sunset Strip. Even better.

Near the long street called Sunset Boulevard, there is a luxury hotel nestling in palm trees with hacienda-like chalets, where the guests languish in home comforts like long sofas and a kitchenette, which they never use. The less expensive rooms (but still costing the Earth, Solar System, Galaxy, and Universe) look out onto a central area that has a swimming pool and bar. These rooms have balconies, so guests can sit and watch the sunbathers and swimmers below who, if they bother to look up, can see the balcony guests looking down *at them*.

The thing is, this hotel is all about *looking*. Looking at people, as the people who get to stay in this hotel are worth looking at. They are all, generally, beautiful. The Beautiful People. Blessed with good looks, of course. Good skin. Good hair. Good body-tone. Good teeth. The pop stars will be looking at the rock stars. The TV stars will be looking at the movie stars. Then, to a much lesser degree, there's the advertising people from the UK who just love this hotel. They will be looking at the pop/rock/TV/movie people, who will *not* be looking at them. Bad Teeth. Bad skin. Not enough orange juice in their childhood. The Beautiful People will not bother to clock the UK admen and adwomen as they are not *faces*. They are not beautiful. Potbellies. Short. Bald.

However, all the guests, whether lowly or highly, will be looking at the hotel bar-staff, who are female, svelte, and dressed from bosom to bum in stretchy Lycra. Men sitting in the bar will find their eyes drawn to the magnetic north of a pair of pert boobs and shapely arse – or 'ass' as the Yanks have it – while women guests will look on with some envy and pull in their tummies and stick out their chests. Anything to rival the amazing bodies on show. The male guests will flirt with the servers, but you have to be A-list Celeb status to make any kind of headway.

Talking of headway, there's a moment when Tone, emerging from the 'restroom', has to flatten himself against a wall – literally *flatten* himself, spread-eagled to the wall – to clear a path for a famous rock singer and his movie-star girlfriend. The rock star doesn't bat an eyelid as he passes by, because to him, Tone just don't exist. Maybe soon he might, if 'Beat, Beat' stays in the US charts another week and RIL appear on more shows. Maybe then the famous rock star might stop and acknowledge Tone, 'Say, aren't you with that Brit Band, "Rock Island"?' And yes, the rock guy might get the band's name wrong, but who gives a fuck? Tone would be *recognised*, a member of the LA elite, an A-list Celeb. Or maybe, B-list; he'll settle for B-list.

Joe has pushed the boat out and booked the guys into this super-swish hotel. Still sharing rooms but 'whaddya-gonna-do-about-it?' as Mickey'd say. They miss him terribly; it's like the loss of a limb. But Phil Sleep is fitting in well, staying in the background. Until one rehearsal when he tries to put in different chords from Mickey's. These chords are of the diminished, augmented, and suspended variety; in other words, jazz chords. Not your usual majors or minors with the odd 7th thrown in.

'Phil, what're you playin' at, boyo?' says Danny B.

'Thought I'd make it more interesting,' says Phil.

'Well, don't,' says Danny.

Enough said. Phil goes back to the usual majors and minors with the odd 7th thrown in. This is what the boys are used to and what Mickey has set in stone. Phil goes back to doing what he's told and doing no more than asked for. He wishes he was more involved though. He'd have liked to have been present at the fracas at the Heavy Metal party, for instance. He'd have liked to help out, especially as he's no stranger to fisticuffs, having learnt to box when he was a kid – although not quite the Queensbury Rules version that Joe was taught. Phil was taught street-fighting, aggressive self-defence, i.e. self-defence that doesn't mean running away but means getting the first punch in and getting it in where it's gonna hurt, like the balls. Thing is, if you're good at boxing, you want to exercise your talent now and then, especially on people who ain't. It's like riding a bike – something you never forget. Boxing's like that. You could go a year or more without a fight, then instinct kicks in, and it's the old one-two-three: belly, bonce, balls. That's what the trainer at the boxing centre he went to after school used to say: if you're in a street-fight, forget the Marquess of Queensbury, son, follow these rules instead:

a) punch to the belly,

b) opponent doubles over, so uppercut or knee to the chin or face,

c) then, as he goes down, the 'coup-de-bloody-grass' – a kick to the bollocks,

d) which he won't get up from for a while,

e) so concentrate on kicking him while he's down,

f) the kidneys are a good target,

g) the bonce is another.

So yes, Phil would've seen off those Heavy Metal wimps, no probs (altho' it sounds like Tank and Danny did all right anyway). So, he moseys along, doesn't make no trouble, tries to fit in. He recognises his time'll be up sometime soon – or maybe it won't? What if Mickey never comes back? What if he's a lost cause? Phil works on Danny, shares his room, acts as his servant, yes Dan, no Dan, three bags full Dan.

At night, the hotel is lit outside by strings of fairy lights. The garden has quiet, unlit corners for couples. Coloured lights under the water of the pool make it look like an enchanted lagoon. Some guests go in for midnight nude swimming – the girls, mostly. When this happens, the overlooking balconies are full.

By day, the boys enjoy sitting by the pool sipping margaritas. They're not allowed to take photos, though. No one is. It's a rule. Reason being, the A-listers don't want their pictures taken, semi-naked, by B-list celebs, or heaven forbid, C-, D-, E-listers etc. It's that principle of *looking* all over again: the pop stars'd take pics of the rock stars, the TV stars of the movie stars, and the rest, if they could, would take snaps of everyone.

So, no pics allowed. Tank has a miniature Pentax SLR, and he surreptitiously clicks away until a manager slides over and insists he desists, stopping just short of asking for the exposed film. When Tank gets back to Boots in England, all the photos are blurry anyway.

There's a rehearsal studio nearby, and the boys go there daily, trying out new things. Tone has a new song they all like, about Mickey's cold turkey time, called 'A Friend's Needs'. Could it be the follow-up to 'Beat'? Evenings are spent in the hotel bar with the slinky servers or at the many clubs along Sunset Boulevard. Music clubs too and jazz clubs. One is where they'll be playing soon, if Joe can negotiate the price – upwards, of course.

As for the mud wrestling? Tank drags them along to a sleazy nightspot where, along with the over-inflated price of drinks, there's an under-inflated rubber 'pool' set on the ground full of some grey goo that's supposed to represent mud. They take their seats around the pool along with the other gawking males, who don't seem to be LA residents but more like Texan tourists in their cowboy hats and Stetson boots. They whoop and holler and stare aggressively at their long-haired hippy neighbours. It's only when they discover that the 'hippies' are from 'Ingerland' that they excuse them, thinking all Brit males are pansies anyway. But if logic prevailed, or indeed any smidgeon of grey cells engaged, they'd figure that these guys can't be gay if they've come along to ogle bikinied beauties wrestling in mud.

Two of these bikinied beauties, one in Stars 'n' Stripes, the other in army-camouflage design, enter the arena to the whoops of delight from the Texans. They step into the ring and start to pretend-wrestle. This is merely an exercise to extract each other's boobs from the bikini tops, and eventually, if enough Texan dollars have been thrown into the 'mud' (to be quickly retrieved by a 'referee'), the bikini bottoms come off too, much to the hysterical excitement of the yee-haw cowboys. And the boys too, it has to be said. You don't get this in the Midlands Working Men's Clubs of 'Ingerland'. After the girls have slopped around for a bit, and after one girl does a pretend winning wrestling move on the other and the referee counts out one-two-three, the girls bow, grab their bikini remnants and exit stage-left. Put it down to experience, thinks Tone, wondering if Aggie would ever... no, of course not!

27
Hey Mickey

One day they're at rehearsals when the studio door opens and who should be standing there but... BUT... Mickey! As they live and breathe, the boys feast their eyes on this vision of health. Mickey, slim and one hundred per cent clean by the look of it. They crowd around him, asking how he is, of course, and they're all beaming fit to burst, and Joe is beaming too, happy to see RIL back together again. Even Phil is smiling; he knows his time is up, but how can he resist the Return of the Prodigal? He's caught up in the moment and almost sheds a tear.

'I'm good, lads. Dry and clean and ready to rock 'n' roll,' says Mickey.

Phil, very kindly, hands Mickey his own Fender guitar and Mickey cradles it lovingly like a long-lost lover, straps it on and plays a solo riff, fast as you like, ending with a shattering *arpeggio* E major 7th. Mickey's back!

He knew about Phil but he was so out of it, well, it just didn't register and quite frankly fellas, I didn't give a monkey's. Pleased that you were still playing, now recording, now a bloody Number One hit in America! He shakes the hand of his fellow guitarist, Phil, who now leaves the studio and joins Joe, Raymond and Jeeves in the anteroom. There are things to discuss: his exit strategy, payments, Official Secrets Acts to sign. Jeeves will sign as a witness (and if Jeeves witnesses a signature, you can bet your bottom dollar he'll be round your gaff sharpish if you don't abide by the agreement).

Mickey finished his second twenty-eight-day rehab with flying colours. As he said, clean and dry. The thorn in his side, Rosie, had been thrown out of the clinic due to the illicit booze she kept smuggling in. Once she was gone, the booze supply dried up, the temptation was gone, and

Mickey could concentrate on stopping. For good. For very good.

Which he did. No alcohol for twenty-eight days and then another two weeks on the outside, and his body is glowing. Such is the resilience of youth. The ability to repair. Like the lungs, which are the only part of the body that can regenerate. Give up smoking, even after twenty years, and after around nine months, the lungs are pink and healthy again like a newborn's – and if *that* ain't an incentive to pack up the fags, what is?

Talking of smoking, Mickey is allowed his daily stash of hash, though. An addictive personality has to have *something* and, compared to drink, pot is relatively harmless. That's what the docs say. 'But don't let the pot lead to cocaine, then heroin, or you'll be back to square one,' the docs also say. And square one is definitely where Mickey doesn't want to be back to. So Mickey has put all his efforts into the second round of rehab: getting up on time, eating healthy, attending group therapy sessions. 'Hi, my name is Mickey and I'm an alcoholic'. 'Hi, my name is Mickey, and I *was* an alcoholic!'

On his last day at the clinic, they bake him a cake. With a single candle on it to signify the first year of his new life. He plays guitar for the patients and staff, singing 'Rock Island Line' and others. Others include a song he'd written for Rosie because, even though she'd been a bad influence, he still had a thing for her so he'd written her a song called 'Rosy Rosie'. A catchy, singalong number with a neat 'hook' – a three-note 'bridge' in between each repetition of 'Rosy Rosie' which becomes one of those tunes that sticks in the brain. They call them 'ear worms'.

He was popular in the clinic and the patients had made him a banner GOOD LUCK MICKEY XX, which near made him cry as he was driven away by Jeeves in the silver Roller. Jeeves had flown all the way from LA to fetch him and then escort him Westward Ho! to where the boys were.

And now, here he stands. As bold as you like. Lapping up all the love and attention.

'I saw the vid,' he says. 'Pile o' shit!'

He's referring to the pop promo video the band made that got shown on TOTP in their absence. If you couldn't appear on that programme, they'd either show a vid or have the dancers on. Legend has it that the first proper pop promo was for 'Bohemian Rhapsody' by Queen, but The Beatles made films for 'Penny Lane' and 'Strawberry Fields Forever', so maybe they were the first?

The vid RIL made was an arty affair, black-and-white footage of the band performing all against black with the boys dressed in black and only their (white) faces standing out (like on the 'with the Beatles' LP cover). Occasionally the image would switch to 'negative', so the white faces were black and the background white. While not exactly a 'pile o' shit', it was, for RIL, pretentious.

'Pile of *arty* shit,' says Danny.

'Pile of *farty* shit,' replies Mickey, and they laugh fit to burst, not because the line is funny but because they're back together again with the same corny sense of humour.

(The clever thing about the video was that the light in the film, what little light there was, pulsed in time to the 'Beat, Beat', so it had a hypnotic effect. In fact, some epilepsy sufferers complained, and the video company had to tone the effect down.)

'Well, if you thought *that* was shit, you should've seen the first idea!' says Tone, and he goes on to explain the first idea:

'We meet with this director who's no more than a kid, barely out of film school. Very full of himself, up his own backside, dressed all in purple with facial piercings like a ring through his ruddy nose like a prize bull. Name of Hugo. Well, it would be, wouldn't it? The video company Joe found for us had just taken this guy on as their "youngest and brightest find", although brightest was something of a misnomer as Hugo liked to "shoot dark" as he put it. "Light is the enemy," he claimed, and banned all artificial lights on his shoots, allowing only natural light, through windows etc. "What about when you film at night?" I asked and his producer, nice girl, said Hugo never filmed at night.'

Danny takes up the tale:

'What an arch-prat! What a prize back-to-the-wall pisspot of an unholy prat! He had this idea, right? for our video promo that he wanted to show us, and he got out this large piece of card with a kind of photo-montage on it, called it his "mood board". All the pictures stuck on the board were of operating theatres and surgeons; there was a cutaway diagram of the human heart and we were beginning to get the picture, have you guessed yet? No? well, I'll tell you; this brilliant whizz kid movie child had this idea for us to play *heart surgeons* about to perform an operation on some poor sod whom we never see as he, or she, is covered in a white shroud with a hole in the fabric where the op is to take place. I mean, heart surgeons! Us? Can you believe it?'

Tone: 'I asked whether we'd be wearing masks and Hugo said yes of course – authenticity – but how will anyone know it's us then? And he said our name would be up front with the title and we said, what title? And he said he didn't know at this stage but there would be a title, then Danny asks how will the viewer know it's him, i.e. Danny, behind the mask and not, say, Tone, and Hugo comes back, with some pride at his obvious *genius*, that the nurses will remove our masks. But you mentioned "authenticity" says Tank, pointing out that nurses wouldn't remove a surgeon's mask mid-op and Hugo says, "Artistic Licence", nodding gravely.'

Tank: 'The *storyboard*! Fuckin' hell, the storyboard! Hugo's drawn what he calls a "storyboard" which is like a comic strip showing the action, and his "drawings" are like kids' stuff, you know, like matchstick figures representing us.'

Danny resumes: 'So, the story goes that as we're performing this heart op, the picture changes to a cartoon of a sad-looking heart, I kid ye not, then there's close-ups, "sense of drama", says Hugo, of sweating brows being mopped by the sexy nurses (did I mention the nurses were going to be sexy?) and various instruments of torture which are being handed to us, the surgeons, at which point the cartoon heart looks scared (did I mention the heart had a face?) and has its fingers crossed (did I mention it had fingers?)…'

'How can a heart have fingers?' asks Mickey.

'Exactly,' says Danny. 'We asked the same thing, but Hugo said as it was a cartoon, *anything's possible*, so this bloody cartoon heart has two arms, hands and fingers and a ruddy face! We can't believe what we're seeing, can we, boys? It's *so* crap, then the nurses hand us, not scalpels, but our instruments, and we mime to the track with the nurses dancing. Then, I have to sprinkle some "magic dust" (we'll solve that in "post" says Hugo) onto the patient and the cartoon heart looks revived, then the patient, who is now revealed to be male and bald and fat, sits up and joins in. Final shot of cartoon heart with a smiley face. Next stop, MTV Awards, Most Outstanding Video, I THINK FUCKIN' *NOT*!'

After all this exposition, baby-director Hugo had sat back proudly, and his producer had sat back proudly, assured that her new protégé had come up trumps with his visualisation of the band's hit song. But Joe, who was, of course, present, sensed that things had not gone well as the boys got up, as one, even Phil was in synch, and walked out of the office and repaired to the nearest drinking establishment and near killed themselves laughing.

'Long story short,' says Danny, 'Joe put us in touch with this other vid director who'd done some award-winning promos, and even though the end result was a mite "arty-farty", I grant you – Bob, as the saying goes, was your father's brother.'

28
Hello Goodbye

There will be a party to celebrate Mickey's return and Phil Sleep's departure.

Held at their LA hotel, where Joe has hired the bar for the night. It's all actually very sedate, maybe because there are a number of 'suits' invited with their wives or mistresses, and people stand around politely chit-chatting, and it ain't like a rock 'n' roll party at all. Joe gives a speech saying 'Hello' to Mickey and 'Goodbye' to Phil, although no one else at the party besides the boys themselves understands the significance. Just a band worker leaving, who knows? The cocktails are flowing – can cocktails flow? – and the boys schmooze the execs and their wives/mistresses, and it's all – dare one say it? – a bit *dull*.

But what is it about the hour of midnight that makes civilised folk turn into monsters? Is it the witching hour? No, that, according to legend, is between three a.m. and four. That is when the witches and demons and ghouls appear. But here in LA, if you're not in bed by eleven p.m., then it's game on, and anything goes. After twelve, if you're still up, still at a party, you'll be there till the early hours. You're committed.

So, past this midnight hour, all is going swimmingly until some of the party guests decide to actually swim in the hotel pool. Is it the enchanted lights underwater that attract them? Is it the cool blue of the chlorination that makes them jump in, some fully-clothed, some less fully-clothed, some not at all fully-clothed. But all are fully-drunk by now. You can trust a margarita to do its work, or a vodka martini. And the bar is still open...

Management is called, staff deployed, perpetrators hauled out, dripping, giggling. Hotel guests, not of the party, complain about the noise which is shrieking and screaming and goddam anti-social. So the bar is closed and management try to disperse the guests, but to no avail,

173

as these party-goers just want to keep on party-going. So off they all trot to the band's rooms to continue the merriment. The band's rooms are next to each other with a connecting door, which is now propped open, so this is a big enough space to house the fifty or so now gathered there.

Mickey has stayed true to his no-drinks routine but is well-stoned with the permitted weed. The others are one thousand per cent pissed. Danny B is punchy as per (they say it's the Irish in him), Tone is philosophical, telling anyone who'll listen about the Cafe Wha? – 'They do *belly-dancing* there now!' Tank is randy, but quite honestly he's too drunk to perform and he should know that by now; and Phil Sleep is... asleep, sparked out on the sofa. Meanwhile, the two mud-wrestlin' mamas from the sleazy joint, who've been invited by Tank, are now doing a repeat performance in the jacuzzi and quite a crowd of onlookers are crammed in the bathroom.

But it's RayRoadieRice who Raises the Roof.

Who'da thought it? The boy-nerd that *was* Raymond is now replaced by a wild and crazy dude who thinks nothing of doing what all rock bands are reputed to do – almost *de rigueur* behaviour with bands – which is to Trash The Room. Sofa upended, Phil upturned. Pissed and pissed, Phil tries to throw a punch at Ray, misses and crashes onto the low glass coffee table, smashing it to smithereens. Jeeves, who's appeared from nowhere, intervenes, cleans up the broken glass, calms Phil down, gives him a knockout drug, pushes management out the door.

But he's neglected to deal with Public Liability Numero Uno, RayRoadieRice, now RayRoomWrecker! Fuelled by cocktails, 'dirty' martinis and mescaline, Ray sets fire to the bedroom curtains. Jeeves finds the fire extinguisher out in the hallway and douses the flames just in time for Joe, who's been summoned from his suite, to deal with the authorities, be they the local fuzz, DEA, FBI, CIA, Mafia – who knows who else? Because the thing is, LA, despite its reputation for debauchery, is relatively civilised – after all, even the mud-wrestlin' ladies *bow* at the end of their performance! And the degree of rabble-rousing going on here till all hours is frowned upon, especially if it's caused by Johnny Foreigners. The movie stars will be getting up at the unearthly hour of five a.m. for a six a.m. call. Same with the TV stars. The Hollywood execs will have their first of many meetings scheduled for eight a.m., and they have to be bright-eyed and bushy-tailed, not bloodshot and limp. This is not Hangover City.

The boys by now are blotto: Mickey doped up to high heaven and low hell, Danny in a dreamy daze, Tank groping women but missing, Tone staring at a picture on the wall of some late-night loners sat at an all-night coffee shop. 'Thass me,' he drools. 'That fella there, thass me!' Ray has gone quiet, slumped by the bed, but now he's suddenly awake and has a target in mind: the room Frigobar, sitting all innocent-like by the TV, now empty of the miniature bottles and candy bars but just sitting there saying, 'C'mon, I dare you!'; and RayRR, who can't resist a dare, rises to the challenge, lifting the Frigobar with both arms, embracing it, ripping the wire out the wall and staggering under its weight to the balcony, hugging the small fridge for all the world like Chief Bromden with the water-fountain at the end of *One Flew Over The Cuckoo's Nest*. It's a cinematic slow-motion moment as everyone in the room stops drinking/snorting/snogging/shagging and watches as Ray crosses the floor, goes out through the open doors to the balcony and tips the frigging Frigobar over.

Consider:

one heavy article of 'white goods' furniture,

one weedy drunkard barely able to stand upright, let alone consign the item to its watery end,

one volume of air between the balcony and two storeys below, the pool,

one pool, perfect recipient of said weighty Frigobar,

and finally, the immutable force of gravity,

which relieves Ray of his burden and the fridge floats freely through the LA air and drops SPLASHHH! into the water below, causing a near tsunami to flood the recliners and ground floor rooms.

'BINGOOOO!' says Ray as he does a bow, then passes out.

By now, the cops have been called and they break the party up, or what's left of it after most have fled the scene, jettisoning what drugs they had in the pool on the way out. It is three-thirty a.m., and Jeeves takes over, putting the boys to bed and clearing up as best he can.

Next morning, the staff dredge the pool for the packages of illicit drugs and pocket most of them.

The Frigobar is a write-off and goes to the local dump.

The picture on the wall with the loners in the coffee bar is straightened back to horizontal.

Carpets shampooed, toilets disinfected, jacuzzi emptied.

Vomit sponged away. Condoms gingerly picked up and disposed of. Abandoned knickers ('panties' in American) similarly disposed of.

Coffee table replaced. New Frigobar installed and re-stocked. Bedsheets changed.

A massive bill for damages presented to Joe, who pays up without protest. Par for the course. If you want an easy life, Do Not Manage A Rock Band.

The boys, semi-conscious, are gathered together in Reception ('Lobby' in American), shuffling, shame-faced, sick beyond redemption, moments away from being turfed out.

Luggage dealt with by Jeeves.

RayRoadieRice waits outside, on probation, as far as Joe is concerned.

Hotel California will only put up with so much.

Suffice to say that no other rock group, be they Heavy Metal band or pop idols, has so far, in this hotel's history, *ever* surpassed the mayhem that UK's Rock Ireland Line caused.

And there's some pride in that.

29
I Love L.A.

'I love LA,' says Danny to Tank as they sit in the bar of the hotel they've moved to – an infamous famous and famed hall of residence and respite, another favourite and favoured haunt of pop and rock and movie stars. The building? Think white. Think Gothic. The reputation? Think Gothic again.

Word on the street, and in the annals of rock legend, is that one band who stayed there hijacked a food trolley to ferry naked girls from room to room – a sort of glorified room service.

A Brit actor returned one night – this was in the '60s – drunk as a skunk and banged on all the room doors, saying that the Martians had landed. He was chucked out, found his belongings on the kerb next day.

Another rock star fell two storeys trying to swing from balcony to balcony à la Tarzan.

Another joker rode a motorbike up and down the corridors.

And yet the inside decor of the hotel belies the bad behaviour therein, being thick columns and arched windows, church-like, but there the resemblance to any church ends.

It is Christmas in Hollywood. Danny and Tank have stayed on as they both love LA. Mickey has gone home to his folks and Tone to his family. The unholy trinity of Joe, Jeeves, and Ray – Der Management – have also gone back to the UK, leaving Danny and Tank to lounge in the winter sunshine of California. Tank is dating the mud-wrestlin' gal and Danny occasionally double-dates with the mud-wrester's mud-wrestlin' opponent. The girls, despite their profession, or maybe because of it, are actually quite prurient and religious. On their Walkmans, they listen to tapes of a particular preacher who has his own TV show where his ranting sermons are of the 'And the Lord shall smite thee asunder' Devil-and-Damnation variety. Heaven knows what awaits these girls in Hell for their nefarious activities. Or maybe mud-wrestlin's just good clean fun.

Rock Ireland Line, in the end, only had one engagement in Los Angeles. They'd been promised several gigs by Joe, but they all fell by the wayside for reasons of money. Joe bargained for bigger bucks but didn't bargain on No Deal. Because LA, at this time, was chock-full of bands, all willing to play the clubs for a pittance as these venues along the Strip and Sunset Boulevard were reputation-makers. The one engagement RIL does get, though, is a good 'un – 'FM Station' in North Hollywood, owned by Filthy McNasty, who also previously owned and ran a music club on the Strip called 'Filthy McNasty's'. FM Station is a legend in its own lifetime, and unknown bands'd give their eye-teeth to perform there, and well-known bands likewise. So the boys are excited to be playing live in such a great establishment.

But they disappoint. Mickey is nervous and rusty. Tank is strangely listless, just no energy or power in his drumming, just a tedious back-beat – no fills, no frills, no thrills. Tone's okay, but Tone's always okay. Who really notices the bass anyway? And Danny's voice cracks, he forgets words, stands pretty much motionless at the mic. Tambourine hanging useless from his hand. The crowd are unforgiving, they expect better than this. RIL play their set of six numbers and go offstage to a smattering of applause. The audience has talked throughout, not bothered to dance much, generally ignored them. It's a sad farewell to LA because they love LA, and they forgive LA for their poor reception as they know they were well below par. Sometimes it happens. Or rather, doesn't happen. A band is an organic thing, it's not a machine. Sometimes the energy doesn't kick in, and sometimes the magic of performing as a whole doesn't gel. Four individuals trying to coalesce as a unit but staying separate. They have a name for these nights – fortunately, not occurring too often – they call them 'death nights' as in, 'We died tonight,' which would be Danny Boy's assessment at their post-mortem. Playing live can sometimes mean you die.

One good thing before they go their separate ways. They record 'Rosy Rosie'.

The recording studio is in a residential street off Venice Beach, which is the seaside resort to the west of LA. There's a two-and-a-half-mile long promenade that runs parallel to the beach called Ocean Front Walk, peopled by street performers, fortune-tellers, artists, and lines of shops and stalls selling tee-shirts, drugs paraphernalia, roller skates and beachwear. It's a hippy environment, mainly young and very 'cool'. There's an outside gym area called Muscle Beach, where oiled hunks lift weights and show off their 'pecs' to admiring onlookers, be they female or gay. They like an audience. Girls on skates whizz by, wearing knee-protectors that look like something out of a Terminator movie and short-as-hell shorts to emphasise their long legs. It's all about body-watching here, and the long boardwalk is a perfect place for speed-skating. Some set themselves tasks, like weaving in between lines of cans set on the ground or shooting up ramps and landing with a skidding halt.

The recording studio is called Gondola, paying lip service to the Venice element, and is like any other studio anywhere in the world – a mess of trailing wires, assorted mics, sound baffles, abandoned coffee cups and stubbed-out cigarette butts. The mixing desk, as per, is in a separate room behind soundproof glass with a sofa and coffee station, water-cooler and tape decks. The reception area of Gondola is smart: photos on walls of bands and singers beside a wireframe 'installation' of a gondola. A pretty girl, tanned and slim, sits behind the desk with only her blonde head visible as one enters from the street. 'Hi, how're ya doin'?' she'll drawl to incomers, regardless of fame or status. Offices along the corridor on the way to the studio area house the 'suits', the managers and money-movers.

Rosy Rosie

Mickey's song about his rehab *amour*. It's all there in the lyrics: the walks in the woods, forbidden visits to each other's rooms, the illegal booze in the clinic, even the attempted stabbing. Nothing is spared, and the melody has a poignant air to it – a love song in a desperate setting. The thorny side of Rosie is laid bare. Used to be called a 'torch song' back in the day. A song of lament, lost love – 'torch song' coming from the expression of 'holding a torch for someone', i.e. keeping the flame of love alight. For RIL, it's a departure as it's mainly acoustic, and Danny's voice is so haunting it brings the hairs up on the back of your neck and tears to your eyes. Like Carl Wilson's heartrendingly beautiful voice on the Beach Boys 'God Only Knows'. Or Lennon on 'A Day In The Life'. Or McCartney om 'She's Leaving Home'.

It's an easy session; the boys play well and get it in four 'takes'. Next day, a string orchestra is brought in to add 'texture' to the track. They all hate it. 'Over-egging', they call it. The idea is abandoned. But the B-side is a revelation. Stuck for an appropriate song, they decide to re-record

'Rosy Rosie' with a more upbeat, harder, electric arrangement. So, Side One is the song pure, Side Two more visceral. The second song is titled, like movie follow-ups, 'Rosy Rosie II'. Horses for courses, opinion is split – some liking the hard edge of the electric sound, others appreciating the unembellished acoustic track. Therein lies the record's success – something for everyone. It also anticipates a trend in later years of commemorative CD compilations that feature alternative 'takes', so RIL is ahead of its time here. The record will top the US Billboard Charts when it's released in the New Year, and when the band meet up again, ready for the next phase in their career.

A day after the final mix is when RIL part company for Christmas.

Danny and Tank, staying on in LA, take their time off seriously. They re-visit FM Station and enjoy the bands. They're recognised now and treated with respect despite their erstwhile lacklustre performance. After all, there's still that Number One hit they have to their name – ROCK IRELAND ROCKS! is one music paper headline.

Meanwhile, it's Hollywood that rocks for the pair. Hollywood Boulevard with its Walk of Fame where movie stars have their names and stars set in the pavement. The giant pagoda of Grauman's Chinese Theatre where film premieres are held and the film stars leave their handprints and footprints in the wet cement. Danny and Tank place their own hands and feet into the prints and take grinning photos alongside the Ming Dynasty lions that guard the entrance. It's all so incongruous in this present-day Hollywood setting, but in 1922, when the cinema opened, it must have been a spectacle. And it is a spectacle now, to Danny and Tank, as they look at all the movie star 'prints', not just hand and footprints but objects too, connected to the individual star: the shape of Harold Lloyd's spectacles, Groucho Marx's cigar, Betty Grable's legs, Roy Rogers' guns, Herbie the VW's tyres. They look, of course, for any 'boob' prints but are disappointed. Surely Marilyn Monroe? But no, she has just left her handprints and the marks of her stiletto shoes – the sole shape and then two dots. 'Maybe they're her nipples!' says Tank as fellow tourists cover their children's ears.

30
American Pie

They love LA. They love LA food.

On Hollywood Boulevard, street number 6667 to be precise, is a legendary diner called Musso and Frank's, reputed to be the oldest restaurant in Hollywood. A classic New York-style bar and restaurant as old as the Hollywood Hills, if not older. 1919, to be precise, is when it opened. High ceilings, pictorial wallpaper above dark wood-panelled walls, yellow shaded lamps, red leather seats in the booths. Charlie Chaplin had his own booth by the only window in the joint. Waiters and bartenders dress in red coats like they've always done. Time has stopped here; it's always 1919 in Musso and Frank's. The colour palette is of browns, reds and ochres.

In the 1930s it was a writers' hangout: Raymond Chandler, Dorothy Parker, F. Scott Fitzgerald, T. S. Eliot, Steinbeck; and, being in the heart of Hollywood, the movie stars flocked there too: Garbo, Bogart, Fairbanks, Valentino, Sinatra, Bacall; later years would see Monroe, Liz Taylor, Steve McQueen. The restaurant even has its own star on the Walk of Fame.

The fare is classic steakhouse. Danny Boy and Tank are perusing the menu. Tank is having trouble choosing as he likes everything. Danny B is having trouble choosing as he is so picky about food. Chaplin's favourite was roast lamb kidneys; he'd challenge Douglas Fairbanks to a horse race down the Boulevard with the winner picking up the tab. Tank goes for steak tartare as a starter and for the main, or 'entree' as it's known here, the classic ribeye. Danny goes veggie with onion soup to start, followed by the Welsh rarebit, then for dessert a 1919 sundae. Key lime pie – a real American pie – for Tank.

They spot no famous faces this lunchtime, just men in suits, power-players, some women in groups. The lads could almost be the most famous here, although the clientele likely doesn't follow the Billboard Charts. It's a warm, cosy venue and the food, even Danny's veg options, is comfort food.

When they were in New York, the band had tried a well-known Deli which was known for its gargantuan portions. They'd looked at the menu and seen the plates of their fellow diners with piled-high steak dinners and roast chickens and decided to play safe and ordered turkey sandwiches. Sandwiches, harmless enough, they thought. What they didn't bargain for was a sandwich around a foot and a half high, crammed with turkey slices and smothered in gravy with fries – a bucketload – on the side. Even Tank was defeated. When the waiter came to take their plates away, still half piled up, he almost sneered. If there was a Union Jack over their table, it would have drooped sadly. However, they did note that the other customers were as gargantuan as the portions, or because of the portions, and they reasoned that rock bands have to be slim; it goes with the territory.

Vegetables

Meanwhile, in Musso and Frank's, the Union Jack has flown proudly, the meals finished, and now they take their time over the desserts. Tank, mindful of Danny's veggie food-faddiness, wonders about its origins, not understanding it himself, being an 'I'll eat anything' kinda guy and lovin' meat. Danny blames school.

'I blame school,' he says. 'When I was seven, my parents sent me away to boarding school – this was in England, in the Midlands, where they'd moved to. They had money and felt an education outside of the old country would stand me in better stead. Ireland, at the time, was becoming more violent and dangerous. Still bad today of course, back home on the mainland as well as Northern Ireland itself, Derry and the like, the no-go areas, the IRA, British troops, internment, "Bloody Sunday". The Troubles. Some of my schoolmates from back home were killed in the bombings.'

Danny looks hard at Tank, wondering whether to continue, knowing the territory he's about to enter into. Schooldays. Bloody schooldays!

'I'd had a happy childhood, in Dublin's fair city…'

Tank completes the sentence,

'… where the girls are so pretty…'

'Pretty indeed! Like my dear mama. As I say, my childhood was happy enough; my Junior Infants school, the pals and gals I had to leave behind when we set sail for the Midlands of England, where my parents saw fit to send me off to a fookin' *English* public school which I hated from Day One, even more from Night One when the prefects, the older boys, would maraud the junior dormitories looking for fresh meat!

'That school was a homosexual's ideal hunting ground, I can tell you. The prefects would have their "boyfriends", a younger kid, who they'd walk around with during the day, almost holding hands, as brazen as you like, and the teachers'd turn a blind eye, probably queer themselves, the way they too looked at the "prettier" boys. And no, Tank, *I* wasn't partakin' of that particular activity, I can tell you. I was an ugly kid with big ears, scrawny too and that probably saved me from the prefects; they could pick and choose. One particular older boy went mad with it all, had to be sent away to a sanatorium.

'Then a new young master came in, third year I was there, and reformed everything. He was shocked at the "goings-on" and put a stop to it. Outed the main offenders; they were expelled. Sent the younger boys, the "bum-boys", to Matron for a good talking-to, then to the Reverend for absolution.'

'I went to a mixed school,' says Tank. 'It taught me to appreciate girls from an early age. Fell in love with a girl two years older than me, aged ten. My first proper kiss. Got to First Base. Felt like Heaven.'

31
School's Out

'You asked me about food and why I'm so fussy,' says Danny, 'and I said I blamed school. Well, the place I was sent to was a straight-out-of-Dickens shithole. Dickens wrote about a school called "Dotheboys Hall". Do the boys, that could've been my school's motto. After all, it's what the prefects did to their bum-boys!

'What this establishment did was to make you eat every morsel of the disgusting "food" they served up, like *rabbit* for God's sake, or you'd get punished, i.e. beaten. If you refused to eat the disgusting food, you got beaten. Only we didn't call it getting beaten; we called it getting "whacked". Sounded friendlier, I guess. Remember that pub we went to in Soho, and I said the landlord looked like Jimmy Edwards who was that headmaster on the telly who liked using the cane? And the programme was called "Whacko!", remember? Well, it was like that at my school – "WHACKO!" we'd say when a boy was sent off to a master's study for a beating. There was this one sadist bastard of a teacher who gave his collection of canes nicknames, like "Ol' Bendy", "Thrasher", that kinda thing. Hilarious. "Nipper" for the one that had a split end that nipped your flesh. And bare flesh it'd be cos the beating'd be on your naked behind. Trousers down boy, pants too, bend over and WHACKO! Some said one of the teachers'd reach around for a quick grope of your balls. Through cunning, or maybe just good luck, I never got beat. It was the humiliation, y'see, not just the pain. The shame of being bare-arsed in a grown-up's presence and getting six of the best. Why, for God's sake, was it "six of the best" when, for fuck's sake, it was "six of the *worst*"?'

Danny toys with his ice cream, losing his appetite. Tank, too, is lost in his thoughts, leaving the remains of the pie. Outside, as if in sympathy, the day has turned grey and it's raining. People rush into the restaurant, shaking their umbrellas, saying how it's cats and dogs out there, gimme a whiskey (American for 'whisky'). The waiters take the dripping brollies and store them in a stand by the door as the men go off to the bar, telling the bartender about the cats and dogs.

'Some real weirdos came out of that school and probably became politicians.'

Danny pauses for a moment, taking in his surroundings and his fellow diners chatting happily away, enjoying Musso and Frank's culinary treats.

'D'you know what my favourite food was back then? Hot buttered toast. When my ma came to visit, she'd take me to a tea shop on the High Street and we'd have piles of hot buttery toast and sweet tea.'

'My favourite food,' says Tank, 'is steak. Rare and bloody!'

'Y'see, that's the worst for me, Tank ol' buddy. Anything that resembles the animal it came from, like a rabbit! Blood or bones or skin or fat. Can't be doing with it!'

'What about fish then?' asks Tank.

'Don't get me started on fish,' mutters Danny and delves into his sundae.

They order coffees. The rain outside has stopped. There's a glimmering of winter sun, although it's never really winter in LA, never below freezing. The warmth of Musso and Frank's smothers them along with the rich fireside colours. All is well with the world until Tank starts to recall his own school days.

'I failed my eleven plus, so I went to a secondary modern rather than the grammar school my parents wanted. Funny really, because my father was a teacher at this secondary modern, so you'd have thought he'd have been happy to have me under his wing, so to speak. But he was not the *happy* sort. He taught Modern Languages and he'd rasp out German phrases loud and guttural like he was Hitler. In fact, he *was* a sort of Hitler, my father. Anyway, what with him being a teacher there, and my buck teeth and four-eyes, I was a target – bullseye! – for the bigger boys and I was bullied sommat awful. I was thin then and small for my age, so that didn't help neither.

'So, I had a pretty miserable time and the only thing that made things

185

better were the girls there – as I said, it was a mixed school. At first, they mothered me as I was so weedy, but as I grew out of my short trousers and excelled in the A-stream, they took notice and became friendly. This was when I developed interest in the opposite sex, which I retain happily to this day!'

It's like a light has shone onto the conversation which has been so void of light. It's like the sun that's now shining through the doorway, sending off the dark clouds. 'Brightening up!' say the new customers brightly. 'That's good, sir,' says the bartender. 'Now, what would be your pleasure?' and nine times out of ten, it's a bourbon. 'Warms the cockles,' says the barman.

But Danny is still in his dark mood.

'Was there corporal punishment in your secondary modern? I assume there wasn't, it being modern and all that.'

'You assume wrong, my friend. Canings, like you. For the girls it was across the palm while for the boys… well, at least we kept our trews on. Trouble was, y'see, I got double helpings. When I got caned by the headmaster, which was often, I then got caned *again* by my father when I got home. So I got caned for getting caned!'

'Your father sounds like a right bastard.'

'Oh, he was. He'd go through each line of my school reports and cane me across the tops of my thighs for each bad comment. Little did each teacher know that when they wrote "must try harder" or "doesn't concentrate" or "easily distracted" or *the worst*, "lazy", I'd get a thwack of the cane. Two for "lazy". My mother tried to protect me, but he treated her badly too, stopping just short of physical violence but would shout her down, yell blue murder at her until she ran to the bedroom, crying her eyes out.'

'Is he still alive? I'll sort him out for you, if you like.'

Danny mimes punching him, one-two. Belly and Bonce. Tank shakes his head,

'He died some years ago. I didn't grieve. Didn't go to the funeral. My dear ma's still going strong. Got married again. Nice fella.'

Tank smiles to himself, at the thought of his ma and her new partner. A kind man. A *gentle*man. But the memory of his cruel father won't let him be.

'D'you know what my father's nickname was at school? "Sticky".'

'Sticky?'

'Yeah. Cos he liked the sting of the stick, I suppose. At home he'd use a garden cane on me with the end wrapped in insulating tape to stop it splitting from the violence of the strokes. It was that old-fashioned woven fabric tape impregnated with black waxy stuff. I can smell it now. Petrol-ly. The edges of the tape, spiral-wound around the cane, would fray and add a sting. I'd be left with purple weals across my buttocks and thighs. I never knew whether to cry out or stay silent during the beatings. Would screaming make him stop or make him carry on all the more? Should I be defiant or give in? Actually, I don't think anything would've made any difference. Crying or gritting my teeth. He was a sadist and that was that. Afterwards, my mother would put Valderma cream on the wounds and kiss me and curse my father behind his back.'

'What did he die of, your father?'

'I think he died of hate.'

And they leave it at that.

He died of hate.

The coffees are long gone.

Gone cold in Tank's case.

The evening is approaching.

They repair to the bar– an appropriate word, 'repair', because they need some salve after this baring of their respective histories.

'What would be your pleasure, sirs?'

Bourbon, bartender, bourbon.

32
Christmas in L.A.

December 25, 1976. The day finds Danny hungover from Christmas Eve celebrations.

As he wakes up on Christmas morning, he wishes it was snowing. Snow in California? Not much chance.

He wishes he was home in Ireland. The time difference makes phoning difficult.

He has woken up, come to, at midday here in LA, so it'll be eight in the evening in Ireland.

They'll have spent their Christmas Day without him.

He calls anyway, speaks to his folks, his mam says he sounds tired, his step-pa thinks he sounds drunk.

Younger sister comes on the line, excited beyond belief with her brother's fame.

Her school pals are *sooo* jealous!

She's full of questions: 'How's America? Have you got a tan? Have you met anyone famous?'

He tries to tell her that he's seen *the back* of Stevie Wonder, sat at a keyboard in the recording studio, and he's been told it's Stevie Wonder, and he recognises the dreadlocks, and he's kicking himself he didn't go over and see *the front* of Stevie Wonder...

... but try telling that story to an excited teenager over a transatlantic phone line with its speech delay and echo, and you're hungover to high heaven to boot.

They all shout 'Happy Christmas!' to him as they sign off, and Danny is tearful. Shakes it off. Grown man crying. Shameful.

He calls for room service. Do you have Guinness? No, they don't have Guinness. Settles for a large bourbon and ice. Waits an age for it to arrive and when it does, he can't face it. The ice melts.

He rings Tank's room but no answer, then remembers that Tank went back to Miss Mud Wrestler's place – what's her stage name? 'Stars and *Strips*', that's it. Clever. Especially as her pre-naked 'uniform' is a Stars 'n' Stripes bikini. 'She stars and she strips' – so runs his muddled mind.

Last night – no, this *morning* – Danny's own mudwrestlin' madam puts him in a cab back to the hotel, near-comatose, good-for-nothing, helped up to his room by hotel staff, thankful not to be thrown up over, who put him to bed, still fully-clothed, then go off to rescue the next Christmas Eve victim.

Then CRASH awake at midday and feeling like he has the plague.

Who invented the hangover anyway, and why hasn't the human body learnt how to cope with it, and how come it ain't been cured yet, what with all the advances of modern medicine?

Truly, you'd make a fortune for one reliable working hangover cure. He's tried them all:

1) aspirin, doesn't work,

2) antacids, the fizziness too much for his delicate stomach,

3) water, you gotta be kidding!

4) a big greasy breakfast, ditto!!

5) coffee? the rule is: if you can stomach coffee, you ain't got no hangover,

6) exercise, presumably to get the poison out of your system, but if you're too ill to even get up…

7) a cold shower, same rule as 6), i.e. if you're too ill to even get up…

8) sleep it off, yes, good plan, postpone today, live for tomorrow.

What was it Churchill said to some aristocratic lady who accused him of being 'disgustingly drunk'? Something along the lines of: 'Madam, you are ugly, but tomorrow I will be sober, while you will still be ugly!' Not very gallant, admittedly, but funny all the same.

Danny's tried Cola, Lucozade, milk – but only one liquid seems to do the trick and that's called Hair of the Dog.

Which is waiting for him on the tray with the ice melted and he downs it in one, grimaces, rushes to the sink and throws up.

So that particular Hair of the Dog didn't work. Or maybe it did because the extreme physical act of vomiting has revived him somewhat.

But he still has a whole day to get through. Or half a day.

What to do to pass the time?

Tank is AWOL.

The hotel almost deserted.

Very few staff as most are home for the holiday.

He calls Mickey, gets Mickey's parents (damn!) who say Mickey's out but they like a chat, and so it goes, 'How are you, Danny?' 'Are you looking after yourself, Danny?' etc etc.

After ten minutes of this, he manages to ring off and calls Tone, who answers, but it's hard to hear what Tone's saying over the noise of his kids squabbling.

Oh, the joys of home life, Danny thinks.

The room TV's showing *It's a Wonderful Life* again.

Danny disagrees with that premise at this present moment in time.

He decides he'll go for a walk down Sunset.

A tramp on the sidewalk yells at him, 'Git the fuck outta here, limey cunt!'

How's he know I'm British? All I've done is give him some money and wish him Happy Christmas – so it was the accent that gave me away, even though my accent is Irish? – is his blurry train of thought.

Maybe it all sounds the same if you're a drunken old tramp.

Not very kind sentiments on this festive day.

Jesus's birthday.

Happy Birthday, Jesus.

This gives him an idea.

Goes back to hotel and picks up guitar.

He only knows three chords: C major, G and G7.

E minor at a push.

Four chords, then.

F should be amongst that mix, but F is too difficult to finger.

So he makes do with C, G, G7.

And E minor. At a push.

Starts writing a song about Christmas.

Christmas in LA.

Takes him all afternoon and into the evening when Tank knocks on his door.

He plays it to Tank:

'Sitting in Musso and Frank
With my Christmas buddy, Tank.
Grauman's Chinese,
Bending to see
Handprints of the stars,
Sunset Strip clubs,
Downtown bars,
Baby Jesus,
Happy birthday,
Yuletide in LA,
LA XMAS.'

The last phrase is sung as written, i.e. LA Ex Mas.

Tank approves, and this song will be the band's Christmas hit in a year's time.

Then their tour will start.

And so, in RIL's history, will a brand new chapter.

33
Touring

There now follow the years of touring. And if it seems repetitive, that's because it is.

There's an old touring cliché about not knowing what country you're in, let alone what city.

There's another one that says what goes on tour, stays on tour. (This is also true of business trips, movie shoots, and conferences. A different location condones different behaviour, it seems.)

But getting back to the repetitive nature of touring. One long round of flights, itineraries, hotels and crowds. Stadiums merge into lookalike stadiums, as do concert halls. Cramped dressing-rooms, narrow corridors leading to an ever-increasing volume of crowd noise. Expectant and excited. Then you burst onto the stage, blinded by the lights, carrying your instruments, ready to plug in. Tank holds his sticks. Danny, his tambourine, harmonica in top pocket. And the audience goes wild; you've kept them waiting twenty minutes or more to increase the tension, which is released a hundredfold at the band's appearance. You run onto the stage, not amble. Full of energy. Wave at the crowd. 'Hello Cardiff. We love you!' (But make sure you're *in* Cardiff.)

You play your set, do a few encores. Banter from Danny. Mickey's solo. Tank's solo. Then Danny's solo with his acoustic while the others go off for 'comfort breaks'. When it's Tank's solo, Danny can go off. If he needs to, though. The sweating means he don't always have to pee. Then it's a mad dash to a minivan parked round the back by the stage doors. Fans banging on the sides. 'We luv u Danny!' Crying tears of worship, clutching hands together as if in prayer. They'll clamber onto the roof if security don't stop 'em. The boys wave, trapped inside the vehicle like caged beasts. They're a mess of sweat, mopping themselves off with towels. RayRR on hand with cool water, ice, fresh towels, wipes.

'Went well?' says Danny, like he always does.

'Went well!' agree the others, like they always do.

Then to the hotel where they're barricaded in their separate rooms. Unable to dare to venture out for fear of being mobbed. Unless heavily disguised. Stupid disguises. False beards, moustaches, glasses, hats. But the fans know they're there and look out for boys in false beards, moustaches, glasses and hats. Rumbled. 'WE LUV U DANNY!!'

One whole hotel floor booked, usually. Costing a fortune. All coming out of the tour 'profits' which they, the band, see little of. But the tour is coining it. Every gosh darned US dollar or Ozzie dollar or Chinese People's Currency or Cardiff pound.

Fame at long last and long may it last.

Hotels: the ways that the band is treated now improve dramatically; they each have their own hotel room for instance, no more sharing, and not just a room but a suite. The sort of suite where you lose your way in the middle of the night en route to the bathroom and end up in the living room. The sort of suite where your pathetic little pile of luggage, one suitcase and a holdall, looks lost in the room's hallway – yes, the suite has its own hallway – deposited there by the obliging and about-to-be-heavily-tipped porter, 'Will there be anything else, sir? Shall I show you how the aircon works?' 'No thanks mate, here's a fiver.' 'Thank you, sir. Enjoy your stay at the Ramada/Holiday Inn/Sheraton etc.'

The TV set in the room welcomes 'Guest, Mr O'Shea' and encourages him to enjoy all the hotel's facilities. The gym? Not likely. The pool? Too much effort. Massage? Ah, now you're talking! A knock on the door, and it's a call-girl or a groupie – some company at least, at last.

Because, for Danny, it's lonely on tour. It really is. Surrounded by roadies and tour managers and assistants and sound-guys and merchandisers and drivers... it's lonely.

And the rest of the band? They're lonely too, in their own way.

Tone, of course, missing his family.

Tank and Mickey? Who knows?

They go quiet, introspective, self-absorbed even.

Mickey likes video games.

Tank reads. And reads and reads.

They don't talk to each other now. At rehearsals, it's business. But no meeting up in the bar after a gig.

They can't anyway. They'd be swamped, 'WE LUV YA MICKEY!'

Transport: during the course of the touring years, the modes of transport have also improved dramatically. The Tour Bus – a cramped, smelly affair with seats too narrow – has become a Tour *Coach*, which is a grander affair with two loos in the back and soft toilet tissue. The loos are chemical and have to be emptied on the way, so there is a general rule that everyone has to abide by which is: Number Ones is okay, but Number Twos is strictly verboten and, if the need arises, i.e. most mornings after breakfast, the occupants have to use truck-stops, or verge or layby if desperate. The coach toilets get blocked easily so female passengers have to store their used sanitary items in plastic bags to be deposited in the nearest roadside bin.

These are the Rules of the Road.

The Rules: another Rule of the Road is to do with smoking. Those that do and those that don't. Mickey and Tank and Danny do, Tone doesn't. So he is allowed some Time Out non-smoking periods being mid-morning ten till twelve and mid-afternoon three till five.

Personal hygiene is another factor; but as hotels have showers, body odour isn't so much of a problem but clothes-washing is. Especially, *socks*! Everyone on the bus (driver included) is encouraged to wash socks and underwear in hotel baths or basins. Or simply buy new ones while travelling and trash the dirty stuff.

On-coach entertainment is easy as everyone has their own Walkman. There's a TV up by the driver that's permanently tuned to some news channel, or maybe one should say *untuned,* as the picture rolls and breaks up on a continual basis. On good days they have singsongs. On bad days they stay moodily silent; some play cards, Tank reads... and reads. Steinbeck mostly. He loves Steinbeck, after Tone introduces him to the wonderful American storyteller. He loves *Cannery Row*, Doc and the boys.

Guests (female or otherwise) in the coach are discouraged as once ensconced on the bus they're hard to get rid of, freeloaders mostly. And then there's your valuables: ripe for the stealing or the taking as souvenirs and hard to keep secure in an area as intimate as a travelling bunch of seats and bunks.

Bunks: for the boys and RayRoadieRice. There's a bunk kept spare for clothes, cases etc. which are piled up in towering heaps. The back area is for general seating and tables, and the very back area is for the toilet cubicles. Towards the front, after the bunks area, there is more seating and the 'galley' for tea/coffee etc. and a fridge for drinks and water. There's a jump-seat by the driver and on occasion he'll invite someone up for conversation to while away the miles. He's an entertaining cuss and full of stories of past occupants, bad behaviour and scandalous gossip. A bit like London cabbies with their 'guess who I had in the back of my cab the other day?' His name is Miles – yes, really, *Miles*, as in 'Miles has been driving for miles' – and he must have one helluva bladder as he never seems to need to stop for a pee. Tone has the nerve to ask him one day how he keeps it in and Miles replies, 'Will power'. Mickey, with his ever-weak bladder, takes note. 'Will Power, who's he when he's at home?' but no one finds it funny. You lose your sense of humour cooped up like this on a coach for days, weeks, months on end.

Everyone sits in the same place, strange that. You'd think they'd swop places, move around a bit for a change, but no. Danny B sits on his own, usually in the front jump-seat next to the driver, but only if invited, otherwise he sits on the couch. Stretches out, lies down, claims it as his own. Tank and Tone sit opposite each other at the back and play cards. Mickey usually adopts a prone position in his bunk or joins Tank 'n' Tone at the table. RayRoadieRice is like a nomad, never settling down in one place, flitting between seats, annoying everyone like a clingy puppy – 'Piss off, Ray,' 'Fuck off, Ray.' Joe does not travel with them as he has his own car, his silver RR, either transported abroad (at great expense), or a similar vehicle, like a Bentley, hired in the country they're touring in. Jeeves driving him as per. He might invite one of the band to travel with him, but none of them appreciates that. 'Like travellin' with yer Dad,' they say.

Winnebagos: as the years roll by and the touring increases, and as the band's fame increases and the subsequent income increases, so does the mode of *personal* transport improve. Each RIL member now travels in his *very own* Winnebago or Recreational Vehicle (RV). Each with their name printed on the side in BLOCK CAPITALS. An RV with TANK on the side causes much ribald comment: 'Don't look much like a tank to me!' or variations, thereof.

A Winnebago is your own luxury over-sized caravan: bed (double) at the back, toilet (single) in the middle opposite the cooking bit, the front has comfy seating with table. TV above the windscreen. Ray now follows in the equipment trailer, no longer a pest to the band.

The money is rolling in and, it has to be said, rolling into their manager's pockets rather than the band's bank accounts. All that 'small print' in the contracts that Alamo Godbold advised them to ignore has now come to fruition. All the hidden percentages and expenses off the gross. Basically, the band is fucked. They don't even own their own songs as 'said songs comprising lyrics and music' are owned lock, stock, and bloody barrel by a music publishing company in London's Tin Pan Alley – being the area around Soho and Denmark Street. So, no royalties.

Joe has his own percentage, negotiated upfront with said music publishing company. No flies on Joe. Performing, personal appearances and other income is swallowed up by the legendary 'expenses'. Well, your own private Winnebago ain't cheap. But enough dosh trickles through to satisfy the otherwise simple appetites of the band – there's no drugs dependency for one thing, which is usually the drain on a band's resources. But they have their whims and fancies which are indulged in what's called the 'Hospitality Riders' or 'Catering Riders' which are the items of food, drink etc. provided in their dressing rooms before a gig.

Riders, or the *Diva List*, as it's also known. Back in the day, dressing-room fare used to be a simple combo of cold meats, dried-up sandwiches, and warm beer. Maybe some fruit if the boat was really pushed out. But nothing exotic like Kiwi fruit. Just Granny Smiths and some oranges – maybe a pineapple if you'd had a Number One hit. But now, with the 1980s approaching, the demands become excessive. Why? Because they're allowed to. Give 'em an inch…

A top band of, say, four members, can easily chalk up a list of eighty items, what with the variations of water, iced teas, breads, cereals, cheeses, sweets, meats. Then there's the domestic beer and imported beer, the gin and vodka, American or Scotch whisky, and the shades and regions of wine: French, Californian, South African... the list goes on. Brand names like Budweiser, Gordon's, Jack Daniel's. And towels of course, lots of towels to mop off the drug-sweats, performance-sweats, and alcohol-sweats. Fluffy towels. White, normally. Who wants coloured towels?

And so the Diva Lists lengthen...

How many different sorts of *milk* can be itemised? Soya, lactose, full cream, non-lactose, skimmed, semi-skinned – it ain't just MILK! Another example, mustards: French, English, Dijon, Honey, Grainy, Brown, American. Paper plates? No, the bands require *china*, white, same with the cups (no plastic) and the cutlery (good quality metal, not wood, def not plastic!).

The items get even more specific: a banquet table, love seat, B-12 injections (nurse or doctor to administer), condoms (flavoured), dumbbells, dumb blondes, strawberry jelly, KY jelly, jelly beans, baked beans (Heinz, of course).

RIL's Diva Lists: well into their touring, the Rock Ireland Line boys now have their own dressing-rooms, of equal size, decorated and equipped to each member's specifications and each room to contain toilet, sink and shower. If these demands cannot be met, promoter and venue forfeit a percentage of their gross profits. But their individual Diva Lists are modest in comparison to others more flamboyant or eccentric:

Mickey. Likes cheese (any variety but not from a goat): cheese 'n' onion crisps, cheese 'n' pickle sarnies and for pudding? Cheesecake! Mickey does like his cheese. To drink: soft drinks, no alcohol. Ointment for his athlete's foot problem. Flowers in clear glass jars but no lilies – death flowers he calls 'em. Room decor? Not fussed, take it as it comes. Just provide him with a comfy armchair and a selection of the day's papers – UK of course, if he's abroad. A radio to listen to the local DJs, it gives him a feeling for the country he's in, the music they like and the sound of the language. Mickey is fascinated by language: the guttural German, where even the most innocent phrase sounds like a command; French, where even the most innocuous phrase sounds sexy; Italian, *beautiful* Italian, where every word is romantic, *bellisimo*; Spanish, with the strange 'th' sound; Chinese, or Mandarin, sounding like a squeaky toy; and American, the accent that sounds the most authoritative and generally is *sooo* slow; finally, English, with all its regional variations – the singsong Welsh, broad Yorks, East End cockney, clipped Upper Class. His most favourite language? Indian. Always so polite-sounding with its ups and downs.

Danny. Insists on vegetarian food, absolutely no meat products. Salad bowl. Fruit bowl. To drink: Guinness (if abroad and not available: alternatives to be provided, for instance, Retsina in Greece). Tap water in jug (no ice and, if tap water is suspect, provide bottled, still). Toaster and white bread (sliced), salted butter and Marmite. Danny Boy loves his Marmite. Decor: black and purple. Medicinal items for his voice – mouthwash to gargle, throat spray, TCP for infections. His greatest fear? A sore throat. His second greatest fear? Losing his looks. His third greatest fear? That increasing waistline. A full-length mirror is a must for our boyo, to practise his moves and, quite frankly, to admire his good looks. And why not? If you're born beautiful, why not appreciate it? Because Danny B *is* beautiful. As a baby, he was bonny and, as a toddler, cute. His schoolboy phase was his ugly duckling one, saving him from homosexual attention, but as a teenager he was acne-free. Now, as an adult, tall, slim-ish, and oh so handsome! Floppy black hair falls across dark brown eyes. Does he know the girls all fall for him? Course he does. Those lingering looks trying to catch his attention. The hand laid on his arm, the standing-too-close. So he revels in his reflection, does Danny Boy. Especially when he's bound up tight in his belly corset.

Tone. Lists Head & Shoulders shampoo plus hair dryer for his luxuriant locks. 'Why do you need shampoo for your shoulders?' asks Tank sarcastically. Tone likes lots of colour in his dressing-room – flowers and *Christmas decorations*! He says to remind him of Christmas with his family. Photos in frames of Aggie and the kids that he puts around the room. To eat, he likes a pizza margherita from Pizza Express if poss. Even in Italy. Coals to Newcastle. To drink, G&T. Tone's tipple. And cans of Heineken please, the beer that refreshes the parts other beers cannot reach, as the advertising slogan goes. He also requests a tea set-up: kettle, teapot (china), Yorkshire Tea, sugar, skimmed milk. Brews it himself, the way his mother made it:

1) bring the pot to the boiling kettle (not the other way round) to retain maximum heat,

2) let the tea brew for one minute precisely,

3) sugar in cup first (one level teaspoon), then the tea, finally the milk,

4) colour: dark brown.

Biscuits to accompany, preferring Nice biscuits which are crunchy, or chewy Garibaldi which get stuck in your teeth. Toothpicks.

Tank. Stipulates a lot of food items, his all-time favourite being cottage pie – not *shepherd's* pie which is lamb, but *cottage* which is beef. 'Lamb tastes of sheep!' he says mysteriously. This menu item is hard to find in most countries, it's true, so RRR sneaks into hotel kitchens and rustles up the dish especially. Which earns Ray plenty of Brownie points, far as Tank's concerned. He also likes eggs, be they fried, scrambled, poached, or boiled. In France, he orders *oeufs sur plat*. In America, *over-easy*. In some far-flung countries though it's potluck – ask for a four-and-a-half-minute boiled egg and when you crack it open, it's either liquid/embryonic or rock-hard. They don't seem to do in-between. But in his rider, he can be ultra-specific, i.e.

1) place egg in boiling water laced with salt to stop egg cracking,

2) boil for four minutes, remove pan from heat and leave to stand for one half-minute,

3) serve with brown toast, cut into 'soldiers', salt *and* pepper.

One essential item in Tank's room is an exercise bike cos Tank would like to be less 'tank' to tell the God's honest. To drink: if in the States, it's Bud. 'When in Rome,' he's prone to say. 'When in America.' Chintz is the style of choice for the room. The flowery patterns that his ma favoured, and his bastard dad hated. Ha! A TV is essential. He loves American TV as there are so many channels to choose from, he loves to 'surf'. Also, he's a fan of the *local* programmes in other countries, but why do they all speak so fast? Tank likes to imitate the excitable Japanese cooking-programme presenters: 'Biii-tooo-ruuu-tooo!' 'What does that mean?' asks Mickey. 'Beetroot,' says Tank.

Beetroot: There is one hard and fast rule the whole band agree on, and that is: NO BEETROOT. This dates back to when they were touring an Eastern Bloc country – well, not exactly 'touring' as they only played one city. They stayed at a tourist hotel: a dark gloomy old building whose only saving grace was the basement which housed The Balalaika Bar. High chairs, tall round tables. This bar served vodka, natch, but also domestic wines. Mickey, with his no-alcohol regime, stuck to tonic, ice and lemon – the reformed alcoholic's version of G&T. G&T without the G. But the others, after a few tastings of the vodka (ice, no tonic, down-in-one), moved on to the local red wine which was robust, to say the least, or 'rough', to say the most.

There was nothing else to do of a weekday night in this Eastern metropolis – where the roads were edged with muddy slush and near everywhere was closed apart from the pricey restaurants where the boys were looked at with some horror by the head waiters who grandly announced, 'All tables booked!' (As the boys clocked the near-deserted room). So, the Balalaika Bar it was, and sure enough, a balalaika player was performing, dressed in rustic garb, singing doleful peasant songs, probably about tractors.

At this time, being the early '80s, they were aware that they were being watched and followed. It couldn't be more obvious. The burly fella in reception who gave them steely glances behind his newspaper, the woman with the shopping bag who stopped to look in shop windows the moment they turned around, that old couple who were *always* sat on benches or on the opposite side of the road. They'd been tipped the wink that their hotel rooms would likely be bugged, and they'd been warned about attractive call-girls who'd lure them into compromising situations, leading to blackmail and spying for the Bolsheviks. So Joe R warned: no girls and watch what you say. Which, after a few bevvies, was a red rag to these bulls, who started chanting anti-Soviet sentiments down the metal table-legs which they reckoned were hollow and hid microphones.

These pronouncements were not subtle: 'Down with the Commies!' for instance.

It was not long before some long-legged Ludmillas sashayed into the bar and started schmoozing around the band saying to giff them drink pliss with promise of good timings, boys, as we Eastern girls luff you cute Western mans. But the cute Western mans, heeding previous warnings, were having none of it, even Tank resisted, and they declared that they were 'gay' – but this was not understood, 'You happy boys, yess?' – then they said 'homosexual' – which was also not understood, 'Sexual iss gud, da?' So Danny put his arm around Tank, and Mickey did the same with Tone, and the girls got the message and slunk off to find tourists anew. But it was not long before some loose-limbed Ivans now showed up, fluttering eyelashes and swaying hips, but the lads basically just told them to fuck off, which they did with their Soviet tails between their legs.

They were three bottles of the vicious local red down by now, and they decided to call it a night and retire to their bugged rooms, outside of which an old Babushka woman in black shawl sat on a chair – wooden, utilitarian – observing the floor's comings and goings. There was an identical woman on each floor. The boys would greet her warmly, but she'd ignore them and carry on with her knitting.

Next morning they met for breakfast, and they were all, apart from Mickey, rather quiet. In fact, *very* quiet. Mickey was somewhat bemused by their passivity but put it down to hangovers. The others exchanged nervous looks, showed no appetite for the boiled eggs, be they embryonic or like concrete. They shifted in their seats.

What had happened was rather alarming. Each of them, apart from Mickey, had noticed a distinct red tinge to their morning waterworks. Was it some deadly disease of the bladder? They contemplated the prospect of death and wished they'd written their wills. Tone was quite teary at the thought of leaving his loved ones bereft, vowing to himself to take out life insurance if he was spared this one time, Lord.

Finally, Tank blurted it out: how his piss was red and was he dying? The others nodded in horrified agreement re the colour of *their* urine, then cooler heads prevailed. Mickey said his piss was normal, so they deduced that maybe, just maybe, the local red wine had affected them somehow. Made sense. It was a dark red red, after all. All three of them: red pee. Mickey: normal. All three of them: local red wine. Mickey: tonic water.

So, having identified the possible culprit, a mighty sigh of relief was heaved, and they proceeded to enjoy their liquid/concrete boiled eggs.

But why the all-out rider ban on beetroot? Well, what happened was this: after the red wine incident, Mickey had felt left out. When he didn't partake of the wine and get the resulting shade of wee – well, he just felt left out. Now, he'd heard, or someone had said, or someone had read, that beetroot had the same effect. Apparently, red beetroot equalled rustic red wine equalled red pee. So Mickey decided to test the theory out. He bought a jar and consumed the whole lot in one go, getting a very red tongue into the bargain. And the next morning? Well, as the saying goes, 'Red beet in the evening, red pee in the morn.' He announced the result triumphantly, and his efforts were applauded. And appreciated. A tight band, f'sure.

But the experience of scarlet piss, now witnessed by all four, was not one to be repeated so an overall ban was introduced. End of beetroot. End of story.

34
Keep On Running

On the run indeed, as they travel from city to city, country to country. They call their tour 'Rock Ireland Line: Travellin' Heavy'. A play on 'travelling light' and 'heavy' rock. Danny's invention. Each tour will then have a number in Roman numerals: I, II, III etc, 'Travellin' Heavy III', for instance.

So, travelling heavy and never travelling light: they, the band, exist now in a complex world of gross potentials, percentages, revenues, advances, contracts, straight guarantees, bent guarantees, fuck-all guarantees, sponsors, buy-outs, rip-offs, load-ins, load-outs, traffic streams, security sweeps, curfews, agents, guest lists, publicists, PR, R&R, Press kits, 'merch' (merchandising), promoters, photo ops, local radio, DJs, BJs... and Tour Managers.

Tour Managers: are the most important, vital, goddam *essential* component of a rock band tour as he/she/they will literally handle everything from the crews (comprising sound technicians, roadies, drivers, gofers, merch sellers plus Uncle Tom Cobley) to the transport, logistics, itineraries, expenses... and not forgetting the band itself because they're the m-fs who're the whole reason for this jamboree. Without those four guys, the sound engineers, roadies, drivers, merch girls *et al* would be out of a job. A good tour manager (TM) considers *health* to be the most important factor of touring as the continued maintenance of same ensures a successful tour. Because whether it be drink, drugs, close proximity to others, exhaustion or bad hygiene, ill-health will wreck a tour. What use is a singer with a throat infection? The TM has to have a private stash of antibios. What use is a drummer with 'the runs' or a guitarist with 'frozen shoulder'? The TM has a stock of medicines and ointments. What use is a bass guitarist with...? (No, bass players are immune, it seems.)

The close environment of a tour is potentially disgusting: the stinking coaches or buses, the cramped dressing-rooms, and as for hotel rooms... well, don't look too close at the mattress, it will have seen a lot of action (and bodily fluids) in its time. The thing is, people who stay in hotels generally aren't there to *sleep*; no, they're either on holiday (which means screwing) or on business (which means screwing). Ever been in a hotel and wondered what the previous occupant has been up to on that hotbed of bacteria? Not your own bacteria but soon-to-become-yours as you touch the bedspread, loo handle, Frigobar and TV remote (especially that well-worn MOVIES/porn button). Best to go in with disinfectant and hand sanitisers for a clean sweep.

So touring, my friend, is one big germ factory, and germs can decimate a tour in one fell swoop as everyone on tour is living cheek by infected jowl, passing on every darned illness known to man. Even the singer with just a cold is the pits – try singing stuffed-up and sneezing.

So the TM must encourage a good health regime:

1) drink plenty of water,

2) avoid 'greasy-spoon' caffs,

3) eat healthy: salads, fruit, nuts etc,

4) have clean laundry (esp. underwear and socks, *esp.* socks),

5) shower, shower, shower.

If someone starts to smell fruity, tell 'em. And the slightest health problem, call the doc. Better still, have a nurse as part of your crew. Be vigilant of drugs, goes without saying really, and be mindful of how much booze anyone is putting away. A good TM is a mix of commandant, dictator, PA, accountant, bookkeeper, problem-solver, counsellor, psychiatrist, parent and best friend. And the golden rule for a TM is: be nice to everyone, where possible. A smile will do more than any sum of money, or harsh word, to smooth troubled waters.

Belinda: introducing the best TM the band has on any tour. Before Belinda comes on board, Tour I is a disaster area in the shape of Johnnie, a willowy male beanpole with an everlasting grin (or is it a smirk?) who says 'Yes' to everything but in the end delivers 'No'. Is the hotel booked? Yes. They get there, no reservations. So, *was* the hotel booked? Er...

couldn't get through, sorry. 'Sorry' should be Johnnie's middle name. Has the venue been checked out? Yes. They get there, performance time changed to one hour earlier due to teenage curfew. Why weren't we informed? He called the venue, he says, but they didn't mention this, sorry. Sorry! They only have an hour now to sound-check, get changed, get charged. The support band (a local band) has to shorten their spot, and they ain't happy as this is their biggest gig to date. They stop short of three numbers, strop off-stage and get rip-roaring drunk, pick a fight in a bar, get arrested, get busted, get a criminal record for possession and public affray. Career over. Sorry, says Johnnie. Then he gets a nervous rash, all up one arm; then, to keep it company, up the other arm. He scratches them endlessly, and the nurse puts on cream. Then he reports that the rash has travelled 'down south' but nursey ain't gonna administer cream *down there* so it has to be *self*-administered, which, given the groans heard from Johnnie's room, is something he perhaps enjoys. Or maybe it's pain, who knows? Who cares? Sorry. Eventually, after a four-all vote, that's what the lads say: Sorry, Johnnie. Your presence on this tour is no longer required, so please would you be so good as to fuck off.

'Joe, we need a new TM!' (Danny B on the blower.)

'I have just the lady,' says Joe.

'A *female*?'

'I believe that is the correct definition of "lady".'

'I'll have to consult the boys.'

But before he gets the chance, or the result of a vote, Joe has acted, arranged a flight, and onto the scene wafts the fragrant figure of Belinda.

She calls them all 'Mister' – Mr Danny, Mr Mickey, Mr Tony, even Mr Tank.

'You can call me Belinda,' she purrs, even though 'Bitch' would be more like.

Picture the scene of this momentous first meet: she is Amazonian, nudging six-foot tall, broad-shouldered, wide-hipped. Long dark hair teased into flowing waves of softness that belie her hard-as-fuckin'-nails character. 'Belinda has more balls than you can shake a rattling stick at!' says Danny later as they discuss their newly-appointed TM.

Picture the scene: she towers above them as they slump in chairs. All decked out in head-to-toe leather, higher-than-high high heels on thigh-high boots, fishnet stockings evident in the unholy gap between top of boots and hem of mini skirt. Mr Tank's tongue, were it long enough, would be lolling out of his mouth; and his eyes, were they on stalks, would be... well... on stalks. Ballsy Belinda will rule the roost over the crew as she gives them the dag-eye from her one unclad eye (the other being behind a pirate eyepatch). She will crack the whip, literally, as she wields a bullwhip – yes, really – a long leather bullwhip, which she cracks like a good 'un. Or like a lion-tamer with a herd of obedient beasts. Crack! Get that gear unloaded! CRACK! Sound-check NOW! CRACKKKK! Why isn't Mr Tank's kit set up? CRACK!

Belinda handles the stage crew like naughty schoolkids, and if they're slacking – well, she hasn't hit anyone with the whip *yet*, just the ground gets the punishment, but sometimes she's within a hair's breadth. Mexican-born, she struts her stuff like a cartel *Capo*. Swears liberally through those ruby red lips, swears like a man, strides like a man, but no brave soul tries to seduce her like a woman. She ain't interested anyway. More into her own kind is Belinda. Rumour has it that she has already sampled the 'merch' girl, she of the pink rubber dress, so the male element of the tour are well pissed off that the two most attractive females on tour are off-limits. The boys in the band, however, think she's great, as she eats the venue managers for breakfast, lunch and dinner, and sometimes high tea as well. Belinda has an appetite for fools, mugs and charlatans.

Groupies or 'Road wives': the groupies who follow RIL are basically yer standard groupies who follow male rock bands around, whose mission in life, whose ambition, whose very *goal*, is to shag as many rock and pop groups as poss. Some will even go for the road crew, tour managers, sound engineers, anyone to do with their favourite group. They will collect shags like autographs; if they're lucky, they'll get a scalp or a souvenir – an indelicate Polaroid or a soiled pair of Y-fronts.

But being a groupie isn't all about sex but something more, something about loyalty. Remember The Liners? Hattie, Bet and Trude. A true fan can *worship*, rather than, say, conquer. A shag is about conquering, but a shag isn't all a dedicated groupie has to offer. Loyalty. Service. A 'road wife'. Offering not just sex but companionship. They all, Danny, Mickey and Tank, have road wives from time to time on their tours. Even ever-faithful Tone allows himself a 'road wife' but not one he has sex with; more for female company in this band of brothers. In fact, to be fair, Tone's road wife is more like a sister to him, and when he gets home, he'll feel no guilt as 'just good friends' will be an accurate description of his on-tour relationship.

This is not the case with the rest of the band who treat their groupies as girlfriends, to be left by the side of the road, so to speak, when the tour ends. Apart from Mickey who, being a hopeless romantic, wants to marry his road wife, make her his permanent wife, but she says not to be so silly, she has other fish to fry, i.e. others bands to sleep with. These girls find other loyalties; they're not just one-band girls.

On departure, Tone will chastely kiss his 'girl' on the cheek, shake her hand, give her a paternal hug and wish her well. She will then go off, surprised at her celibate role and, feeling somewhat sexually frustrated by now, will seek further employment. 'I was with this bass guitarist for, like, four weeks, and we never had sex!' she'll say as she shares a post-coital joint with her next conquest, who'll then say, 'Tone from Rock Ireland Line, was it?' 'Yeah, tee-total Tone,' she'll reply.

Meanwhile, the others would've plied their road wives, now their ex-wives, with signed posters of the band, free tee-shirts, records, souvenirs, Polaroids of their pricks. Quid pro quo.

Family: on one leg of the tour – the Eastern part of the pan-European concerts – Tone brings his family on board, and this simple act changes the whole dynamic.

However, the night before they are due to arrive has been a memorable one for the road crew, who find a sleazy strip joint in the old part of the city where they flash their kopeks on private lap-dances and terrible 'champagne' which, when they're presented with the bill, turns out to cost the Slavic equivalent of £100 per bottle.

Like most road crews abroad, a call to the local cab company and a request to the driver to take them to the nearest strip club – with the miming of 'big boobs' (hands cupping imaginary breasts) surpassing any language difficulties (even though the words 'strip club' are universal enough) – results in a drive-around-the-houses and an exorbitant large taxi fare and a shrug of the shoulders from the driver when his passengers try to complain.

But no matter for they are now deposited at the purple doors of the 'Strip-A-Go-Go, Nude and Lap Dance Club' which in reality is *literally* just around the corner from their hotel but the cab driver has taken them on the 'scenic route' thereby earning himself and his grateful family the exorbitant fare from these rich Westerners who now stand outside the purple doors while a bow-tied bouncer frisks them for fire-arms then welcomes them into a passageway lined with photos of naked girls and onwards to a small booth where a middle-aged Eastern dame informs the crew that they 'will be required pliss to sign on as our lifetime member' of said club for a mere £25 equivalent per and from there to a table facing and very close to a pole-dancing pole which is being gyrated upon by a topless girl who is coincidentally also a Pole as this city is indeed in Poland. A Pole on a pole. Coals to Newcastle.

They are served free beers but before long are joined by skinny gals in nightdresses who want the 'club champagne' which is brought in ice buckets but is warm and sugary and the skinny gals down their glasses and are served more fizz and thus the evening progresses as whispers in ears result in members of the crew being taken off for 'private' lap-dances from which they return with grins all over their mugs and a nod and a wink to the rest to follow suit as 'it's worth every rouble!'

But when the final bill arrives they question it along the lines of 'What the fuck's all this? You trying to rip us off?' referring to the champagne cost as the private lap-dances have been reasonable enough (£50 per) and the beer was free so why the fuck is the warm and sugary 'champagne' (of which they ordered four bottles) over £100 per so they are well out of pocket?

Now, being a Brit crew and burly to boot, they don't take kindly to this over-charging and take issue with the management who, being a kind of East European mafia, do not understand the cockney vernacular of 'You takin' the piss?' (the poor translation into Polish by a semi-English-speaking waiter being, 'Are you drinking your own urine?').

At this point, the British contingent (x 3) opt to hop it without paying for the bottles of pricey fizz (x 4) whereupon the Bolshevik bully boy bouncers (x 5) descend upon the Brits with knuckledusters and batons and one even pulls out a handgun with which he tries to 'pistol-whip' the roadies whereupon all hell lets loose and an ugly brawl moves from the club lobby area all the way down the corridor to the purple doors and out into the street where the bloodied and bruised roadies are deposited in the gutter. Time for reinforcements.

They stagger back to the hotel locating it by some primeval homing instinct where they rouse (at four in the morning) the rest of the road crew (x 2), the sound engineer and the drivers (x 4) – this whole band of brothers being led by RayRoadieRice armed with a tyre lever (x 1). Imagine this marching band of limeys in the historic city marauding the cobbled and narrow streets and passing ancient buildings which they swear they recognise as landmarks en route to the Strip Club A-Go-Go – or they *think* they recognise as landmarks because by now they've been walking for fifteen minutes or more – so they stop the last dregs of the night's drunken passers-by to ask the whereabouts of the Club A-Go-Go but there is no one of a sound mind or sense of direction who can guide them.

They parade up and down the Strasses singing a ribald version of 'Show Me The Way To Go Home' involving bed, board and a lusty landlady not being tired but still wanting to go to bed. They hail a cab but the driver knows better than to pick up drunkards in the early hours. Finally they realise they'll never find the purple doors of the Strip A-Go-Go – it has truly A-Gone-Gone – and anyway it would most likely be closed by now so they hightail it back to the ranch which is a sound plan were it not for the fact that they can't remember where the ranch is by now.

They try this way and that, trying to recognise the route back to the hotel but the medieval streets all look the same, the historic buildings offer no clue and the street signs are all in 'foreign'. The city is fast asleep, apart from two police cars who, having been alerted by members of the populace woken from their slumbers, have tracked down this Johnny Foreigner menace. It is now that a breakdown in communications ensues as the police (x 4) call for reinforcements (x 6) in a police van, and in order to suppress any violence from metal tyre levers, baseball bats and the odd item of hotel cutlery, the Local Plod set about the Brit Crew with no mercy and flailing truncheons, after which friendly treatment the offenders are bundled into the van and taken to the nearby nick where some additional jolly foreign coppers assist the boys into the cells with the aid of boot, club and knee. An especially muscular sergeant then plays footer with one of the crew's heads.

Next morning Joe Rainbow is summoned from his suite to bail out the prisoners whose wages are docked for the next few weeks. RayRR is in disgrace (again!) as being leader of this army, although secretly amongst the RIL lads he is much admired. Showed guts and loyalty to his crew. For a while, he is dubbed 'Napoleon'.

Also on this next morning, as the battered crew take to their hotel beds, and in sharp contrast to the erstwhile debauchery and violence, Tone's family arrives from the airport to be greeted with hugs and kisses by father and husband.

And so the dynamic, for the next couple of weeks, changes.

Bruises fade, cuts heal, prides are restored. After all, the Brave Brits reason, we *were* threatened with *guns*! Not a fair fight by any means, as the number of bouncers, in their memories, increases to a dozen or more, and *armed* forfuckssake!

In this new atmosphere of 'bonhomie', Joe relents and pays the crew's wages, 'Par for the course,' he reasons. 'Boyos will be boyos,' according to Danny's vernacular.

Back on the road, Tone's sons love their pa's transport, the shiny Silverstream trailer that they liken to a space rocket. They've had one night in the hotel with room service of burgers and cola, sharing a room with Aggie, who makes a few conjugal visits to hubby's room while Belinda babysits the seven-year-olds.

And what of Belinda? The bullwhip is retired as it'd scare the kids (heck, it scares the adults!) and the leather gear is replaced by trouser suit and silk blouse. She becomes positively maternal as the twins call her 'Auntie' – Belinda likes being an auntie.

Meanwhile the twins take turns travelling in the other trailers as the lads make a fuss of them, treating the young boys as special guests, trying to outdo each other as they spoil them with ice cream or cartoons or fancy pizzas. Mickey hires a clown, so Danny hires a magician. Then Tank hires a superhero with a cloak and a deep voice.

The groupies have left, obv. Long gone. Shipped off to the next venue, which will be when Tone's family departs. The efficient Belinda has arranged this, the calendar re-scheduled. They'll all meet up again soon.

Meanwhile, Tone is in seventh heaven having his brood around him but all good things blah blah blah and the day comes when he waves his family off at some airport somewhere, bound back to England whereas Tone is bound for... he doesn't care, just wishes it could be anywhere near Aggie and his sons. The lads try to cheer him up, to no avail, he mopes and shuts himself in his trailer – alone now in his silver space rocket. But it was only a space rocket when his boys were there; now it's just a trailer.

But a good song comes out of this. Tone, alone with his acoustic twelve-string guitar, writes a poignant ballad that'll feature on the forthcoming album – a farewell song about home and love, which'd bring a tear to the eye of the hardest bastard.

One Song: the years go by fast in a blur. The new decade has begun. The '80s. The mix of touring, recording, home leave, holidays, then back on the merry-go-round of TV appearances, interviews and photo calls. They love it; they really do. A tight band, as ever. No tour fatigue for them. This is the life they dreamed of, and the dream come true. Some bands say the touring dream turns into a nightmare of monotony but not RIL. Sure, Tone misses his family, but there are enough breaks when he spends his family time one hundred per cent. And still, 'Tone the Phone' calls home every night.

The band rehearses endlessly. Perfection is their aim. Their latest album has been created by Tone as a 'concept' album in that all the tracks will run together as one. Inspired by the Beatles medley at the end of the 'Abbey Road' LP, Tone has taken twelve tracks and composed musical bridges, or segues, between them to make one whole song in effect. If they're in different keys, he modulates. The problem of Side One and Side Two is overcome by the first side ending on an orchestral drone fading out then fading up on the second side. For the touring concerts, this album presents something of a challenge as playing the twelve songs continually would take an exhausting 38 minutes and 23 seconds, so they treat them as individual songs but play them religiously in the same order as on the record. Which, by the way, is titled 'One Song'.

They all now write their own material and, in true democratic fashion, list all four as the composers in alphabetical order regardless of who actually composed any particular track. In fact, they tend to pair off in their writing: Danny and Tone sitting opposite each other with acoustic guitars, Mickey and Tank likewise tho' Tank can't play guitar so he usually writes the words. But all's fair in love and bands so all are credited alphabetically: *Johnston, Mills, O'Shea, Sandercock.* And what's most important is that they now own copyright to these new songs. They've lived and learned.

They write their songs while travelling, and in the downtime on tour. Of which there is plenty. Some say it's all downtime. As the conventional wisdom goes, touring is five per cent performing and one hundred per cent WAITING (yes, do the maths). They should add WAITING to the itinerary: waiting to check into the hotel, waiting for transport, waiting for meals, waiting for waiters, waiting for the sound-check, waiting for the support group to finish – talking of which…

Support Group: their favourite 'opening band' or 'support group' is a five-girl group of real beauties. And God created Woman. Did He ever! There is talk amongst the crew of them being 'lesbos' but Danny B puts paid to that by bedding two of the girls – at the same time. The girls' act is simple – sexy-strutting around, singing live to backing tapes in the least amount of clothing possible without breaking US State Laws. Japan goes wild for them as the laws are more liberal there, so the least amount of clothing becomes almost non-existent – PVC, leather and *Geeee*-strings!

Offstage, bizarrely, they're all religious nuts, just like the mud-wrestlin' gals of all those centuries back. They attend the local chapels and churches dressed like Sunday School teachers. They are something like '5th Adventist Baptists' although no one has confirmed this to any great degree of accuracy. Certainly 'Baptist' comes into it and Danny swears he heard 'Adventist' mentioned. 5th? Who knows? No one dares ask the girls, but they're not common-or-garden C of E or even RC – their religion is more complex and fanatical. The fire 'n' brimstone variety. Maybe they think this is the way to avoid eternal conflagration – a salve for their wicked ways. Because on stage, they certainly have wicked ways. Maybe they confess a lot, says Mickey. 'Forgive me Father for I have cavorted unseemly!' Say ten Hail Mary's, then back into the S&M gear. Their band name gives the game away: 'Rawnch'. A neat play on words of 'raw' and 'raunch'.

Belinda loves 'Rawnch' and even joins them on stage at one gig, cracking her bullwhip and smooching with the girls. The Jap crowd, mainly boys, are hysterical, and it's a case of follow-that for RIL. How can they? Their solution is to extend the interval then delay their own stage entry by twenty minutes, by which time the audience is baying for: 'Rock-Ireland-Line… Rock-Ireland-Line… ROCK-IRELAND-LINE..!' Clever ruse.

At the end of that particular show, Rawnch (plus Belinda) join them on stage and dance along to the music. The crowd goes wild again and this is not a thing to be repeated, the lads agree afterwards, as it somewhat steals RIL's thunder but just this once…

(Aggie never gets to hear of this opening band and just as well – what happens on tour etc).

So the touring is going well until the devil of happenstance joins them and tragedy strikes.

35
King Of The Road

It didn't happen on a Friday – that traditional unlucky day. It wasn't on the thirteenth either. There'd been no portents or omens. No black cats crossing paths or magpie sightings. No ladders to walk under.

But tragedy struck from nowhere on that not especial day.

The tour had moved to the Netherlands, and the venue they were due to appear in was like a stadium-in-the-round. Circular like a Roman amphitheatre. The stage was in the middle of the circle so the audience would be seated all around. To complete the circular theme and to ensure each section of the audience got their fair share of a view of the band, the stage was a mechanical 'revolve', designed to rotate a quarter distance for each quarter section of the performance. There was something like it in an early Beatles concert, according to resident pop historian Tone – this took place in Washington D.C. in 1964. Ringo's drums were set up on a revolving platform that had to be turned by hand by muscular roadie Mal Evans.

The boys had been alerted to this revolve, and even though they took issue normally with such theatrics, they recognised they had to be fair to their fans to get a good look-see at them. The revolve would solve this.

RayRoadieRice is there early with his crew for the load-in while the boys book into their hotel. When Ray gets to the stage area, there is a flurry of activity around the revolve because, apparently, as they are told in complicated Double Dutch, the revolve *won't revolve*. It's stuck in one position. Something's got jammed in the gearing mechanism and the platform just judders in the same place, trying but failing to release itself. Something of a disaster as the band can't turn themselves around physically to face each section of the audience, not with all the cables and the immovable amps, let alone Tank's gargantuan drum kit.

There is much foreign shrugging of shoulders and spreading of arms out wide in a 'what's-to-be-done?' gesture, so ever-enterprising RRR decides to take his crew down below with some heavy tools, a wrench and hammers, anything weighty enough to free the jam. There's a side entrance on the stage that leads down steps to go underneath the revolve, and with flashlights they're able to see that the gearing has been fouled by a metal strut that's come away and been bent by the force, stuck deep into the cogs.

They call up for the mechanism to be turned on, and immediately the violent 'hiccupping' of the cogs starts up as the gearing tries to free itself from the embedded strut. The jerking back and forth is erratic – loud, grinding metal – and in fear of the whole shebang rupturing, Ray quickly calls 'OFF!' and as soon as the gearing settles out of its epileptic fit, Ray and his crew set about attacking the metal strut, trying to prise it out with the wrench but it won't budge.

They go back up and arrange for a metal-grinder to be delivered ASAP and meanwhile they smoke roll-ups and lounge about with the Dutch boys until the grinder arrives. It's a heavy-duty bugger, and Ray agrees that the most brawny of his crew will operate it. Down they go again into the depths below the stage and the bruiser member of the crew starts metal-grinding away, sparks flying everywhere; the noise is screeching until suddenly the strut is sawn away and springs out and the cogs meet up again, grateful, it seems, to be free. Then there is only the wrench, now stuck in the teeth of the smaller cog, to be removed.

They're just about to attend to this when the unthinkable happens. A cry of triumph from Ray, when the strut is removed, has been interpreted above as an instruction to turn the revolve back ON, and when the switch is thrown, the gearing, with the wrench still wedged in, goes into a heaving spasm and erupts sideways, sending the teeth of one of the cogs into Ray's chest. One whole side of the cog is now embedded in his chest like some prehistoric monster head. Ray doesn't scream or even cry out, just looks down at the metal thing wedged in his chest, now part of his body, as blood starts to trickle, then pour out. He is impaled, white-faced, in shock, bleeding out, as the crew yell, 'STOP! TURN IT OFF!!' and the mechanism judders to a halt.

Ray has fallen backwards now; the murderous cog drops out under its own weight, leaving a gaping hole in the boy's caved-in chest. Ambulance called, don't move him, is he breathing? only just, stem the bleeding with anything you can find, ambulance on its way, keep him awake, talk to him, talk to his wild staring eyes, talking him alive, stay with us bro, you're gonna be okay, help is on its way, stay with us – but Ray is fading unconscious. The medics arrive and stretcher him out from the underworld of the revolve as the crew clamber out in despair – if the machine hadn't been switched on, if Ray hadn't shouted in triumph, if he'd been maybe a foot to the left so the cog would've missed him, if they hadn't taken it upon themselves to repair the fuckin' thing. If only…

By now Joe has been called and arrives on the scene. A figure of authority, quizzing the venue's technicians, inspecting the revolve, taking photos for evidence. Who's to blame? Who's gonna take the rap? The main venue guy holds his hands up and speaks in hurried jerks in his stilted English, 'It was not our fault! Not our error! Your men were not patient! They *should've waited*! You weren't the experts! Our own technician was on his way! You should've fuckin' WAITED! WHY DIDN'T YOU WAIT?'

The Dutch crew are all shouting now, pointing fingers, squaring up, and the Brits move forward, ready for a fight, but Jeeves bars their way. With Jeeves now caught in the middle, holding both groups back, the Brit crew now turn on the Dutch. 'The machinery was fucked, kaput, crap. We weren't to blame, WE WERE JUST TRYING TO GET THE BUGGER GOING!' Then they stop. Go silent. The boys of Rock Ireland Line have arrived and they gather helplessly at the scene, turning to Joe, their protector. Then the enormity of what's happened dawns on them as Joe fills them in with some details. 'Ray's in a bad way. He might not make it. Sorry, boys. It was just an accident.' And the band stand together, upset and shocked as they love RRRice.

RIL L. RRR.

In the hospital now, RayRoadieRice is put in a coma. Induced, it's called. The surgeons have done their best to repair his shattered breastbone, punctured lung, internal bleeding, and heart damage. His parents are there. No parent should suffer the loss of a child. There should be some immutable law set up by God, the Cosmos or Gaia – whatever you believe in: No Parent Should Suffer The Loss Of A Child. Ray's ma holds his hand, *grips* his hand, holding on for dear life, whispers to her darling boy that he'll be fine, he'll get better, stay strong my Raymond, we love you more than God or the Cosmos or Gaia – whatever you believe in. His father stands, struck dumb, head bowed. A younger sister sobs quietly.

The band are there of course, staying in the background, silent as the grave. Oh God, not the grave! Don't say the grave. But he slips away. A last heaving breath. The machines go into frenzy, beeping and alarming. The nurses and doctors rush in, push the relatives away, and apply heart-starters. 'Stand aside… clear!' Jolt, shock, the wracked body arches, then relaxes. 'Stand aside… clear!' Jolt. Ray's body arches. The machines have flatlined. 'I'm sorry, Mr and Mrs Rice,' says the doctor. The nurses look down, hide their faces, maybe hide their tears. Patient deceased. No one needs to lose a patient. The doctor records the date and time like a news bulletin. The mother howls like a wild animal. The father slumps down in a chair. The sister goes to hug her mother. A scene of human devastation. The nurses try to quiet the mother as other patients will be alarmed, but there's no quieting her.

The band, as one, leave the parents to their grief but outside they separate, the tight band now becoming unwound. One goes to the exit, one to the canteen, another to a lonely corridor, the other to a coffee machine but doesn't buy anything. Just to get away. Joe Rainbow bustles in, sees Mickey's face by the coffee machine and knows the worst. Joe is brilliant, hugs Mickey, asks where the others are, 'They've left, I dunno.' 'Which room?' he asks, so Joe joins the parents and is like a parent himself, such was his love for Ray, his protégé. He embraces the father, then gives all his attention to the mother and sister, then lays his hand on

Ray's forehead just before the nurse covers his face. He leaves to find his boys: Mickey is still by the coffee machine, Danny in the canteen. Jeeves finds Tank outside, Tone in the corridor. And once more gathered together, Joe takes them off to the nearest pub, where they hardly drink at all. Just sit silent. A terrible day.

The funeral is beautiful though. Flowers everywhere, courtesy of Joe. Tank, Danny Boy, Mickey and Tone carry the coffin; Ray doesn't weigh much. Joe Rainbow delivers a homily – affectionate, fatherly almost. The boys of Rock Ireland Line perform *a capella* the song 'King of the Road' by Roger Miller; the words aren't really appropriate, being of cigarettes and boxcars and brooms, but no matter, sung real slow and in four-part harmony, the song delivers. There's the hymn, 'In The Deep Midwinter', and a short poem read out by the preacher, 'If I Should Go', then a recording of 'Rock Island Line' by the band. The parents sit staring and unbelieving. The sister in tears throughout. Mickey, being the most empathetic, moves to sit beside her and hold her hand.

Outside the church, as the coffin is lowered into the grave, a lone bagpiper plays a Scottish lament called 'The Dark Island' (there's some Scottish ancestry apparently). Such a sad sound, the drone and wail of the pipes. And after? No wake. No trip to a pub or nearby hotel. No curled sandwiches and hushed chat. The parents have declined, despite Joe offering to pay, and that is respected. So, all that happens is everyone peels off and goes their own way. Which makes the value of a wake the more clear. The modern term is 'closure'. There needs to be a The End.

Well, there *is* an End. And it's an end to the touring.

They just stop.

Venues are cancelled, penalties paid.

It costs them a fortune in fines and lost revenue and costs already incurred that they won't get back.

Joe tries to reason with them but no joy.

That's the trouble, there ain't no joy now.

RIL is left in debt and with no income.

Record sales plummet as the band disappears. Off the radar.

Rule Number One for a band: never disappear.

Joe survives through other bands he's signed.

Like 'Rawnch', who make the Top Ten, then Number One.

The lads separate, just like they did at the hospital –

Tone to his family, Mickey to his folks, Danny back to Ireland and Tank to his dissolute life.

It's the end of the road. 1982.

36
Girl

Mickey remembers seeing her face in the crowd. One night of the long tour 'Travellin' Heavy III'. He thinks he gets a glimpse of his rehab love, Rosie. Then he spots her again, on another night. There, in the crowd. Or maybe it's not her; the long hair is now a buzz-cut. But the face, surely, is unmistakable. An oval face going down to a pointed chin – and those eyes. Huge eyes. Set apart by more than an eye's width. And talking of eyes, she doesn't try to catch *his* eye. She looks off into some distance, lost.

Lost and found, though, because if this is Rosie returned, Mickey could not be more pleased. Even though she stabbed him, or tried to.

Most nights, they play his song, 'Rosy Rosie', but she doesn't react. And by now, Mickey is certain that the face in the audience *is* that of Rosie of Rehab, despite the shorn hair. She dresses sloppily, like a man, in dungarees out of Steinbeck's *Of Mice and Men*. Open-neck check shirt and bandana around her forehead. No make-up. Can't see her feet, but he imagines biker boots. One night, as the spotlight plays over the crowd, he reckons he makes out a red dot between her eyebrows. Like a Bindi.

But no contact is made or attempted by either party.

Until the postcards start arriving.

Every city where the band appears has a postcard waiting at the venue – a picture of the city on one side, WISH U WERE HERE X on the back. Which is weird because he *is* here. He don't get it. Does she mean 'here' meaning 'with her'?

Then there's the small gifts. Kinder Surprise Eggs with a toy inside that has to be assembled. Easy for a kid's small fingers but not so easy for Mickey's stubby digits. Each city, a new Kinder Surprise. They don't say who from, but who else?

'The sweet-toys didn't last long, though,' says Mickey, some years on, as he tells his folks about Rosie – the girl he's soon to marry. Or co-habit with, as Rosie don't respect institutions.

'I have to admit, things got a little strange from then on…'

Why in God's name is he telling us all this? his parents wonder. Talk about a hard sell. But there's more, and worse, to come: the A4 brown envelopes being posted to his dressing-room or sometimes left there, with no postage. One contains dog-ends with red lipstick on the filters.

'But I thought, "Since when does Rosie ever wear red lipstick"?' His parents look at each other, wondering what their dear boy is letting himself in for.

'It was quite funny really, as the envelopes kept on coming. I remember one had torn-up bus tickets, another had a shopping list that had just two items on it: Lipstick and Kinder Eggs. Her little joke, I guess.'

(But the parents aren't laughing.)

'Then another had a torn-up promo photo of me, then another had a torn-up photo of me taped together, then a taped photo but in the wrong order. By now, I was thinking "stalker" and the lads kept an eye out, especially Danny who was worried Rosie had "gone rogue" as he put it – "looney-bin material" he reckoned…'

'Did you call the police?' This is Ma.

'Have 'er sectioned?' This is Pa.

'I didn't want to get her into trouble.'

'But surely it was obvious she *was* trouble?' says Ma.

Mickey shakes his head.

'I couldn't.'

Mother pours tea. Offers her son a Jaffa cake, his favourite. The father, first name Bill, lights up his pipe. Puffin' Billy.

'The envelope contents became weirder,' continues Mickey, thinking maybe he should hold back a bit, but he's in too deep now and anyway this is a sort of confessional. 'Dead insects, feathers, chicken bones. Spooky stuff. Danny called the cops and we showed them the envelopes but what could Dixon of Dock Green do? No proof, no evidence who sent the envelopes. Danny said to take fingerprints, but they said, "Wasting police time. Leave us to do proper copperin'." That's what the boys-in-blue said to us. So we left it at that. Then the envelopes stopped.'

Ma: 'Thank goodness for that. But you still want to *marry* this girl?'

Mickey sets her straight.

'Well, not "marry" exactly. Rosie says marriage is archaic so we're moving in together. I've bought a flat near the town centre. You must come visit when the sale is through.'

'She's just after yer money!' says Puffin' Billy. 'Greedy slag!'

'Language!' exclaims Ma.

'Harrumph!' goes Pa, disappearing behind a cloud of pipe smoke.

'Where'd Dad go?' jokes Mickey, but no one laughs.

What *doesn't* he tell his parents? What does he leave out? The threats, for instance, or what seemed like threats. By now, the touring is finished, done for. The band, The Police, have a new single out called 'Every Breath You Take' about the singer watching someone closely, and Rosie takes the words literally and posts each line to Mickey at his home address. There are thirty-five lines in the song, words about longing and losing, belonging and heartaches, and this accounts for the thirty-five post-it notes she sends, one a day, all signed 'Rosie' with a red X drawn in lipstick. These are the first missives that have actually been signed by her or acknowledged as being from her, so it's some kind of breakthrough. He tells his parents it's fan mail. Then the phone calls start…

'We've been getting these funny phone calls,' Ma says one day. 'Silence on the end of the line and I say "Hello, who's there?" and I swear I can hear breathing.'

'Probably just fans, too scared to speak…' says Mickey, but he knows who's calling. Sometimes in the early hours too. So he gets his parents an answerphone, but his mother can't get used to the contraption and picks up the phone anyway.

'Hello, who's there? Hello?'

'It's all in the past now,' says Mickey. 'She was going through a bad patch but now she's fine, as right as rain!'

Puffin' Billy has the last word though.

'A leopard don't change its spots.'

Cloud of smoke, and he's gone again.

But what Mickey *also* hasn't told them is what happens when he goes off to stay in a hotel, supposedly to write his autobiography in peace and quiet and seclusion. 'But you can get peace and quiet here,' Ma protests. 'Just close your bedroom door.' 'No, Ma. I need to get away. I've got a deadline to meet. The publisher's given me six months to complete.'

The working title of this opus is 'Mickey's Riffs' ('riffs' being the short melodic lines or phrases on the guitar) but it never gets completed, 'me bein' no bleedin' Hemingway', Mickey says. It never gets past page nineteen, in fact, but because RIL has gone into hibernation, he needs to do something to fill the time and maybe there's a market for a rock star bio.

Then Rosie tracks him down to the hotel – turns out she called at the house and Ma gave the game away. 'Such a nice young girl, shame about her hair though!' 'Bald as a coot!' says Pa. The next phase in her stalking is to send crates of booze to the hotel, c/o Mr M. Mills, Room Seventeen. Alcohol being verboten for Mickey though, so he donates it all to the hotel bar. Seven crates altogether, one a day, with different booze each time: lager one day, then beer, red wine, white wine etc. The hotel is grateful but suspicious of these deliveries. 'Fans!' explains Mickey.

But where else could these deliveries be coming from, if not from Rosie? A giveaway is the red lipstick 'X' on the cards that come with the crates. But how can she afford all this? Then Mickey remembers something from their rehab days – something about family money and Rosie being the offspring of double-barrelled parents, the surname of whom she's abandoned, changing her name by deed poll to Rosie Posie.

When the booze crates cease, Mickey is on tenterhooks as to what might be coming next and it's not long before he finds out. As he goes for his afternoon run ('gotta keep fit, can't sit writing all day') he becomes aware of a figure some way behind him, also running, and when he stops and looks around, the figure also stops, tying a shoelace or relieving cramp or stretching. If he goes towards the figure, who by build and posture is clearly female, she runs off in the opposite direction. He's sure it's Rosie and calls out to her, but she just stops still, hands on hips. Sometimes he tries to catch her out, turns a corner and waits, but some instinct must be guiding her because he ends up waiting a long time until he gives up and looks back around the corner. And there in the distance, she is standing, hands on hips.

Then. It happens one night. He's got back to his room after a puzzling exchange with the receptionist who asks if his wife found her room key? He points out he's not married, he's there on his own, and the receptionist shrugs and just says she must've got the wrong room number. Goes back to her gossip mag.

So he gets to his room, sniffs the air, something not quite right, but dismisses the thought and gets ready for bed. Sometime during the night, he is woken by the sound of snoring. Not from a neighbouring room but close by. The bed he is in is a mock four-poster with space underneath and as this seems to be where the snoring is coming from, he switches the light on and takes a gander underneath... to see a curled-up figure in a parka, curled up like a foetus, shaven-headed, fast asleep and snoring.

He can see the Bindi on her forehead, which belongs to the unmistakeably pretty face of Rosie. Under his bed. He gently nudges her, and she screams awake. Shh, it's okay, don't worry. She crawls out and stands shamefaced, and he hugs her.

They talk through the night, sitting side by side on the edge of the bed. They eat snacks from the fridge and the morning breakfast biscuits. They drink all the tea and coffee. She has given up alcohol too, so no booze. She tells him that she can't get him out of her head ('Like Kylie,' Mickey remarks – the only joke of the whole long night), and he says that he thinks of her a lot, which isn't quite the same thing. She was just trying to get his attention she says, but was too scared (of rejection) to approach him. She says how she was moved by his song about her – it was about me, wasn't it? Of course it was. She tells him of her name change to Rosie Posie. He thinks it's cute. She tells of shaving her head 'like a nun'. Do nuns shave their heads? She doesn't know; she thought they did, otherwise hair would show under their, what do you-call-'em? 'habits'? Mickey reckons 'wimples' but he doesn't know how he came by that info. Anyway, she says, it was her act of contrition for trying to stab him in rehab. 'You weren't in your right mind. Are you now?' 'I just want to be with you.' 'Me too.'

And with that, after their long night, as dawn comes up, they undress

224

and get into bed, and their newfound relationship is sealed.

I Should Be So Lucky

Rosie has hair down to her shoulders now. The Bindi is gone. She dresses softer too, more feminine. No more dungarees or parkas but wears dresses, yes, *actual* dresses, which make her look young. Colours and patterns too. No more blacks and greys. Her wide eyes look upon Mickey with adoration and he looks upon her with amazement – that he should be so lucky. He's living in a Kylie Minogue world of the future: from 'Can't Get You Out Of My Head' to 'I Should Be So Lucky'.

They will move in together once the purchase of the flat near the town centre goes through. They meet with Mickey's parents at a Steakhouse. Rosie, of course, is vegetarian, so sticks to salad. 'You need to eat more, dear,' says Ma. 'You're all skin-and-bone.' Mickey's ma, who is far from 'skin-and-bone' is, however, 'on a diet' she says, rather sanctimoniously, as she devours her Minute Steak – is it called 'Minute' because that's how long it takes to cook, or is it because it's small? Puffin' Billy likes his sirloin 'well-done', as he tells the sneering waiter, 'incinerated, son', and the waiter goes to tell the chef to find the worst portion of meat in the fridge. 'If it's bloody, it's undercooked,' Pa proclaims proudly. A man who knows his meat. Mickey respects Rosie's aversion and opts for tofu in lasagne form. It's disgusting – who invented tofu? – but he pretends you can't tell the difference.

Rosie is at her most feminine. She charms Pa and cosies up to Ma. 'I like your hair. Where do you get it done?' and, 'You must be so proud of your famous son!' 'We always thought Mickey'd do well,' Ma says, 'he was always so musical, we got him a little ukulele when he was five and he could pick out a tune straightaway!' Beaming, she is.

Pa: 'He's done good, the lad, altho' there ain't much moolah to show fer it.'

He still thinks Rosie is after his money ('bloody gold-digger!') and that she suspects there is more of it around than Mickey lets on, but he's warming to the lass and by the end of the meal he's getting quite hot, 'You mark my words, young lady, you won't do better than m' boy here!'

So that's the story of Mickey and Rosie. A happy ending.

And do they live happily ever after? Yes, they do. Rosie can't have kids, so they live in each other's pockets; they're one of those couples who're rarely apart – Mickey 'n' Rosie. Even though they never marry – Rosie is still anti-conformity – she changes her surname *again* by deed poll to his name and likes being called 'Mrs Mills'.

In the intervening years, before the band re-forms and goes on the road again and she takes over Aggie's former role as de-facto manager and gig-arranger, phoner-upper and money-taker, Rosie works in a library while Mickey works nights baking bread. Baking bread to make the bread, is how he refers to it. But that's another story...

37
9 to 5

And so the years go by as the band goes into hibernation, rarely making contact, barely keeping in touch.

They have jobs now, nine to five, as the touring money (or what was left of it after all the penalties and Joe's slice) has evaporated. Joe has moved on to other bands and, as the lads suspected, has had Jeeves move in with him; they are now officially a couple and happy together. Country mansion, fleet of cars, servants. Jeeves plays the role of squire, mixing with the huntin' 'n' fishin' fraternity, hobnobbing with the nobs. Jeeves gets on with everybody – it's that prison training. The posh-set adore his roughshod ways while the hoi-polloi recognise him as one of their own. He dresses in Harris Tweeds, wears spats, peaked cap (the expensive variety) and affects an odd mix of accents, somewhere between Streatham and Surrey.

Joe Rainbow is entranced by his partner. He takes on more bands and earns a fortune doing it. However, the good life gets to his belly, then his heart, and in his early fifties he dies. Massive heart attack brought on by cocaine overdose. Classic. Leaving Jeeves bereft but as rich as the veritable Croesus. As he grows older, living alone in the big house, Jeeves develops a penchant for rent boys, one of whom, instead of sniffing the 'popper' – the sex-enhancer amyl nitrate – takes it orally. Not to be recommended, in fact generally *verboten* in the drug-taking lexicon, 'sniff don't swallow' being the maxim. But this kid hasn't heard the lexicon or read the manifesto and dies accordingly. Jeeves, as supplier of the drug and 'more responsible adult', never mind the fact that the poor kid is only fifteen, is charged with manslaughter – *boy*slaughter it should be – and 'under-age sex', and is banged up in prison again with a long sentence. What goes around, comes around.

In prison, he's a target because of the 'kiddie-sex' label and, despite being segregated in the protected wing, is knifed in a lunch queue that he shouldn't have been in anyway, but the warders turn a blind eye and a deaf ear to his dying screams. This, indeed, is a sorry tale and not one that this history takes any pleasure in telling, but for the sake of truth and accuracy.

38

All Night Long

But back to the nine to five jobs. Or, in the case of Mickey, five to nine as his job is night-shift work starting at five p.m. when he has to get up, and finishing next morning at nine a.m. when he goes to bed – which is a backwards way of living, f'sure.

In these days of the mid-'80s, before the mass-market manufacture and supply of our daily bread by conglomerates with factories churning out loaf after plastic-wrapped loaf, there were still local bakeries that delivered your bread fresh-as-you-like after a night's baking. The local corner shop would hand you your bread, sometimes still warm, and if there is one pleasure in life, it is surely fresh-baked, still-warm bread. (However, you had to be up early to catch that first batch.)

So, working in a bakery, which is what Mickey is doing now, is a night job – a bit like security guards and prostitutes. After sleeping a good part of the day, Mickey gets up at teatime, has a cuppa, then cycles to the bakery to clock on at six p.m. along with the rest of the bleary-eyed crew, numbering four, who also spend their lives upside-down, who also don't get to see much of their wives and kids, but who get paid well for the punishing hours.

By the time Mickey gets home in the morning, Rosie has already left for her job, and on the table waiting for him is cereal and toast and a flask of tea and the newspaper which he'll fall asleep reading if he's not careful. Then earplugs in, eye-mask on, curtains drawn and try to ignore the everyday noises that threaten to keep him awake: the cheery chatter of passers-by (why do they have to *go on* about the weather?), the traffic (why do they keep blasting their horns?), milk bottles (why do they have to be glass?), whistling postmen (why so cheerful? shut-the-fuck-up!), barking dogs (he hates dogs!), squeaking brakes (lubricate the buggers!), squealing kids (he hates kids!) – they're all out to stop him sleeping so he dozes fitfully. Then, at midday (in effect, his midnight), he has a snack and watches TV. Then a final short doze from two till four.

No wonder he's going mental.

'But the money's good,' he says to Rosie.

'You mean, the *dough's* good!' says Rosie, who is not normally one for jokes.

The rest of the bakery crew are certifiable. Their topsy-turvy world does weird things to the mind, like a permanent jet lag. Their humour is warped, obscene of course, jokes delivered starey-eyed, deadpan, dead-eyed. They work like automatons at their baking tasks, oblivious to the heat from the ovens. They dress for winter in jumpers and thick trews. They don't sweat, even when the oven doors open and blast out heat, they don't sweat.

Boris is enormous. Built like an Orca whale. Worked there forever. 'Baker – born and bread!' he says. 'Geddit? "Bread"!' and they're all supposed to laugh. His great gut hangs over his jeans, leading his nose by a good eighteen inches. He scoffs doorstep sandwiches made by his mum, stuffed with hunks of cold beef and horseradish and yet... and yet... out of this bulk of flesh and internal plumbing, he emits the tiniest of farts – they're pipsqueaks of parps, *parp*squeaks! – raising one bum cheek or, if he's standing, one leg, and letting rip, saying, 'Thar she blows!' But it's hardly 'letting rip', this tiny trump. Mickey puts the pitch at a high C, but there's no one musical enough in this bunch of losers to argue the toss. Boris deals these 'bottom-blows' without a hint of embarrassment, and the rest of the crew bat not a droopy eyelid.

Finally, to draw a line under this unsavoury subject, it has to be noted that the farts mercifully have no smell. But anyway, how could they compete with the delicious aroma of newly-baked bread? – something Mickey would relish every night, were it not for the presence of rats and mice sharing the long mad-crazy night with them.

Another member of this baking fraternity is worth a mention. Brian sells pineapples. Imaginary ones, that is. 'Come and get yer juicy pineapples!' he shouts. No one knows, or cares really, whether Brian believes he has pineapples to sell. Such is the level of apathy in this lunatic asylum.

Finally, introducing baker number four, Donald 'Dogger' Dodds. Famed for his ventriloquist tricks.

He can 'throw his voice' so that it appears someone is trapped behind the sacks in the storeroom. 'Help! Lemme out!' goes the tiny voice, fooling

Mickey the first time he hears it, and he rushes into the storeroom, tearing sacks away and scaring the mice. Another trick this amateur 'vent' does is imitate a dog barking outside, 'Bloody dog!' he says, then barks some more. He does this act *every* night, and it never fails to fail as the other bakers sit blank-minded in their tea-breaks. Boris explains to Mickey in a rare lucid moment that that's how 'Dogger' got his nickname – 'imitating a dog,' he explains rather unnecessarily.

As to Dogger's supposed antipathy to the canine fraternity, he explains as follows:

'I've always had a thing about dogs. The racket they make, 'specially those little yappy ones. Can't keep their gobs shut. Cats, I like. A gentle purr, an occasional meow when they want food. Otherwise, shtum. While as for dogs... dogs are a different kettle of fish.'

So saith Dogger on the subject and having exhausted the topic he goes back to: 'Help! I'm trapped!'

One night, Mickey the Angry decides to get his revenge on the noise-makers, both human and animal, that interrupt his daily sleep. Giving the excuse of needing to get his asthma inhaler (he doesn't have one) for his asthma (he doesn't have it), he takes advantage of a half-hour tea break in the early hours to cycle home. Once there, he pedals at speed the whole length of the street, blowing his cycle horn and ululating like a police siren. Looking over his shoulder, he sees bedroom lights coming on and faces peering out of windows. He is satisfied. He has woken up the whole street and got his revenge.

'Was that you last night?' asks Rosie.
'Was that me what?' replies Mickey.
'That made all that noise at – God! two a.m. Woke me up as well as the whole bloody street!'
'I was at work.'
'Someone said they saw a chap on a bike.'
'Could've been anybody. Anyway, I was at work.'
She eyes him suspiciously.
'Well, don't do it again!'
Rumbled.

39
Art For Art's Sake

In the Red room, the occupants, encouraged to wear as much red clothing as possible, are playing Rolling Stones records like 'Street Fighting Man' and 'Sympathy For The Devil' full-blast. Some have smeared red lipstick over their faces like war paint, which is an apt allusion as they argue, shout, and rant at each other, stopping just short of actual violence. They play the Stones songs as loud as they're allowed, but they keep nudging the volume up, which disturbs...

... the Blue Room, where all around is dark blue and the mood is sombre, the occupants quiet. Morose. The music is Leonard Cohen – that 'Master of Blue Magic' as Tone calls him. The 'Sisters of Mercy' have not departed or gone; they sing to the blue people, sitting cross-legged on the floor, swaying slightly. The music really ought to be the Blues, 'Woke up one mornin',' etc, that kinda thing. But someone brought in Cohen albums, so Cohen it is. And the songs *are* beautiful...

... meanwhile, in the Yellow Room: *mayhem* reigns! Yellow – not mellow at all but the colour of madness. The colour of the plague when Galleons of Olde would fly a yellow flag to warn other seagoers of contagion. Or 'to tie a yellow ribbon' is the symbol of what? Hostage-taking? Prison release? Or is yellow the colour of a smiley sun? But the people ensconced in this environment are not sunny, far from it. It's fair to say they're hovering on hysteria, throwing yellow toilet paper around like crazy streamers and playing Ravi Shankar sitar music at 78rpm. They babble incessantly, as if on speed.

These three rooms/environments are a social experiment imposed by Tone on his 'lab rats', being the art students at the Technical College where he is now teaching. His art school background, plus his fame, has secured him this dream job teaching Art and Rebellion to impressionable ex-Sixth Formers.

His purpose, as he sees it, is to open their minds to Art with a capital 'A' and get them to think beyond the watercolour/charcoal methodology of school Art 'O' Level. Picasso, DADA, Duchamp, Matisse rather than, say, Constable. Or Turner, as opposed to Constable. 'Do you see the difference? Constable *represents* while Turner *feels*...' Also to go beyond the conventions of classic life-drawing – for instance, for one Life Class he's brought in apples, not an apple for the teacher in this case, but apples for the students. His instruction is to draw 'beyond the physical', to imagine themselves *inside* the apple. Well, before they can get their teeth into that concept, they, being starving students, get their teeth into the apples instead, until only chewed cores are left. 'Doesn't matter,' says Tone. 'Now the apple is inside *you!*'

Being students with immature minds, Tone knows he can get away with any ol' gobbledegook, and they will fall for it. Getting 'inside the apple', for instance, is something the students accept, and no one dares to question the absurd philosophy, even if there is any. 'Wow, he's so deep, our tutor!' 'Yeah man, soooo deep!'

One girl, who calls herself 'Moron IV', produces highly detailed miniature drawings of male genitalia. Intricate pencil portraits of penises she has presumably known and blown and committed to paper. Each picture four by four inches square. She calls it 'Cock Art'. The college governors get wind of this and try to shut her down or get her chucked out, but Tone counters with 'censorship' claims, so they let it go. But he does question Moron IV about the repetitive nature of her 'Cock Art', and she, in her defence, cites Monet and his twenty-five canvasses of the same two haystacks depicting the changing of light. 'It's the same with cocks,' she says boldly. 'All the same, but different.' And Tone can't argue with that. (Her series eventually becomes famous and each portrait sells for thousands of dollars, making her one rich moron.)

Generally though, he tells his students they can't 'draw for toffee'.

'You think you're good at drawing,' he says. 'Your teachers admired your efforts, your parents proud of their talented offspring. They'd say: "Oh, he's very artistic is Billy!" or "She's so good at getting a likeness!" or "They're like photographs, as good as!" but lads and lasses, you're

CRAP! Your drawing is stilted. You have to free up *the line.*'

Tone likes the fact he has long hair like his male students, who adopt a mode of dress, a sort of uniform, of donkey jacket, jeans and fisherman's jersey; while the girls wear baggy shirts or XXL tee-shirts with M&S cardigans draped over shoulders, but ass-tight jeans (well, you've got to have *some* pride in your appearance).

'Can you help me with my shading, Mr Johnston?' This is a blonde bombshell with big boobs who all the boys lust after and pester her to model for them but Sara is having none of it, being shy of her bosom and the attention it attracts. Tone has dropped the double-barrelled element of his surname – this is an egalitarian college; you don't put on no airs and graces. Politics is Labour bordering on Communist. The Tories are evil, and Liberals are wishy-washy. Most of the students want revolution, though they don't know what it is. 'WHADDA WE WANT? REV-O-LUTION! WHY DO WE WANT IT? HAVEN'T A FUCKIN' CLUE!' They like sitting on the floor in the canteen, ignoring chairs, a form of rebellion, one supposes, so Tone introduces some bentwood chairs into the studio and tells them to paint them. Literally. They adorn the chairs with complex patterns.

'Can you help me with my shading?' asks Sara, all flirty-like, but Tone is not falling for it. Never mind the absolute verboten rule of getting involved with your students – there's always Aggie to contend with. Ever-faithful Tone and all credit to him. Sara, after all, is quite a temptation. 'Didn't you used to be famous?' she asks in her posh, private-school voice, and he mentions Rock Ireland Line, who she's never heard of but, on prompting, remembers 'Beat, Beat, Beat' from some ancient history. He likes his fame, proud of it. Starts up a college band called 'The College Crew' and they hold occasional Friday night gigs in the gymnasium.

But back to the coloured rooms. The idea is to investigate the influence the primary colours – red, yellow, and blue – have on people if they are *immersed* in those colours, how it affects their moods. So, in three corners of the large studio, Tone has had his students create uni-colour room sets, each totally decorated in the colour prescribed. The walls and floor are papered or painted accordingly; objects of the chosen colour are brought in or painted – a stool, for instance or an old cabinet. Clothes have to be of the same colour, faces painted etc, so in each room, the occupants *live* that colour. And the results are wonderfully predictable – red: loud, aggressive; blue: quiet, melancholic; yellow: hysterical, crazy.

After a while, the students are encouraged to visit each other's rooms, so the colours get mixed but even then, once in any given room, they revert to type, i.e. the red people, in an all-blue environment, turn gloomy; blue people in red world become loud, and so on. Lab rats, conforming to the norm. We are all influenced by colours. The week's social experiment over, Tone gathers his flock together and explains:

'This is the power of the primals. But secondary colours don't have the same power; if you mix, say, yellow and blue, you get...?'

'Green,' one of them choruses.

'Green, exactly. Mild-mannered, down-to-earth green. Red and yellow makes sunny orange. Red and blue? Pleasant purple. These secondary colours are ordinary compared to the extremes of the primals.'

'What if we'd had White and Black rooms?'

'Again, just as predictable. White: clean, ascetic, cold. Probably playing Bach for the purity of vision and mathematical precision. And as for Black... well, we wouldn't dare go there, would we? No music at all, or funereal like Mahler. Or Heavy Metal.'

One evening, and gradually the students disappear one by one. Tone is busy perfecting a life drawing of a female nude in charcoal. The class occasionally are subjected to the horrors of Life Drawing; at their tender age they're embarrassed by the presence of a naked model, even if the models are always female (the thought of a male model!), never mind the moment when they have to draw the actual *tits*!

Tone (to a shy male student): 'Where's the nipple?'

Student points to a dot on the paper.

Tone: 'That's just a dot, a full point, that's not a nipple. The woman's got a nipple, not a dot!'

Student blushing horribly. Girl students sniggering.

So, this particular evening, Tone is working away when he realises

235

there's one person left in the studio and that is Sara. She's experimenting with colours. She stops, moves across to Tone and surveys the drawing.

'Not bad,' she says, 'especially the nipples.'

Tone is surprised at this normally shy girl's boldness.

'Er… thanks,' he replies, then goes back to his shading (keeping well away from the nipple area).

Sara steps back to admire, or scrutinise, the drawing from a distance, head leaning to one side, hand on chin.

'When I get to Art College,' she says, 'will I have to draw *male* models?'

'Of course.'

'Will they be completely nude, you know, with their… *businesses* on show?' (She hesitates over the word 'businesses'.)

'Often they'll wear a sort of jockstrap.'

'Why?'

'Modesty, I suppose. That's what happened in my Art College days. Mind you, that was… ooh… twenty years ago. Maybe they let it all hang out now.'

'Yuck!' exclaims Sara. 'I like the female form, with all the curves and smooth skin.' As she says this, she smooths her long hair coquettishly.

Tone, keen to change the subject, continues: 'Mind you, it was the '60s and our tutors liked to shock us out of our "middle-class suburban security blanket", as they liked to put it. They were all extremely radical, left-leaning, some Communist, very "right-on" individuals. They sat us down once and put on a *porn film*. I mean, not just soft-porn like those *Diary of a Milkman* films – remember those? no, of course you don't, before your time – no, this was hardcore: tits, bums, and all points in between!' (He realises that he hasn't succeeded in changing the subject at all.)

'What happened?'

'In the film, you mean?'

'No. What happened with the students? What did you all do?'

'Predictable. The girls walked out and the boys stayed, lapping it up.'

'Did the tutors think you'd learnt anything? Or been *taught* anything?'

'Well,' Tone laughs, 'for boys just out of Sixth Form, it was certainly an education!'

Sara stands, looking at the nude sketch, index finger in her mouth, toying with her lower lip.

'I'll pose for you, if you like.'

Tone is uncertain how to take this. Or maybe he isn't.

'What do you mean, Sara?'

'I'll pose for you.'

'What, now?'

'Now. I'll pose naked.'

Shocked. A line has been crossed. Tone recovers.

'Sara, that's against all the rules, you know that.'

'No one's around. Who's to know?'

'I'd be thrown out of college.'

Why he's even saying this, why he's not saying 'No!' immediately is beyond him. No, Sara, he should be saying, don't be crazy. Go home. Let's forget we ever talked about this. But instead, he's offering up a possibility... he'd be thrown out of college... if... IF...

'Anyway, it's not right, it's wrong. You're a student, a teenager, for chrissake!'

'I'm an adult.' Then she takes off her jumper and unzips her jeans, reaches behind and, eyes fixed on Tone, unclips her bra, then takes down her knickers and stands naked before her stunned art teacher. After all the touring years of temptation thrown his way, how could he let this go on? But she's so beguiling, and that body... art for art's sake, surely? Why not?

'Art for art's sake,' Sara says.

'Art for art's sake,' Tone repeats as Sara reclines on a sofa and he starts to draw, his mind in turmoil, never mind what's happening down below. But he draws fast, like on automatic pilot. And even then, he can't help his analytical mind assessing the subject before him. For all her beauty, she is top heavy. The breasts are ludicrously out of proportion to the slim legs and small frame. If da Vinci had drawn the Vitruvian *Woman,* he wouldn't have used Sara as a model.

'Finished,' he says.

'May I see?'

She stands so close to Tone, still naked, surveying the drawing.

'But you've made my boobs so small!'

'Artistic licence,' he tries to joke. Pathetic.

'May I keep it? For a kiss?'

He must be mad. But, thank God, all she does is peck him on the cheek, then calmly dresses. Rolls the drawing up. Then leaves, giving him one last look over her shoulder, 'See you tomorrow.'

He rushes home. Makes love to his wife – no, that's not accurate – not 'makes love' but *fucks*, hard and urgent! 'Where did that come from?' Aggie asks afterwards. But he doesn't say, of course he doesn't say; after all, nothing happened, and he thanks his lucky stars.

Next day, Sara acts as normal, and the boys continue to ogle her magnificent body. If they only knew…

There's one more story to tell about Sara and it's not a pretty one.

She's at a student party, and most of the people have left. It's gone midnight and she's quite drunk, sat on a couch between two guys from the same college who're on another course; she doesn't know what. She's feeling rather woozy and goes to get up to leave, but one of the guys holds her back.

'Don't go yet. Have another drink.'

'I have to go.' She tries to get up but is held back. 'Lemme go!'

'We don't want you to go, do we, Chas?'

Chas doesn't want her to go and puts his arm in front of her, barring her way.

'Tell you what,' says Chas, 'we'll let you go if you give us a snog.'

Now she struggles, kicks out, but then a third guy stands in front and holds her legs, 'Yeah, me too,' he slurs. 'I wanna snog.' He is swaying, braying, laughing, and drunk.

She fights now against all three of them, but she's pinned down. Chas is trying to snog her, slobbering-pissed, but she bites his lip. He reels back, bleeding, 'Bitch!' he cries.

'Tell you what,' says Chas's mate, realising that a snog may not be such a good idea after all. 'How about this? We'll let you go if you give us a feel of yer tits.'

She's outnumbered, she's already drawn blood, this could get even worse, so she acquiesces. 'Okay then, but only on the outside.' Chas's mate gropes her boobs while Chas holds her down, then the third guy, who's been holding her legs up to now, moves in for his turn. He tries to put his hand inside her jumper, but in letting go of her legs, she can now kick out; she catches his shin and he yelps and falls on Chas who lets go of her arms. Chas's mate manages to pull up her jumper and he snatches her bra down, revealing her bare breasts. 'BINGO!' he snorts. Now Sara is all flailing arms and legs and nails, and the boys have had enough; for their pains they've had their fun, and she escapes. Runs back to her digs, crying, furious, spitting mad, tells her flatmate who knows who the boys are. They plot revenge.

Never underestimate the power of a beautiful girl who's been wronged to find a few Sir Galahads to fight her corner. Never underestimate the power of two girls (Sara and her flatmate) to collude in the punishment of the party boys. In fact, it's four brave knights, one of whom is her flatmate's brother, who waylay the sofa guys as they come out of a pub, and the knights lay into them with ye olde knuckleduster and steel-toed boot, resulting in bashed-in bollocks, blackened eyes, busted knees. Unable to walk properly for a few weeks after A&E have patched them up – can't see properly either and to piss is agony. The standing guy, the third lad, who held her legs, is similarly given the Order of the Boot and Fist. He ends up in hospital, he's so badly beaten. And Sara, the Damsel in Distress, is content; all thanks to Sir Bashalot, Sir Kickshin, Sir Smashbone and Sir Kneeballs.

At the end of the A-level course, most of Tone's students get to Art College. He is proud of his success rate as a new bunch of 'can't draw for toffee' students arrive. He will never make the same mistake again. But then, he'll probably never meet the likes of Sara again. She gets into St Martin's in London, a top Art College. Gets a breast reduction on the NHS and is much happier. A weight lifted, literally. Ends up in advertising, as an art director, eventually becoming Head of Art in a big American-owned ad agency. Moves to Madison Avenue to the NY agency. Marries an American, has kids… but that's a whole other story.

40
Please Mr Postman

Another five to nine job, or thereabouts, involves Tank getting up ultra-early to deliver the post and clocking off at noon after filling in the remaining hours in the sorting office. It's a lonely job being a postie but fascinating for all of that. Wandering the quiet streets and watching the lights gradually come on as people get up to start their day. First, a bedroom light, then bathroom, then kitchen. Same pattern in every house in the winter months when it's dark till eight.

He's aware of dogs – what postie isn't? The curse of being a postman.

Rule One: never stuff your fingers into a letterbox – slavering jaws with sharp teeth may be lying in wait,

Rule Two: 'Beware of the Dog' on a gate means just that, so rattle the gate first to see if a bundle of fur and teeth comes rushing out,

Rule Three: if you hear a dog barking on the other side of the door – and as long as no one's looking – scrape the bottom of the door with your shoe to make the critter go bananas,

Rule Four: if you get bitten, get back to the Post Office Depot sharpish for treatment (you may even be entitled to compo),

Rule Five: like most diminutive beings (people, for instance), shortness is a sign of aggression, so small yappy dogs will nip at your ankles while the bigger dogs don't have to compensate – inferiority complex exists in mutts too,

Rule Six: if a dog rushes down the path as you go to open the gate, DON'T open the gate! Just walk on by and deliver tomorrow (if it happens all the time, consult your manager for advice),

Rule Seven: talking nicely to an aggressive dog won't help, shouting at an aggressive dog won't help, but having some doggie snack to chuck and lure said beast as far away as poss will usually do the trick –

preferably in the direction of a busy road (sorry, dog-lovers!).

Yes, dogs are the bane of a postman's life. Cats aren't. Cats usually like a stroke and will purr accordingly. Dogs snarl and bite. Tank encounters the same dam' dog every morning of his round but still the beast treats him as a stranger. He carries a water pistol, and if no one's watching...

Owner: 'Oo, Butch – is it raining outside?'

Before one morning's delivery, Tank's supervisor takes him to one side and hands him an envelope outlined in black. He says it is most likely a death announcement, especially as the address has been written in black and in an elegant hand. Tank is told to knock on the door and warn the recipient that this may be bad news. He dwells on this as he does his rounds, getting more apprehensive as he approaches the address. Should he tell the person to sit down? Should he be prepared for someone breaking down or collapsing? He approaches the front door, knocks; a middle-aged lady answers, 'Yes?'

'I'm afraid this may be bad news.'

'Omigod! Has someone died?'

'Do you want to sit down?'

'No, no, omigod!'

The woman rips the envelope open, reads the letter frantically, then sighs with relief.

'Oh, it's only Uncle Harold! Hang on...'

She gives Tank a £1 tip.

But this isn't the only benefit-in-kind Tank receives as a postie. In the lonely early mornings, he will often get to see a housewife *déshabillé* in her kitchen. And, it has to be said, in some cases, deliberately *déshabillé*. And Tank will find himself 'invited in' for a cup of tea, but not really for a cup of tea, as the *déshabillé* state quickly becomes *un-habillé*. This used to be the realm of milkmen, probably still is, but in the case of postmen these days it's unlikely, as their rounds are now more mid-morning time and *neighbours could be watching*. But in the mid-1980s, when Tank is a mailman, early morning deliveries mean in-the-dark.

They actually leave signs, some of these willing women, like a vase of flowers in the window. Knock, knock. Who's there? Your morning mail. Or is it 'male'?

Debbie, at number 42, answers the door in a transparent negligee.

Janice, of 'Mon Repos', has on a dressing gown, which she lets fall open.

Hugo, of 12A… well, he should be so lucky!

For the remainder of the day, Tank goes to a gym. Now, this isn't some fancy-pants club-type gym with treadmills and women-in-leotards and suchlike, but an all-male enclave that has a boxing ring and weights and punchbags. It's a gym of sweat and muscle. Tank, being built like one, wants to stay that way and turn his bulges into brawn. He also needs to build his strength up for the daily Debbies and Janices. So he joins 'BICEPS', and initially works the weights and punchbag and takes stock of the other men there. Some of the guys recognise him and word soon gets around and he becomes the celebrity of the establishment (this same celebrity status has also been the reason for all the Debbies and Janices, who all want to please Mr Postman).

'BICEPS' is housed in part of a warehouse, the other three-quarters of which is a mix of storage facilities. It's a one-storey building, all-metal, with girders for a ceiling and no windows. Fluorescent strip lighting hangs from the girders. It's as cold as hell but you soon warm up. In summer it's as hot as hell. Muscle and sweat. There's a bar, unlicensed of course, but who's going to tell? Some local bobbies are members and they turn a blind eye for a few 'on the house'. Posters on the walls are of boxing heroes and musclemen but also of wrestling legends like the famous TV wrestlers, Big Daddy, Giant Haystacks and Kendo Nagasaki.

Tank gets talking to a bruiser at the bar who leans over all confidential-like,

'A little birdie tol' me that you was once in a pop group – what-was-its-name?'

'I was in a *rock band*, not a pop group. There's a difference.'

'How's that, chief?'

'Rock bands play rock. Pop groups play pop. The Rolling Stones for instance – a hundred per cent rock band. You wouldn't call them a pop group.'

'What about them Beatles?'

'They're unique. They made the mould, writing their own material, giving up touring for recording. We gave up touring for different reasons.'

'So, what was your group – sorry, *band* – called?'

'Rock Ireland Line.'

'That were it! Rock Island Line!'

'Rock *Ireland* Line.'

'Yeah, what I said, Rock Island Line – after the song. Saw you on the telly. Bit heavier then, weren't you?'

'They say TV puts pounds on you.'

'More like pounds in yer pocket! You were the drummer, right?'

'Right.'

'Thought so. Said as much to me sparrin' partner, that you was once famous, on the telly and the like. I were nearly on the telly, y'know. Got *this* close…'

He mimes with his thumb and forefinger a tiny millimetre apart. Tank tries to place him.

'What? In a band?'

'Nah. Give you a clue: Seconds away. Round One.'

'Boxing?'

'Nah, not that wimpy sport with those big-girls'-blouses-gloves that're so padded they wouldn't hurt a fly.'

Tank would beg to differ, looking round at the posters of all-time Boxing greats: Muhammad Ali, Sonny Liston, Joe Frazier, Joe Louis et al, but his companion soldiers on.

'I'll give you another clue: two falls, two submissions, or a knockout.'

The penny drops.

'Wrestling?'

'Nail on the head, my friend. Nail on the head. The grapple game. I were billed as "Rocky Racoon" – after the song. I was all due to be signed up by the promotions company that handled the wrestlers who appeared on the telly. Ever watched it? *World of Sport* every Saturday teatime, professional wrestling with that Kent Walton fella doing the jabberin'?'

Did he ever watch it? Did he ever watch it, *indeed*? Tank was a big fan of this hour's worth of pugilism – tho' he hasn't watched it for years – with its heroes and villains and it was always the heroes that won. Who cares if it was meant to be 'fixed' according to the Sunday rags? It was dam' good entertainment over a cuppa and crumpet.

Rocky: 'I was what was known in the trade as a "Heel", meaning the bad guy, the villain, the one the audience loves to hate cos I'd break the rules, hit the man when he was down, even hit the referee sometimes! Me opponents was always a "Blue Eye", meaning the good guy, the handsome fella the women in the crowd'd lust after and cheer on. They were the worst, y'know, those women in the audience – who'd have thought they could be such *animals*? They'd scream and cuss like a trooper and they'd charge the ring and hit you with their handbags or worse, their high-heeled shoes! Try having one of them stiletto bastards drilling a hole in yer noggin – Christ, that smarts! Mebbe *that's* why the bad guys were called "Heels"!'

Rocky Racoon as was, but plain Reggie Jones as is now, laughs at his joke, one he's clearly made before, then slams his empty glass down on the bar top, which is a cue for a refill. Tank does the same and shoves a fiver across the counter. But the barman waves the money away. Rocky, and whoever's with him, don't have to pay for no drinks.

'One of a kind,' says the barman. 'If he could've got on the telly, he'd have been a star.'

Tank takes a moment to survey his drinking buddy, noting the cauliflower ears. Rocky sees him looking.

'They're murder,' he says, 'right bloody murder! Mick McManus – now *there's* a wrestling great!'

Tank remembers Mick McManus from the TV programme. A real tough nut, a Heel, known as 'the man you love to hate', but very popular nonetheless. Sported two magnificent cauliflower ears and hated having them attacked by his opponents. 'Not the ears, not the ears!' was his catchphrase.

'Because they're full of blood, y'see, and a blow to these lugholes is sheer bloody torture,' says Rocky, fingering one earlobe gingerly. 'They're like thick ears – like yer pa'd say, "I'll give you a thick ear, cowson!" and then whack you round the head. It hurts so much because that thickness is congealed blood, gone solid, like.'

'Is that what stopped you appearing on TV?' Tank asks. 'An injury, or what?'

'It were a bad bout. What's called a "shoot", meaning the real thing. Not some rehearsed-beforehand duck 'n' dive but a grudge fight that turned nasty. It were against a Blue Eye as usual, me being the Heel as I've said previous, but he were a mean bugger, not a good guy at all, in fact the most vicious piece of work you'd ever have the misfortune to meet in the ring – in the "groin" as it's known, and ain't that apt as that's where Mr Nice Guy aimed his boot! And when I were down, writhin' in agony, he grips me in a headlock, pulls me head right back, near dislocating me shoulder so I calls for submission, but he wouldn't stop, the bastard. The ref breaks the hold and I gets to me feet but instead of matey boy goin' back to his corner like he's meant to do, he charges and delivers a drop-kick to me right knee, dislocating the bugger and tearing a few ligaments into the bargain. I were out of action for months, had to have surgery and that put paid to me TV career as I couldn't wrestle after that. I teach it now, to young lads wanting to get into the game. Anyway, nice talkin' to you, gotta go, fish to fry!'

And off he goes, saying 'fish to fry' – which is quite accurate as he owns a fish 'n' chip shop.

Tank now turns his mind to the *World of Sport* wrestling programme on the telly which he would watch religiously every Saturday at four – a teatime treat for 'grappling fans' as the commentator put it. Apparently, the Queen watched it too. Kent Walton, the genial host with his relaxed Canadian drawl, sat ringside at a small table with his microphone and was often a target for wrestlers pitched over the ropes, to fall pell-mell onto the TV monitor, scattering notes and microphones and often poor old Kent himself.

Tank remembers the famous wrestler, Big Daddy, weighing in at thirty-five stone – real name Shirley Crabtree ('Shirley' being a man's name in 1930 when he was born). Big Daddy started off as a Heel when he tag-teamed with Giant Haystacks, then became a Blue Eye, entering the ring with cheers from the crowd, chanting his catchphrase, 'Easy, easy!'. Over his huge frame, he wore a white leotard that featured his name BIG DADDY writ large, and on his head he sported a sequinned Union Jack top hat. Tank recalls Big Daddy's signature move, 'The Splash', diving onto his floored opponent, full-body, full-weight, more of a crash than a splash, from which the winded recipient never got up.

Then there was Giant Haystacks, one-time tag-partner of Big Daddy but now his arch-rival, all forty-nine stone of him, looking like a wild man of the mountains in fur cloak, ragged dark hair, beard, and scowl. Haystacks used his massive six-foot-eleven body to slam any opponent, and when finally there was a grudge match between him and Big Daddy, it consisted of just three minutes of one body-slam after another, one catching the tiny ref and knocking him out, whereupon Daddy goes to help, only to be kicked by Haystacks, which now makes the crowd bay for his blood, SOCK IT TO EM it says on the back of Big Daddy's leotard, and so he does, pitching Haystacks over the ropes and onto a table incongruously covered with flower bouquets. 'Easy, easy!' chants Big Daddy as Giant Haystacks is counted out.

And how could you forget Kendo Nagasaki? The masked Samurai warrior whose real name was Peter Thornley, so not Japanese or Samurai at all but from Shropshire; who wore a striped red mask and carried a Samurai sword, scattering salt around the ring for some ceremonial reason. Kendo Nagasaki, as well as being a mystical figure and fanatical about any attempt to remove his mask, was known for his strength – in one match, lifting Big Daddy (at that time twenty-six stone) up onto his shoulders and then performing his 'Kamikaze Crash', winning the fight. Big Daddy eventually got his revenge in a subsequent bout, ripping Nagasaki's mask off and revealing a shaven tattooed head and strange-coloured eyes (thanks to tinted contact lenses). Tank remembers it well; he watched the match at a Butlin's Christmas gig, thrilled to witness this longed-for unmasking.

41
The Name Of The Game

The bartender sidles over.

'You that drummer as was?'

'Guess so.'

'With that rock band?'

'Guess so.'

'Wan' another drink?'

'Guess so.'

The bartender pulls another pint.

'Have to charge you for this one tho'.'

'Guess so.'

The conversation is going nowhere until the bartender, whose unlikely name is Silas, tries another subject.

'Say, what's your name again?'

'Tank.'

'Tank?'

'Tank. As in "armoured fighting vehicle powered by tracks".'

'Could be a good wrestling tag.'

'What do you mean?'

'Like, you have to have a memorable name in the wrestling game: Big Daddy, Giant Haystacks. Tank is a good moniker. Here, have this one on the house.'

Passes over the pint, refuses the proffered money, and then pours himself one too.

'Might as well keep you company. Any friend of Rocky's…'

'Cheers, er?' (Looking for a name badge).

'Silas.'

'Really?'

'Yeah, Baptist parents.' (As if that explains it.)

Silas takes a long pull of his pint, then smacks his lips with satisfaction.

'First of the day, can't beat it! You have the build, y'see,' says Silas.
'For what?'

'For wrestling. You seemed interested in what Rocky was sayin'…'

'Yeah, I was a fan of the grapple game, back in the day.'

But Tank is starting to think. Tank… that *does* sound like a good wrestling name. After all, he's halfway there already with 'Tank'. *Titanic* Tank maybe, could be. Then, what does 'Tank' rhyme with? (Apart from the obvious.) Plank. *Tank the Plank.* Like one of those wrestling moves, like a body splash, like the move Big Daddy was famous for: thirty-five stone of body crashing, *splashing*, down on his opponent – total wipe-out!

'Silas,' he says, 'I think I have seen the future.'

'Well, I'll drink to that!' says Silas. And he does.

The future:

Tank will train to be a wrestler and Rocky Racoon will train him.

He's already thought of his signature move, 'The Plank': holding his body flat like a plank to land on his opponent lengthways. He reckons it could work but needs to check with Rocky. And his signature move has given him the stage name: 'Tank the Plank'. He needs to put on muscle and brawn, that much is obvious. Get his muscle-weight up and flab down.

So Tank engages Rocky, who puts him on a high-protein diet, weight-lifting and hours spent in the ring learning how to fall, how to roll, how to turn a move to your advantage, how to get out of trouble.

'The Rules,' says Rocky. 'One: never underestimate your opponent's strength, he may be stronger than he looks. Two: don't assume your opponent will fight clean just because he's a Blue Eye. Three: if you're caught in a submission hold and it *fuckin' hurts*, SUBMIT before any permanent damage is done. Four: adopt your stage persona and stick to it. Don't confuse the audience; if you're a Heel, be a *bad* Heel. Five: create a signature move, or throw, that you'll get known by, i.e. Kamikaze Crash (DONE: The Plank). Six: keep away from the Ring Rats, they'll sap your strength.'

'Ring Rats' is the slang term for wrestling groupies, and as if Tank didn't have enough experience of groupies in his touring days, now there's a new sheriff in town – difference is these ain't young gals but mature women. One minute they'll be screaming for your blood from the ringside seats, next minute they'll be shagging the life out of you, 'Ooo Tank, give me your best moves!', 'Show us your plank!', 'How about a crotch-lift?' etc. These women may be crude but they're good-hearted and most are post-menopausal so no pregnancy worries. Tank is in his mid-thirties now so he's a toyboy to a lot of these Ring Rats, but with age comes experience and boy, do these women have that in spades!

After a year's training, Tank is ready for his first public bout. In his adopted role of Heel and in keeping with his name, Tank comes on dressed military-style like General Patton with a smart army tunic, fake medals, GI helmet, jodhpurs and boots. He holds a 'swagger stick' that he thrashes against his thigh. All of this extra clothing has to come off, of course, so the jodhpurs are 'velcro-ed' to take off easily, as is the tunic. He's chosen good music for his entrance – the theme tune to *633 Squadron,* a stirring bombastic piece that he struts along to.

His opponent for this very first fight is, naturally, a Blue Eye – a blonde Adonis, who actually *has* blue eyes and sports a fake tan and minuscule gold trunks (which are undergoing the Battle of the Bulge). It is in this fight that Tank makes a big mistake, misjudging a move and receiving a knee-drop to the base of the spine. An electric shock judders through his back and he loses by a technical knockout. He can't get up, has to be carried from the ring, and endures a month of physio before he can go back to fighting. Rocky berates him for his carelessness and, once recovered, makes him go through the same routine again and again. He won't make that mistake twice. Twice beaten, twice shy.

One of the Ring Rats – a particularly voluptuous lady of forty-odd – captures his attention. He notices her in the front row seats, always dressed in a fur coat. It's only when she appears at the door of his hotel room that he sees that nothing is under the fur coat. She becomes his manager eventually, arranging the matches, collecting the money (this is so like being 'on the road' again) and even accompanies him into the ring at the start of each bout, dressed, of course, in her fur coat.

The years go by. Years of 'two falls, two submissions or a knockout'. Of 'Six five-minute rounds' and 'Your second public warning'. Years of *633*

Squadron and being booed, heckled, and prodded by spectators. Of bouts of physio after bouts of gruelling punishment. How much can a body take? Well, a lot if you're of Tank's build.

He was conscious of being recognised, felt it might compromise his standing with the band if the outside world cottoned on to who he was. Appearing live in venues, though, he was pretty much disguised and even when he shed all the General Patton regalia, he wore his hair in a ponytail and had grown a Viva Zapata moustache. Some people thought they recognised him, but he'd quickly deny it, 'What? Me? A famous drummer? What would I be doing in this game if I was?'

The last match he ever fights is with his new tag partner, Hank the Yank, a.k.a. Henry from Huddersfield. They've assumed an American identity because of the Patton uniform. To wolf-whistles and cheers, Tank's manager strides into the ring, as always in her fur coat, but now she opens it to show off a stars-and-stripes bikini. More cheers and wolf-whistles. Tank and Hank, being Heels, will face a clean-cut blue-eyed duo, the Blondie Boys, who, in contrast to Tank and Hank's US uniforms, just come on in their tight trunks, showing off their toned physiques. The front row of the audience, being mostly women, find this rather titillating as the trunks also show off obscene bulges, but the rest of the crowd find the clean-cut duo not quite as thrilling as Tank and Hank, who strut around the ring discarding their velcro-ed outer layers like male strippers. Essential difference being this: Tank and Hank, in their stars-and-stripes leotards, are a spectacle, while the Blondie Boys just aren't.

The MC, in his sparkly suit, pulls the microphone down from the ceiling and intones in a weird, slow voice:

'Now it's tag-team time… twenty-minutes duration… two falls… two submissions… two knockouts… decides the winner… in the red corner… the two wrestling Romeos… the Blondie Boys… Billy and Bobby… and in the blue corner… those battling bruisers… Hank the Yank and… Tank the Plank!'

The referee does his usual shtick of checking soles of boots (for hidden weapons?), briefly explains the rules to both teams, then steps away as the bell goes for Round One. There now follow the usual opening moves of bodychecks and body-slams with a ringside announcer, who fancies himself as a Kent Walton, commentating:

'Hank is first in the ring with Billy from the Blondie Boys – and a body-slam sends Hank into the corner-post – he's caught his knee badly and Billy's spotted it and is going for it now – kicking that weak spot...'

Hank is now *crawling* across the ring, trying to tag his partner to take over, dragging his injured leg with Billy stomping on the stricken knee and the ref trying to pull him off; then Hank reaches the salvation of Tank's corner whereupon Tank *bulldozes* in, body-slamming *both* the Blondies – which is fair game as Bobby has entered the ring *illegally*, rules being that only two wrestlers from each team are allowed in the ring at the same time.

And so it goes. There's a glorious moment when all four wrestlers are exchanging blows *outside* the ring, earning them all public warnings from the ref but do the public care? no, they're too busy kicking and shoving the wrestlers, the women of the crowd baying for blood, loving every minute of it; this is what they pays their money for! Then, back in the ring, the normal round of forearm smashes, headlocks, throws and strangleholds, then Hank is tagged and... well, let the commentator take over:

'Hank's looking pretty dazed after that last devastating body-slam from Bobby – maybe his partner was a bit premature in tagging him back in – Bobby has Hank now in a full-nelson...'

(A full-nelson being a half-nelson but using *both* arms, executed from behind and putting immense pressure on the back of your opponent's neck – illegal in some amateur wrestling due to the possibility of serious injury.)

'... Hank is trying to tag his partner – who's straining at the leash to reach him – but Bobby's holding Hank back – straddling him like a horse – now he's on all fours – giddy-up there, cowboy!'

Two women have got up from their seats and are waving their fists by the edge of the ring, looking like they aim to enter it themselves, but some stewards lead them back to their seats. Their language is not becoming of a lady but these harridans could hardly be described as ladies. They sit back in their seats, still screaming and shaking their fists.

Meanwhile, poor beleaguered Hank is crawling inch by painful inch as the crowd urges him on, and his arm extends like Michelangelo's Hand of God to meet Tank's outstretched finger and Bingo! contact is made, and Tank *bounds* into the ring, body-slamming Bobby who crashes into Billy (who's now entered the ring) who falls like a falling tree, prostrate on the deck, which is Tank's cue to execute his signature move, The Plank, stretching himself vertically then, stiff as a board – as a plank – landing full-square onto Billy who is counted out, one… two… three and the bell goes.

Now, what should've happened is that Billy, albeit winded, would stagger up, helped by his partner, and the bout would continue. That's what should've happened. But Billy doesn't get up. Bobby, seeing this, rushes over, trying to revive his partner with a water bottle. One of the 'seconds' goes over too, cradling Billy's head. 'Are you okay? Are you okay?' Tank joins them; clearly something is wrong as the second is now pumping Billy's chest. The St John's Ambulance people arrive and Billy is put onto a stretcher. Members of the audience stand up to see better; the front-row seat ladies are excited – this is real drama! The MC quickly announces the next bout: there's a whole evening's entertainment ahead and, well, these things happen in wrestling, it's not kid's stuff, it's men fighting according to the Grecian tradition. You gotta expect a few bumps and bruises.

But Blondie Billy has more than a few bumps and bruises. He is in hospital in an induced coma because of swelling on the brain caused by trauma incurred during The Plank. Tank had landed square on Billy, as per, but had accidentally head-butted him and Billy's head, in direct contact with the canvas, had nowhere to go to lessen the force. He is on a ventilator and hooked up to the whole spaghetti junction of drips and feeds and tubes. Somewhere, underneath all those wires, is a wrecked body.

Tank goes to visit him and is horrified to find Billy's wife and kids there. He introduces himself to the wife – young, pretty, tiny – expecting a tirade of hatred and blame, 'Look what you did to my Billy, you monster. I thought you weren't meant to hurt each other, that's what Billy told me etc etc,' but she says nothing, just looks at him blankly. So Tank sympathises, tells her it was an accident, wrestling's not a kid's game, but she doesn't need to hear that, she knew the risks, never used to watch the fights, couldn't bear it. The kids are silent, just toddlers, not knowing how to react. The body in the bed doesn't even look like their daddy, so how can they react? 'Daddy's not very well,' she has said to them. 'He bumped his head. He'll soon be better.' They look at the bandaged head, the wires and tubes and the machines going beep, beep, their lights flashing, and they don't understand. Tank leaves, devastated, vowing never to enter a wrestling ring again. He stops at the nearest pub and gets pie-eyed.

After two weeks the swelling has gone down and Billy is taken out of the coma and seems as right as rain, the nurses say. 'Such a strong young lad,' they say, half-fancying him. He has no memory of the fight, which is a blessing, his last memory being before the actual bout when his wife wished him luck and kissed him on the doorstep. Tank is mighty relieved. If the big lad had died, well, he'd never have forgiven himself. 'Tank the Plank' seems trivial now – no, worse, the name and what it represents seems criminal. He calls Hank. Hank is okay, tag-teamed with another bruiser. Tank leaves the gym, leaves Rocky Racoon, puts all that behind him, and resolves to go back to being a postman.

But one good thing comes out of the situation. Present in the audience of that final match is Mickey. He'd known of Tank's new career, Tank'd kept in touch, and Mickey had gone to watch some of the fights, cheering his old bandmate along. So, Mickey sees the accident and tries to call Tank, but Tank never picks up. Goes round to his flat but no answer. Two weeks go by. Then, with Billy out of his coma and recovering, Tank answers his phone at last and tells Mickey the whole story, and Mickey hears the guilt. They meet in a pub.

This is a new Tank to Mickey. He's always been big, has Tank, but this muscular version is something of a revelation – one he's seen, it's true, from a distance at the bouts, but upfront and close, it's like sitting next to a giant (not helped by Mickey being a short-arse, anyway).

They talk, they reminisce, they sit in silence. Mickey with his untouched lager-top, Tank with his barely-touched beer. When they do talk though, Mickey is a good listener and Tank pours his heart out, and Mickey responds kindly, in kind.

'It's all in the game tho', ain't it? That's what wrestlin' is.'

'It's not a game. Not when you hurt a fella like that. He could've died.'

'He knew the risks.'

253

Mickey has come along with an agenda. It's now the early '90s, and he feels that maybe Rock Ireland Line ain't finished yet, not by a long chalk. Maybe RIL has done enough hibernating. Maybe it's time to come in from the cold. Re-form. Play clubs, small venues, whoever'll take a comeback band. They still have fans, Tone has said, as Aggie handles the fan club. The letters and emails ask, 'Will they ever get back together?' Never say never, is Aggie's standard reply.

And surprisingly, given Tank's current frame of mind, he is receptive to the idea. Maybe it's the crutch he needs, that close camaraderie, as he now feels so lost. He listens and nods, says he'll think about it, but in truth he's already decided yes. Has Mickey approached Tone or Danny? No, you're the first. Which makes Tank feel good. He takes a pull of his beer, then downs the rest in one. Mickey goes to get another, and when he returns, Tank has questions. Does Mickey know what Tone's up to? He teaches art. What about Danny Boy? Went back to Ireland, back to Dublin, but Tone, ever-efficient Tone, will have his address.

When Mickey gets home, he puts it to Rosie: what if the band re-forms? What if he gives up his bakery job? How will they manage? Rosie says she'll just work longer hours at the library. 'Are you sure?' asks Mickey. 'I didn't fall for no baker,' she says.

Next day, Tank gets his drum kit out of storage and sets it up in his flat. His neighbours are in for a shock as the first cymbal crash heralds in a new era of almost constant practice. They complain, so Tank keeps to daylight hours, when most are at work. At night, he practises on cardboard boxes. 'It's just like getting back on a bike,' he thinks. You never forget. The muscles that had got used to wrestling now adapt, and sitting at his drum kit loosens up his tummy and he gets his paunch back. 'Hello, old friend,' he says. But the muscles in his arms, built up with all those wrestling holds, now make for powerful drumming.

Mickey picks up his guitar for the first time in years. The tips of his fingers have softened with non-use but soon harden with the steel strings of his acoustic. When he finally plugs in his electric guitar, it all comes back. The first fast riff flows along the fretboard, and Rosie smiles.

She didn't fall for no baker.

42
Mother

While little may be documented of the various parents of the members of RIL, be they middle-class like Mickey's folks or more lah-dee-dah like Tone's, there is one parent who deserves some attention, or at least some recognition, in this history, and that is Danny Boy's mother.

Before the world welcomed the squawking Daniel Patrick O'Shea into its presence, his mother had spent most of her adult, or in fact, not to put too fine a point on it, most of her *teenage* years, as a high-class prostitute. 'Courtesan' would've been the old-fashioned word. Colleen, especially in her teenage years, was a beauty. Dark hair, soulful eyes (they say that, don't they? 'Soulful'. Well, they were really just dark eyes, not giving anything away, but they were big and set wide apart, and that is ever the attraction). Her figure was generous, as indeed was her nature. Her voice, despite her young years, was deep but softly spoken, with a gentle Irish lilt. She knew how to flatter men, look into their eyes with her own eyelids slightly lowered in mock deference. She would lay a delicate hand on a male shoulder or arm, and the recipient would usually fall hook, line and sinker. Or rather, *hooker*, line and sinker. She would pout, preen, praise and pander.

Colleen was no common streetwalker. She would accept gifts of jewellery, say, rather than hard cash. Or men would *loan* her money, to help her aged mother, she might say. She mixed with the male powers-that-be of Dublin society of the late 1940s (she, being aged sixteen, but looking twenty) like some gilded prize. She would attend receptions, parties, dinners, functions – always on the arm of some dignitary (because these affairs were closed to the wives), always looking sophisticated. But those-in-the-know knew she was for hire. Known to the Garda, she was well-in with the official hierarchy, so was safe from prosecution or persecution. Indeed, some of her clients were high-ranking officers.

They say, don't they, that if you enjoy your work, then you're usually good at it. It doesn't take a mile to smile, her dear mama would say. Grin and bear it, her dear papa would say, as he climbed into ten-year-old Colleen's bed. Until she told her mama of 'their little secret' and Mama threw Papa out, saying she'd report him to the Garda if he came near the house or his daughter again. Last seen in a betting shop in Grafton Street, drunk out of his skull, then thrown into the gutter for trying to smash a TV screen when his horse didn't come in. Kicked in the kidneys for good measure. Then died of internal bleeding in some godforsaken A&E. When Colleen heard about it, she just shrugged and said the bastard got what he deserved. But her mother was bereft with grief. There's no figuring human nature.

So when they say that if you enjoy your work etc etc, they could've been talking about Colleen who really did enjoy the physical side of love-making, no matter how repulsive the partner. 'If the boyo's got a cock that stands up, I don't give a monkey's as to what's at t'other end,' she'd say to her girlfriends, then she'd giggle coquettishly, as if embarrassed at her crudeness. Her clients would come away not only satisfied (that part was easy) but also happy, and naturally they became regulars. Her little black book could bring down governments and the judiciary, along with TV personalities, anyone who was anyone: a judge who liked to be spanked, a quiz show presenter who dressed as a woman. Colleen would never make her clients wear a condom as she considered it impolite. Like putting on a plastic mac to go swimming, she'd say. So she used a cap for herself, not being a practising RC, and as to venereal infections? she was lucky. After all, her clients were respectable, so infection-free. They had wives to consider and try explaining away a dose of the clap to your nearest and dearest. 'Toilet seats' just don't swing it.

Colleen considered it part of her calling to indulge every whim of her customers, and after all, the kinkier the whim, the bigger the bangle, she'd say. If they wanted to dress in an oversize nappy with a dummy in their mouth then suck on her tits, then so be it – 'I'll be Mummy,' she'd say. The customer is always right, no matter how wrong, was her maxim. If they want to be ridden like a horse on all-fours with her dressed in jodhpurs snapping their behind with a riding crop, then Tally-Ho! If they wanted to be punished for being a naughty boy, then Matron Colleen, or Headmistress Colleen, would oblige with a 'bend over and six of the best!' Or she'd play Sadie the Sadist. Grist to the mill. And even though she'd find the practices hilarious – what fools men are! – she would put on a straight face because men *do not* like to be laughed at. She learnt that early on. She'd tried laughing at her father once and got a black eye for her trouble. 'Walked into a door she did, clumsy gal,' lied her papa.

Straight sex was rare. That was for the up-against-the-wall streetwalkers. Wham-bam-in-the-alley. Colleen didn't have a pimp, but she had a 'business manager' as she called the job, more like an agent, who made the bookings and handled the finances. This manager was a woman, a few years older than Colleen, a housewife and a mother and a dam' good manager – 'You're my *wo*manager!' Colleen would joke. They made a heap of money, Mrs O'Brien taking her twenty per cent, and Colleen declaring a portion for tax purposes, citing her job as 'Professional Hostess'.

She only ever had one problem client, a new one introduced by a regular, who turned out to be a sadist rather than a masochist. In other words, rather than being happy to be on the receiving end of punishment, he preferred dishing it out. Turned out he was a judge. Anyway, he started slapping Colleen around – he was wearing his judge's wig at the time, but otherwise was a fat flabby thar-she-blows naked blubber whale – harder and harder he slapped her until she reached underneath her pillow, where she always kept a flick-knife which she plunged into his thigh, luckily missing the main artery, otherwise the blood would've been like Niagree Falls. Judge Blubber wailed and screamed and high-tailed it out there, clutching a towel to his wound, running out into the street, stark-bollock naked with his clothes underneath his arm, leaving his judge's wig behind as a souvenir, which Colleen decorously draped over the lavatory cistern. Of course he didn't report it and anyway it looked worse than it was, once a large plaster had stemmed the blood flow.

However, with the knowledge that Judge Blubber had friends in high places and fearful of repercussions, Colleen booked a round-the-world cruise: South America, the Suez Canal, and various points North. For the first time in her life, she was free; she could afford it, and she relished the break. A cabin with a balcony so she could have the sea all to herself and no one to ogle her as she lounged in her dressing-gown, sometimes without her dressing-gown, feet up on the balcony rail. By now, she was age twenty.

Dressing for dinner was fun, as she knew she was being admired every time she went down in the evening to the shared table – shared with couples, some single older ladies. On board were many eligible young males, for some reason accompanying their mothers, and she made merry for a while, picking them off, shocking the mothers, until she became acquainted one evening, over 'dirty Martinis', with a businessman from England, a decade older than her, clearly well-off. Turns out he had a factory in the Midlands making boots and shoes – 'People'll always need something on their feet,' he'd say. 'We weren't designed to go barefoot,' he'd say, and she'd laugh prettily; and soon she would enrapture this smart man who was a Good Catch – she could tell from the envious glances from other unattached females on the ship. 'And maybe it's time I netted a good catch,' she thought.

His name was Unwin, and his factory was called 'Unwin's Boots and Shoes'. The advertising slogan – he was proud of this – was 'Happy Feet Win With Unwin's!' He delighted in telling her this, and she delighted (or pretended to) in hearing it – 'So clever!' she said, laughing prettily. Then he drew a foot on his napkin with a smiley face – 'That's our logo,' he said, 'meaning our brand symbol. A happy foot!'

Terrence Unwin was easy to seduce. Colleen set about 'fascinating' him. An example: one evening there was to be a 'Black and White Ball', idea being the passengers were required to dress in variations of black and white. Simple enough for the men, as all their evening clothes were variations of these shades – a white tuxedo, black trousers, black bowtie and so on. Ladies would conjure up a black sparkly evening dress, say, with a white chiffon scarf, that kind of thing. Monochromia, Colleen called it. But never one to follow the crowd, she diversified. She covered her face, arms, hands and what was visible of her chest (which, being Colleen, was *a lot*) with *black* stage make-up which she borrowed from the entertainment crew. In the 1950s this wasn't seen as racist, it was just upholding a music-hall tradition of 'blacking up' like Al Jolson.

So there was Colleen resplendent as a blacked-up siren with fiery red lipstick and wearing a white ballgown with long white gloves. She looked like a bride. A black bride. The shock of the other passengers, in their traditional evening wear, was palpable, but Terrence was fascinated. That night they consummated their relationship, with Colleen pretending she didn't know *quite* so much about the act of love – the act of *fucking* – but still Terrence ended up with black make-up all over his body.

From then on, for the rest of the cruise, they were inseparable, arranging their own table-for-two, but nevertheless courted by the Captain and his officers to join them at *their* table as this couple were a cut-above, both in terms of obvious wealth (on Terrence's part) and style on Colleen's. Also because T. Unwin Esq., owner and proprietor of Unwin Boots and Shoes, was a witty raconteur and as for Colleen? well, she was just *fascinating*. Flirty with the men, gossipy with the women.

They disembarked as a couple, to Ireland first, then eventually moving to the Midlands where they set up home. A mansion in the countryside outside Northampton. They never married, never got around to it, or maybe Colleen was wary of tying the knot. 'Let a man still think he has his freedom,' was her maxim.

Daniel Patrick O'Shea was conceived on the cruise – Colleen getting confused about her contraception. The year, 1952. Danny was born in Ireland – Colleeen having moved back there to have her baby, with Unwin in tow. The boy took his mother's name, proud to be Irish; Terrence had to accept that, he had no choice really. For a while, they adopted 'Unwin' as a middle name, but Danny Boy dropped it in later life. Terrence had offered marriage, but Colleen had prevaricated. Which was a mistake. Because when Terrence died suddenly of a stroke, when Danny was just in his early teens, the business and the money went to relatives, none to Colleen and the boy.

But the family were kind; they liked Colleen – everyone liked Colleen – and they let her and Danny stay in a wing of the house, and they let out the rest to business corporations for their meet 'n' greets and staff-training sessions. Danny was due to move on to Technical College to finish his exams, so it made sense for them to stay in the Midlands. Anyway, life in the mansion, albeit confined to one wing, was pleasant enough.

Technical College is where Danny meets Mickey. Despite Danny being younger than Mickey, they are on the same technical drawing course which requires them to draw plans with rulers and ink pens. It's tedious work and the ink pens blot and the perspectives look all wrong, so instead they skip classes and indulge their mutual love of rock music, sitting in Mickey's bedroom on his bed – Mickey with his acoustic guitar and Danny playing 'harp' (the colloquial word for the harmonica). They try to write doo-wop songs and fail. They try to write Dylan-esque songs and fail. But they play Dylan songs, and Danny discovers he has quite an okay voice, and Mickey finds he's quite an okay guitarist. The rest, as they say, is…

Meanwhile, undaunted as ever, Colleen has hooked up with a French dude over on business, called Jean-Baptiste, who she quickly marries (she wasn't gonna make the same mistake again) and he whisks her off to his chateau in the Dordogne, leaving Danny to fend for himself until Terrence's 'rellies' join forces and chuck him out of the wing, saying they need to extend the business facilities.

So he goes to stay with Mickey and his folks, who night after night have to put up with 'Blowin' In The Wind' and 'Hey, Mr Tambourine Man' and, worse, some self-penned horrors, played and sung at full vol upstairs while they're trying to watch *Emergency Ward 10*.

Were there to be one of those 'So-and-so Lived Here' blue plaques on the wall of Mickey's home, it would read: ROCK IRELAND LINE (ROCK BAND) STARTED HERE 1967-2019, because it is in this very house, nay, this very bedroom, that Danny Boy, self-proclaimed Leader of the Pack, puts it to Mickey that, hey, they should start a band.

'We'll be like The Beatles,' he says. 'A band of four, so we'll need a drummer and a bass player…'

'But,' says Mickey, 'most bands have *two* guitar players besides the bass. They have a rhythm and a lead guitar.'

'Well,' says Danny, 'unless I can learn a few chords, you'll just have to do both.'

Which is how Mickey learns to do both, mixing chords with solo riffs because Danny never does learn more than a few chords, sticking to harp and tambourine. Danny's dream of a band finally comes to fruition a few years on when Mickey gets his first electric guitar.

Rock Ireland Line. 1967-2019.

43
The Leader Of The Pack

Danny is back in Dublin. He has visited his family – Ma Colleen (now in her fifties but looking thirty) and his stepdad, or step-*père,* Jean-Baptiste. They had eventually left the Dordogne Chateau when Jean-Baptiste's wine export business went down the Swanee, and they moved back to Ireland, living in a more modest two-up, two-down, taking their new daughter with them – now age twenty-two but still an ardent fan of her once-famous stepbrother, demanding autographs soon as he stepped through the front door.

He is sitting supping Guinness in the John Mulligan pub ('Mulligan's') in Poolbeg Street, wondering what to do with his thirty-three-year-old life now that RIL is AWOL. He misses his fellow band-members. Misses Mickey's jokes like: 'Knock, knock! Who's there? The Doors!' (you have to know your rock groups to get that one). He misses Tone's lugubriousness (is that a word? he wonders, 'lugubriousness'? or should it be 'lugubriosity'?). He settles on 'glum'. Misses Tank especially, his LA companion.

Danny is one quarter of a whole, so he doesn't really feel whole any more. He calls them from time to time but it ain't the same: 'How's baking going, Mickey? Earning an honest crust, haha?'. 'Hey Tone. Discovered any budding Picasso's?'. 'Tank, ol' fella, how's the grapple game going?' One for all, all for one, like them Musketeers.

He has some money saved up, enough to keep him *in* mischief, he tells the bartender, who doesn't get the joke. 'Didn't you used to be in a band?' he asks instead. They all ask that. He hates the 'used to be'. 'I still am,' he answers, but the barman has gone off to serve another customer.

Danny is here to meet a mucker of his from the old days, an Irish boyo he knows from his childhood, before he was taken 'across the water'. Sean is a 'culchie', from the countryside, while Danny is a 'true

Dub', a Dublin boy; and here Sean is now, bursting through the pub doors crying out, 'DANNY BOY, YOU *BEAUTY!*'

And Danny Boy *is* a beauty, takes after his ma, sat there in his tight-fit black suit, narrow lapels, black polo neck, black hair slicked back from his forehead and behind his ears, probably to show off the ear-piercings. While Sean is *not* a beauty unless you like purple. Because Sean, bouncing into Mulligan's, and attracting a few stares, or *glares* more like, from the customers, is rigged out like a Beau Brummell dandy with a bit of pirate thrown in. This fopster dares to go around, *in broad daylight,* through the thoroughfares of Dublin's fair city, decked out in decorous fashion.

To paint a picture:

1) travelling in a southerly direction from the northernmost point, the hair is the first port-of-call; it is in mullet-style, which is short at front and sides but long at the back. Never an attractive look but one that was à la mode back in the 1970s and sported by the likes of David Bowie, Rod Stewart, Keith Richards, and Paul McCartney, and still around at this time,

2) the face is made-up with eyeliner and mascara – and as if the clothes aren't enough to enrage the customers of Mulligan's, a man wearing *make-up* really takes the biscuit,

3) a silk frilly 'fop shirt' is semi-covered by a purple military tunic, straight out of the Dragoons, with gold braid across the front and worn draped over the shoulders,

4) trousers are tight-fitting Regency-style in light-coloured fabric, showing more than they should of what lies beneath; these are tucked into…

5) … black leather Highwayman's boots with heels to elevate the wearer by a good coupla inches.

Sean carries all this off with a careless air, like he couldn't care less what people think, because he is a *New Romantic*.

'What the fuck?' is the first thing Danny says in greeting his old buddy.

'What do you think you fuckin' look like?' is the second thing Danny says.

'I'll have a pint of Guinness and a Manikin cigar,' says Sean, sitting himself down at the bar beside Danny and hitching up his trews to prevent creasing.

'They're moleskin, y'see,' he explains, as if moleskin was a rare commodity (not that they're made of moles' skins anyway). 'Pricey,' he points out. 'All the New Romantics are wearing 'em!'

'I assume,' says Danny, 'that by "New Romantics", and by the way you're dressed, that you are referring to the New Romantic movement in popular music – oh, and buy your own fuckin' cigar!'

'Correctamondo, my friend. Not only have I adopted the Romantic look hook-line-and-sinkerooney but I have my own New Romantic band called "The Dandy Dimonts" and, in keeping with said movement, this is the way we all dress; and as to why I'm dressed in this enviable fashion at this very moment in time is because the next stop on my onward journey after our little tête-à-tête – (pronounces it 'tate-ah-tate') – is a gig this very evening, which is an hour's drive away and I am being picked up by my horse-and-carriage to convey me there; and as to the Manikin cigar, don't be such a tight-fisted bastard, you're a famous rock star and can afford it while I'm not and can't!' All this without drawing breath, which Sean does now, extravagantly. Then he slaps Danny on the back, all matey-like but with considerable force.

'But the New Romantics went out with the ark,' says Danny, recovering from the choking fit brought on by trying to drink at the same time as being delivered the power-slap by Sean because Sean is a big fella and a slap from him is a serious slap. 'In Rock Ireland Line we never followed trends. We ignored Punk and, as we predicted, it had all but disappeared in a moment. We never dressed up and we never changed our music neither. We ploughed our own furrow, Sean, and what's more, let me inform you, speaking from experience and as one who's been through the mill, you're behind the times, boyo! The New Romantic groups, as was, have now moved on. Duran Duran wear sharp suits, as do Roxy Music. Bowie looks cool now – mind you, did he ever otherwise? Boy George has his own eclectic style. So why are you clinging on to something that's old hat?'

'It may be old-hat in trendy London, Danny Boy, but there are clubs here in Dublin and around-abouts that fair lap it up. The ladies especially – suckers for a spot of good old-fashioned romance! Like the gig this evening – hey, why don't you come along? Come and see us: The Dandy Dimonts. Appearing Tonight!'

'What's with the name? What's "Dimonts"?'

'Actually, it's a breed of dog, the Dandie Dinmont – D-A-N-D-I-E, D-I-N-M-O-N-T – Scottish as it happens. Pesky little buggers. Some sort of terrier. Spelt different, but we like the way "Dimonts" sounds like "Diamonds".'

'So why don't you call yourselves The Dandy Diamonds?'

'Good question, and one I have no answer for, as I didn't choose the name. Our singer, Cat – we call her "Crazy Cat" – she chose the name.'

'A *girl* singer?'

'Yeah, she looks so fuckin' cool – shaves her hair on either side of her head, piercings like you wouldn't believe, wears a pink tutu.'

'Fuckin' hell! Maybe I'll come along, maybe give you the benefit of my…' but he doesn't finish as Sean interrupts.

'Great! The club's called "The Blitz", after that Covent Garden wine bar that ran a "Club for Heroes". Did you ever play there?'

'We didn't do the clubs. We were too busy touring, I guess. Then we stopped.'

'Yeah, that's right. You stopped, all of a sudden. Why was that?'

But Danny can't bear to tell.

'We just stopped. Got pissed off.'

'You still together? As a band, I mean?'

'Well, we're not apart, as such, but we're going our separate ways at the moment.'

'I loved your band. "Beat, Beat" was a great track.'

'It wasn't bad.'

'Not bad? It was fuckin' great! The bee's bollocks! Actually, we do our own version of it, hope you don't mind, different words o' course and a different "sound-profile" as we call it. Dandy Dimonts is into "synthpop" in a big way. We have two synths. I play one, Mad Matty plays the other. Then there's Conor the Cunt on bass guitar – we have these wild nicknames, I'm Shagger Sean, for obvious reasons!'

Sean winks and taps the side of his nose – 'Know-what-I-mean?'

But Danny is not amused and is wincing.

'Synthpop? What, like Kraftwerk?'

'Yeah, something like. Kraftwerk was our inspiration. And Gary Numan. Didn't you just love "Cars"?'

'Yeah, "Cars" was good.'

'And Adam and the Ants, and Spandau Ballet, surely?'

'Yeah, they're all good,' admits Danny, 'Kraftwerk, especially. I liked Ultravox's "Vienna". It was, like, *symphonic*, y'know?'

Sean hums part of the song, sings some of the words about meaning nothing to me, then he goes silent, sort of reverential-like at the magnificence of that ground-breaking track.

'Ground-breaking, that's what '"Vienna" was. It sure meant something to *me*! Listen, I'm getting picked up in half an hour. Why don't we have another pint, then we'll piss off to The Blitz and then you'll really hear "symphonic". It's what The Dandy Dimonts do best. Those synths, why, they sound like whole *orchestras*, they'll blow your mind!'

'So what happened to drum, bass and guitar?'

'Well, my friend, talk about "going out with the ark"!'

Danny sighs, suddenly feeling old and 'past it'. The world has moved on, as it's wont to do, and it's moved on without him. Drums, bass and guitar, I ask you! Versus a glorified electric piano that sounds like a full orchestra. But the discussion is curtailed as two labourer-types have entered the pub and are giving Sean hostile looks.

'Time to hit the road, Jack,' says Danny, and they exit stage-left without their extra pints and walk around the block until their ride arrives. No horse-and-carriage this, but a beat-up fucked-up rust-bucket of a Ford Escort driven by a maniac.

The Blitz is a seedy joint in a backstreet in Drogheda, which is an hour's drive up the M1 if you're a normal driver and half an hour if you're a maniac. The Blitz looks like it's been the victim, indeed, of the Blitz. Ramshackle, dusty, broken furniture, holes in the walls, plaster falling off, damp coming in, an air of siege about the building. It's dark inside apart from orange-shaded lamps on upturned beer barrels which serve as tables. The lamps are empty Mateus Rosé bottles that one time must've held candles as wax has dripped down and solidified. A one-armed bandit in a corner provides some extra illumination as it flashes and pings. A fag machine is empty of wares. A jukebox is not plugged in, there's no plug anyway. It's fair to say that the Blitz has seen better days and better nights too.

By the time Danny and Sean arrive, it's gone six, and a panel in the front door slides back in response to their knocking. An unseen character challenges them, 'What do you want?' Sean utters the immortal phrase: 'We're with the band.' 'What band?' is the reply. 'The band that's playin' here tonight.' 'Well, get your arse in 'ere then.' Panel slid back, various locks and bolts, then the door creaks open and a man-mountain in a white tuxedo jacket and, bizarrely, spangly pink hotpants beckons them in and slams the door shut.

'The Garda,' he explains, 'got their beady eyes on us for drug-dealing, so they say. As if...'

He sniffs in that cocaine-way. As if indeed...

Danny whispers to Sean.

'What's with the hotpants?'

'Don't ask.'

So he doesn't.

They wait. Danny and Sean. A roadie arrives with amps and the synths, plugs them in, job done. Sean tries a synth out, adjusts the volume, sits down. Conor the Cunt turns up, takes his bass guitar out of its case, plugs it in, tries a few notes, adjusts the volume, goes off to change into his New Romantic gear (he will be a Highwayman tonight). Mad Matty shuffles in, tries out his synth, and turns the volume up. Once Matty's gone off for a pee, Sean turns the volume up on *his* synth, not to be outdone. Matty returns and takes his coat off. Matty is a gypsy king with spotted scarf and waistcoat.

They wait. Where is Crazy Cat? They start to panic, phone her home but no reply. They panic more. Starting in an hour. They usually use this hour to do a run-through, but no Cat so no run-through. A half-hour has gone by. Sean looks at Danny. Could he step in?

'Don't be ridiculous,' says Danny, 'anyway, I don't know your material.'

'Yes, you do, we cover songs, you'll know them – one of them's yours for fucks sake!' Sean lists a few songs.

'But I don't know the words...'

'We'll write the words out for you, no probs.'

Matty, Conor and Sean start writing full pelt, they know the words.

So Danny steps in. Temporary singer for one night only.

'Good evening, folks. We are The Dandy Dimonts and if you know us, you'll see we have a new addition to our line-up. Please welcome our guest singer, Danny!'

Him in his plain black suit. Them, done up to the nines in dandy finery. But no matter for Danny's voice, even if it's been unused for a year or so now, and without any warm-up, *sings* out. A tad hoarse against the artificiality of the synthesisers, but it sounds natural. His high notes crack, but it's *real*. Cat's singing style was robotic to go along with the synths, but by contrast Danny's voice has emotion. Come to think of it, he looks a bit like Adam Ant, same chiselled features (they say that, don't they, about features – 'chiselled'), same boyish good looks. The gig is a success, and Danny feels the buzz of performing 'live' in front of an audience. The cheering and applause.

And so it comes to pass that Danny Boy becomes a member of the Dandy Dimonts. This development he keeps from the rest of RIL for fear of breaking the rule of solidarity which is: *the band stays together, doesn't stray, does NOT set up with a new band or perform solo without a unanimous YES vote*. Danny, for the sake of an easy life, stays shtum.

Meanwhile, him joining the Dandy Dimonts has a profound effect on this band, sartorially-wise, as Danny refuses to change his mode of dress (i.e. go 'Romantic') so the Dandy D's are forced to catch up with the times and get sharp-suited-up like Danny – and indeed like Duran Duran and Roxy. And, to be honest, they look the better for it. They get to perform in more swish venues, and Danny develops a liking for so-called 'torch songs', sentimental love songs that the ladies in the audience appreciate, like Cole Porter's 'Every Time We Say Goodbye'. At the end of any gig, just like the final smoochy number in any dance hall, Danny gets his 'Torch Time'.

'Ladies,' Sean will announce, 'get your hankies at the ready because our handsome croonster, Danny Boy, will now touch your hearts with a heartfelt love song. Gentlemen meanwhile, we suggest you repair to the bar. Now, bring the lights down low...' and then a gentle chord from Sean's synth, set for 'muted violin ensemble', plays the chord of D major, the loveliest chord, then into A7, and Danny hugs the mic, 'I've Got You Under My Skin...', and as for the ladies, he's got 'em f'sure.

One evening, Crazy Cat is in the audience. She don't look so crazy now as she's let the hair grow out on the sides of her head, toned down the Goth make-up, and removed most of the piercings. Dressed casually in parka and jeans, black beret and hiking boots. When she goes to talk to the band in the interval, they don't recognise her at first, but it's her Brummie accent that gives her away. Sean greets and hugs.

'Crazy Cat! As I live and breathe, where the fuck you been?'

'Aww man – I needed some space – went to a retreat in the Himalayas – meditation, yoga, and pot – had to sort my shit out.'

'And that did it?'

'Yeah that did it – it's a spiritual thing – you go into yerself – know what I mean? – anyways, who's this dude?' She's referring to Danny.

'Well, we were suddenly without a singer, weren't we...'

'Yeah sorry 'bout that guys – it was kinda weird – y'know I had an out-of-body experience – kinda floated up outta my body – and looked down on meself...'

'You do that all the time don't you, Matty?'

'What?' says Matty.

'Look down on yerself.'

Matty doesn't appreciate the joke.

'Fuck off.'

'So,' continues Sean, 'we had to find a new singer pronto and Danny Boy stepped in. Don't you recognise him? From the '70s band, Rock Ireland Line?'

'Shit – I loved that band when I was a kid – posters on me bedroom wall – what was that song? – "Beat, Beat" or sommat.'

'Danny,' Sean calls him over, 'come and say Buenos Dias to our ex-singer – AWOL and MIA!'

'Hey, sorry I took your place.'

'It's cool.'

'Are you coming back? I mean, I don't mind stepping aside.'

'Naw – I run discussion groups now – therapy, like – junkies and dropouts is my speciality.'

Everyone has a story to tell. In the intervening years since Crazy Cat didn't turn up and serendipitously Danny was the substitute, Cat has 'found' herself and then helped others 'find' themselves too. She has given something back after the gift of the retreat. So now she reckons it's her turn – 'Hi. I'm Terry and I'm a junkie,' 'Hi Terry – welcome to the group – I was a junkie too.' In the meantime, she has married her partner Beth and soon they intend to joint-mother a child. The father is yet to be chosen, as is the intended 'birth-mother'(but most likely it'll be Beth as she's never done drugs while Cat took them for breakfast). Beth is in the audience too, dressed more feminine than Cat, the pair having settled on a distinction between the more masculine Cat and the more feminine Beth. Some same-sex couples look the same deliberately, making no physical distinction between 'male' and 'female', but not these two.

'Why not join us on stage, Cat? You know the songs.' This is Sean.
  'What? – join you bunch of gimps in yer wide-boy suits?'
  'Yeah.'
  'Okay.'
  'Ladies and gents. For those of you who've followed us through the years – our loyal fans, the "Handy Dandys", you know who you are – you'll remember our first singer, Crazy Cat. Please welcome her back, for one night only (unless we can persuade her otherwise) – to sing with Danny – you know him, you love him, we love him too *and* we love Cat – ladies and gents, give a big hand to Cat and Danny and The Dandy Dimonts!'
  They go down a storm. The blend of voices is strange as Cat's voice is the deeper, being more of a mezzo-soprano, while Danny has a tenor's range. The same was true of husband-and-wife duo Sonny and Cher with their hit song 'I Got You Babe', with Cher's voice being deep and smooth and Sonny's voice higher and rougher which made for a great combo. Danny's voice is smooth as the veritable silk and he and Cat together sound like Heaven has pulled up and pitched its tent.
  At the end of the set, Cat brings Beth over and they all end up around

a big table in the pub where the gig has taken place and, at closing time, the landlord adopts a 'closed door' policy whereby the doors are shut to the general public but open till early hours for them what's still inside. It reminds Danny of Mickey's joke he always tells: 'Knock, knock, who's there? The Doors!' and he gets a tad wistful, recalling his band's sitting around a similar table in anypub, anywhere – and Mickey's jokes:

'Knock, knock.'

'Who's there?'

'The.'

'The Who?'

'Yup.'

The years go by. The gigs go by. Cat and Beth have a kid; the father's identity is not known, but the best guess is Sean. Especially as they call the boy Sean. No one cottons on to Danny's real identity; he looks different anyway now, hair cut short and a moustache, coincidentally like the one Tank has adopted (maybe it's the influence of the Fab Four in their Sergeant Pepper days). Occasionally there's a 'weren't you the singer in… ?' 'If I was,' replies Danny, 'why would I be singing in *this* band?' So people shrug. 'Well, you look a bit like what's-is-name?' 'Well, if you can't remember his name…' says Danny.

The years go by. The gigs go by.

It's the early 1990s, and one day, out of the blue, comes Mickey's call.

44
Come Together

'Hi Danny, how's tricks?'

'Tricks are fine, Mickey, how 'bout you?'

'All good. All good. Listen. Been talking to Tank and we reckon the band should hook up again. Play some gigs. What do you think?'

'I dunno. Maybe. You talked to Tone?'

'No, called you first.'

Danny feels flattered; it's his band, after all.

'Well, happens you *called* me first, but you *talked* to Tank first.'

'Point taken. Apologies. So what do you think?'

'I think… it's a good idea.'

He doesn't mention his association with The Dandy Dimonts, but the lads know anyway. How would you keep a secret like that in the tight-knit world of bands and their followers?

'We heard you were singing with another band,' says Mickey.

'Ah… er, just filling in time, nothing permanent.'

'Weird name.'

'Yeah, weird. New Romantics.'

'That's what we heard.'

'You know what, Mickey? It's all synth music and you know what? I reckon "synth" stands for "synthetic"! I asked them at the start if they had a drummer? Nah, they said, you get a drum track on the synth. What about guitar? Nah, they said, synth effect with distortion, fuzzbox, the lot. But not like you, Mickey! They do have a bass guitarist, but I reckon that's just for show. They couldn't replicate a singer though, not on a synth.'

'We ain't changing for nothing, Danny. Tank on drums, me on guitar, Tone on bass – and you, Danny?'

'I'm in, boyo. It'll be great to be back to good ol' rock 'n' roll and *real* instruments. Count me in.'

Mickey calls Tone.

'Tone. How're you doin'?'

'Doin' okay. Bored, to tell you the God's honest.'

'RIL are getting back together.'

'No kidding?'

'No kidding.'

'Fuckin' A!'

'You in?'

'Hundred per cent!'

'Your garage? This Friday at six?'

'You talked to Danny?'

'Yup, Tank too. We're all up for it.'

'Gimme a few days to sort the garage out. Been using it for storage.'

'Me and Tank'll help.'

'Fuckin' A!'

'What will Aggie say?'

'About the garage?'

'Nah, about you bein' in a rock band again.'

'I reckon she'll say, "I didn't marry no teacher!" '

And, as it turned out, that's exactly what she did say.

45
Sailing

It's called 'The Hollyday Cruise 1994'. In honour of Buddy Holly and for diehard fans of that rock legend. Those fans who call themselves the 'Buddies'.

Little does Danny know that he was conceived on a cruise; ironic really, as he gets seasick. On calm seas he's okay, but as soon as there's some roughness – technical term 'pitch and roll' – boy, does he suffer! While hardier passengers are swaying in the corridors, bouncing off the walls and holding onto handrails, Danny would be holed up in his cabin waiting for death.

But as this is a river cruise there's not much swell so he'll be okay. It's a small ship, not one of those transatlantic liners like his ma was on, so maybe two hundred or so passengers. The route is along the Danube, which has no relevance to Buddy Holly and is really just an excuse to be on the boat. Quite honestly, they could've stayed put dockside, but a river cruise it is, so they have to cruise a river. Along the route, they'll take in towns in Germany and Austria, ending up in Hungary.

RIL have been booked to headline the cruise as manager Rosie has answered an ad in the music papers requesting a Buddy Holly tribute band – which RIL are now, according to Rosie, who presents the band in glowing terms as hardcore Holly fans. The boys like the idea of a cruise, the pay is good, and they *do* like Buddy Holly. Who in the pop/rock business doesn't? Those in the know proclaim Holly and his band, the Crickets, as the precursor of the modern pop line-up of drums, bass and two guitars – even though, in Holly's day, being the late '50s, the bass was one of those giant stand-up double-basses as tall as the player. Electric bass guitars came in later, much to the relief of the bass players – after all, the stand-up version, more like a bigger cello, was more akin to orchestras than to rock bands. The other feature of the visionary Holly was his ability to write his own songs. Unheard of in Tin Pan Alley in them far-off black-and-white days. Or more like grey-and-white as the TVs were grey and life was pretty grey too. Then along came 'Peggy Sue'!

The lads learn all the Holly songs, pack swimming shorts in the hope of some Bavarian sun and set sail. The cruise company has only allowed for two cabins, so it's back to the sharing of the old days: Mickey with Tank, Danny B with Tone. The cabins are next to each other though, and have the luxury of balconies so they can hang out together during the day watching the Danube go by – a tight band once more.

'So, how shall we do this then?' asks Danny. (This is before the cruise, during one of their Holly rehearsal sessions.)

'So how shall we do what?' says Mickey.

'Well okay, we're going to play Buddy Holly songs and maybe with a bit of intro as per – but how much intro is what I'm thinking? Should we tell the whole Buddy Holly story?'

Tone chips in,

'I gather the cruise will hold several lectures on his biography so ours would be redundant.'

'Unless we do it a different way,' says Tank. 'Look, I got this idea.'

Which is unusual for Tank, who is not a great begetter of ideas.

'I got this idea,' he continues, 'that we play the parts of the various people, including Holly himself, who figured in his history – the other band members, for instance. I could play the drummer, Jerry Allison, and demonstrate the machine-gun rhythm of "Peggy Sue", you know, to show how it motored the song.'

And he does a quick demo, performing those classic paradiddles on the snare.

'Danny, you could be Holly himself. You're not unlike him, tall and skinny – well, skinny-ish – just put on a pair of horn-rimmed specs, slick back your hair. Might need cutting a bit though. And Mickey, you could tell the story about the famous Fender Stratocaster that Holly played.'

'That could work,' says Danny, warming to the idea, especially as he gets to play the legend. 'How much shorter though?' he asks nervously, fingering his long hair.

Tone: 'How many nights are we on?'

Mickey: 'Four is what Rosie's agreed. It's an eight-day cruise and we'll be on every other night.'

Tone: 'Have we learnt enough songs?'

Mickey: 'Say, six a night then repeats.'

Tank starts counting on his fingers. Tone, impatient, butts in –

Tone: 'That's *twenty-four* songs altogether! How many have we got so far?'

Danny: 'We got ten. We can learn another fourteen easy. There's a month or more before we sail.'

Mickey: 'Your garage will never be busier, Tone.'

Tone: 'I'll have to break it gently to Aggie.'

Tank: 'Buy her some flowers from us.'

Tone: 'Lot of good that'll do!'

Danny: 'C'mon Eeyore, a bit of schmoozing'll work wonders.'

But Eeyore is not convinced.

So, a month or more goes by. Aggie has been bribed, boozed, and schmoozed, the garage has echoed with sweet music, the boys have caught a flight to Germany, and ahoy there, they're on board ship! 'We are sailing,' sings Mickey in his own version of the Rod Stewart song.

'"Sailing",' pronounces Encyclopaedia-of-Rock Tone, 'released in 1975 but originally recorded by The Sutherland Brothers in '72. Rod Stewart was a fan of theirs and recorded his own version for his "Atlantic Crossing" album, later to be released as a single and staying at the Number One spot for four weeks, if memory serves. The song was played as a background to the Falklands War Task Force leaving Portsmouth Harbour in 1982 to great patriotic approbation, the song being quite anthem-like in its nature.' And as per, Tone lectures to an unappreciative and unlistening audience.

There's a welcoming party on board where they dress up in tuxedos and meet The Captain, who looks the part in his crisp white uniform with gold epaulettes and peaked cap which he nestles underneath his arm. They shake hands with him like they're meeting royalty and he says, 'So you're the pop group, are you?' and the lads cringe but let it go, no point in trying to explain to this example of the Admiralty the difference between a rock band and a pop group.

The Captain is very tall, clearly from Central Casting, and they suspect the *real* captain (with a small 'c') is a weedy fella probably aged twelve. The other passengers fawn over Central Casting Captain, especially the ladies, who link arms with him and get their photos taken and ask if they might have a turn at the wheel and 'drive the ship'? He, the Captain, is chivalrous and a mite flirty, and promises the younger females a visit to the bridge. 'Is that a euphemism, do you think?' says Tone.

(It turns out, they hear later from a gossipy passenger, that said Captain, despite his womanising demeanour, is a closet gay and lives with a Hungarian sailor called Bruno. So the gals are wasting their time as he is no ladies' man. Come to think of it, Danny says, he's sure he saw the Cap'n wink at him. 'Any port in a storm,' quips Tank, and they all laugh, as usual, fit to burst.)

They're assigned their own 'butler', or 'steward', as he's called, who'll look after their every whim, make up their beds and serve their meals in-room if they so desire; but they desire instead to take their places in the ultra-luxurious Dining Room, with their own table-for-four, every night they're not performing. The Dinner Menu is different each night and boasts culinary delights par excellence but is a considerable threat to the waistline. 'Well, you only live once,' says Tank, tucking into a giant fillet steak. 'And not for long the way you're going,' says Tone, and they laugh fit to burst.

'Charles Hardin Holley – Holley with an 'e' – born 1936, died 1959, aged just twenty-three.'

So begins Danny in his first intro of their shipboard performances. He is dressed Holly-style in grey suit (sharp-fitting), white shirt and black bowtie, slicked back (short) hair and those famous horn-rimmed spectacles. He switches to first-person narrative now, adopting as much of a Texan accent as a Dubliner can muster.

'Lubbock, Texas was mah hometown. I came from a musical family with mah elder brothers, who nicknamed me "Buddy", performing in Talent Shows playing Country and Western music with me on violin. Trouble was, I couldn't play the violin none too well so one of m' brothers'd grease the strings so's no one could hear m' caterwaulin'!'

The assembled 'Buddies', the hardcore fans, laugh, accepting this lookalike (and reasonable soundalike) of their hero.

'I got me a *gui-tar* and after learning enough chords necessary to play a half-decent number, I teamed up with mah school buddy Bob Montgomery. We called our act "Buddy and Bob". We got onto the local TV station, and we mixed in some R&B with the Bluegrass. By this time, I'd met mah future drummer, Jerry Allison – we all called him "J.I.", his middle name being "Ivan" – and we opened shows for Presley and Bill Haley. I reckon it was their influence that led me to Rock 'n' Roll. So, in a short spell, we went from C&W to R&B to R&R. This was 1955, but let's break off now and play one of those early songs.'

They play 'Blue Days, Black Nights', which for such Holly-aficionados as the Buddies is a fine start to proceedings, being none too obvious a choice.

'Some Nashville scout then caught the act and I got signed to the great Decca Records, and you know what? in the contract they spelled mah name without the 'e'. So it was Buddy H-O-L-L-Y from then on in. On m' first Decca recording sessions for "Blue Days" and "Love Me", the producer guy took charge and wouldn't pay me no mind. I didn't take kindly to that!'

The Buddies clap along to 'Love Me' with its swing-along beat. They are all of an age, these Buddies. Pretty much the same age as RIL because these are the guys and gals who grew up listening to Buddy Holly on Radio Luxembourg on their transistor radios; the signal would fade in and out, hopefully not during the spectacular 'It Doesn't Matter Anymore' – but what the heck were those strange plinky sounds on that song? Not *gui-tars*, surely? To the untrained ear of a pre-teen in 1958, those pizzicato strings were a strange brew indeed.

In terms of their 'look', the Buddies adopt the fashion of the era with the ladies wearing their hair in ponytails like '50s high-school girlfriends or they wear it as bangs or bunches. But these are women in their sixties or seventies so it's an incongruous image, them trying to look like teenagers, not to mention the wide beam-ends stuffed into toreador pants. They wear tight jumpers and pointy bras and the male Buddies just love it.

The men try to be Holly lookalikes, most wearing wigs or the lucky ones with their own hair use dye. The cruise company has bought a load of horn-rimmed frames with no lenses. Little do they know that they have echoed the reality of Holly's own glasses, found in a field after the plane crash, also without their lenses. Art imitating life, you might say.

Danny injects some Hollyisms into the songs like the 'hiccupping' way of singing and Mickey plays down-strokes on the guitar. And yes, Mickey has brought his red Fender Stratocaster for the cruise, this being Holly's trademark. And it is this very guitar that Mickey (as himself and not playing any part) now introduces:

'You all know it, don't you? Buddy's famous Fender Strat. Two-tone Sunburst model. Taken up by Hank Marvin of the Shadows and then by future guitar gods like Clapton and Jeff Beck. Holly had his own style of guitar-playing, fast downward strokes like I've just been playing,' Mickey demonstrates, 'which is quite a different sound from the normal up and down strokes – hear the difference? – by keeping his wrist locked in position and strumming hard and DOWN he kept up a driving rhythm.'

In the course of the evening they've played Holly songs, the less well-known ones like 'Crying, Waiting, Hoping' and 'Take Your Time', and they finish with that show-stopper 'Rave On'.

The Buddies rave on, even after Rock Ireland have left the stage.

In between performances, the lads join the tours of the stop-off cities like Nuremberg and Vienna and Budapest and in the evenings they sign autographs at their table and pose for photos with the other passengers who stop by to swop Buddy stories; and some even remember the band's former stardom with the usual, 'You were famous once, right?' shtick.

'In the 1950s,' (this is Danny on their second performance), 'there weren't bands as such, but backing groups behind a singer, like Bill Haley and his Comets, Cliff Richard and the Shadows. So Buddy had his own backing group, The Crickets, also known as "The Chirping Crickets", with his old pal J.I. on drums; and this was the norm, singer plus backing group... and talking of norm... may I introduce you to Norman Petty...'

Danny waves on Tone to the mic (pony-tailed to hide the long hair and wearing a check shirt and jeans) who assumes an American accent tinged with Surrey.

'Hi, I'm Norman Petty. I own me a recordin' studio in Clovis, New Mexico. Name on the door. I've already recorded stars like Roy Orbison

– the big "O". It's 1957 and who should walk into my reception but a gangly young guy looking like a high-school teacher. Neat as a button.'

Danny/Holly: 'Neat as a button, that's me. Dress smart, tidy hair. Well turned-out, like I was brought up. Mah daddy always wore suits, collar and tie, he owned a tiling company – anyways, as Mr Petty was sayin'…'

Tone/Petty: 'So in walks this guy in glasses who says he wants to make some *dee-mos*. I like the fella so I say "sure" and he plays me "That'll Be The Day". Kinda catchy. Seems that some DJ in Lubbock has told Buddy about mah studio. State-of-the-art, vacuum tubes, ribbon mics. Folks like m' pink ceiling tiles. Call it the Pepto Bismal Palace! I charge by the record not by the hour like most studios do, so no time constraints. Which suits Buddy to a tee as he is a PERFECTIONIST! Swops mics around till he's a hundred and ten per cent happy. So Holly and his band come in and record "That'll Be The Day".'

'D'you know how we got that title?' says Danny/Holly, adjusting his horn-rimmed specs. 'Me and J.I. went to the movie house to see John Wayne in *The Searchers*, and in that western, the Duke used the phrase several times like it's some sorta catchphrase.'

Tank, sitting at his drums (as always in faded denims and shorts so already looking the part) now assumes the role of J.I.: 'Yeah, when the hombre with the knife says, "I hope you die," Wayne says, "That'll be the day!".'

'Right, so after the film, me and J.I. go back to his place for a jam session – me on acoustic and J.I. on the drums. It ain't common for the singer of a band and the drummer to have a *simpatico* relationship but me and J.I. – (here, Danny goes over to Tank and stands beside him) – we have something special as he plays those drums like a guitar or piano. Plus, we've been best buddies since I-don't-know-how-long so we kinda gel. Then, what do I say to you?'

'You say, "J.I., we're gonna write us a song".'

'That's right. And what do you say in reply, as cool as y' like?'

'I say, "That'll be the day!".'

The Buddies laugh at this.

'And we reckon, hey that's a good title, and in thirty minutes that song is written and pop history is written too.'

This is the cue for the band's performance of the classic that their audience has been waiting for, and that was Holly's first Number One. The RIL boys provide the vocal backing throughout, and at the end, Holly's 'oo-oo's' are echoed by the Buddies themselves. Could these be the very 'oo-oo's' that inspired the Beatles' falsetto 'ooh's' in their early songs that would have the screaming fans go into overdrive? Or maybe influenced the similar 'woo-woo' choruses on the Stones 'Sympathy For The Devil'?

Tone/Petty: 'I took the dee-mo to New York, sold it to Brunswick Records, became Buddy's manager. Many other hits came out of my studio, like this 'un...'

They play 'Not Fade Away'.

'... but that was the B side to "Oh Boy" so it never charted as a single.'

They play 'Oh Boy'.

Tank/J.I.: 'Buddy says that I played the drums like a musical instrument and that's surely true as I saw the role of the drums not just fer timekeepin' but instead as a fourth player. Take the beat of "Peggy Sue" – (cheer from the crowd) – that song started off with a Latin rumba beat, like so – (he demonstrates) – but when we recorded it, we changed it to these kinda relentless paradiddles – (demonstrates) – it was originally titled "Cindy Lou" after Buddy's niece but Peggy Sue bein' my girlfriend, later to be m' darlin' wife, we changed it around so I guess poor ol' Cindy Lou missed out on im-mor-tal-ity.'

Tank starts the song with the drumming, singing 'Cindy Lou', then Danny takes over: 'Peggy Sue, Peggy Sue...' At the finish of the final four beats, Tank/J.I. continues:

'One day I was sat in reception and I was workin' out the rhythm of the song we were about to put down called "Everyday", and I was slappin' on mah knees and thighs when Norm came out and said...'

Tone/Petty: 'Let me put a mic on that.'

'... and he trailed a cable all the way from the desk and said...'

Tone/Petty again: 'Don't play the drums on the record, just slap your thighs like you're doin' now.'

And so the Hollyday Cruise resident Buddy Holly tribute band (who've called themselves 'The *Crock*ets' in honour of Holly's band and with due deference to their ages) end the session with 'Everyday', with Tank slapping his thighs like a good 'un.

46
Everyday

Every day there are on-board activities announced first thing in the morning on the ship's PA by sleazebag cruise director, one Vic 'More Strings To Me Bow' Viola, who sickly-smiles his way through the frolics on offer for the day. And every evening, when RIL are not performing, there are special Theme Nights, introduced by MC slimy Viola. There's the PEGGY SUE BALL, dress code 1950s America, balloon skirts and Bobbysox. A karaoke night where wannabee Holly's sing to the background tracks. A rather dry lecture on *The Short Life and Death of Buddy Holly*, accompanied by slides and some archive footage, is followed by Quiz Night, IT'S *NOT* SO EASY, posing questions like: What was Holly's dad's profession? What was the original title of 'Peggy Sue'? What was the film that inspired 'That'll Be The Day'?

Daytime activities include THAT'LL BE THE DECK!, an on-deck quoits tournament, there's hairstyling for the ladies TRUE LOVE WAVES, and American Diner cooking lessons and Dirty Bop dancing classes. Also, for your delectation, dear cruisers, a lecture on eating bugs called THE CHOMPING CRICKETS (samples provided). SPECS APPEAL is the name of the ship's shop that sells Holly memorabilia and souvenirs.

And so it goes. For Rock Ireland's third session, 'It's So Easy' and 'Heartbeat' cover off Holly's romance with his soon-to-be bride María Elena then the move to New York, leaving J.I. and The Crickets behind. Then the sacking of Petty, his manager, followed by the momentous 'Guess It Doesn't Matter Anymore' with the pizzicato strings. Holly is now in charge of his recordings and has a whole orchestra – well, eighteen performers – to play with.

Danny/Holly: 'I'd already experimented with different instruments like the celeste on "Everyday". That was played by Norman's wife, Vi. I'd also used swirling strings on "Raining In My Heart" and "True Love Ways".'

Cue Tone on hired synthesiser, emulating the violins and celeste as the band perform the songs. Then Danny/Holly finishes off his intro.

'Took up the offer of a tour, forming a new line-up of The Crickets. Billed as the Winter Dance Party tour. Mark that word well: *Winter*. This was January and February in the Midwest with temperatures below forty degrees! Twenty-four concerts in as many days. María Elena was pregnant so she couldn't go with us.'

'True Love Ways' ends the evening on a sombre note.

That fateful tour and RIL's account of it on their last performance of the Hollyday Cruise is prefaced by the one thing that all cruise ships dread: an outbreak of norovirus, also known as the 'vomiting bug' (which is putting it mildly as the condition involves *projectile* vomiting as well as stomach cramps and diarrhoea). The virus spreads like the proverbial through the confines of the ship where the passengers are living at such close quarters. The lads come down to breakfast to find some of the crew all togged up in protective clothing, head to toe, wearing masks, and swabbing every surface with disinfectant. 'Just a precaution,' says one, then, 'make sure you've washed your hands,' and points to the hand sanitiser.

The swabbing detail have left by the time more passengers arrive, but they're all discussing that morning's announcement by Vic Viola, who misspeaks his way through 'a mild case of sickness that has affected a small portion of the ship's passengers who are confined to their cabins'. 'Put in quarantine, more like,' says a know-it-all passenger. That word 'quarantine' strikes a doomful note with its connotations of plague, negating the so-called-by-Vic 'mild case', which doesn't fool anyone as long queues form at the sanitisers. The same know-it-all – there's always one – says, with some relish, that once the virus gets hold of a ship, then everyone gets it. This is evidenced by the sight of crew members cleaning bannisters and spraying door handles. Vic V gets back on the PA and announces that, although the captain will be available for meet 'n' greets, he won't be shaking hands. 'The last person you don't want holed up in his cabin is the captain,' says Mr Know-it-all. Those passengers in hearing-range return to the sanitisers. Then one unfortunate clutches her stomach and rushes to the loo. Everyone looks scared.

In the afternoon, a Code Red is called, although the passengers are not informed of this; it's for crew's ears only, and will mean no self-service in the buffet (meals are served by the staff wearing gloves), doors to the public toilets are wedged open (to stop people touching the handles), the library is closed, and anyone showing symptoms (and it's hard to hide them) is sent to their cabin and told to stay put.

Tone gets the band together and issues rules:

1) Try not to use the public loos, use your own in the cabin,

2) Open doors with tissues, avoid touching bannisters,

3) Use your knuckle to press the LIFT button or, better still, use the stairs,

4) Keep a safe distance from other passengers,

5) Wash your hands for as long as it takes to sing 'Happy Birthday' – twice.

Hands to face is the most common way this virus transmits. 'Just take a half-hour in any day and count how many times you touch your face,' says Tone, 'we're conditioned to it,' and he points to Mickey with his copy of *The Sun*, licking his fingers each time he turns a page.

By the evening the passenger numbers are so decimated there's just a handful of Buddies attending RIL's final performance and, just to rub it in, Mickey's getting the cramps, has overdosed on anti-diarrhoea pills but still gets nauseous and has to excuse himself during Danny's intros.

'Now we are here on the day the music died.' The Buddies know full well what's coming. Some are already dressed in mourning.

Danny/Holly goes on to describe the events of February the second, 1959. First, he introduces the 'new' Crickets, formed especially for the tour: Waylon Jennings on bass (Tone takes a bow), Tommy Allsup on guitar (Mickey is absent so Danny points to his abandoned guitar leaning against the amp, creating a mild feedback), and Carl Bunch on drums (Tank waves his sticks in the air). They're all in casual American-type clobber: jeans, tasselled cowboy shirts, trainers. Tank sports a Stetson, which is a bit OTT, but who's complainin'?

The tour is chaotic, Danny says, covering the mid-western states of Minnesota, Wisconsin and Iowa in the depths of the harshest winter, zigzagging on a madcap meandering route for thousands of miles in unheated buses. And yet the line-up of the tour is top-notch with the Big Bopper (hit song: 'Chantilly Lace'), Ritchie Valens ('La Bamba') and Dion ('Runaround Sue') starring, let alone Buddy himself.

Danny points to Tank: 'Carl here goes and gets frostbite in his toes sitting in that icebox of a bus. Has to go to hospital. Lucky he don't lose his toes. We burn paper in the aisle just to keep warm. We get to our next venue late as the bus breaks down. This is the Surf Ballroom in Clear Lake, Iowa.'

Tone/Waylon: 'It's midnight when we finish the show and Buddy wants to charter a plane to get to the next place, fuck the bus! Sit in the warm, get there early, shower, change of clothes.'

Danny/Holly: 'Yeah, the plane is a Beechcraft Bonanza, seats three of us at thirty-six dollars each. Mah fellow passengers'll be Waylon and Tommy. Hey Tommy, you take up the story…'

Mickey, having returned to the stage, steps forward to the microphone. This is his first role-play, so he speaks all deep-voiced American (which near makes the band crack up as they're more used to squeaky Mickey):

'Richie Valens keeps begging me to give up mah seat so we toss a coin for it and heads, he wins. Big Bopper's suffering with flu so Waylon sacrifices his seat too. Course for me it was the luckiest coin toss. In later life, I owned me a restaurant. Called it "Heads Up".'

The Buddies know these details backwards – maybe not the last one – but the devil is in the detail, and the devil now enters the scene.

Danny/Holly: 'We're in a snowstorm, nil visibility, but we feel safe, we're in a plane and planes fly, right? And planes land, right? But just five miles out from Mason City airport, the plane just gets lower and lower – altho' we ain't aware of that. Nothing to see out the windows. Not the field with the stick-fence that's getting closer and closer until… until… well, you don't survive a crash like that. I was lying near to Ritchie, and the Big Bopper had been thrown right over the other side of the fence. Pilot trapped in his seat. I don't remember much, didn't feel a thing, just one minute looking anxiously out the plane window, next

285

minute nothing. M' darlin' wife had a miscarriage when she heard. Mah funeral was four days later in m' hometown at the Tabernacle Baptist Church where the Reverend Johnson, who'd married us not six months previous, presided.'

The Buddies are quiet, some sobbing. The death of their hero. Such a fuckin' waste. Just think what the great Buddy Holly would have achieved had he survived!

'Among the pallbearers was mah friend J.I., also Sonny Curtis, who was mah original guitar player, and Bob Montgomery of "Buddy and Bob". The headstone in Lubbock cemetery spells Holley with an 'e', and there's a carving of a Fender Strat, and the inscription says, "In Loving Memory Of Our Own Buddy Holley", I sho' like that.'

The band finishes their final performance with the old favourites – 'Peggy Sue', 'Guess It Doesn't Matter', 'Everyday' and 'Raining'. It was raining in everybody's hearts that final night of the Hollyday Cruise.

They finish with 'American Pie' by Don McLean – the day the music died.

The Buddies join in the choruses, then file out almost in a procession like it's a funeral.

But then again, it kinda is.

47
Sick As A Dog

A paler shade of white. Or rather, a greener shade of green. Because by the next day, the last day of the Hollyday Cruise, the lads have all got it. When they disembark in Hungary, they're whisked off to hospital and put in a quarantine ward. Rosie has to re-arrange their flights home, and their music equipment has to be stored. It all costs a pretty penny. When they're discharged from hospital, they feel too ill to fly, so the flights have to be re-re-arranged. Rosie is going mental because insurance won't cover the virus. Act of God, apparently. Thanks, God. Most of the profits from the cruise are swallowed up, and any reparation on the part of the cruise company is declared null and void, claiming another Act of God. When the boys finally get home, they swear they'll never go 'sailing' again.

48

To The Beat, Beat, Beat Of My Heart, Heart, Heart (Reprise)

The 'red-tops' – so-called because of the red banners at the top of their front pages – are the populist papers, mass-market, middle-of-the-road, and not so full of news that you're scared half to death over your boiled egg. The number one red-top, *The Sun*, for as long as any male reader can remember, always had a Page Three 'stunner' to brighten your day. She would be topless, usually just wearing the bottom half of a bikini, smiling sweetly, with a brief description of 'Becky from Biggleswade' who liked nothing better than a game of chess – check*mate*! Actually quite sexless and innocent, never a suggestion of lust. But the PC powers-that-were eventually got the Page Three girl covered up, from then on appearing in both bikini bottom *and* top. It was a sad day for mankind. What would the opposite of 'topless' be? Top-full? Top-more? Topped? Anyway, the Page Three girl would now be chastely dressed for the beach, and no cheating folks – no see-through garments or wet tee-shirts, no nipples, no sirree! The punters were disappointed for a while but weathered the storm and still looked at *The Sun*, although lingering less over Page Three, featuring now-covered-up Becky from Biggleswade.

Thus it was, one morning in the early days of December 2017, that Mickey, over his boiled egg, turned the pages of his red-top paper and stopped short at a story that greatly concerned him. The headline was confusing: HAPPY CHRISTMAS 1977! but the sub-line struck a chord: IF YOU CAN'T BEAT, BEAT, BEAT 'EM! Under a picture of a small boy and a large seabird was the accompanying 'exclusive' about a new Christmas TV commercial for a supermarket chain that would be featuring that 1970s hit, 'To the Beat, Beat, Beat Of My Heart, Heart, Heart' by veteran group, Rock Ireland Line. 'Where are they now?' came the question, but answer came there none. The song had been 're-imagined', the report said, by a hip-hop girl singer, popular at this time. Mickey was not familiar with her work, even though the paper listed some recent hits, but then, how long since he'd listened to a pop channel? The paper had a picture of her, and she sported orange hair and a teenage scowl. The visual side of the TV ad was shown in the form of a comic strip and made little sense as the supermarket was keen on keeping the advert under wraps until its 'premiere' in a prime slot during a TV talent show in a week's time.

Now, what Mickey was aware of were the following facts:

1) Rock Ireland no longer held the rights to the song, hadn't for donkey's years, as Joe Rainbow had sold them off to a music publisher,

2) The reason the band had not been informed of the forthcoming song's commercial usage was due to point 1) above,

3) However, even though there would not be any financial gain for RIL, there would be publicity and possibly a comeback for the band,

4) Songs featured before on these supermarket Christmas ads usually made the charts.

So even though the girl with the orange hair and teenage scowl had possibly made a dog's dinner of their hit – and to be fair, Mickey was yet to hear it – the future suddenly looked bright and full of promise. Without turning further pages of his paper and abandoning his boiled egg, now gone cold anyway, Mickey got straight onto the phone to Danny Boy who was in the shower and didn't hear the chirrup-chirrup of his mobile. Mickey called Tone. But Tone's mobile was OFF as he liked to conserve the battery. Bloody typical! Then Mickey tried Tank, who answered straightaway and received the news with a 'Hoozah!' as he too recognised the import. By this time, Danny was out of the shower, and Tone had turned his phone ON and thus it was that all of RIL were now appraised of the info, so they assembled in Tone's garage to digest and discuss. They agreed with all four points laid out by Mickey and brought in their de facto manager, Rosie, who was waiting in Mickey's car. Invited into the holy-of-holies sanctum that was the RIL HQ, she considered the status quo and the modus operandi but not speaking Latin, translated as follows: 'Guys, you're gonna be famous again.'

49

The Morning Papers

By the afternoon, all the papers were trying to track down this once well-known band, and the calls started coming in, put through to Rosie on her gig-arranging answering service. The papers were astounded that the band didn't have its own website, email address, Twitter, or online web chat link. But Rosie came up trumps, acting out the big-time manager and being offhand, 'Play hard to get,' she said and played accordingly. At times, she used comedy, emphasising the lads' infirmities – like when she was asked how much they charged for interviews, she said, 'They don't get out of bed for less than…', naming a figure, then following up with, 'actually, at their age, they don't get out of bed!' Other times she was a hard-bargainer. 'You've gotta be kidding, try making that figure *per* band member, then double it.' Then, panicking, and not being good at maths, she'd hope the other side would make the right calculation and if it sounded okay, 'You gotta deal, honey.' God, she was good. The boys would listen in, gesturing to her to take the money, the first sum offered, but Rosie'd tap her nose and wink like a market trader.

One of the newspapers that first carried the story didn't need to do much digging as Rosie rang them, getting through to the reporter of the article and offering him an exclusive 'Where are they now?'. He said he was delighted all were, at least, still alive. 'Oh, alive alive-oh!' sang Rosie down the phone and captivated the reporter. A photographer was sent round to the garage and the band posed with their instruments; but when the feature ran, the paper cruelly dug up some old photos of the lads in their heyday and put them side by side with the new ones. Well, not many folk can survive before-and-after pictures like that, not when they're separated by four decades. It just emphasised their age. And to cap it all, they ran the headline: ROCK AROUND THE CROCKS! Rosie put a ban on that paper and never returned the reporter's calls.

But there were plenty of other rags ready to get onto the band's wagon. The posher papers consulted some modern composers and experts to analyse the structure of 'Beat, Beat', some declaring it to be 'modal', others that it was 'Dionysian' as opposed to 'Apollonian'. 'I thought it was in E,' said Mickey. One magazine tried to interview Aggie to get the female angle and got a flea in their ear when they waylaid her on the way to Tesco cos no one, but *no one*, gets in the way of Aggie when she's on her way to Tesco. Imagine this cub reporter holding his mobile phone aloft, trying to record Aggie's bon-mots as she wheels her trolley along the pavement. Because Aggie has her own shopping trolley and, in this case, used it effectively as a battering-ram. The reporter retired hurt, nursing bruised shins.

Rosie, on the other hand, and by now a mature beauty, was willing to pose for pics to publicise the band. She smelled money, quite simply. One paper made a meal out of Tone's upper-class background, dubbing him 'Posh' after they rooted out his full moniker: TREDWELL DOES WELL! ran their headline. POSH ROCK! was their follow-up when they secured an interview with the sister in Surrey. A particular snooping rag sought out Tank's 'illegitimate' daughter, hounding poor Kath outside her flat. When she angrily confronted them, the headline ran: TANKS A LOT, DAD! Tank was furious and hit back, literally. TANK ATTACK! was the report next day, showing a blurry photo of Tank with flailing fists. He banned that paper. Great, thought Rosie, two papers down. So she put a ban on any further banning, rang the rags concerned and made peace. Lesson one, she thought, never ban the media. As a consolation prize, she offered them both 'specials' on Danny Boy's Irish background, but they didn't bite, instead asking if she had any childhood snaps of the band, more before-and-afters. She told them to fuck off.

A housekeeping mag wanted to photograph the lads' homes, promising a free make-over with an interior designer on hand to 'spruce up' if necessary. Rosie thought that a lot of 'sprucing up' would indeed be necessary, thinking of her and Mickey's untidy hovel and, as for Tank's digs – well, it didn't bear thinking about. So she declined, and the housekeeping mag was well miffed. Then a mag specialising in male fitness wanted to do an article on 'Ageing Gracefully', they said. It was good money and the premise seemed promising to the lads, but the snapper who was aged about ten made them dress in tight tank-tops and tee-shirts and 'wife-beater' vests, so rather than disguising paunches and sagging flesh, the photos emphasised their senility. 'More like Ageing *Dis*gracefully,' said Tone. And no one laughed fit to burst. So, they held their stomachs in and battled through. When the feature appeared, they saw it was sponsored by a male hair-dye product, which amused Mickey no end, being follicly-challenged. 'Never say dye,' he joked, and this time they did laugh fit to burst. A guitar periodical did a big picture spread on Mickey's guitar collection, highlighting the Fender Strat and, of course, mentioning the Holly connection. The pictures of Mickey with his Strat next to Holly likewise, pleased him no end.

50
Good Morning, Good Morning

The world of television soon beckoned. Breakfast TV, for example, needs constant material and an ageing rock band, catapulted back into fame, is perfect breakfast fodder. They're first invited on to an early-morning regional breakfast show that requires them to be picked up at four a.m. to arrive at the studio by five. Hair and make-up ready by six, transmission-time. 'Good morning,' says the breezy female presenter to her waking audience and goes on to list the forthcoming treats in store, including the famous rock band who'll be appearing later on in the show. How much later? the boys wonder as they lounge about in their dressing-room which is no more than a cupboard really. Plastic cups of lukewarm coffee. Morning papers. They find that they're hungry. Croissants arrive. They ask the runner what time they might be on and he shrugs, 'Lap of the gods, guys. It's a lottery out there.'

They watch the show-in-progress on a monitor. The only mention of the group is a passing reference to the Christmas TV ad, and the band behind the song will be on shortly, stay tuned. That was around seven-thirty. A politician gets grilled via the large screen; he's not in the studio but stands in front of the Houses of Parliament, which make an impressive aren't-I-important backdrop. He evades and squirms and repeats himself constantly while never answering the direct question – a politician's trick: only say what you want to say, not what *they* want you to say. 'As I said before…' and he repeats what he said before. 'But you haven't answered my question. 'I've already answered your question.' But he hasn't. And round and round it goes, getting nowhere slowly. 'What I want to say is…' Then he says nothing at all. Job done, he thinks at interview end.

Meanwhile, a report on waste incinerators: are they a good thing or a bad thing? Everyone agrees they're a bad thing apart from the representative from the waste-recycling company, whose solution is to burn every goddam thing and stuff the harmful emissions and is adamant that burning plastic is 'green'. 'Lying bastard,' says Tank. 'What do you know about incineration?' asks Danny. 'It's a burning issue,' says Mickey, and they all laugh fit to burst. The waste-rep settles back at interview-end, 'Thank you, Mr Bullshitter,' puffed and pleased that he's pulled the wool. Next up is an item on cruises, and shiver me timbers, if it ain't ol' Vic 'More Strings To Me Bow' Viola, entertainments director on the Hollyday Cruise of many moons ago. 'Fuck me, it's that smarmy bastard from our ship,' says Tank. The smarmy bastard is quizzed about the norovirus, there's been a well-publicised outbreak recently, and Vic says, 'Very rare. Hardly ever happens in my experience.' 'Didn't he get it as well?' asks Danny. 'Word is, he locked himself in his cabin with the female contortionist,' says Tank. 'Any port in a storm,' says Mickey.

There's a competition offering the prize of a luxury hatchback and holiday in Ibiza. All you have to do is phone in (premium rate at £1 a call), no questions, no skill involved, just phone or text COMP. Mickey texts then worries that he might be excluded as he's part of the show. 'Wasted a bloody pound,' he moans, but at that moment the runner pops his head round the door, 'You're on in fifteen, guys. Final checks,' which is the cue for hair and make-up to administer the smoothing hand and concealing brush, not a call for late payment.

On in fifteen. On in thirty. Finally, at eight forty-five, they're pushed on with only fifteen minutes of broadcast left. The presenter, who seems to have been briefed wrongly, thinks the boys are American. She's too young to remember them from their glory days, and her sidekick, also too young, doesn't correct her. He seems wrapped up in his 'running order' and when the cameras are off him, he calls in wardrobe to check his tie, jacket, trousers, god-knows-what. He's a fidgety bugger, which the TV company probably attribute to high energy and 'fizz'. But really, he's just fidgety. They're like children, these two baby presenters. 'Just out of nappies,' says Mickey. 'Probably still in 'em,' says Tank. Cue: laughter fit-to-burst all round.

Meanwhile, Tammy – for such is the lady presenter's name – continues with her confusion: How did you lose your American accents? How come you sound so English? You say you've been here a long time, when did you come over? You were born here, really? So, when did you move to the States? And so on. You all seem to have English names?

The lads, getting an inkling of what's going on, play games: Mickey says he's from Boston. 'Massachusetts?' asks Tammy, showing off her knowledge of American cities. 'No,' Mickey replies deadpan, 'Lincolnshire.' Have you seen the commercial yet? No, says Danny in his broadest Dublin brogue, we don't get British ads over there. In the US, you mean? No, Ireland.

Five minutes left to perform their 'Beat, Beat' song, which they mime to. Their guitars are unplugged and they mime deliberately badly, fluffing lines or not bothering to mime at all. At one point, Tone turns his guitar the wrong way round and 'plays' the back and the others get the giggles.

Rosie is waiting for them outside the studio.

Tank: 'We got up in the middle of the fuckin' night for *that*?'

'Worth its weight in gold, my friend,' and she waves him off as she has fantastic news.

'Decca want to re-release "Beat, Beat" and they want *you* to record it! Guess where?'

Who knows? Some studio in Soho? The Bahamas, maybe?

'Abbey Road,' she says triumphantly, 'only ABBEY *BLOODY* ROAD!'

The home of The Beatles. George Martin. The famous zebra crossing. The classic final LP. Abbey bloody Road!

51
Albatross

Before this momentous event, they finally get to see the TV ad. It's posted up on YouTube just before it's screened so they can watch the full sixty seconds several times. Needs must, as it's a complicated story involving a boy, an albatross, and a Cornish seaside village at Christmas. 'I'll call you Andy,' says the boy to the albatross, 'as long as you're not a girl.' Andy the albatross has full vocal powers and tells the boy that he got lost on his way South, turning North instead, as he fell asleep on the journey. There is some truth in this, Tone comments, as birds do sleep on long flights. 'Much like people,' says Danny. The albatross is worried about missing Christmas in South America and puts on a weepy face, courtesy of CGI. It's all done by computer, Tone explains, CGI standing for Computer Generated Imagery. Anyway, back to the plot: this being a supermarket ad and this being the tide of Yule, a large dollop of schmaltz is in order, so the kid looks sad too. 'What's the matter, Tommy?' asks the warm-as-toast mummy, and the next thing we know, the mummy is in said supermarket buying something (which is not shown). Cut (technical term) to Christmas Day, and Tommy is presenting Andy the albatross with a small Christmas gift-wrapped parcel with kid's writing on it, 'To Andy, X'. Then, somehow either through computer wizardry or fake wings, Andy opens his gift, and it's a tin of tuna. 'Better than turkey,' the albatross says. 'Talking of which,' Danny says, 'that's what that ad is.' And after laughing fit to burst, they can only but agree.

52

The Beat Goes On

Abbey Road. Abbey bloody Road.

They're going to walk there all the way from the pub in West Hampstead where they have two rooms. Distance a couple of miles from West End Lane to St. John's Wood which is where Abbey Road Studios resides. This is the West Hampstead of their early days when they came down to London seeking fame but never, in the end, fortune. Maybe this time around? But first, they take a look at their old 'digs' in Kingdon Road and it's looking smart now, the peeling paint on the old front door now replaced by a glazed oak number. The building is no longer a hive of bedsits but apartments with their own buzzers. The roof has a loft conversion optimistically called 'The Penthouse'.

'Bet they can't keep pets up there now!' This is Tank, cracking an elaborate joke, which relies on the appreciation of two factors: first, that their old digs banned pets; and second, that the girly mag *Penthouse* had its own nude 'Penthouse Pets'. The lads get the references and nod in appreciation, 'Nice one, Tank'.

So, on the morning of the recording, which is due at midday, and after a pub breakfast of considerable proportions, they stroll into the sunshine along West End Lane passing Asian and Thai restaurants, artisan bakers, the pub where they had their first West Hampstead drink all those years ago, the supermarket where they couldn't afford the food. They cross over the railway bridge and on their left is a lane, not really more than an alleyway, that they don't remember, or at least they don't remember its name, being Billy Fury Way. 'Not in our day, it weren't called that,' says Mickey. In fact, they don't think this narrow thoroughfare was called anything back in their day. As they pass by, cue Prof Rock:

'Billy Fury, as you may recall from Danny's intros, was a pop singer of the late 1950s. Real name Ronald Wycherley but re-christened by his manager, Larry Parnes. Billy Fury was tall, handsome, hair with a quiff, smart suit; the girls worshipped him. A pop idol. Fury's hits were "Halfway To Paradise", "Jealousy", "It's Only Make Believe". He was in films, *Play It Cool* was one, and *That'll Be The Day*, which had Ringo Starr in it.'

'Starring Ringo Starr,' comments Mickey unnecessarily, but Tone is not to be put off.

'Sad to say, Billy Fury started having heart problems in his thirties and these health issues plagued him during the 1970s and he died of a heart attack aged just forty-three, if memory serves. He was a keen birdwatcher – not a lot of people know that.'

'I'm a keen birdwatcher!' Delivered with a wink, this is not one of Tank's best jokes so he is ignored. Meanwhile, Tone is checking on his mobile.

'Billy Fury Way, it says here, was a previously unnamed alleyway, once an ancient footpath connecting West Hampstead to the Finchley Road, but was christened in honour of Billy Fury by Camden Council. It boasted a magnificent mural of the pop star, but this was defaced and the alley has since become daubed in graffiti. I reckon Billy would be ashamed to be associated with such an eyesore.'

'Why?' chimes in Danny.

'Why what?'

'Why's it named after him?'

'He recorded near here. Decca Studios, Broadhurst Gardens. We passed it a way back.'

Their conversation, by now, has got them into St John's Wood – an affluent neighbourhood of mansion blocks and townhouses. To the right is the less affluent area of Kilburn. They pass a grand church, St Mary With All Souls, further on down is the New London Synagogue – all denominations catered for in this neck of the woods. Now they're in Abbey Road itself, rich suburbia, another church, Baptist this time; then on the right their ultimate goal, Abbey Road Studios.

And there it is! Only Abbey bloody Road!

Number Three, an elegant Georgian mansion, white-walled with a grand doorway up a flight of stone steps. The building is set back behind railings and a low wall which is covered with fans' graffiti proclaiming their love for the band that christened the former EMI Recording Studio, 'Abbey Road', after their final album. Amongst messages like BEATLES FOREVER and @MALCOLM, there are the more angry signings, LOVE MUSIC HATE RACISM is one such, DON'T KILL ROCK 'N' ROLL is another. One simple message, I (HEART) JOHN (with a drawn heart), has an added political touch worthy of John himself: inside the 'o' of John is a 'Ban The Bomb' symbol.

But how can one talk of the famous Abbey Road without including the even-more-famous zebra crossing across which the fab four strode for their album cover? Where every tourist since has had their photo taken, holding up traffic; and now the lads do the same, with the photographer being their record producer, a cool young dude called Musgrave. Right guys, legs in synch – CLICK!

Musgrave needs describing: he's Black, slim and smart and quite short, pencil moustache, wearing a blue suit and red polo neck, scarlet baseball cap bearing a large white M, espadrilles with no socks. He is smoking a pipe. A pipe! Who smokes a pipe these days? Outside the studio, he's as nice as pie, but inside he becomes a tyrant.

They climb the steps and enter *Nirvana*.

Through the doors, a modern reception area. Girl behind a desk where they're asked to sign in, but Rosie is already there to do the honours. She looks cool in a leather 'bomber' jacket, worn and creased in all the right places. Dark leggings. Hair scraped back in a ponytail. Huge hoop earrings. The 'look'? – Rock chick, of course. This reception area could be for any large corporation, with a giant TV screen set to a music channel. Above the long desk are the words writ large and proud: ABBEY ROAD STUDIOS. But it's not designed to intimidate, this reception area, like some multinational companies. The curved lines of the desk and a sweeping lighting feature in the ceiling make for a friendlier feel. There's an Art Deco clock above double doors that lead, presumably, to some inner sanctum. Above the leather sofa is a geometric mural, the design of which is reminiscent of a musical stave. Perhaps that's intentional. As the lads await their call, leafing through music mags on the coffee table, a man with a cello case strapped to his back signs in, then goes through the double doors. He knows the receptionist by name, and she likewise – 'Morning Joe.'

Musgrave gathers them together and leads them through the double doors down a corridor lined with black-and-white photos of bands and album covers in frames. They want to stop and take a look, but time is of the essence, says Musgrave, and Rosie hurries them along from behind, herding them like sheep. Another part of the corridor has vintage recording desks and tape machines up against one wall – maybe these were the four-track machines The Beatles used!

Then, to the very seat of Heaven, Studio Two, where the Best Group In The World (in the boys' opinion) recorded most of their music; a world of 'Revolver' and 'Sergeant Pepper' and that delicious swansong 'Abbey Road'. They are in the booth (there should be a blue plaque dedicated to George Martin here) that's high above Studio Two itself, which they can look down on through a big picture window. Light-coloured wooden flooring, tall plain white walls, spotlights on racking, cables and wires and headphones that hang in loops. Everything neat and professional. They descend the long flight of stairs into the studio where their instruments are waiting for them next to sound-baffles, placed to deflect extraneous sound, and behind which each will play. They look back up to the picture window at Musgrave who has now removed his baseball cap to reveal a shaved head. Natch. He looks like he means business as the engineer, who will work the desk with its multiple sliders, knobs, and dials, enters. They know each other, hug, and do a 'fist-bump'. This massive desk boasts more tracks than these four instrumentalists will ever need. But wait, what are all those chairs doing in rows next to the grand piano?

Danny calls up to Musgrave, 'These for another session?'. 'Wait 'n' see,' comes Musgrave's voice through the intercom. That slow American drawl. Musgrave is, of course, with a name like that, American.

They tune up, then it's Take One for the backing track. The singing – from Danny first, then Mickey for the 'B' side, being his 'Rosy Rosie' song – will be added after. In a weird volte-face, the arrangement of

'Beat, Beat' now has to match the version put out by the girl singer on the ad. So the song is now in waltz-time (3/4), which goes back to Tone's original acoustic rendition, and has a more romantic feel. A softer, gentler beating of the heart. Danny's vocals, which he adds later, match the mood sublimely. How his voice has matured over the years! Mickey harmonises, and Tone and Tank provide a wordless drone in D major, the new key of the song. Then, Mickey takes over the vocals for 'Rosy Rosie'. His voice has deepened (slightly) over the years and roughened, like a Tom Waits vibe, and it fits the heartache of his song. After a few takes, Musgrave is happy, and he beckons the boys up into the booth for mixing the tracks.

They look down on the deserted studio, imagining the ghosts of Lennon and McCartney, Harrison and Starr. But the vision is broken by the boisterous entry of twenty women holding music sheets, with bags and chattels, chatting noisily. The rustle of coats being discarded, the scraping of chairs, laughter, 'hello's' and 'how are you's'. They put on the cans, taking care not to muss their hair. 'Have you changed your style?' 'I had it cut shorter.' 'Looks fab, where do you go?' 'Toni does it.' 'She's great.' 'I like your coat.' 'What, this old thing?' And so on and so on, only to be interrupted by Musgrave appearing amongst them, which causes a flurry of 'Hi Musgrave!' and 'Cool espadrilles, honey!' and so on and so forth. Which Musgrave just *loves,* as he sets up a music stand in front of them and, for chrissake, he has a conductor's *baton*! Where the fuck did that come from? Puts on his cans. 'Playback,' he calls out, and through the speakers comes a rough mix of 'Beat, Beat', which Musgrave hums along to, demonstrating the parts that the women's chorus will sing. He conducts as the women follow the music sheets and join in. Harmonies, sometimes pianissimo, sometimes forte, swirl around the track, complementing Tone and Tank's D major drone and adding more emotion to Danny's soulful voice.

'Fuckin' hell,' is all Tank can say.

'Musgrave done good,' is Danny's summary.

Mickey's song is polished off with a kind of staccato singing arrangement, almost tribal, adding a percussive note to emphasise the edginess of Mickey's Tom Waits-growl.

The session is done. After a final mix of both tracks, the designated two hours is up. The woman's chorus has long gone, all huggy and kissy. 'Bye, Musgrave sweetie!' 'You *really* understand female voices!' etc etc. And just as quickly, Rock Ireland Line are ushered out onto the street again – little people looking back at The Temple, hardly believing they could be this fortunate at their time of life.

'We're some lucky boyos,' says Danny, and the lads can only agree.

As they walk away, back to West Hampstead, some tourists – a gaggle of giggling Chinese this time – cross back and forth over the black-and-white stripes, holding up traffic; while in Studio Two, the ghosts of the best-bloody-group-in-the-whole-wide-fuckin'-world, who are part of the very atmosphere of the place, like the Ghosts of Versailles, call up to 'George', asking if they should do another take. The urbane Martin, in white shirt and tie, looking like a schoolmaster maybe or an RAF Group Captain, handsome features, combed-back hair (the very opposite of the Beatles' fringe), messages down to 'the boys', in his upper-class accent, that he's happy and 'let's move on'.

53
Hallelujah

'Hallelujah!' is the cry from the crowd that greets Rock Ireland's Second Coming.

'Hallelujah' is the Leonard Cohen song that the band adopts for the end of the set. This song that speaks of a secret chord.

But for RIL it's more like a battle-cry – onward Christian soldiers! – onward the aged who battle on despite ailments, various. A rallying call.

Or is it an epitaph? They're all knocking on a bit now. Rocking on a bit too. When they can. For in this Yeare of Our Lorde 2018, Tone has moved into his seventh decade, now seventy-one. Mickey is next, on the cusp at sixty-nine. Tank is sixty-seven, and Danny Boy still a boyo at sixty-six.

But 'Hallelujah!', they can at least stand up for two hours straight (and not too bent) which is the length of their set at the festival. And 'Hallelujah, Viagra!' is Tank's mantra as a new breed of groupies require his attention – talk about standing up for two hours straight!

Hallelujah is an anthem, and the band deserves an anthem now. To have lasted this long.

The Beginning, way back in the Sixties, then success in the Seventies, followed by the wilderness years of the Eighties. The Nineties saw the Reformation, and now the Noughties, their Renaissance.

To have lasted this long and still stayed together. 'Like A Rolling Stone' is the Dylan song, and like a Rolling Stone is their creed as an example of that everlasting band: Mick, Keith, Ronnie, and Charlie. So yes, an anthem is deserved. They are worthy.

Their 'Beat, Beat' single goes into the Top Ten, then climbs to the Number One slot in a week. It's released in America and gets in the top five of the Billboard charts, thanks to online video streaming. Rosie handles the money side like a born-again accountant, and the band have a whole new audience now – the web chat generation who revere this bunch of cronies. They replay videos of the group's yesteryears and love the retro music. So things are going well for RIL.

It is at this point that Alamo Godbold, erstwhile head of YoungDudes Records, appears back on the scene in the shape of his son, Cisco.

To backtrack: when Alamo Godbold marries Sandy the receptionist, he adopts her two children, a girl and a boy. He is allowed to re-name the youngest – the boy – 'Cisco', after his Romani roots. That is Alamo's reasoning to Sandy at the time – 'Cisco' sounding appropriately Bohemian, in his humble. When Alamo dies (in 2010), he leaves a significant portion of YoungDudes to his adopted son who'd started working with his father some years previous. So Cisco, at the age of 26, is MD, Chairman and Dictator of the company, which is now a management and talent agency, having jettisoned the records side some years back (hence the dropping of 'Records' from the company name).

Cisco, in his new position of power, proves to be a right bastard to work for. He fires the older staff, saying that 'old people', i.e. people over forty, make him feel old. 'To stay young, I need the elixir of youth,' he is wont to say. He hires cool young guys – young dudes – and all are guys, as Cisco, being one hundred per cent gay, is only partial to the 'apposite sex', as he puts it. They look alike, generally dark-haired short-cut, sallow-skinned, slim of course. They wear a uniform of sorts: black suit, black polo neck, black slip-ons. He models them on staff he's seen in those trendy New York hotels, the kind that like to keep the reception area tidy: no suitcases, no scruffs, no clutter – image being the be-all-and-end-all (the sort of hip hotel where it's the guests that let the side down).

In deliberate contrast to his underlings though, Cisco has an aureole of permed hair, like Hendrix, and favours white suits. He likes to call himself 'President Poof' as in 'President Poof no longer requires your services,' as he fires someone for being too old or just for effect or because he's found out they're straight.

So, enter Cisco Godbold onto the scene who, being aware of his father's early success with RIL, wants to bring the band 'back to the fold,' he says, to represent the band in a managerial capacity. First stop: Rosie. He susses out where he needs to attack initially and this is their present manager-elect. Gets his underlings to arrange a 'meet'. Rosie declines. Calls Rosie's 'office', i.e. her answering service, but his calls aren't returned. Gatecrashes an album launch held at a top-end London hotel. The band's new album is called 'Rock Ireland Line. RE-BIRTH' and the front cover has family photos of the fellas as babies. Introduces himself to Rosie. Knows she's the one to schmooze. There's a heap of ground he needs to cover with her – first off, his father's launch of RIL, his nurturing of them, how he stopped them going punk, how he made them a success. Water under the bridge, my friend. The noise of the gathering makes it impossible for him to make any sense though, he's reduced to shouting in her ear and Cisco don't go a bundle on shouting. He is a gentle assassin. All Rosie gleans from their brief encounter is this smarmy character who's earholing her. She does not like. Cisco moves off with a 'catch you later' and introduces himself to the boys – they seem so *old*, he thinks. They give him the time of day, in honour of the Rt. Hon. Alamo G, but no more than that. Defeated, Cisco leaves them his gold-embossed business card and says he'll 'be in touch'.

Next day, they tell Rosie about their history with Alamo and YD Records, and what they've heard about his son taking over the firm and what a right bastard he is. They call him the Cisco Kid, after a TV Western of the '50s. But they've had their fill of high-powered management, Joe Rainbow and his ilk, and want to stick with streetwise Rosie. The Cisco Kid bites the dust.

Does this narrative now break off to tell the history of Cisco Godbold? Does this narrative care? If his were a dull story, it would not. It wouldn't waste time over it. But Cisco's story is extraordinary indeed: in short, Cisco finds God.

His Path to Righteousness begins with him becoming ultra-sensitive to electricity. The condition, which doctors disown, has a fancy name: Electromagnetic Hypersensitivity. It even has initials, which all the best ailments have: EHS. Doctors and those-in-the-medical-know believe the condition to be 'imagined'. All in the mind. Like that joke about the annual Hypochondriac Convention, where no one turns up as they've all called in sick.

But for Cisco, and others like him, EHS is real enough. He experiences an unusual reaction to electricity, starting merely with mild shocks from door handles, then progressing to stronger shocks from touching anything metal, shocks that make him pull back his hand sharply. He hears a crackle as this happens and puts it down to static electricity from the office carpets, so he has them all taken up and wooden flooring put down instead. But still the shocks continue and get worse. People get a shock *off him* when they shake hands, for instance, and they reel back, feeling the shock going through their whole body. He feels his hair stand on end, and his skin burns hot. If he touches a light switch, there's a visible spark.

The next phase causes fuses to blow. He only has to touch a plug, and 'BANG!' the whole circuit board is blown. By now he's read up on EHS, but finds his symptoms don't match other sufferers who, in the presence of ordinary household appliances, get violent headaches, migraines, blurred vision, prickly skin with rashes, 'pins and needles', aching muscles, chest pains, vomiting. But none of them seem to actually *store* electricity like Cisco, because that's what seems to be happening. The build-up of electricity in his body is palpable and increasing. 'This is crazy,' he says to his private doctor, who says to wear rubber-soled shoes, rubber gloves, don't walk near pylons, take painkillers – 'that'll be £200, Mr Godbold.'

He consults an online forum, which recommends a form of holistic medicine, dating back thousands of years, promoting a balance between body and mind. Cisco just wants a balance between his body and the electrical outside world, but 'mind' might be relevant as he's wondering if his condition is indeed psychosomatic. Managing YoungDudes and being a right bastard is stressful, after all.

The online forum lists holistic doctors in Southern India, so he gets on a plane, where he keeps getting the shocks off pretty much anything he touches. A stewardess asks if any passengers have their mobile on, i.e. not set to 'Airplane mode', as the pilot is encountering electrical interference – nothing to worry about, though. Nothing to worry about?

306

Electrical interference on a plane flown by electrical instruments? Cisco has taken to carrying a metal key clip, which seems to diffuse the worst of his shocks.

The first holistic doctor he finds works by feeling the feet and diagnosing medical problems by touching the soles and the toes. He asks if Cisco has any issues in the 'anal area'? Unnatural growths. Cisco confesses to haemorrhoids. This condition is indeed God's punishment to Mankind, probably for seeing off His Only Son. Also known as 'piles'. Hard to say which is the worst word.

As the Indian doctor massages Cisco's feet, he suddenly gets an almighty shock. Jolts back, staring at his tingling hand as if it's infected. He tentatively touches the foot again and gets another shock.

'You, my friend, are like a battery. You absorb electricity like a car battery, so every time you touch something electrical or are in the vicinity of something electrical or an electromagnetic field, you store up the power in your body. This is not a problem of the mind, my friend, it is of the body. I can feel that you are now overloaded, and my advice is to get away from modern life with all its appliances. We are, in this modern world of ours, surrounded by currents. Here in my surgery, the electric fan, radio, computer, phones, and you are draining their power. I therefore recommend you go to a monastery in the foothills, where you can live the simple life away from that which harms you. If you ignore this advice, you will likely burn up; you will become so saturated with electrics that you will explode in flame. I cannot cure you with my ancient arts. Go in peace.'

He goes in peace, becomes a monk, and finds God.

That is Cisco's story, worthy of inclusion here.

But what became of him, might be the question? Did he live the humble life into old age? No, is the answer. He dies young. In his forties. As the electricity leaks out of him like a draining battery, he loses strength and power until, one by one, his vital organs shut off and fail. His fellow monks mourn his loss, not just because he has become one of their own, but because they loved him. For Cisco changed when he found God, as people often do.

It is Cisco's sister who tells this story, so it must be Gospel.

They once knew a man, one of their road crew while touring, who they called 'Mr Volto'. He was lanky-tall and clumsy as hell. If there was anything around to bump into, he'd find it. Usually at crotch level, which made for high-pitched squealing as he doubled over in agony. If there was a beam or some such skyward obstruction, his head would connect with it. He'd knock things over, spill things, burn himself. But this wasn't why they called him Mr Volto. They called him this because, in the presence of anything electrical, disasters would happen. Spotlights would blow, bulbs explode. Recording equipment would malfunction, sometimes tape would be partially erased or suffer interference. On the mixing desks, the dials would go apeshit, crashing into the red, even though there was no sound. Everyone swore that he drained batteries. Brand new batteries placed in a device would be flat in seconds if they were in the presence of Mr Volto. They had to sack him as he was causing havoc. Ended up working for the National Grid. Somehow his strange facility worked in an environment that was wholly electrical. Maybe it reversed the polarities or something. RayRoadieRice, who was his boss while touring, said he'd never seen the like in all his born days. But then, RRR was only a kid in his twenties. Anyway, that's the true story of Mr Volto. The Human Dynamo. 'Should've been on the stage,' was Mickey's view.

54
Rock Of Ages

There are offers of touring, but the members of Rock Ireland, being on the brink of seventy and beyond, have to consider whether they can take the rigours of being 'on the road'. Been there, done that, when they were young. But now?

They call a garage-meet with Rosie excluded as the discussions might get a mite personal.

Mickey is first to put in his two pennies' worth.

'It's my back strain I have to think of.'

'What about your piss-poor bladder?' says Danny.

'I have no problem in that area. Anyway, peeing frequently is a sign of a good working bladder. It's when you can't pee there's a problem.'

Tank chips in, 'I'm beginning to notice that. I wanna go but then I can't, and I stand there for bloody ages till at last there's a pathetic trickle like I didn't need to go after all.'

'Well, that sounds like your prostate,' says Mickey. 'You should get it checked out.'

'What, and have a doctor stick his finger up me bum?'

'It's not that bad. Bend over, close your eyes and pretend it's Marilyn Monroe.'

'Marilyn Monroe with rubber gloves. Oo, matron!' says Tank.

They laugh; it's a good image.

Tank again: 'Doctor Monroe, I'm *in love!*'

They laugh. It's a good image to linger on – the blonde bombshell in a white coat or, better still, a *Carry On*-type nurse's outfit. They go quiet for a while.

Mickey: 'But I have to think of my back. I can't sit on a plane for hours on end as it gets my back real bad. Just here.'

He indicates his lower back. Tone massages his own back in the same place.

'It's called the sacroiliac joint.'

'Who's gotta joint?' asks Tank, coming out of his Monroe reverie.

'No one's got a joint, Tank,' says Danny, 'go back to sleep.'

Mickey continues: 'No long-haul flights for me, is what I'm saying.'

Danny: 'You'd have to sit near the loo.'

'THERE'S NOTHING WRONG WITH MY BLADDER!'

Another pause. Who's going to be next to admit to another symptom of old age?

Danny: 'You all know my problem: remembering the fookin' lyrics! If I've got them written down, I can't see them properly from a distance. And I can't very well stand there holding bits of paper. Not the coolest of cool.'

Tone: 'Why don't you wear glasses like Buddy Holly?'

Danny: 'Not bloody likely. Not *Buddy* likely!'

(On a scale of one to ten, joke-wise, this isn't up with the eight's but more of a three or four maybe.)

Danny (cont'd): '… and before anyone mentions it: no, I can't wear contact lenses. Can't touch my eyes, freaks me out.'

Tone: 'Try learning the words off by heart and if you forget them, I'll prompt you. Just give me a sign.'

'What sign?'

'Like a pointing to the head like your brain's gone dead.'

'Like this?' and he mimes the pointing.

'Yeah, like that.'

'I guess that'll work, but you know what? I just don't feel comfortable playing any stadium gigs no more. Like, in a pub I can have the words close-up on a stand in front of me. But not in a huge arena.'

Tank's turn. 'And there's my hearing, shot to hell and back. Pretty much all I get all day is a high pitch buzzing like a dentist's drill. It's getting worse too. I can't deal with touring. I'd end up stone-deaf!'

There's a pause as Aggie brings in a pot of tea and Jaffa cakes. Tone starts to pour.

'Shall I be mother?'

Mickey: 'Does anyone else get sore feet?'

They all get sore feet.

Tone: 'Bunions, corns, the lot. I get those foot pads from Boots.'

Tank: 'Those Boots are made for walkin'.'

He's sung the title of the Nancy Sinatra hit.

Tone: 'Released in 1966, if memory serves, with that great descending bass line, not on the electric bass, as you might expect, but on a proper stand-up double bass.'

Mickey (ignoring the history lesson): 'What foot pads?'

Tone: 'It's a rubber pad you hook around your big toe. As I said, Boots do them.'

Tank: 'Boots are good for feet, yeah? That could be their slogan.'

Danny: 'Y'know, I might try those rubber pad things too; my feet kill me these days.'

Tank: 'You should stop wearing stilettos!'

Danny looks at him like something the cat dragged in.

Mickey: 'Wrenched my knee t'other day.'

The others wince in sympathy; they've all been there.

Tone: 'That's a killer, when your knee goes. You know you can get a support bandage for that?'

'From Boots, by any chance?'

'Yeah, from Boots. Everything from Boots. They should have a section: AGEING ROCK BANDS.'

Tank: 'Mickey, have you tried CBD oil for your knee?'

Mickey: 'Is that like hemp?'

'It's got the hallucinogen taken out. Relaxes the muscles.'

'You know what I heard?' says Tone, 'that CBD oil makes men, y'know, *last* longer…'

'You mean…?'

'Yeah.'

Tank: 'Man, if I lasted any longer, you'd have to call a priest.'

Mickey: 'I'll give it a try. Where can I get it?'

'BOOTS!' they all shout.

Danny holds up his right hand, palm outwards.

'Look at this, fellas. I've got this swelling on my palm.'

Tank smirks: 'You know what that's from!'

Danny ignores him.

'I went to the doc, and he said it's called something something

311

syndrome and can't be cured. Look at my hand, I can't get me fingers straight,' and sure enough, Danny's fingers are curled into a fist. 'Works for holding the mic, though. It's a weird condition that came over with the Vikings, the doc said, so it's in my blood.'

'The Vikings invaded Ireland then?'

'Fuck knows.'

There's a moment's pause where, like telepathy, they all think the same thing. Tank is the first to introduce the subject.

'What about the other thing, y'know, like "down below"?'

'You mean "piles"?' says Tone with a grimace.

'You got piles?'

'No, I *don't* have piles!'

For Danny, the coin drops.

'Tank means "I Can't Get No Satisfaction".'

'Yeah, or "A Hard Day's Night" maybe,' says Tank, 'c'mon, admit it, fellas. That little blue pill that works miracles? Be upstanding for Viagra! Show of hands please – who takes Viagra?'

The hands go up, one by one. Danny, the last. He, he thinks, being the youngest, shouldn't have need of Man's Little Helper. Hallelujah, Viagra! The Birth of the Blues.

Tone: 'In France, they have a version of the little blue pill that lasts *all weekend*. They call it "Le Weekend" – especially for husbands and their mistresses.'

Tank wriggles his fingers.

'I swear I'm getting a touch of the Arthurs. Look at my hand!' (Bent, crooked fingers.)

Danny: 'Arthur-itis? Me too, in my shoulder.' (He moves his shoulder around, groaning.)

Tone: 'Listen, I'm the oldest out of you lot. Who's the youngest? I can't remember…'

Danny puts his hand up and immediately yelps as the movement of his arm catches.

Tone: 'That's "frozen shoulder" you got there.'

Danny massages his neck where it meets the shoulder.

'Bloody ageing, bloody shoulders, bloody everythin'!'

Tank: 'Y'know, most old people say that in their minds they're still twenty-five. Well, let me tell you, in my mind my mental age is my real age, sixty-seven – a grumpy old bastard, intolerant, cantankerous, mean, angry, and generally pissed off with all that life, politicians and the Inland Revenue can throw at you.'

This is probably the longest speech Tank has ever made, and the others sit in stunned silence.

Danny: 'I always thought your mental age was ten.'

This breaks the ice. Danny continues.

'Are we all agreed then? No touring. No "on the road". Short-haul flights only.'

All agreed.

'Let's bring Rosie in.'

55
A Kind Of Magic

Rosie is not surprised. In fact, to tell the truth, she is relieved. She doesn't want to be the cause of Rock Ireland reaching the end of the Line by insisting on touring. The rigours thereof. But she has an idea up her sleeve. A call has come in from a popular rock festival in the summer, the Thorfield Festival, or 'Thor', as it's known for short. It claims to be 'more glam than Glasto but without the mud'. Held in a generally dry part of the countryside with well-drained grounds, part of a country estate that's fallen on hard times and needs the dosh that a festival brings.

'You'd be the penultimate act before the main set,' and here Rosie mentions the name of an American rapper who the boys haven't heard of. 'He's big in the States, big over here too, so it's prestigious you being on the main stage before him. You'll be on at seven, him at nine.

'So a two-hour set,' says Mickey.

'Yes, a two-hour set; think you can manage that?'

'Sure,' says Danny.

'Sure,' says Tone.

'Sure,' says Tank.

'Guess so,' says Mickey doubtfully.

'What's the problem, Mickey?' but she knows; she's married to the guy after all.

'There's an offer – well, more of a suggestion from the festival organisers – that you might do a surprise set on a smaller stage the day before. Sort of a *dry run*,' she says, trying not to look too meaningfully at her husband. 'You wouldn't be billed, so it'd be more like a mystery band. Savvy?'

They savvy and quite like the idea.

So, onto the logistics. Where would they stay?

'You have a choice,' Rosie continues, 'you could either have a tour bus on site in amongst the other tour buses. Problem is: noise till all hours from the other buses as they'll be likely to party. Or you could go "glamping", which is posh camping in Bell Tents with double beds. Problem is: same as the tour bus scenario, namely noise as festival-goers don't go to bed at nine o'clock – in fact, word is, they don't go to bed.'

Word is, indeed. As if Rosie hasn't been to enough festivals in her wilder days. You don't go to no festivals to *sleep*. She doesn't mention the abundance of drugs either: weed, MD, coke, as this will worry some of them – not Tank, but the others. She also doesn't touch on the sniffer dogs, police checks, dazed crowds, and the terrible loos.

'What about the terrible loos?' asks Tone.

'Ah, you've heard about them. Well, if you go for the glamping option, the loos are much better, they even have soap in them.'

'Any nearby hotels?' asks Danny.

'That's option three. Not a hotel but a very nice B&B in a pub near to the site. I've checked and they have two rooms available, which I've put on hold. Sorry guys, it'd mean sharing again.' Story of their lives.

'How far from the site?'

'A few miles, granted. Problem is: traffic. You'll get caught up in the daily festival jams. Especially on the last day. But I have a solution: helicopter.'

'Can we afford a helicopter? Surely that'll blow our fees?'

'Not as pricey as you may think. There's a field near the pub, it could land there then fly the short distance to the helipad on the site.'

So that's the decision: two rooms at the Bell & Dragon. Helicopter to the site. Good night's sleep, decent breakfast. Sorted.

It goes well. The surprise set goes well. The crowd cheers when they see who the mystery band is, and the reception is great. The set is only an hour. Even Mickey can 'hold on' for an hour. No pints of lager-top beforehand though. Danny remembers the words and Tone's back holds up. Tank wears his hearing aids, Mickey his piss-pad. Then a good night's kip at the B&B.

Next day, the helicopter whisks them off to the site. How exciting to see the crowd from that height and see the people looking up, wondering what star is arriving! And then the lads do that thing of overdoing the ducking as they leave the helicopter, holding onto hair, hats. They walk to the holding area, signing autographs, to then wait for their seven p.m. slot, feeling good about being once more in the Presence of Gods. They recognise some bands, nod to ones they know well, nudge each other as a big Black guy with a huge entourage swans in, 'Is that the rapper?' 'Yo, fellas,' drawls the deep deep voice of said rapper. 'You Rock Ireland Line? I'm a big fan.' He high-fives and hugs each one of them, and don't they feel just grand!

These minutes of waiting before going on have never stopped them feeling nervous. Mickey strums his unplugged guitar, checking and re-checking the tuning. Tank paradiddles on his thighs – slap-slappity-slap-slap. Tone hums a bass line, tries it out on his mute guitar. Danny is doing his voice-warming exercises – meeh, meeeeh, meeh, meeeh. A festival runner ambles in, 'Five minutes, guys. Have a great one!' Have a great one, indeed. But this is no easy pub gig, or even the club venues they've been doing lately, this is MASSIVE. Mickey rushes off to a corner and throws up. 'Sorry, lads.' It's a sign of weakness and the terror can be catching, 'It's okay, Mickey, we all feel the same.'

'And now… the band you've been waiting for, the band of the moment, let's give a beat, beat, beat to…'
    This is the announcer, whose last words are drowned out by a deafening chord from Mickey's guitar and RIL not so much run on as saunter. (They're like the Stones, but more strolling than Rolling.) But they're not met, as they hoped, with a great cheer of welcome from the crowd. The crowd are silent and it becomes clear, as the band plays, that this is a rapper-fan crowd who are impatient for their hero to appear. The main act, not the one before. This audience just doesn't 'get' this long-in-the-tooth group; they're young and hip and only appreciate street-talkin' rappers, not an old-fashioned past-it bunch of pensioners. Jeez, these guys are older than their *grandparents*! And didn't that song just get used on a supermarket ad? Which is not cool. Not 'street'.

A performer knows when they're not going down well. It's in their psyche. Danny senses it first when he scans the faces in the front. Bored, drugged-out, pissed. Talking to each other, not listening, not watching. A girl gets more attention when she pulls her top up to show her tiny tits. There's no applause in between the songs, no response when Danny says, 'Clap your hands'. Tone notices it and hides behind his bass guitar, holding it upright, pointing due north as per. Mickey turns his back on the crowd and plays to the amps. Only Tank is oblivious, lost in his tinnitus-world.

Then they start throwing things, this audience. Just some half-finished food at first, but then the missiles start, bursting onto the stage, showering Danny in piss. It turns out it's a favourite with this crowd, and also this festival, that's more 'sham' than 'glam' as there's no law or order on this last day, no control over booze, let alone drugs as the sniffer dogs have gone back to their kennels. The cops are nowhere to be seen. Anarchy rules. The piss missiles – or 'pissiles' as the louts in the audience call them – are emptied-out water bottles filled with urine. Like a Molotov cocktail, they burst on impact, hence the piss-shower. They may be small plastic water bottles but once filled up and lobbed with force, they're deadly. The lads have to duck the bottles, Mickey hides behind the amps, Tone hides behind Mickey. Tank is protected behind his barricade of drums but one bottle catches him on his ear, making his hearing aid howl – just another crazy tinnitus sound. Furious, he stands up, throws the bottle, which hasn't burst, back into the crowd. Bad idea as this just encourages the crowd to fight back; and now a barrage of bottles hit the stage, full of piss, full of water, beer – who cares? as long as the bottle's got some weight to it. They explode as Danny calls for calm, and the bottles seem to miss him – the luck of the Irish, they say much later, safe in their B&B, taking turns to use the one shower, piss-stinking like old tramps.

A festival organiser comes on stage and tries to stop the onslaught but is hit himself, 'right in the breadbasket,' Mickey notes later; he doubles up and limps off to cheers from the mob. But this band will never admit defeat, they've had worse audiences in pubs. With a nod from Danny and a sign meaning 'wrap up', they launch into 'Hallelujah'. Their anthem.

Then something magic happens. One of those movie moments that wouldn't happen in real life, but now it does. At the first chords and then the first few lines of Danny's ethereal voice, the crowd quiets down. Some girls stay the hands of the bottle-throwers. They start to sway and join in the singing. There's now a chanting that echoes Danny's singing as an early dusk, for this has been a grey sort of day, descends and the lights on the mobile phones glow like fireflies. The song ends quietly, Danny has ramped the band down with his hands, no crescendo to end but a soft fade to nothing. Then a fresh chant begins and increases, and they can make out the words 'Beat, Beat,' repeated over and over. They have some fans in the audience, after all! So naturally, for who can resist such a call to action, they oblige with their hit song and, because they now like the crowd and wish to give them a Grand Finale, they let off the confetti cannons that Rosie has provided. 'It's raining confetti,' says one spaced-out girl.

And then… and then… as if enough magic hasn't happened already, an aerial display that was meant to be for the main act arrives early: two World War II Spitfires fly low over the arena in tight formation, and the sound of the planes comes through the speakers and still echoes after they have passed, and the crowd look up in worship. 'They're like birds,' says the same spaced-out girl.

Tank says afterwards, 'I don't know about "Beat, Beat," but you can't beat that.'

And they can but only agree.

The Thorfield Festival is the one and only festival the band ever do. Even though there are some more that Rosie has in the pipeline for the forthcoming year. But for now, Rock Ireland have triumphed, and that night, what's left of it, is celebrated royally in the pub bar where even teetotal Mickey dares to drink something more serious than his usual lager-top, until Rosie puts the kibosh on that.

56
Flying

And so it came to pass, in the year 2019 AD, that from the lands of the Nether came the pop prophet Tim Smit, and he saith unto the disciples of The Lord Danny and unto the Lord Himself, 'Why dwellest thou forever in the place of thy birth? For it is beholden upon thee to visit Kavos, being the part of the Isle of Corfu, which is much given to feasting and dancing and has many Temples of Music. And thou shallst come with me, as brethren, to tread the righteous path.'

Tim Smit, the interviewer from Radio Amst, is now DJ-ing in a swanky nightclub in the part of Corfu that's known for its wild nightlife, and Tim, being an RIL fan, has invited the band to 'guest spot' for three nights as a special appearance for interviews and general chit-chat in his one-hour nightly Rock Ireland Line slot. As it's a short-enough-haul flight, the band decide it will be a nice easy break, and Corfu is a pleasant temperature this time of year, being early September. Also, the worst of the Kavos crowd would've been in the summer months.

Their flight from Gatwick is an afternoon one, so no getting up at stupid o'clock. Rosie sees them off: be good, don't get into trouble, and if you do, don't call me for help. She has no desire to go on this jaunt and anyway, this is one just for the boys. She is always careful not to 'crowd' them or be 'mother'.

When they get to the airport, they hear reports of bad weather on mainland Greece and neighbouring Corfu and the other islands, and at one point, the flight is nearly cancelled because of 'electrical storms'. But the flight goes ahead, albeit delayed, and the journey over is smooth until they reach Greece, when the turbulence kicks in and the seatbelt lights go on and passengers are advised to stay in their seats.

The stewardesses quickly gather up the half-finished coffees and alcoholic drinks, and the plane is set tight in lockdown for any dips and dives, jolts and judders. Of which there are plenty, as the turbulence gets worse as they approach Corfu; and there's Mickey scrutinising the safety leaflet, memorising the Brace position and lifejacket instructions.

The pilot's voice comes on, calm, and reassuring everyone that it's 'just a bit bumpy'. What he doesn't mention is that the wind is topping thirty-seven knots, which on the Beaufort Scale is a near-gale, not quite a gale, but try telling that to a cylinder of metal at the mercy of the elements.

Apart from Mickey, the boys are making light of the situation. They are split across the gangway – two seats by the window and two seats in the central section. Danny with Tone, Tank next to Mickey, who's nearest the window.

Now they are circling in a holding pattern. They should've landed an hour ago, but the pilot says he's waiting for a break in the wind. Tank makes a joke about eating beans, but no one laughs. A knowledgeable passenger – there's always one – says that Corfu has one of the world's shortest runways at 2,400 metres, so the pilot doesn't have much leeway for error. The know-it-all's use of the word 'error' alarms his neighbours.

Mickey feels under his seat for his lifejacket, he's never learnt to swim and panics when he can't find it, but the stewardess tells him it's further back – you'll be able to reach it if need be but don't worry, sir, you're in safe hands. But the turbulence is becoming severe, sudden sharp drops accompanied by expressions of shock from the passengers. 'These crates can take it,' says the expert. 'I've been in worse, this is like a walk in the park.' Whoop! Down plummets the plane for what must be twenty metres or so.

Then the announcement comes through that they're about to land, phew! The flight staff strap themselves in and there's the clunk of the landing gear deploying. The plane is being buffeted badly, though; armrests are being gripped, and it's dark as dark outside, just the flashes of lightning. Lightning? Isn't that dangerous? Is that what they meant by 'electrical storms' back in the safety of Gatwick?

They can see the lights of the airport's surrounding buildings through the rain-lashed windows and thankfully they're about to touch down, but just when the ground is nearing – that welcome return to Mother Earth – the plane suddenly accelerates and surges upwards. Upwards not downwards. Back into the storm.

The passengers gasp – this isn't meant to happen! They'd all been prepared to applaud the flight crew on landing, like they always do, but now they're frightened. The plane soars upwards at what seems to be a crazy angle, and the knowledgeable passenger says he's been through this before, it's not that unusual, it's what's known as an 'aborted' landing. No one likes that word, 'aborted'.

Now the lads look at each other nervously as the plane climbs and the engines roar their protest. Danny Boy smiles his Lucky Irish smile, Tank is drumming on his thighs, Tone has his arms folded tight against his body, Mickey is shaking.

The pilot comes on again, nothing to worry about, folks, the gusting was a touch too strong, your safety is my responsibility, the wind was coming from the wrong direction, we'll have another go. The turbulence is now dynamic, it's like they're in a massive food blender or tumble dryer, shaken about as the plane circles for another attempt.

The flight staff stay strapped in their seats, looking tense. A baby is crying. An elderly couple, separated by the aisle, reach across and hold hands. Married for thirty-five years but they'll be together at least, at last, if something happens. But it won't, will it?

Clunk! as the landing gear comes down again.

Just a few feet from the tarmac, the plane lurches to one side then screams upward once more. Some passengers are trying to stop themselves crying out, don't scare the kids.

They're in the air. Mickey says to get their passports out of their bags and put them in their pockets – 'if we ditch it's the most important item to keep'. They see the sense in this and rummage in their bags but only Mickey can find his before the wheels clunk down again.

But first, the pilot sets out the options: either to divert to the nearest airport on the mainland which is Thessalonica or make one more try at landing. But Thessalonica, he says, is also experiencing heavy weather so he'll go for third time lucky, folks, and if that fails, he'll go for Thessalonica. He says all this in a homely manner as if it's all par for the course but there's an edge to his voice.

A lightning strike seems to hit the plane causing it to swerve – if swerving is possible in the air. They're now being shaken about worse than ever, lockers come open, bags and clothes fall out. The flight staff say to assume the Brace position, just as a precaution, and everyone bends down in their seats, then the oxygen masks drop down and dangle lazily in the leaning motions.

'Have you got one last wish?' This is Danny trying to make light of the situation.

'Yes, just to be back performing in pubs,' says Tone.

'Just to be back performing,' says Mickey.

'Just to be back,' says Tank.

And then, as the engines complain about the pressure they're under, and the wind banshee-howls outside, and the rain streaks like rivulets against the windows blurring the welcoming lights; and as a stewardess hides her face in her hands, obviously in tears, and more children are crying, and prayers are being muttered, 'Dear Lord, in our hour of need'; and as the pilot repeats his mantra, 'Third time lucky folks', trying to keep a smile in his voice; as all this is happening, in one split second, the band, Danny Boy, Tone, Tank and Mickey, for the first time in their long lives together, for the very first time in their history, reach across and hold each other's hands, tight.

They were always a tight band were Rock Ireland Line.

57
The End

Chapter/Song Title

It will likely not have escaped the notice of pop and rock aficionados reading this book that all the chapter headings and sub-headings are song titles. Some obvious, some not so.

To address any frustration and relieve the reader of the need for excessive Googling, here is a list of the songs and the artists. I have left out details of songwriters and record companies as these can easily be found online.

The important thing is the singer and the song.

Rock On. David Essex 1973
1. Rock Island Line. Lonnie Donegan 1961
2. Summer Holiday. Cliff Richard & The Shadows 1963
3. Hey Joe. The Jimi Hendrix Experience 1967
4. On The Road Again. Canned Heat 1968
One More Cup Of Coffee. Bob Dylan 1976
On The Road Again (reprise)
5. Waterloo. ABBA 1974
6. Rock Around The Clock. Bill Haley & His Comets 1956
7. Rock The Joint. Bill Haley & His Comets 1952
8. Anarchy In The UK. Sex Pistols 1976
9. To The Beat, Beat, Beat Of My Heart, Heart, Heart. Rock Ireland Line 1976
10. Bricks And Mortar. The Jam 1977
11. Never Ever. All Saints 1997
12. Let's Spend The Night Together. The Rolling Stones 1967
13. Be My Baby. The Ronettes 1963
14. Crying. Roy Orbison 1961
15. Drums. Johnny Cash 1964
16. Bits & Pieces. The Dave Clark Five 1964
17. Daddy-O. The Fontane Sisters 1955

18. Remember The Alamo. Donovan 1965

Gypsy. Van Morrison 1972

Here, There and Everywhere. The Beatles 1966

Sandy. The Hollies 1975

19. Sunny Goodge Street. Donovan 1965

20. Homeward Bound. Simon & Garfunkel 1966

21. Guitar Man. Elvis Presley 1967

22. Cold Turkey. Plastic Ono Band 1969

23. Strange Brew. Cream 1967

Rehab. Amy Winehouse 2006

24. Substitute. The Who 1968

25. New York, New York. Frank Sinatra 1979

Leaving On A Jet Plane. Peter, Paul and Mary 1969

Honky Tonk Woman. The Rolling Stones 1969

Glory Days. Bruce Springsteen 1984

It's My Party. Leslie Gore 1963

26. Going To California. Led Zeppelin 1971

27. Hey Mickey. Toni Basil 1981

28. Hello Goodbye. The Beatles 1967

29. I Love L.A. Randy Newman 1983

Rosy Rosie. Rock Ireland Line 1976

30. American Pie. Don McLean 1971

Vegetables. The Beach Boys 1967

31. School's Out. Alice Cooper 1972

32. Christmas in L.A. The Killers 2016

33. Touring. Ramones 1981

34. Keep On Running. Spencer Davis Group 1965

35. King Of The Road. Roger Miller 1965

36. Girl. The Beatles 1965

I Should Be So Lucky. Kylie Minogue 1987

37. 9 to 5. Dolly Parton 1980

38. All Night Long. Lionel Richie 1983

39. Art For Art's Sake. 10cc 1976

40. Please Mr. Postman. The Marvelettes 1965

41. The Name Of The Game. ABBA 1977

42. Mother. Pink Floyd 1979

43. The Leader Of The Pack. The Shangri-Las 1965

44. Come Together. The Beatles 1969

45. Sailing. Rod Stewart 1975

46. Everyday. Buddy Holly and the Crickets 1957

47. Sick As A Dog. Aerosmith 1976

48. To The Beat, Beat, Beat Of My Heart, Heart, Heart (Reprise). Rock Ireland Line 1976

49. The Morning Papers. Prince & The New Power Generation 1992

50. Good Morning, Good Morning. The Beatles 1967

51. Albatross. Fleetwood Mac 1968

52. The Beat Goes On. Sonny and Cher 1967

53. Hallelujah. Leonard Cohen 1984

54. Rock Of Ages. Def Leppard 1983

55. A Kind Of Magic. Queen 1986

56. Flying. The Beatles 1967

57. The End. The Beatles 1969